DESTROYING ANGEL

THE SECRET WAR

BRIGHAM STONE

Disclaimer

This is a work of fiction. While this story may draw inspiration from real organizations, public figures, and historical events, the plot and all incidents are entirely fictional. In particular, the religious beliefs, practices, factions, and conspiracies depicted are products of the author's imagination and are not intended to represent the official doctrine, beliefs, or internal workings of any real-world religious institution.

Any resemblance to actual persons, living or dead, or actual events is purely coincidental. The views and opinions expressed by the characters are their own and do not necessarily reflect those of the author.

Brigham Stone's Testimony

Dedication

To my wife, the reason for the world and the answer to the riddle.

CONTENTS

Chapter 1

THE HOMECOMING

The Rio de Janeiro mission office, a small yet inviting suite, provided a cool haven within a bustling office building, a true respite from the thick, humid Brazilian heat. The air-conditioning sighed as a handful of missionaries worked with hurried reverence at their desks.

A soft whisper broke the silence. "Did you hear if the Copacabana spot is opening up?"

Another elder quickly shushed him, but the question hung in the air.

Transfer time was near. The thought echoed in every corner of the office. Every phone ring made heads turn, every footstep from the president's office caused a collective, indrawn breath.

By the entrance, a small administration desk offered a polite greeting to arrivals. A whiteboard along one wall presented a gallery of dedication—passport-sized photos of each missionary paired with their companions. A large map of Rio de Janeiro, bold and colorful, commanded attention, a powerful visual echo of the vibrant city just beyond the pale walls and the deep sense of purpose that resonated within the office. Religious texts and filing cabinets lined another wall, their presence a quiet testament to the devotion and dedication that permeated the space.

In a small waiting area, slightly removed from the administration desk, sat a couple from Utah, their eyes fixed on the door. Sarah smiled with anticipation, smoothing the front of her modest dress. Beside her, Jason, solid and quiet, held a small bouquet of brightly colored flowers. They had arrived early, the two years of waiting feeling like an eternity in these final moments.

Then, the door opened, and a figure stepped in, wrestling with two large, well-worn suitcases. He was taller and broader than they remembered, his white shirt wrinkled from the journey, but his missionary tag was still crisp. He looked around the old office, a familiar, kind smile spreading across his face. It was Elder Rockwell Barnes, arriving from a crowded public bus, just another missionary finishing his service.

"Rockwell!" Sarah cried, her voice breaking with emotion. She surged forward, navigating around a stack of boxes.

Rockwell dropped his bags and met her halfway, wrapping his arms around his mother. He buried his face in her shoulder, a scent so familiar and comforting after so long. Tears streamed down Sarah's face as she held her son, murmuring his name like a prayer.

Jason joined the embrace, his strong arms enveloping both Sarah and Rockwell. It was a silent, powerful hug, conveying years of missed moments and unspoken pride.

Rockwell pulled back, looking at his stepdad with affection. "Jason," he said, his voice thick with emotion.

"Welcome home, son. Well, almost home." Jason clapped Rockwell on the back, a gesture of deep approval.

Rockwell's smile softened, his gaze growing distant. "This *is* home, Jason. Being together again. I imagine this is what heaven feels like."

Sarah pulled back, holding Rockwell at arm's length, her eyes shining. "Oh, Rockwell, look at you! You've grown into such a handsome young man."

Rockwell grinned. "Two years of walking everywhere and...well, let's just say the members here are excellent cooks." He chuckled, looking between them, his heart full. "It's so good to see both of you."

They stood there for a moment longer, a small island of pure happiness in the bustling office. The mission was complete. They were together again.

A moment later, a voice boomed from across the office, cutting through the gentle hum of activity. "Elder Barnes! And the proud parents, I presume!"

Mission President Peterson, a man whose rotund frame seemed to fill the doorway of his office, waddled toward them, his face beaming. He wore the standard white shirt and tie, but on him, it looked less like a uniform and more like an extension of his personality. His soft features were set in a smile that reached his eyes.

"President Peterson," Rockwell said, stepping forward to shake the older man's hand. "It's good to see you, sir."

"Elder Barnes, my boy!" President Peterson clasped his hand. "You've done a *magnificent work and a wonder* here. Truly magnificent." He turned to Sarah and Jason, his smile widening. "And you must be Sarah and Jason. It's such a pleasure to finally meet you. We've heard so much about you from Elder Barnes. It's always a joy to see fellow Utahns, especially after being down here for four years." He gestured toward his office. "Please, come in. Let's get out of the thoroughfare."

He led them into his spacious office which, despite being a workspace, had comfortable chairs and a large window offering a view of the city. Once they were settled, President Peterson leaned back in his chair, a twinkle in his eye.

"Now, Jason," he began, his tone jovial, "just because Elder Barnes is finishing his mission doesn't mean he's off the hook just yet." He paused for effect, a smile playing on his lips. "According to mission policy, a missionary still requires a priesthood-holder companion until they're officially released back home. And since you're here," he gestured to Jason with a flourish, "I'm officially transferring Elder Barnes to be your companion for the journey home. Congratulations, Elder Taylor! You're the senior companion."

He chuckled at his own joke, and Sarah and Jason smiled, appreciating the man's lightheartedness.

"Seriously, though," President Peterson continued, his voice softening. "We're incredibly proud of Elder Barnes. He's touched many lives here. To celebrate his faithful service, and to welcome you to Rio, we'd be honored if you'd join my wife and me for dinner tonight. We're having a small gathering at our home. Nothing too formal, just a few close friends and some of the other missionaries who are finishing up. It's a little ceremony to honor those who are heading home soon."

He paused, looking at them expectantly. "Our place is...well, it's got a bit of a view. A penthouse on Lagoa de Freitas. We'd be absolutely delighted if you could make it."

"A penthouse on Lagoona Gee Fritos?" Jason repeated, a puzzled look on his face. "I know what a penthouse is, but...Lagoona Gee Fritos? I've been to Lagoona Beach. Is it like that?"

Rockwell and President Peterson exchanged a subtle smirk. Rockwell quickly stepped in. "No, Jason, it's not a waterpark. It's a beautiful lake in the middle of the city. I'll help you with the pronunciation later."

Jason shook his head sheepishly. "Can't say I'm not disappointed there won't be waterslides. But we happily accept your invitation and look forward to meeting some of the people from Rockwell's mission."

Rockwell smiled, happy to see his parents so pleased.

After gathering Rockwell's well-traveled suitcases, they said their goodbyes to President Peterson and headed out of the mission-office building toward the parking structure. The steamy air hit them as they stepped outside, a stark contrast to the air-conditioned office. Along with the heat, the air carried the city's less pleasant aromas, a mix of exhaust fumes, the distant scent of street food, and something sharper, like stale urine and the acrid tang of burning tires.

"All right," Jason said, jingling a set of keys, "got us a rental. Even got upgraded to the American-sized car—for free! What a day." He led them toward a sleek, black SUV with dark-tinted windows.

Rockwell whistled softly as they approached the vehicle. "Wow, Jason. Haven't been in a car this big since you dropped me off at the airport back in Utah." He ran a hand over the cool metal. "It's going to feel weird not walking everywhere or hopping on a bus. I swear, I don't think I know how to navigate this city unless I'm on my feet."

Sarah smiled, linking her arm through Rockwell's. She couldn't take her eyes off him, just wanting to soak in his presence, to talk to him and hold him and make up for two years of missed hugs.

As Jason navigated the rental car out of the parking structure and into the flow of Rio traffic, his gaze was drawn to the stunning, yet sometimes unsettling, landscape. He pointed toward the hillsides cemented with tightly packed structures. "What about those, Rockwell? The...the slums?"

Rockwell followed his gaze, his expression becoming more serious. "Those are the favelas, Jason. They're...complex. A lot of people live there, often in really difficult conditions. Homes built right on top of each other, a maze of narrow alleys." He paused, choosing his words carefully, minimizing the danger for his mother's sake, though he had seen and experienced things in the past two years that would have terrified his parents. "There can be issues with gangs and safety, but the people themselves are often just trying to make a living, raise their families."

"Fascinating," Jason murmured, his eyes scanning the hills. "Quite the difference, seeing this next to that. These incredible beaches, the fancy buildings, and then...this. Right on top of each other."

"So," Rockwell said, turning back to his parents with a brighter smile, eager to shift the topic. "Before dinner, I was really hoping we could go see the Christ the Redeemer statue. I've seen it from a distance a hundred times, but I'd love to go up there with you guys."

Sarah squeezed his arm. "That sounds wonderful, honey. Anywhere with you is perfect."

Jason chimed in, captivated by a row of shining shops. "Check that out, Sarah! It's stunning."

But Rockwell's eyes were drawn to a side street where a group of young men with hard eyes watched their black SUV pass. He saw one of them subtly touch his hip, where the bulk of a pistol was visible beneath his shirt. Rockwell said nothing, not wanting to alarm his parents, but a familiar coil of caution tightened in his gut. He quickly turned his attention back to his mother, forcing a smile. "You'll love the view from the statue, Mom. It's...peaceful up there."

They spent the afternoon visiting the iconic Christ the Redeemer statue, taking in the breathtaking views of the city spread out below. It was a peaceful and memorable experience, a moment of shared beauty before the evening's events.

Later that evening, the black SUV pulled up to a gleaming, modern apartment building overlooking the serene expanse of Lagoa de Freitas. The contrast between the bustling streets they had driven through and the polished elegance of this address was striking. A doorman in a sharp uniform greeted them with a polite bow, his smile welcoming.

"*Boa noite*," the doorman said in Portuguese, switching to excellent English when he heard their accents. "Good evening, may I help you?"

"We're here for President Peterson," Jason replied. "The dinner this evening."

The doorman's eyes lit up with recognition. "Ah, sim! The president is expecting you. Welcome. Please, allow me." He buzzed them into the building, providing clear instructions to the penthouse suite.

As they walked through the lobby and waited for the elevator, Sarah and Jason couldn't help but marvel at the building's opulence. The architecture was sleek and modern, unlike anything they were used to seeing in Utah. Stone-clad walls met polished granite floors, and large windows offered glimpses of the city lights beginning to twinkle as dusk settled over Rio.

The elevator ascended smoothly and silently, opening into a private foyer on the penthouse level. A moment later, a friendly housemaid, dressed in a neat uniform, greeted them. "Welcome," she said with a kind smile, gesturing for them to enter. "Please, come this way. The president is in the salon."

She led them into a grand room that took their breath away. Floor-to-ceiling windows spanned the entire length of the space, offering a panoramic view of the lagoon and the city beyond, a glittering tapestry of lights against the darkening sky. The room was furnished with high-end, comfortable pieces, arranged around a long, beautiful stone dining table that could easily seat a dozen people.

And there, near the balcony, stood President Peterson. He was holding a small plate of mini-corndogs and, with his mouth slightly full, waved them over. "Ah, if it isn't Elder Taylor," he said, a warm smile spreading across his face, a hint of playful formality in his voice, "and his junior companion, Elder Barnes! Come in, come in! Don't just stand there!"

Elder Barnes smiled and approached, his parents following closely behind. As they entered the spacious salon, Rockwell's eyes scanned the room and landed on a few familiar faces—missionaries with whom he had started his journey two years ago. There was Elder Watts, his good friend and MTC companion, looking a bit thinner but with the same earnest expression. And over by the window, looking slightly bored, was Elder Wendt, the one everyone knew spent more time in the mission office as a secretary because proselytizing just wasn't his forte.

While Rockwell exchanged nods and quiet greetings with the other departing missionaries, Sarah and Jason engaged with President Peterson.

"This is a beautiful home, President Peterson," Sarah commented, taking in the stunning view.

"Thank you, Sister Taylor," he replied, finishing his mini-corndog. He wiped his hands on a napkin held by the housemaid. "We feel very fortunate to be here. It's quite a change from Utah, as I'm sure you can imagine."

"It certainly is," Jason agreed. "If you don't mind me asking, President, what did you do back in Utah before your call to serve here?"

President Peterson chuckled, a deep rumble in his chest. "Not at all, Jason. I always tell people I mess with the dead." He paused, letting the humor hang in the air before his smile returned, softer this time. "I own and operate one of the largest mortuaries in Utah County. Been doing it for over thirty years."

Sarah and Jason exchanged a brief, surprised glance but quickly recovered, nodding politely.

"It's...a demanding profession," Jason offered.

"It has its moments," President Peterson conceded. "But it's also a service. Helping families through difficult times. Much like the work these young men do," he added, gesturing toward the missionaries. "Though their focus is on a different kind of eternal life. Don't get me started on the advancements of chemical embalming."

"Trust me, I won't," Jason joked.

"Ah, and here's my better half," President Peterson said, turning as Sister Peterson entered the room. She wore a long, flowery dress that swished around her ankles, and the scent of her overpowering perfume—a mixture that could only be described as lilac and bottled grandmother—reached them even before she did.

"Oh, Bem-vindos Elder-eeees and Sister-eeees!" she exclaimed, her voice pitching high like a cheerful preschool teacher greeting her class. Clapping her frail hands in welcome, she declared, "Isn't it just a lovely evening? The view here is pretty good, but I'd trade it for a Walmart within walking distance any day."

Amused glances passed between Jason and Sarah, and Rockwell couldn't suppress a chuckle.

"You're absolutely right, Sister Peterson," Jason said, a smile playing on his lips. "This view pales in comparison to downtown Provo—Walmarts as far as the eye can see."

Sister Peterson's eyes sparkled with aloof warmth as she focused on the Taylors, yet her gaze still seemed distant. "And you must be Elder Barnes's parents! It is so truly wonderful to meet you." Turning her kind gaze to Rockwell, she added, "Rockwell's been a real ray of sunshine in our mission. I recall one time he actually found a box of newborn stray kittens abandoned by the train tracks and absolutely insisted we find them a home before we could even begin our Zone Conference."

Rockwell smiled at the memory. "They did find a home," he confirmed. "A lovely couple in my area took them in and named the two surviving kittens Elder Barnes and Elder Lesueur, after my companion and me. I've never felt more honored."

President Peterson clapped his hands. "Well, shall we get started? We have a few other guests arriving shortly, but I wanted to begin with a little program to honor our departing elders." He looked around the room. "Perhaps we could begin with a word of prayer? Jason, would you like to offer our opening prayer this evening?"

Jason nodded. "Certainly."

After the prayer, President Peterson smiled. "Thank you, Elder Taylor. That was lovely. Now, for our opening hymn... Is there anyone here who might be willing to accompany us on the piano?"

A silence fell over the room as the few missionaries present looked at each other.

Then, Sarah, a shy smile on her face, tentatively raised her hand. "I can play the melody, President," she said. "Any song from the hymnbook. I just... I can't do the bottom hand anymore."

Rockwell's eyes met his mother's, an air of understanding passing between them. He remembered the hours spent at the piano as a child. "Remember, Mom?" he chimed in, stepping closer. "When we used to sit on the bench together, and I'd play the bass notes for you so you could do the melody? I can't play all the notes on the bass clef, not like you could, but I can at least read one or two at a time. We could do it together."

Sarah's smile widened. "Oh, Rockwell. I'd like that very much."

They moved toward a beautiful grand piano in the corner of the salon, a stark contrast to the keyboard Sarah had at home. Sarah sat on the bench, carefully positioning her left hand, which lay still and slightly curled in her lap, a silent testament to the injury she had suffered years ago. Rockwell sat beside her, his larger hands hovering over the lower keys.

President Peterson announced the hymn, and as the others in the room opened their hymnbooks, Sarah began to play the familiar melody of "Be Still My Soul" with her right hand, her fingers moving with a grace that belied the stillness of her left. Rockwell, concentrating, found the simple bass notes, adding a foundational harmony. Together, mother and son filled the luxurious penthouse with the simple, heartfelt music of a hymn, a poignant blend of Sarah's enduring talent and Rockwell's loving support.

As the final notes faded, a comfortable silence settled over the room, broken only by President Peterson's warm smile. "Beautiful," he said, looking at Sarah and Rockwell. "Simply beautiful. Thank you, Sister Taylor, Elder Barnes." He cleared his throat, his demeanor shifting slightly as he prepared to address the departing missionaries. "Well, elders," he began, his voice carrying a tone of sincere appreciation, "it's been a privilege to serve with each of you. Two years is a significant portion of your young lives, and you've dedicated it to something truly meaningful." He paused, looking at each of the missionaries in turn. "I'd like to say a few words about each of you who are heading home this week."

He started with Elder Watts. "Elder Watts," President Peterson said, his smile warm, "I remember when you first arrived, full of enthusiasm, perhaps a little green. But I've watched you grow over these two years, become a dedicated and dependable missionary. You've faced challenges with faith and perseverance, and you've touched many lives through your quiet example and diligent work. You became a missionary I could always depend on."

Moving through the group, President Peterson offered heartfelt acknowledgments to a few more missionaries, recognizing their unique talents and dedication to the work.

He proceeded on to Elder Wendt. President Peterson's smile held a wink of amusement. "And Elder Wendt. Well, Elder Wendt has a unique talent for organization. The mission office has never been quite so...streamlined since you took on those responsibilities." He chuckled. "Whether that's because you truly loved the work, or perhaps," he winked, "because you appreciated the air-conditioning, we may never know. But your efforts behind the scenes have been invaluable to the smooth operation of this mission."

Finally, President Peterson's gaze settled on Elder Barnes, his smile returning, deeper this time. "And then there's Elder Barnes," he said, his voice full of warmth and appreciation. "Rockwell. You have a gift, son. A sincere and genuine way of connecting with people that is truly remarkable. I knew from early on I could trust you with our new missionaries, the green ones, the discouraged ones. After spending just a few weeks as your companion, they would learn what true, charitable mission work was. You became a teacher, a mentor, a counselor to the young men who arrived here." He paused, as if swept away in a fond memory. "You were a senior companion from the time you were here only three months. We called you the 'Baptizer of Kings.' It seemed every area you went to, you baptized a King Lamoni." He chuckled. "But it was never about the numbers for you, was it? It was about bringing full families, families that could be together forever, to the one and only true Church of Jesus Christ."

He looked at the small group of departing missionaries, his expression turning more serious. "Each of you has contributed in your own way. You've served faithfully, and you've made a difference. As you return home, remember the lessons you've learned, the growth you've experienced, and the love you've shared with the people of Brazil. I say these things in the name of Jesus Christ, amen."

A sense of warmth and contentment settled over Rockwell and his parents as they left President Peterson's stunning apartment building. The evening had been perfect, a beautiful capstone to Rockwell's mission and a joyous reunion. They were filled with more love for one another than they had experienced in years. The week ahead promised an exciting journey, a chance for them to visit all the areas of Rockwell's mission.

As Jason drove, the city lights of Rio blurred past. They were heading back to their hotel when the screen on the GPS flickered, displaying a garbled map before going dark.

"Well, shoot," Jason said. "Guess the free upgrade didn't include a reliable satellite connection." He squinted into the darkness, confident. "No matter. I've got a pretty good sense of direction. I think it's this way."

He turned off the main thoroughfare. The smooth asphalt gave way to uneven cobblestones that jostled the SUV. The streetlights grew sparse, then disappeared, replaced by the dim, yellow glow from a few scattered windows. The buildings, once separated by sidewalks and air, now pressed in on them, rising like canyon walls of unpainted brick and corrugated tin. A tangled web of illegally tapped power lines hung overhead like thick black spiderwebs.

"Huh," Jason murmured, slowing the vehicle. "Looks like I took a wrong turn. I'll just find a spot to turn around."

Rockwell, however, felt dread wash over him. The air seemed thicker here, heavy with the smell of charcoal, damp earth. He recognized the specific style of graffiti on a wall—a symbol he recognized. Then he saw the entrance ahead, a narrow constriction between two redbrick sentinels. His breath caught in his throat. It wasn't just *a* favela. It was *Morro Diabólico*, English translation: Devil's Hill.

Rockwell had spent two years in Rio, walking miles each day, spreading his message in neighborhoods that ranged from the wealthy to the destitute. His latest and last mission area covered a wide swath of the city, including the Morro Diabólico, but he'd always avoided this particular section. Missionaries were given explicit instructions to never, ever proselytize in the Morro Diabólico due to its reputation for danger. It was a no-go zone, a place whispered about with an edge of fear and respect.

As the car crept further into the maze-like streets, Rockwell's unease grew. He had never seen this part of his area at night or from the inside of a car. It was alien and hostile in its unfamiliarity. He noticed the crumbling brick walls and the narrow alleyways where shadows seemed to stretch longer than they should. His heart pounded.

"Jason." Rockwell's voice was tight, barely a whisper. His hand shot out and gripped the seat in front of him. "Dad, stop. Please. You have to back out. *Right now*."

Jason glanced at him, his brow furrowed in confusion. The black SUV with its tinted windows was a symbol of authority here, of police. Rockwell knew this. "Relax. It's just a neighborhood. We'll be quick."

"No!" Rockwell shouted, the sound raw in the confines of the car. "You don't understand! This car...they'll think we're *polícia*! They'll think we're BOPE! Dad, please, *turn around*!"

But as they entered the narrow street, the brick walls closing in, it was too late. The car was committed. High above, on the rooftops, figures moved. Young men, barely more than boys, perched like birds of prey. Jason noticed them, a slight smile on his face. "Look at that," he quipped, misreading the situation. "Isn't it a little late for them to be flying kites?"

Sure enough, Rockwell saw what looked to be a nine-year-old boy sending a blue kite into the air. By that time, it was too late. "We either need to back down or get down."

Almost at the same time, large traffickers moved in behind them with big truck tires and placed them behind the SUV, making it impossible for them to back out. Rockwell heard a commotion of screams and shouts that sounded like tactical maneuvering. He heard the words "Policia," "BOPE," "FBI," "CIA" being passed around outside. Normally, those words would have been comforting to him, knowing that there was protection around, but in Devil's Hill, the police were powerless. The traffickers were the police of the Hill. They had been in an open conflict with law enforcement for years, with dozens dying each day from the all-out war between the drug traffickers and the police trying to keep them out of their beautiful city on the ocean.

Then, a shot rang out.

The windshield shattered in a spiderweb pattern around a single bullet hole on the driver's side. Jason's right shoulder slumped down, and material from the seat behind his shoulder exploded into the air. Jason looked over his shoulder, aghast. "Golly," he said, his voice filled with disbelief. "I think he fetching shot me."

Rockwell grabbed his mother, covering her body with his own as best as he could and diving toward the floorboards to shield her. For Jason, it was already too late. A hail of gunfire erupted, riddling the car with bullets from AK-47s, handguns, and shotguns. Jason didn't have a chance to form another thought as a high-powered bullet tore through his head, creating a wound that Rockwell's older brother, Angelo, in his grim line of work, would have recognized instantly: a "JFK." The top of Jason's head flopped to the side like a soft-boiled egg being cracked open for eating.

Thankfully, Sarah never had to see this. She screamed in terror, a raw, piercing sound, and Rockwell rumbled in fear, his words a jumble of desperate prayers and reassurances.

He felt searing stabs in several parts of his body—his legs, his chest. It felt like he was getting the crap beaten out of him, but all he could think about was protecting his mom. He worked his hands onto her head, his fingers fumbling, trying to give her a blessing.

As he did this, Sarah's eyes found his. Her lips formed his name in a silent, desperate prayer: "*Rockwell*." It was the last thing she did.

Another shot rang out, a distinct, heavy-caliber sound, and he could see, through the shattered glass and chaos, that this one had hit her directly in the heart. He felt the impact simultaneously, the same bullet piercing his side after passing through her. He finished giving the blessing to her lifeless corpse, his voice barely a whisper amid the fading echoes of gunfire, and whispered "I love you to the moon and back" over and over.

As Rockwell lay in the back seat, gasping for air, bright-red blood bubbling from his lips, he prayed for the people committing the atrocity. He knew the dire circumstances they came from; he knew this was a case of mistaken identity, a tragic misunderstanding fueled by the brutal reality of the favela. In a moment of clarity, amid the pain and the fading sounds of the attack, he prayed to God for their forgiveness. In his mind's eye, he could see another reunion, a heavenly one, with Jason and his mom—a tight hug, a feeling of home even greater than he had experienced that morning.

The car door was wrenched open. A large, strong figure loomed above, silhouetted against the dim light of the favela street. He had tattoos snaking up his arms and a terrifying presence. It was Rogerio Da Silva Fogo. He was the general on the scene, and he pulled Rockwell out of the wrecked SUV.

"Shit," Fogo spat, his eyes scanning the scene, taking in the white shirt and name tag. "These motherfuckers are with Jesus, not the fucking police."

Fofinho, chubby and sweating, despite the cool night breeze, scurried up beside him, his eyes wide with alarm. "Whoopsie," he squeaked, the word sounding absurdly out of place amid the carnage. "They're not American, are they? Please say they're not Americans. We don't need this shit."

"Of course they're Americans, look at them!" Fogo snapped, gesturing toward the car and its occupants. "They're Mormons."

"Old missionaries, though," Fofinho mumbled, looking bewildered. "I've never seen such old ones. How was I supposed to know? I saw that guy with the salt-and-pepper hair, the tinted windows...so I told the little lookout to set up the kite. I was just following protocol." He gestured back down the street. "We all thought they were police. They crossed the line. This isn't my fault."

Fogo's gaze fell back on Rockwell, who was still alive, gasping and mumbling under his breath in Portuguese. "This saint is still praying," Fogo said, a hint of interest in his eyes. He leaned closer, listening, expecting to hear the familiar pleas of the dying. A look of surprise, then perhaps a glimmer of something akin to confusion crossed his face. "No," he said, straightening up. "He's saying,'Forgive them, for they know not what they do.'"

Fogo stared down at the dying missionary, a strange expression on his face. "We may not have known who you were," Fogo said, his voice low, a chilling finality in his tone, "but I know what I'm doing now. I have to finish it." He pulled out a sawed-off shotgun, the metal gleaming in the faint light. He pointed it into Rockwell's chest.

Rockwell, his eyes fluttering, heard the words. He saw the shotgun. His lips moved, a faint whisper against the foaming blood. "In the name of Jesus Christ, amen," he said.

Fogo paused for a fraction of a second, a glint of penitence flashing in his eyes. Then, he bowed his head, crossed himself, and muttered, "Amen."

He pulled the trigger.

Chapter 2

That's Not the Way It Feels

Angelo "the Operator" Barnes stood in his apartment high in the Burj Khalifa. The view was breathtaking—a sprawling panorama of Dubai, a glittering tapestry of modernity stretching to meet the hazy line where the desert kissed the sea. Sunlight, filtered through the windows, illuminated dust motes dancing in the cool, still air. This was Angelo's world, an organized sanctuary of wealth and control, far removed from the life he'd left behind in Utah.

The silence of the apartment was shattered by the insistent ringing of his phone. It wasn't a standard ringtone, it was the jarring, mechanical sound of an old operator-disconnected line: *beep-boop-beep, the number you have called has been disconnected, please hang up and try again.* It rang once, twice, three times. On the fourth ring, Angelo reached out and picked up the call.

"Hello," he said in a low murmur. "You've reached the Operator. How can I direct your call?"

The voice on the other end was hesitant. "Oh, I'm so sorry. I...I thought I was calling the number for Moroni Barnes. Can you... Do you have a number for Moroni Barnes?"

Angelo's eyes narrowed. The name. He hadn't used that name in years, not outside of official documents he rarely looked at. A cold edge entered his voice, cutting through the practiced "Operator" persona.

"I do," Angelo responded. "But I can guarantee you, if you call him Moroni and he finds you, you'll find out how hard it is to wipe your ass with a cast on both hands."

The caller stammered, clearly taken aback by the sudden shift in tone. "Oh! I...I'm so sorry. Yes, please. Could I get that number?"

Angelo's eyebrow twitched. "Just dial nine," he said, his voice returning to a more neutral, albeit still firm, register.

A pause on the other end. "Just, nine?" the caller said, confusion replacing the fear.

"Yeah," Angelo replied, as he toyed with the caller. "Just hit nine on your number pad. On your little phone there. And I'll put 'em on for you. But he goes by Angelo these days."

Angelo waited, the line going silent for a moment, then came a faint beep. He imagined the caller fumbling with their phone, pressing the digit. A moment later, the secretary's voice came back on the line, crisp and professional but with an underlying tremor.

"Mr. Barnes?"

Angelo's chipper "nice guy" persona snapped into place. "Hello! You've reached Angelo Barnes. What can I do for you today?"

"Oh, thank heavens I reached you," the voice said, relief evident. "I've never had to call Dubai before. I'm a secretary in the Church Office Building in Salt Lake City. Your name is on the rolls, but it doesn't say anything about Angelo. It has another name here that I'm not going to say, but I'm pretty sure I have the right person."

The Church Office Building. The words clicked into place, and a flicker of dark, cynical amusement cut through Angelo's confusion. Of course. The tremor in the man's voice, the palpable fear... He was some straight-laced, temple-recommend-holding Peter Priesthood who had likely never spoken to anyone who had threatened bodily harm and used the word *ass* in the same sentence. The poor guy was probably terrified he'd get struck by lightning just for being on the same phone line.

"Yeah," Angelo responded, his tone flat once more, the brief burst of cheerfulness gone. "You have the right person."

"Right," the secretary said, taking a shaky breath. "Well, I...I have a very important call here for you. From President Hatch of the Quorum of the Twelve Apostles. I would appreciate it if you would take his call. It's of the utmost importance."

Angelo was silent for a beat, his mind racing. An apostle? Calling him? He hadn't stepped foot inside a church since he was young. He couldn't even name the current apostles, let alone imagine why one would be calling him. Confusion warred with a sudden dread.

"Is he calling about collecting all the back tithing I owe?" Angelo asked, a sardonic edge to his voice. "Because if he is, he's gonna have to get in a long line of other people who think I owe them something."

The secretary's response was humorless. "Mr. Barnes," he said, his voice firm this time, "I wish I could banter along with your levity and light-mindedness, but unfortunately, I'm quite certain that this is a very serious issue. Please hold for President Hatch. I will put him on immediately."

A click, and the line went silent for a few agonizing seconds. Then, a new voice, calm and measured, despite the gravity it held. It was President Hatch.

"Brother Barnes," the voice began, deep and full of a quiet compassion.

Angelo bristled at the name, at the formality, at the title.

"I'm afraid I have some tragic and heartbreaking news. And there's no easy way to say this, but I've learned that honesty isn't only the best policy but the only policy."

Angelo's blood ran cold. He gripped the phone tighter, the knuckles of his free hand turning white.

"As you know," President Hatch continued, his voice heavy with sorrow, "your brother, Rockwell, was faithfully serving his mission in the Rio de Janeiro North Zone. He was set to come home this week, and your parents, Sarah and your stepfather, Jason, went down to pick him up. Unfortunately, there was an incident. A...a terrible incident. It tragically ended with Rockwell, your mother, and your stepfather all losing their lives."

President Hatch paused, allowing a moment for the devastating news to sink in. The silence on Angelo's end of the line was absolute, but inside, his world had collapsed. For a second, his breath caught, a sharp hitch in his chest. The opulent room around him seemed to tunnel, the glittering panorama of Dubai fading to a dark, closing ring at the edge of his vision. A physical pain, sharp and hot, clutched at his heart—grief, raw and unwelcome. He felt his composure, the fortress of "the Operator," begin to crack. With a surge of will that was pure instinct, he shoved the feeling down, locking it away behind a wall of ice. He forced his vision to clear, the room snapping back into sharp focus as the apostle continued, his voice filled with heartfelt compassion and empathy.

"Brother Barnes," he said softly, "I can only imagine the pain and suffering you're feeling in your heart and soul right now. And I don't want to minimize that, not in the slightest. But I also know, deep, deep in my heart, that they were welcomed with open arms by their loving Heavenly Father. And they will rise again with perfect bodies." His voice softened further, a gentle comfort entering his tone. "I understand your mother was a piano player. And I'm also aware of the injuries and difficulty she had with her hand." He paused, a tender thought seeming to cross his mind. "But I imagine that right now, she's in heaven, playing the most beautiful organ, surrounded by angels and loved ones."

As Angelo listened, his expression stony, Hatch's talk of heaven and celestial organs was a dull, sickening roar in his ears, drowned out by a memory that clawed its way to the surface, vivid and vile. *Her hand*. The words weren't comforting, they were a fresh twist of the rusty, jagged knife that was Oren Barnes, his biological father.

He was no longer in his sterile Dubai apartment. He was fourteen, small and terrified, the scent of Oren's rage—a mix of cheap beer and hypocritical piety—filling their cramped Utah kitchen. Oren's face, contorted and purple, inches from his own. The shouting hadn't been about a broken dish or a bad grade. No, it had been about something far more damning in Oren's eyes: public image. Angelo, in the innocent honesty of a child, had mentioned to his primary teacher that their family didn't really *do* Family Home Evening, not like they were supposed to. The teacher had sympathetically mentioned it to the bishop. The bishop had spoken to Oren. And Oren's facade of the good Mormon father had shattered in his own mind.

"You made me look like a fool!" Oren had bellowed. "You little bastard, airing our dirty laundry!"

Then Sarah had stepped in, her small frame a shield. "Oren, stop it! He's just a boy! It's *not* his fault!" Her voice, usually so soft, trembled with a desperate courage.

Oren's fury, denied its initial target, had swiveled, latching on to her with terrifying speed. He grabbed her arm, his fingers digging in. "This is *your* fault too! You coddle him! You don't teach him respect!" He'd dragged her then, through the kitchen, toward the garage, Sarah stumbling, trying to pull free.

Angelo, crying, a knot of terror and helpless rage tightening in his small chest, had followed. "Leave her alone! Dad, please!"

The garage stank of oil and trash. Oren, his face demonic in the dim light filtering through a grimy window, had forced Sarah's left hand, her music hand, flat onto the scarred surface of his cluttered workbench. She'd whimpered, pleading, but Oren was beyond reason.

He'd picked up the heavy claw hammer from its pegboard hook.

Angelo screamed, lunging forward, but Oren backhanded him, sending him sprawling into a pile of greasy rags.

"You watch, boy," Oren had snarled, eyes fixed on Sarah's pinned hand. "You learn what happens when you disrespect your father, when you shame your family."

Then the sickening, wet *crunch*.

Sarah's scream, a sound that had ripped Angelo's world apart, echoed in the garage, a sound that still haunted the deepest recesses of his nightmares. The sight of her hand, mangled, bones shattered, bleeding onto the workbench, Oren sneering in triumph...

Rockwell never had to meet him, Angelo thought, a cold, bitter thankfulness twisting in his gut. *Thank God for that, at least.*

The Operator's cold mask settled firmly back into place, the raw memory shoved back into its dark cage. Inside, a storm of grief and a much older, colder rage was gathering. Hatch's words about heaven and perfect bodies landed on him like stones, meaningless platitudes in the face of this raw, earthly pain. He didn't believe in any of that. Not anymore.

He took a slow, steadying breath, his voice tight when he finally spoke. "Thank you, President Hatch," Angelo said, the formal title feeling alien on his tongue. "I...I appreciate you calling. Can you tell me how it happened? Was it...was it peaceful?" He knew, with a chilling certainty, that it hadn't been.

"Brother Barnes," President Hatch's voice was gentle, but the hesitation was back. "It... it was not peaceful. It was a violent incident. Involving... involving local gangs." He didn't elaborate on the specifics, perhaps unwilling to share the gruesome details over the phone. "The local authorities are investigating."

"Local authorities," Angelo repeated, the words laced with a cynicism President Hatch likely missed. "Right." He paused, his mind already shifting, processing, planning. "What are the next steps?"

"Well," President Hatch said, sounding relieved to move to practical matters. "The Church will, of course, assist with all the arrangements. President Peterson, the mission president in Rio, is already working with the authorities and the embassy. We will ensure their...remains are handled with the utmost care and transported back to Utah for burial." He paused. "President Peterson has also offered the services of his mortuary in Utah County. He is a...very capable man in these matters."

Angelo felt a cold, hard knot tighten in his gut at the mention of a mortuary, of remains. "I see," he said. "And the mission office in Rio? Can you give me the address?"

President Hatch provided the address, his voice still gentle, offering further condolences and support from the Church. Angelo listened, his expression focused, jotting down the information. He thanked President Hatch again and ended the call.

The instant the line went dead, the mask dropped. The breathtaking view of Dubai became a meaningless blur. Grief hit him, not like a wave but like a physical blow that buckled his knees. A guttural sob, a sound he hadn't made since he was a boy cowering in a garage, tore from his throat as he collapsed onto the floor. For a few precious seconds, there was no Operator, only Angelo. He wailed, a raw, private agony for the void that had just been ripped open in his life. The pain was a living fire in his chest, consuming him. He had lost brothers before, good men who had fallen beside him on dusty, blood-soaked battlefields. He knew this agony. And he knew the only way to survive it was to power through, to complete the mission in their honor. The burning sadness in his chest twisting into a white-hot rage. His family. Dead. Murdered. The grief was still there, a heavy stone in his gut, but the rage was now a fire propelling him forward.

It was time to get to work.

He pushed himself up from the floor, his movements stiff at first, then fluid and purposeful. He didn't waste a second. His apartment, a testament to his dangerous profession, was also a highly organized operational hub. He moved with practiced efficiency, his mind already racing, calculating, planning. He went to a hidden panel in the wall, revealing a compartment filled with weapons—sleek handguns, combat knives, silenced submachine guns. He selected a few key pieces, checking their weight, their readiness.

Next, he accessed another hidden compartment, this one containing body armor, tactical gear, and a collection of fake identities—passports, driver's licenses, credit cards, all meticulously crafted. He chose a passport, a name, a history that would allow him to move through the world undetected.

He went to his walk-in closet, filled with expensive tailored suits. He chose a dark, well-fitting one, putting it on with practiced ease. Beneath the jacket, he secured an underarm holster, the weight of the pistol a familiar comfort.

His mind raced as he got ready, his grief channeled into a cold, focused energy. He had set out on missions countless times, for clients, for money, for the thrill of the hunt. But this time, the mission was personal. This time, his heart was in it.

He picked up another phone, a secure satellite line. He dialed a number he knew by heart. It rang twice before being answered.

"Hey, boss," Angelo said, his voice back to its usual calm, professional tone, devoid of the turmoil churning inside him. "Got some personal business to take care of. Gonna be out of town for a few weeks."

There was a brief pause on the other end. Then, a voice, exotic and authoritative, replied. "Of course. Anything you need, Angelo."

Angelo ended the call and moved to the integrated communication system built into his apartment. He called for a heli-taxi, specifying the pickup point on the Burj Khalifa's helipad. While he waited, his mind was already mapping out the next steps: a quick flight to the company airfield, chartering a private jet to take him across the world to Rio. But first, a necessary detour. He had a friend to pick up.

Chapter 3

THE FAMILY WE CHOOSE

The arid Texas landscape stretched out under a vast, pale-blue sky, the heat shimmering off the dry earth. The only sounds were the buzzing of insects and the rhythmic *crack-thump* of gunfire. Shawn Martinez, younger than Angelo but with a similar intensity in his eyes, stood at his personal outdoor firing range, a high-powered rifle in his hands. Before him, arranged on stands, were several ballistic gelatin heads, each one already bearing the gruesome marks of previous shots. He was meticulously testing different calibers, observing the cavitation and penetration with a detached, professional interest.

He lowered the rifle after another shot, the gelatin head shuddering on its stand. He was about to make a note on a small pad when he heard the distant rumble of an engine growing steadily louder. Shawn didn't flinch, his eyes tracking the sound. It wasn't the usual ranch hands.

A few minutes later, a rugged, black Jeep bounced down the dirt access road, kicking up a plume of dust. It pulled to a stop near the edge of the firing range, and the driver's side door opened. A figure emerged, tall and lean, dressed in a dark suit that seemed impossibly sharp and out of place in the dusty Texas heat. Shawn recognized the controlled stride, the air of quiet danger that surrounded him. Angelo.

Shawn waited, the rifle still in his hands, a knowing smirk. He knew that Angelo wouldn't just show up without a reason, and that reason was never good. The figure approached, the silence between them filled with unspoken history and understanding.

Angelo stopped a few feet from Shawn, the dust settling around his expensive shoes. The two men stood in silence for a moment, the dry air between them thick with anticipation.

Shawn finally broke the silence. "Well, look what the *haboob* blew in," he said, his smirk widening. "To what do I owe the pleasure, Operator? Did someone forget to pay their bill in Dubai, or did you just miss my charming company and the smell of burnt gunpowder?" He gestured to the gelatin heads. "Just doing a little market research. Always good to know your product."

"Shooting jelly with a fifty cal? What's your product, Jell-O salad? Trying to spice up the potluck with firearms?" Angelo knew that "ball busting" was Shawn's love language.

"What's a Texas picnic without a little shooty-shooty gooey-fruity?" Shawn responded without missing a beat.

"Did you just come up with that name for your salad on the fly, you quick son of a bitch?"

"Nah, like I said, market research. Learned you gotta take shit seriously. Had this mentor I used to work with, old fart, kind of like a Dumbledore with guns. Real mean, real ugly, smelled like a butt all the time, had a lame-ass comic book nickname too. Called himself the Switchboard Girl or something... No, wait, I think he named himself the Operator," Shawn said, goading Angelo.

"Old? I'm ten years and eight days older than you, you little shit. And you're barely old enough to rent a U-Haul."

"Ooooh, so you *do* know when my birthday is, you crusty asshole! It came and went this year, and you didn't even send me a set of socks and sandals so we could be matchy matchy, you geriatric fuck," Shawn fired back.

All right, all right, my balls are sufficiently busted. Haven't busted my nuts this hard since I stumbled across your mom's OnlyFans page."

"That's not funny!" Shawn said, feigning anger and starting to pretend to cry. "My mother died ten years ago." Shawn's face lightened into a grin, showing he was only kidding. They both knew Shawn's mom was alive and well; they could probably even smell her cooking from Shawn's gun range.

The joke, however, landed with a thud. Angelo's expression didn't just become serious, it cracked. The mention of a mother, even in jest, was a gut punch he hadn't braced for. An image of his own mother, Sarah, flashed in his mind—her smile, the way she used to hum while she cooked, the feel of her hand on his cheek. Now gone.

Shawn's grin evaporated. He saw the change, the raw pain that Angelo, the master of control, couldn't conceal. Shawn straightened up, turning his body to face Angelo squarely, his teasing demeanor replaced with the focused stillness of a soldier sensing a threat. "Hey," he said, his voice dropping low, empathetic. "What did I say? Angelo...talk to me." He saw the flicker of emotion, the raw grief of the man, not the cold steel of the Operator. "This isn't business, is it?"

"Something's happened, Shawn," Angelo said, his voice low and devoid of its usual dry wit. "My family," Angelo continued, the words tight. "My mother. Jason. And Rockwell."

Shawn's eyes widened, and he lowered the rifle, resting the butt on the ground. "Angelo...what happened?"

Angelo took a breath, the dusty breeze at his back doing little to cool the fire building inside him. "They were killed," he said, the word raw. "In Rio. A wrong turn. A favela." He paused, the images from President Hatch's call flashing in his mind. "Knowing what *I know*, the *enemies* I have made, I can't shake the feeling It might have been a setup, not sure yet. They were murdered."

Shawn didn't say anything for a moment, his gaze fixed on Angelo's face, reading the pain and the cold, hard resolve etched there. He knew Angelo. He knew what this meant.

"Rio," Shawn finally said, the single word a question and an acknowledgment.

"Yeah," Angelo confirmed, his jaw clenched. "I need you, Shawn. I need you with me on this."

"Done. I'm in. Do we at least get to take your company's private jet? Or do I have to go through TSA and store all my drugs in my asshole?"

"Oh, we have the company's full resources at our disposal. So, no need to prep your prison wallet. But...do you think we can eat first? I think I smell carnitas and I'm starving."

Shawn's grin returned, though it was tempered with the seriousness of Angelo's news. "Carnitas it is," he said, nodding toward the ranch house. "Mom's been cooking all day. We can talk business on the plane."

Hours later, the hum of the private jet's engines was a low thrum beneath them as Angelo and Shawn sat in plush leather seats, the lights of the North American continent slowly receding below. The initial shock of the news had settled into a quiet, potent grief for Angelo, a feeling Shawn understood better than most. They had eaten, the familiar comfort of Shawn's mother's cooking a strange anchor in the storm, and now, with the serious conversation looming, they found themselves falling into old patterns, using dark humor and shared memories as a shield.

"Remember that job in Prague?" Shawn asked, swirling the ice in his glass of water. "The one with the miniature schnauzer and the poisoned umbrella?"

Angelo gave a faint smile. "Ah, yes. The 'Barking Assassin.' Client was a bit...eccentric."

"Eccentric?" Shawn scoffed. "The guy thought he was a character in a spy novel. Had a secret lair in a clock tower. Almost blew us up with a self-destruct sequence he probably stole from a Saturday-morning cartoon."

"*Almost* is the operative word," Angelo said. "You disarmed it with three seconds to spare. While taking a bullet in the thigh."

Shawn shrugged. "Comes with the territory. Besides, you got the shot. Clean through the optic nerve from three hundred meters, in a crosswind, after rappelling down a gargoyle."

"Details, details," Angelo murmured, but there was a shimmer of appreciation in his eyes. They were silent for a moment, the unspoken acknowledgment of their shared history.

"Your brother," Shawn said, his voice softer now, the humor gone. "You didn't talk about him much. Knew he was a missionary. Good kid, right?"

Angelo nodded, his gaze fixed on the dark window, seeing not the night sky but Rockwell's smiling face. "The best," he said, the words barely audible. "Pure. Good. Everything I'm not." He paused, a bitter edge entering his voice. "And they killed him. And Mom. And Jason."

Shawn reached over, placing a hand on Angelo's arm. "I'm sorry, man," he said, his tone sincere. "I know what family means. Even the complicated ones." He didn't pry, didn't mention Angelo's biological father, about the past that had shaped him. He didn't need to. They had their own language, their own understanding.

As the plane continued its journey, the silence between Angelo and Shawn was not uncomfortable. It was the kind of silence that only existed between people who knew each other inside and out. Their bond, forged in countless life-or-death situations, allowed them to communicate without words.

Angelo leaned back in his seat, closing his eyes. He thought back to the first time he and Shawn had worked together. They had been thrown into a mission with little preparation, tasked with infiltrating a high-security facility in Moscow. Despite their different backgrounds and temperaments, they had quickly found a rhythm.

"Remember Moscow?" Angelo asked, not opening his eyes.

Shawn chuckled. "How could I forget? You almost got us caught because you couldn't resist that damn chessboard."

"It was a valuable piece. It was used in a game between Kasparov and Karpov! And, besides, it was you who tripped the alarm trying to disable the security system."

"Details," Shawn said with a smirk.

The truth was, their partnership had been serendipitous. Angelo's precision and meticulous nature complemented Shawn's improvisational skills and quick thinking. In combat, they moved as one unit, anticipating each other's actions.

During an operation in Buenos Aires they had been followed by a group of armed guards. Without a word, Angelo had scaled a rusty fire escape, taking the high ground while Shawn laid down a blistering volley of covering fire, drawing their attention. Angelo's sniper shots were perfectly timed with Shawn's movements below, each muzzle flash from an enemy position answered by a silent, deadly retort, picking off the guards one by one until the path was clear.

Undercover ruses were another testament to their synergy. In Istanbul, they had posed as rival businessmen vying for a lucrative contract. Their banter had been so convincing that even seasoned operatives were fooled. Angelo played the stoic strategist while Shawn took on the role of the brash negotiator, their performances seamlessly intertwined.

"Sometimes I think we could do this blindfolded," Angelo said.

Shawn bowed his head. "We've been through enough that we probably could." He looked at Angelo, his expression serious. "And we'll get through this too."

Angelo opened his eyes and met Shawn's gaze. There was a silent agreement between them—no matter what lay ahead, they would face it together.

Their bond went beyond mere friendship; it was an unspoken promise to have each other's backs, no matter the cost.

"This isn't just about revenge, Shawn," Angelo said, turning to look at him, his eyes hard and cold. "This is about making them pay. Making them understand what they took." He leaned back in his seat, grim determination settling over him. "We're going to Rio. And we're going to find the people who did this."

Shawn nodded, his expression serious. "All right. Usual approach? Loud and messy?"

Angelo shook his head. "No. Not this time. This is different." He paused, choosing his words carefully. "This...Mormon world. It's not like ours. It's quiet. Subtle. They operate differently. And the situation in Rio...it's complicated. More than just a simple mistake." He thought of President Hatch, of the unexpected call, of the glimpse into a world he'd left behind. "It's going to require finesse. Tact. We can't just go in guns blazing. Not if we want to get to the truth. Not if we want to make sure all the right people pay."

Shawn leaned back, considering Angelo's words. "All right, Operator. You always did have a flair for the dramatic. So, what's the play?"

Angelo's gaze was distant for a moment, already formulating the initial steps of an unconventional plan. "We start by playing along," he said, his voice low. "We get close to the source. We find out who's at the top. And then...we make them and anyone involved regret the day they ever heard the name Barnes."

Chapter 4

Personal Effects

Angelo and Shawn disembarked the jet at Rio de Janeiro–Galeão International Airport, the Brazilian heat a thick blanket after the sterile cabin. A black Range Rover waited on the tarmac, quickly whisking them away. The vibrant, chaotic energy of Rio enveloped them as they drove, the city a blur of color and motion, the lush, green hills dotted with favelas a constant backdrop. Their destination: the Rio de Janeiro mission office.

They were directed to a waiting area, and after a delay, Mission President Peterson emerged from his office. He was just as Rockwell had described in his letters, a man whose presence was as substantial as his reputation. His initial expression of professional sympathy shifted as he took in Angelo and Shawn, their sharp attire and confidence bearing a stark contrast to the typical grieving family members he had encountered.

"Mr. Barnes?" President Peterson said, extending a hand, his voice soft and full of condolence. "And...your associate?"

Angelo took his hand, his grip firm. "President Peterson," he said, his voice smooth, adopting the persona he had chosen. "Angelo Barnes. Rockwell's brother." He gestured to Shawn. "This is Shawn Martinez. My...valet."

Shawn, standing beside Angelo, a faint, mischievous glint in his eyes, piped up, "Actually, President, Angelo is *my* valet. I just let him think he's in charge sometimes."

President Peterson blinked, a wobble of surprise crossing his face before he recovered, a polite smile returning. Angelo, without missing a beat, played it cool.

"We're partners, President," Angelo clarified, his tone light but with an underlying firmness. "I just like to give Mr. Martinez here a hard time." He looked at Shawn, a silent message passing between them—the game had begun. "We're in the finance world. Businessmen."

President Peterson nodded, his gaze lingering on them, perhaps sensing something beneath the polished surface. "Right, yes, of course. Please, come in. My deepest condolences, Mr. Barnes. This is a...a terrible tragedy." He led them toward his office, the bustling mission work continuing around them. "We've been doing everything we can to cooperate with the local authorities."

He settled into his chair behind his large desk, gesturing for Angelo and Shawn to sit opposite him. "Rockwell was a remarkable young man," President Peterson said, his voice filled with warmth. "A true light. He touched so many lives here in Rio. And your mother and stepfather...they seemed like wonderful people. Rockwell spoke of them often and with such love." He paused, his expression softening further. "I know this must be incredibly difficult for you, Mr. Barnes. Losing your entire family like this...there are no words."

He leaned forward, his hands clasped on the desk. "We are, of course, doing everything in our power to assist with the investigation. The local police are involved, and the embassy is providing support." He paused, his tone becoming more reassuring, perhaps a little too much so. "There's really no need for you to feel like you have to stay and oversee things personally, Mr. Barnes. The mission is perfectly capable of handling all of Rockwell's personal effects and coordinating their return home. We'll ensure everything is taken care of and that there can be a beautiful service for Rockwell, Sarah, and Jason back in Utah." He cleared his throat. "In fact, I understand you were the one who generously provided the funds for Rockwell's mission. On behalf of the Church, and personally, I want to thank you for that sacrifice. Your contribution allowed a wonderful young man to bring so much good into the world for two years."

Angelo listened, his face a mask of polite grief, but his mind was already working. He needed information. "Thank you, President Peterson. Your words mean a great deal. And yes, Rockwell was... He was a good kid." He paused, choosing his words carefully. "Regarding the investigation, has there been any progress? Any information on who was responsible? Or a motive?" He leaned forward, his gaze direct. "And Rockwell's personal effects? Are they being held by the police? Is there a way I could retrieve them?"

President Peterson sighed, a look of weariness crossing his face. "It's still very early, Mr. Barnes. The police are being quite tight-lipped at the moment. It appears to have been a tragic case of being in the wrong place at the wrong time. A random act of violence, unfortunately, which happens in certain areas of the city." He avoided Angelo's gaze. "We're expecting an update from the investigating officer soon. Officer Mauro. He's the lead on the case." He shifted in his chair. "As for the personal effects, they're being held as evidence by the police. It's standard procedure in these kinds of investigations. But rest assured, as soon as they're released and the investigation is complete, we'll get them to you back in Utah. There's no need for you to concern yourself with those details." His tone was reassuring, perhaps a little too eager to dismiss the matter. "And if there's any financial advice that you have for a...a mortician like me," President Peterson added, attempting to make a connection, "I'm more than happy to talk. What kind of finance do you do, Mr. Barnes?"

Angelo offered a polite smile. "Venture capital, President. I invest in promising start-ups, help them grow." He paused, letting the implication hang in the air. *People are far more forthcoming with information when they think you might be willing to pay them for their ideas*, he thought.

"Really? That's interesting because I have some pretty unique ideas about chemical embalming. I think there is a real market for my proprietary technique. You see—"

A knock sounded on President Peterson's office door, sharp and authoritative.

"Come in," President Peterson called out, slightly perturbed by the interruption.

The door opened. Officer Mauro stood silhouetted in the doorway. He was a man who radiated a different kind of authority than President Peterson, a hard, military-like bearing, his movements precise and economical. He was middle-aged, his face etched with the grim realities of his profession, a stark contrast to the softer features of the mission president. His eyes swept over Angelo and Shawn, assessing them before stepping inside, closing the door with a definitive click.

"President Peterson," Mauro said, his voice curt and professional.

"Captain Mauro," President Peterson said, standing up. "Thank you for coming. This is Mr. Barnes, Rockwell's brother, and his associate, Mr. Martinez. They just arrived from Dubai."

Mauro gave a brief, almost imperceptible nod to Angelo and Shawn. "Mr. Barnes. My condolences." He turned back to President Peterson. "I have an update on the investigation."

He paused for a beat, his gaze steady. "The culprits have been dealt with. We conducted an operation in the Morro Diabólico. My team from BOPE engaged the gang members responsible for the attack. Fifteen of them were neutralized." He said the word with a chilling lack of emotion. "All were implicated in the incident involving the Barnes family."

He paused again, letting the weight of his words hang in the air.

"The case is considered closed," Mauro continued. "Justice has been served." He gestured toward the doorway. "I have a team outside with the family's personal effects. They've been processed as evidence. You can arrange to have them sent back with the remains, President Peterson."

Angelo and Shawn exchanged a glance. "Dealt with." "Fifteen neutralized." "Case closed." The words lingered, reeking of a cover-up. Angelo's jaw tightened, his eyes fixed on Mauro, a dangerous glint appearing in their depths. This wasn't the truth. This wasn't justice. He could feel it in his gut.

Despite the fury simmering beneath his skin, Angelo forced himself to maintain the facade. He rose to his feet, matching Mauro's height, and extended his hand. "Thank you, Officer Mauro," Angelo said, his voice sincere.

Mauro clutched Angelo's hand for a moment before placing his other hand on Angelo's shoulder, a gesture that was less a comfort and more a claim of dominance. He squeezed, just once. "It is my duty."

Angelo turned to President Peterson. "And thank you, President Peterson, for everything you and the Church are doing. It means a great deal during this difficult time." He paused, allowing a touch of vulnerability to show. "It's hard to hear that they're gone, but knowing the culprits have been apprehended...that brings some small measure of comfort." He swallowed, appearing to compose himself. "Regarding the personal effects," Angelo turned back to Mauro, his tone shifting, becoming more businesslike, "as the next of kin, I'd be happy to take possession of those now. I'll be heading back to Utah shortly to be with the rest of Jason's extended family and make the necessary arrangements for the service." He gave a mournful smile. "President Peterson mentioned he owns a mortuary in Utah County. He's offered his services, which is a great blessing."

He paused, then, drawing from the memories of his roots, he looked at President Peterson. "Speaking of mortuaries and Utah," Angelo said, "president, with all your experience, do you happen to have a great recipe for funeral potatoes? I know it's a strange question at a time like this, but it's a Utah tradition, and Mom always made them for family gatherings."

President Peterson, looking slightly taken aback by the abrupt change in topic, but perhaps relieved to move away from the grim details, chuckled. "Funeral potatoes? Oh, yes, Mr. Barnes. Of course. My grandmother practically invented them, or so she always claimed." A warm smile came across his face as he thought of it. "It's a closely guarded family secret, but for Rockwell's brother, I think I can be persuaded to share."

"Absolutely, we'll have to talk sometime," Angelo said, his smile broadening, playing into the persona. "You can tell me all about funeral potatoes and...embalming techniques. I can't thank you enough for your offer, President." He paused, leaning back in his chair, affecting a thoughtful air. "And, yes, I think I even have some space in my venture portfolio for innovative biochemistry applications." He glanced at Shawn.

"I figured *bio* meant living things." Shawn piped in with a smirk, his dark humor cutting through the polite conversation. "Is it still biochem if it's for corpses?"

Angelo chuckled, a dry sound. "Forgive my partner, President," he said, turning back to Peterson. "He always seems to know the exact wrong thing to say." He stood up, signaling the end of the meeting. "We better grab those personal effects and get going. A long trip back to Utah ahead."

The car was silent for a few blocks as the driver navigated the busy streets. Angelo stared out the tinted window, his brow furrowed, the polite smile he'd worn in the mission office replaced by a grim, focused intensity. Shawn sat beside him, his gaze sharp, observing Angelo and the city outside.

Finally, Shawn broke the silence. "Well, that was a grade-A load of bullshit."

Angelo nodded, his eyes still on the street. "You got that right." He turned to Shawn, his gaze piercing. "Okay, let's break down that shit show. First, Peterson. Trying to give us the brush-off from the moment we walked in. 'No need to stay, Mr. Barnes, we'll handle everything.' Like he wanted *us* gone yesterday."

"Definitely eager to send us packing," Shawn agreed. "And the whole 'police are tight-lipped, early in the case' routine? Then *boom*, minutes later, Captain Hard-ass Mauro shows up, case closed, fifteen dead guys, all tied up with a neat little bow."

"Exactly. And Mauro. BOPE. Special operations. Like a SWAT team but with more autonomy."

"And less paperwork."

"Precisely. BOPE doesn't lead investigations. They're muscle. They go in hard, clean up, and leave. An investigator should be leading this, someone from the regular police force, maybe homicide." He paused, a thoughtful look on his face. "Mauro's interesting, though. Stone cold. An operator. He's someone who operates in our world, Shawn. Just on someone else's payroll right now. We need to be careful around him."

"No doubt," Shawn said, his eyes flicking toward the back of the driver's head.

"And the personal effects," Angelo said, the anger simmering. "Evidence? Held for further processing? Why hand them over to Peterson, who then hands them over to *us*, within hours of the supposed 'resolution'? That doesn't add up. Not standard procedure. Not unless someone wants that evidence gone. Or controlled."

"Definitely fishy," Shawn said. "And Peterson's little slip about Dubai? When we came directly from Texas? And then keeps trying to shovel us off to Utah?"

Angelo's eyes narrowed. "That's the part that bothers me the most. Peterson knows more than he's letting on, enough to know about Dubai. He either got that information from the Church, or someone has eyes on us." He ran a hand over his chin, the gears in his mind turning. He couldn't shake the sickening feeling that this wasn't a random attack but something deeply personal—a consequence of his past, aimed squarely at his family. "No. This isn't a simple random act of violence. This smells like a cover-up. And President Peterson is involved."

Shawn leaned back in his seat, a grim look on his face. "Yeah," he said, his voice low. "BOPE officers in Rio are no fucking joke. Those guys are the real deal. I have no doubt they killed fifteen gangbangers or something to close the case, but there's no way in hell they got everybody involved in this. And you're right, the evidence thing...why hand it over? Why put it in our hands right now? Did they plant something in it, are they tracking us or something?"

"They want it gone," Angelo said, his voice hard. "They want us gone. Back to Utah. Grieving. Out of their hair." He looked out the window at the passing city, the vibrant colors now seeming muted, dull.

Shawn nodded at the rearview mirror. "They're making sure. We've picked up a tail."

Chapter 5

Small and Simple Things

"Amateurs," Shawn scoffed, though there was a serious edge to his voice. "A tail this obvious? They must think we're just nosy grieving relatives."

"That's their mistake," Angelo said with a cold smile. "Let them follow. It tells us they're anxious about us." He leaned back in the seat, his gaze calculating. "We need to lose them. Discreetly. We can't afford to have Mauro's goons watching our every move."

Angelo leaned forward, tapping his private driver on the shoulder. "Excuse me, could you take us to the Fairmont on Copacabana Beach? We need to make a quick stop."

The driver, a professional accustomed to the demands of Angelo's world, nodded. "*Sim, senhor.*" He adjusted his route, navigating the Range Rover through the dense Rio traffic toward the iconic coastline.

The Fairmont Rio de Janeiro Copacabana stood as a beacon of luxury against the backdrop of the famous beach. Palm trees swayed in the breeze, and the sound of the ocean provided a stark contrast to the recent tension. The black car pulled up to the elegant entrance, doormen in crisp uniforms immediately opening the doors.

Angelo and Shawn exited the vehicle, each taking one of the two suitcases from the back. Angelo scanned the arriving and departing guests. A well-dressed businessman, engrossed in his phone, had a key card nearly sticking out of his pocket. Shawn gave him a bump that appeared accidental. Simultaneously, Angelo's movements were fluid, almost imperceptible. His fingers deftly picked the key card from the businessman's pocket while his other hand crumpled a hundred-dollar bill. He bent down and pretended to pick the bill off the ground. "Excuse me, sir, I believe you dropped this."

The businessman glanced up, startled, spotting the cash in Angelo's hand. "Ah, thank you so much!" he said, taking it without a second glance, already returning to his phone. Nobody complains about being pickpocketed when they come out ahead in the deal.

Angelo gave the driver a dismissive wave. "Thank you. Wait close by." He and Shawn walked toward the elevators, the key card a secret in Angelo's hand.

Inside the hotel, they found the room number written on the envelope: 28-9. They rode the elevator up, the bags heavy with the weight of tragedy and potential clues. The key card worked. Angelo placed the suitcases on the smooth marble coffee table and opened the first one. He went through it methodically, his movements precise, his expression focused. He wasn't looking for clothes or souvenirs, he was looking for pieces of his brother's life that might shed light on his death.

He found them nestled among Rockwell's neatly folded white shirts and ties: the worn missionary badge with Elder Barnes engraved into it, a well-used copy of the missionary handbook, several leather-bound journals filled with Rockwell's looping handwriting, a thick binder overflowing with letters from home, and his brother's quad-combination of scriptures—the Bible, the Book of Mormon, the Doctrine and Covenants, and the Pearl of Great Price.

Angelo put the items in the backpack and set it aside, a sense of grim purpose settling over him. These were the small, simple things, the artifacts of a life dedicated to faith and service, a life brutally cut short. He would keep these.

"All right," Angelo said, turning to Shawn, his eyes hard. "We ditch the bags. They're tracking these, I guarantee it." He gestured to the suitcases. "Probably a simple GPS tracker, maybe something more sophisticated. Doesn't matter. They won't be tracking *us*."

Shawn nodded with a smile. "Classic switcheroo? Simple but effective. I'll google a discrete place to make the switch." After a few moments. "Got it, Tunnel do Joa."

Angelo closed the suitcase, then picked up his phone and made a call, his voice low and efficient. He arranged for a black BMW Gran Coupe to meet them at a specific point within the Tunnel do Joa and to keep the back doors unlocked.

Angelo picked up the suitcases again. "Let's take these down, get in the Range Rover, and head for the tunnel."

Once they reached the tunnel their SUV crawled through the congestion, the air thick with exhaust fumes. Their tail had fallen several cars back as their experienced driver created as much space as he could subtly manage. Traffic was stop-and-go, just as Shawn had predicted. Through the tinted windows, Angelo spotted it—the Beamer he had ordered, also stuck in the traffic jam, precisely where he had instructed it to be. Their driver methodically positioned the car beside their target.

Angelo spoke quickly to their driver. "Head to the airport, put the luggage on the plane, tell the pilot to head to Utah and lose the bags once he touches down."

Angelo and Shawn waited, eyes trained on the rearview mirror, tracking the tail car's movements. The tunnel's dim lighting flickered, casting long shadows that played tricks on the eyes. Cars honked impatiently as traffic ebbed and flowed. Each pause and advance was a test of their patience, but both men had long mastered the art of waiting. Once the tail car's view was momentarily blocked by a delivery truck, they made their move.

"Now," Angelo said, his voice calm, eyes fixed on the target vehicle beside them.

With practiced coordination, honed by years of operating in hostile environments, Angelo and Shawn moved. Angelo opened the rear driver's side door of their Range Rover just as Shawn slipped out and opened the rear passenger side door of the adjacent BMW. In the chaos and anonymity of the tunnel traffic, the exchange went unnoticed. Angelo and Shawn slipped out of their SUV and into the waiting BMW, leaving the suitcases on the back seat of the Range Rover.

Angelo leaned forward, speaking to the new driver. "Grand Hyatt in Tijuca."

The driver nodded, navigating the luxury car away from the gridlock as a small gap opened in the traffic.

Angelo watched as the SUV moved forward in the tunnel, heading toward the airport and a flight back to Utah. A cold satisfaction settled over him as they saw the tail follow the suitcases and not him. Mauro thought he was sending Angelo home, grieving and out of the way. He was wrong. Rockwell's badge, his journals, his scriptures were all he needed. The hunt had truly begun.

Later that evening, settled into a quiet corner booth at the bar of the Grand Hyatt in Tijuca, Angelo and Shawn nursed traditional Brazilian caipirinhas. The vibrant energy of the hotel on the pristine beach felt a world away from the mission office and the harsh realities of the favela. Angelo held Rockwell's missionary badge in his hand, turning it over and over, his gaze distant.

The smooth plastic of the badge felt alien in Angelo's calloused hand: ELDER BARNES. His brother, the good one. He remembered a hunting trip years ago when his little brother was just a boy. Angelo, efficient and brutal, had blown a jackrabbit practically in half with a shotgun shell meant for bigger game. Rockwell, ten at the time, had cried. Not just for the rabbit but at Angelo's cold satisfaction. Another time, Rockwell had accidentally winged a rabbit, trying to miss, as usual. Angelo, impatient, had urged him to "finish it." Rockwell had stood his ground, his face pale but resolute, confronting Angelo's cruelty. He'd taken the wounded creature home and nursed it in a homemade hutch. Damn kid even managed to tame the wild thing; it would eat out of his hand. No one else in their dusty town had ever seen a tame jackrabbit.

Different paths, Angelo thought, the ice in his caipirinha clinking. Rockwell got Jason, the quiet, steady stepfather who had taught him to fish and camp. Who showed him a different kind of manhood than the violent ghost of Oren Barnes. Angelo got...the military. And then, the trade.

Angelo set down the badge. He knew which path he was on. It wasn't the one that led to taming rabbits.

"So," Shawn said, swirling the ice in his glass, "plan's in motion. Bags are on their way to Utah, complete with tracking devices. Mauro and his boys will be scratching their heads when they realize their pigeons flew the coop."

Angelo took a slow sip of his drink, the tartness of the lime a sharp contrast to the sweetness of the sugar and the bite of the cachaça. "They'll figure it out eventually," he murmured, his eyes still on the badge. "Mauro's not an idiot. He's just...compromised. And Peterson, he's hiding something big. I can feel it." He paused, a dangerous glint in his eyes. "I need leverage. Something to put pressure on Peterson, on anyone who's trying to bury this."

"Leverage," Shawn repeated, nodding. "Against a mission president? Against the Church? That's a whole different ball game, Operator."

"It is. This isn't about hitting a cartel or taking down a corrupt businessman. This is about navigating a world built on faith, reputation, and secrets. A world Rockwell believed in." He clenched his fist around the missionary badge, then relaxed his grip. "I need to blend in. Become part of their world. Understand how it works from the inside."

"You? Blend in with the missionaries?" Shawn raised an eyebrow as well as his glass, a hint of amusement in his voice. "White shirt, tie, bicycle? You think you can pull off the 'elder act'?"

"*We* can pull off anything *we* need to," Angelo said, an idea sprouting in his mind. "We've worn plenty of masks. This one just happens to be clean-shaven and comes with a name tag." He gestured with his caipirinha toward the city. "And it means operating differently. Most of our usual party favors—the heavier firepower, the armor—went back on that jet with the suitcases we ditched. We knew coming in we might need a lighter touch, and now it's a necessity."

Shawn nodded. His hand brushed the small of his back where his own sidearm was concealed, mirroring the comforting weight Angelo felt from his personal handgun beneath his jacket. Shawn also had his trusted blade, an ever-present companion. "So, one handgun apiece and my trusty pig-stick-er," he summarized, a glint in his eye. "Makes the whole 'meek and lowly servant' routine more convincing, I guess. Less clanking." He smirked. "And if the flock turns out to have wolves among them that require a bit more...persuasion?"

Angelo met his gaze, a cold resolve settling in his own. "Then we adapt, like always. Rio's not exactly short on unofficial supply chains. For now, this approach buys us access and anonymity. Our best weapons right now are the ones no one can see until it's too late: surprise and underestimation." He looked out at the beach, the sounds of the city a distant hum. "But to do that, I need to make sure Peterson is...cooperative. He has access, connections, a whole network of his own type of operatives—missionaries."

Shawn leaned back. "Blending in makes sense. If we go in as missionaries, we keep Mauro and his guys off our ass. They won't suspect two elders. Plus, we get access to people who knew Rockwell best."

Angelo nodded. "Yeah. People avoid missionaries like the plague because they don't want to be preached to. We'll be invisible to most. But to those who were close to Rockwell, we'll be seen as allies, trusted immediately."

"And Peterson?" Shawn asked, raising an eyebrow.

"We need enough dirt on him to keep him in line," Angelo replied, a confident determination in his voice. "He'll cooperate once he realizes we're not bluffing."

"So, we dig," Shawn said, understanding dawning in his eyes. "We find out everything there is to know about President Peterson. His past, his secrets, his weaknesses."

"Exactly." Angelo took another sip of his caipirinha, the resolve hardening in his eyes. "We'll use the few things Rockwell left behind to guide us. And we'll use Peterson's dirty laundry to get us where we need to go. This is about uncovering the truth. And making sure everyone involved pays."

He set the missionary badge down on the table next to his adult beverage, the small plastic rectangle a stark symbol of the two worlds colliding. "First step," Angelo said, his voice quiet but intense, "I have a call to make."

Angelo picked up the phone and dialed a contact he knew would provide results. The line connected and a voice answered.

"Company extension, please."

"Hello," Angelo said, his voice flat and devoid of warmth. "This is the Operator. Get me in contact with the Cable Guy."

While the call was waiting to connect, Shawn whispered, "You guys and your fuckin' silly nicknames, man." He then mimed picking up a phone, holding it to his ear, and spoke in a dumb-faced, mocking tone, mimicking Angelo. "Hi, This is the Orkin Man, get me Cap'n Pap Smear immediately." He punctuated it with an exaggerated grin.

Angelo nearly choked on his drink, trying to stifle a laugh. In jest, he flicked the lime wedge at Shawn, which hit him in the face with a splat.

The next morning, sunlight streamed through the panoramic windows of the hotel room, illuminating the contents of Rockwell's backpack spread across the large desk. Angelo sat hunched over the journals, his brow furrowed in concentration. Shawn was across the room, meticulously cleaning his fingernails with a wicked-looking knife, his eyes occasionally glancing toward Angelo.

Hours had passed since they'd arrived at the hotel, the initial adrenaline of the escape giving way to a quiet, focused intensity. Angelo had spent hours that night poring over Rockwell's journals, the missionary handbook, and the letters from home. He was searching for anything—a name, a place, a subtle hint—that might connect Rockwell's life, and death, to the murky world of cover-ups and corrupt cops they had glimpsed.

Angelo tapped a finger on one of the journal entries. "Brett Sawyer," he murmured, more to himself than to Shawn. "Rockwell wrote about him a lot in the last few months. Ward mission leader in his area. Ex-army ranger." He looked up at Shawn. "Could be a solid resource. Military background, likely has a different perspective than the typical member, and he's American, so no cultural barrier."

Shawn grunted in acknowledgment, not looking up from his task.

Angelo thumbed through another section of the journal, stopping at an entry with a name that he had highlighted: Ricardo de Aparcido. "Ricardo," Angelo said, his voice thoughtful. "This guy could be a potential resource. Rockwell mentioned him several times."

Shawn finally looked up, curiosity piqued. "What's his story?"

"Get this." Angelo leaned closer to the journal, searching the page with a finger before reading aloud: "May twelfth. I'm so proud of Ricardo! We've been working with him on the Word of Wisdom for a few weeks now. Last night, he walked into his favorite bar, held up his new Book of Mormon, and told his old friends he was trading his cachaça for church permanently. He told them they wouldn't see him there again unless he was bringing them a copy of their own. I remember when we met him while tracting. He opened the door so drunk he could barely stand. There was a sadness in his eyes, but a spark of goodness too. I wasn't sure he'd remember that he invited us back, but we felt we needed to return. To see him now, it's a miracle. I have never felt the Spirit so strongly. This is why I'm here."

Angelo fell silent, the cheerful, faithful words of his brother hanging in the air.

"Sounds like quite the transformation," Shawn acknowledged.

"It gets better," Angelo continued, eyes scanning the page. "Ricardo has influence in Rio. Friends and acquaintances in government." He closed the journal and leaned back in his chair. "He can provide people, information, resources."

"Sounds like he'd be an instant ally," Shawn said, sheathing his knife with a practiced flick of his wrist.

Angelo's gaze was distant, picturing his brother, the pure, earnest Rockwell, teaching and baptizing in this chaotic city, a stark contrast to the violence that had ended his life.

He gathered the journals, returning them to the backpack. "These are the threads, Shawn," Angelo said, his voice low. "Little things. But they're all we have right now."

Shawn looked up, meeting Angelo's eyes. "And the dirt on Peterson?"

Angelo gave a grim smile. "The Cable Guy came through. Like his name implies, he connects us to the information superhighway of secrets that are buried deep." He paused, a glint of satisfaction in his eyes. "He did some serious digging overnight and got back to me early this morning. Let's just say he found something *very* juicy, buried somewhere he never expected, literally. We have the leverage to make President Peterson *very* cooperative."

"Fun!" Shawn said, a predatory look in his eyes. "So, where do we start?"

Angelo picked up Rockwell's missionary badge again, the plastic cool against his fingers. He looked at his brother's name, then out at the sprawling city. "We start by having an interview with the president."

Chapter 6

FOR AS IN ADAM ALL DIE

The mission office was usually a quiet place, a few missionaries diligently working at desks. But today, President Peterson's office was particularly quiet. He sat behind his large desk, a beacon of Christlike concern, facing a young sister missionary whose hands were clasped in her lap. Elder Wendt, the only mission secretary present, guarded the waiting area. President Peterson had conveniently arranged a brunch outing for the others, including the sister missionary's companion. Wendt sat stiffly in the waiting area daydreaming of catching his flight home later that week.

In the privacy of his office, President Peterson leaned forward, his soft features set in a gentle, encouraging expression. "Now, Sister Cohen," he said, his voice a low, comforting murmur. "You mentioned you had something weighing on your conscience. Something unresolved." He paused, his smile warm. "The Savior's atonement is for all of us, Sister. No sin is too great that it cannot be overcome through sincere repentance."

Sister Cohen swallowed hard, casting her gaze to the floor. "Yes, President," she confessed, her voice trembling. "I...I've been waiting for this day. To clear my conscience. To finally get something off my chest." She wrung her hands together. "But I'm so worried...about the repercussions." Her voice grew more urgent. "I'm concerned for my soul, President. And...and I'm so worried I'm going to get sent home."

With a practiced, almost imperceptible adjustment of his expression, President Peterson maintained his facade of loving concern as he passed her the box of tissues he kept on his desk for just such occasions. While her face was covered in shame, a brief, unsettling smile touched his lips, and a cold, calculating glint entered his eyes. This was not compassion, it was opportunity. "Go on, Sister."

"I...I can't believe I have to say this," she whispered, the admission tearing at her. "The stress, it's been crushing me. Between the struggles in my area and the helplessness I feel about everything happening back home—the things I can't fix—I haven't had a moment's peace, barely any sleep." Her voice cracked, the shame palpable. "I was so overwhelmed, so weak, that one night...I gave in. I succumbed to temptation, to an act of self-abuse. The shame is...it's overwhelming." She buried her face in her hands, her body racked with sobs. "Please," she choked out, the plea muffled, "please don't send me home."

He waited for her to regain her composure, his expression shifting back to one of practiced sympathy, though the cold calculation remained hidden just beneath the surface. He offered a gentle nod. "Sister," he said, his voice soft, almost paternal. "First of all, take a deep breath. No one is going home." He paused, a note of tactful levity entering his tone. "If I sent home every missionary who confessed to...well, to masturbation, we wouldn't have any missionaries left, would we?" He leaned back, a comforting, yet strangely disturbing, chortle under his breath. "It's a common struggle, Sister. A very common struggle indeed."

"Thank you, President Peterson, that helps. I was so worried, but I can literally feel the weight lifting from my shoulders," Sister Cohen said, her eyes red and teary.

President Peterson smiled. "It's funny you mention weight lifting, Sister, because just like building muscle, true repentance takes work. Are you ready to do that work? The acts that prove your faith?"

"I'd do anything, President Peterson, for the Spirit to return its comfort."

"*That* is the attitude I like to see. Now, I still have some questions I need to ask you. We need to fully understand the nature of this challenge. How often does this happen? Is it a frequent struggle for you?"

"No, not frequent, just the one time recently. Not since before my mission and only that one time during."

"Good, Sister. That's important context. Thank you for your honesty." He nodded, his gaze steady. "When...these things happen, what thoughts are in your mind? What do you find yourself thinking about?"

Sister Cohen hesitated, looking down. "I...I don't see why that's relevant, President. Do I really need to say?"

"Sister," his voice was firm, "we cannot hide anything from the Lord, and we cannot truly repent of what we are not fully honest about. Trust the process. Opening everything to the light is the only way to truly cleanse the wound. You'll feel a deeper peace when we're finished, I promise."

She wrung her hands, then spoke quietly. "Just...boys I knew back home. My first boyfriend sometimes."

President Peterson leaned forward, his voice dropping. "Do you ever think of...more depraved things? Or perhaps look at impure pornographic material?"

"No, President."

"Really, Sister? Actually, it's quite common, even here in the mission field. It's normal to be curious about sex."

Sister Cohen shifted uncomfortably in her chair.

"I'd skip these questions if I could," Peterson continued, his voice softening, "but it's very important that you remain honestly engaged with me. Just a few more, and we can put this all behind us."

He waited for her to give a slight nod of compliance, then proceeded.

"Homosexual pornography, two girls at a time, multiple partners? Did anything like that ever enter your mind or your view?"

"No, President," she responded, her head snapping up. "I would never."

"And do you ever fantasize about older, powerful men?" He paused, his eyes searching hers. "Sister Cohen, you don't have to be afraid to be honest with me. The Lord wants you to be truthful, and He has given me the gift of discernment. I'll know if you're holding anything back. And if you lie to me...you know that's not a contrite heart. While I'd never send a missionary home just for struggling with the pleasures of the flesh, I might have to send someone home if they fail to show true humility or choose to be dishonest with their priesthood leader. I worry about your dear mother's heart, Sister, and what would happen if you were sent home from your mission dishonorably because you couldn't be fully truthful."

The fear spread across her face as the realization took hold of what was happening. The conflict filled the empty mission office. The trap was sprung, and President Peterson knew there was only one escape. Comply.

Outside the mission office door, Angelo and Shawn stood near the entrance, usually a beacon of quiet order, it felt charged with a different kind of energy today. Angelo glanced at Shawn, a grim determination on his face.

"All right," Angelo said, his voice low. "He's in there. With Wendt and...a sister missionary."

Shawn nodded, his gaze sharp, taking in the scene through the glass window in the door—the bored-looking Elder Wendt at the front desk, the closed door of President Peterson's office. "Just Wendt? And a sister? Looks like Peterson cleared the decks."

"Exactly," Angelo replied, an edge in his voice. "And he's got that sister missionary in there. Alone." He paused, the implications hanging heavy. "Knowing what we know about Peterson, that doesn't sit right with me."

"Doesn't sit right with me either," Shawn agreed. "So, how do we play this? Go in quiet? Gentle tap on the door, 'Excuse me, President, do you have a few moments to talk about our Lord and Savior Jesus Christ?'"

Angelo considered it for a moment, his eyes scanning the office. "Reverently and quietly might work. Catch him off guard. But..." He looked back at Shawn, a dangerous look in his eyes. "He's got that sister in there. And Wendt's the only one out here. If we go in quiet, he might try to play games, stall, maybe even call for backup. We need to make an impact. Make it clear we're not here to play by his rules."

Shawn's grin returned, though it was a mischievous one. "Raucous and rowdy?"

"Raucous and rowdy," Angelo confirmed with a cold smile. "We need to make enough noise to ensure that sister missionary knows something's happening. Enough to make Wendt uncomfortable. Enough to make Peterson realize we're not just here for a polite chat about funeral potatoes." He paused, mischief in his eyes as he glanced at Shawn. "Are you ready to...put on a show?"

Shawn cracked his knuckles, a low, satisfying sound, his grin widening. "My favorite kind of entry," he said, eyes gleaming with anticipation. "I don't have any pea soup, but I can improvise. Let's go crash an ice cream social."

Angelo nodded.

Together, they burst through the doors of the mission office, the sound echoing in the quiet space. Elder Wendt looked up, startled, his eyes widening as he saw the two terrifying figures entering.

Angelo lunged forward, his face contorted in a mask of desperate concern. "Elder! Help us! It's my friend! Something's wrong!"

Shawn, beside him, played his part with conviction. He stumbled into the office, his body stiff, eyes wide and unfocused. He let out a guttural groan, a sound that was less human and more like something struggling to break free. He twitched violently, limbs jerking.

Elder Wendt, startled by the violent intrusion and Shawn's disturbing display, yelped, jumping up from his desk like a startled cat. His eyes were wide with fear, fixed on Shawn's thrashing form. "What in the...doody!" he stammered, his voice high-pitched and trembling.

Angelo grabbed Elder Wendt's arm, his grip strong, pulling him further into the chaotic scene. "He just...he just started acting like this! I don't know what's happening!" Angelo's voice was laced with a convincing panic.

Shawn let out another unearthly sound, his head snapping back, eyes rolling. He began to babble, a stream of distorted, nonsensical words that sounded demonic.

Elder Wendt, terrified and out of his depth, stumbled backward. As if by reflex, he raised his right hand to the square, his arm bent at a ninety-degree angle—the gesture of priesthood authority. His face was pale, sweat beading on his forehead. He closed his eyes, muttering under his breath, then straightened, his voice gaining a shaky resolve.

"Out, Satan! Out!" Elder Wendt shrieked, his voice trembling but growing louder. "In the name of Jesus Christ and by the power of the Melchizedek Priesthood, I cast you out!" He took a step forward, his hand still raised toward Shawn.

Angelo and Shawn advanced just enough to maneuver Elder Wendt into a corner near a sturdy metal filing cabinet. Shawn continued his performance, thrashing and groaning, drawing Elder Wendt's full, terrified attention.

Then, in an instant, the act vanished. Shawn's body relaxed, his eyes cleared, and the demonic sounds stopped. A wide, cheerful grin spread across his face. "Hey, look!" Shawn exclaimed, his voice bright and normal. "I'm cured! No more demons!" Shawn proceeded to awkwardly high-five Elder Wendt's still-raised hand.

Elder Wendt, caught off guard by the abrupt shift, stared at Shawn. A look of bewildered relief fluttered across his face, his mouth agape.

It was all the opening Angelo needed. As Elder Wendt stood frozen in surprise, Angelo stepped forward and delivered a sharp, open-handed slap across Elder Wendt's face. The sound cracked in the quiet office. Simultaneously, Shawn, with lightning speed, grabbed Elder Wendt's raised hand, twisting it in a swift, painful wristlock.

Elder Wendt cried out in pain and surprise, his brief relief replaced by shock and confusion. Before he could react further, Angelo produced a zip tie from his pocket and, with practiced efficiency, secured Elder Wendt's wrist to the handle of the nearby filing cabinet.

Elder Wendt was left standing in the corner, his arm awkwardly raised and bound, his face a mixture of pain, confusion, and disbelief. Angelo and Shawn stood over him, their expressions now cold and businesslike, the facade of panic and possession gone.

"Sorry about that, Elder," Angelo said, his voice devoid of apology. "Just needed to make an entrance. And make sure you didn't interrupt our conversation with the president." He glanced toward President Peterson's office door. "Now," Angelo said, his voice dropping to a whisper, "it's time to have our up close and personal priesthood interview."

Shawn mockingly knocked on the door to President Peterson's office and announced, "Excuse me, sir, do you have a few moments for us to share a brief message with you? I promise, it will change your life."

"Go away, I'm busy," President Peterson said, sounding frailer and more sheepish than the wolfish ghoul he really was.

"Fuck that!" Shawn giggled as he kicked open the door with a thunderous smash. "You're going to listen to what we have to say!"

The door to President Peterson's office slammed inward with a crash, the sound echoing through the stunned silence of the mission office. Inside, President Peterson jolted in his chair, eyes wide with alarm. Across from him, Sister Cohen flinched, her hands flying to cover her mouth, her earlier distress replaced by terror.

Angelo and Shawn stepped into the room, the door framing their imposing figures. Shawn moved to the doorway, pulling a glinting knife from his jacket and taking up a position that blocked the entrance. He glanced at the bound Elder Wendt, visible in the outer office, a silent warning in his gaze, before settling on the scene inside. Sister Cohen, her face pale, tried to shrink back in her chair while looking between the intruders and President Peterson, clearly wanting to disappear.

President Peterson, his face rapidly cycling through surprise, fear, and a shiver of disbelief, finally found his voice. "You...you're still here?" he stammered, eyes fixed on Angelo. "Mauro said... He said you were confirmed to have touched down in Utah. The luggage...it was tracked."

Angelo ignored the question. He walked further into the room with a slow, deliberate stride that radiated controlled menace. He stopped a few feet from the desk, hands clasped in front of him, a picture of calm that was far more terrifying than any outward aggression.

"President Peterson," Angelo said, his voice low and smooth, a chilling contrast to the violence of their entry. "We need to talk. About my family. About what happened. And about your...extracurricular activities."

President Peterson stiffened, his attempt at feigned innocence already crumbling. "I...I don't know what you're talking about," he said, his voice shaky. "I've told you, it was a tragic accident. The police have closed the case." He glanced nervously at Sister Cohen, then back at Angelo. "And I have no idea what you mean by 'extracurricular activities.'"

Angelo's smile didn't reach his eyes. "Oh, I think you do, President," he said. "See, when I told you I was in venture capital, I wasn't entirely lying. I do my due diligence. Especially when considering investing in...innovative biochemical applications." He leaned forward, his voice dropping to a near whisper, but the words were sharp and precise, cutting through the tension in the room. "Tell me, President, as someone who's spent decades in the mortuary business, someone with a keen interest in advancements in chemical embalming...what exactly can you tell me about Embalmadol-Exo?"

The effect of the name was immediate and devastating. President Peterson's face drained of color, his eyes widening in terror. His facade shattered, and he recoiled in his chair, mouth opening and closing.

Sister Cohen, though she likely didn't understand the significance of the name, felt the sudden shift, the palpable fear radiating from the mission president. She kept her head down, trying to make herself invisible.

Angelo watched President Peterson's reaction, a cold satisfaction settling in his gut. He had him. The knowledge of Embalmadol-Exo, a name Angelo had learned from Cable Guy, a name tied to the darkest rumors surrounding Peterson's mortuary, was the key. It was proof that Angelo knew the secrets Peterson had buried, secrets far more damning than coercing sister missionaries to compromise themselves.

"I see that name rings a bell, President," Angelo said, his voice still quiet but now laced with a dangerous triumph. "Funny, isn't it? How a simple chemical compound can open up a whole world of...possibilities. Possibilities for investment. Possibilities for leverage." He paused, letting the full weight of his words sink in. "Hey, Shawn, you're a Hooked on Phonics kid, right?" He glanced over at President Peterson. "Shawn's been working real hard on his reading comprehension, Do you mind if I quiz him?"

President Peterson stared, as white as a ghost.

"Yay, that stupid look means *yes*." He then directed his attention to Shawn. "Shawn, my companion, could you please tell President Peterson what we read this morning in that little report we found? The one that used to be buried deep in the Church quarry vault?"

"First off, Angelo, I'd like you to know that I aced my reading SAT with a score of go-fuck-yourself," Shawn said with a taunting grin, then continued to recite from memory the highlights of the report, his voice conversational. He pushed off the doorframe, taking a step into the room. "Fascinating stuff, President. Really. Like, get this." He paused, as if recalling an interesting fact. "In one hundred percent of deceased subjects, Embalmadol-Exo was able to raise the core body temperature to an exact 98.7 degrees Fahrenheit. Delayed rigor mortis too, left the corpses warm and supple for up to seventy-two hours." Shawn's voice dropped to a conspiratorial tone. "And eleven percent of subjects recorded measurable, though insignificant, motor function and neuroelectrical impulses." He shrugged. "Potential for medical applications, they said. Organ transplants, even life extension."

"Thank you, Shawn, for sharing that passage with us. What did it make you feel when you read that?" Angelo asked as if he were leading an elders quorum discussion.

Shawn's expression shifted, becoming more pointed. "Well, two things that come to mind," he stepped closer to the desk, his gaze fixed on Peterson's terrified face, "A: the criminal underworld would love something like that. Messing with time of death, muddying evidence. Real handy. *Or*," he leaned in closer, his voice dropping to a stage whisper, "B: someone wants a warm, soft, defenseless body to..." Shawn took a slow, deliberate breath, then belted out, his voice filling the office with a sudden, booming operettic sound "Fuuuuuuuuuuuuuu-uuu—"

"I never!" President Peterson shrieked, his voice cracking. He recoiled, his chair scraping against the floor. "I never did *that* to the deceased! I would never!"

Angelo stepped forward, his voice low and dangerous, drawing closer to Peterson's ashen face. "But you allowed it to happen, didn't you? You fucking necro pimp." The derogatory term, delivered with chilling precision, seemed to physically strike Peterson. "A few high-powered, ghoulish individuals? The good old Mormon Mafia families from Salt Lake?" Angelo's voice was a venomous whisper now. "What did they offer you to whore out your stash of warmed-up dead girls and boys in your upstanding mortuary? Money? Callings? Maybe a mission presidency with a general-authority option?"

President Peterson buried his face in his hands, his body shaking with sobs. A dark stain spread on his trousers. "I didn't have a choice," he choked out. "They would have ruined me anyway. My name was on that BYU paper, and our methods weren't exactly...reviewed. And you're right about the criminal element. I didn't want to, but some very scary people from the underworld made me cooperate with hiding evidence." He looked up, his eyes red and streaming. "Sure, there was money, but I didn't want to," he repeated, a pathetic whimper.

Angelo's expression remained cold, unmoved by Peterson's tears or his soiled trousers. "Oh, doesn't it feel nice to confess?" Angelo said, his voice devoid of sympathy. "Here you are again, with very limited choices and some *very* scary people." He leaned down, his face inches from Peterson's. "Either you help me get to the bottom of my family's murder, or you are going back home to your mortuary before you know it, but this time you'll be the warmed-up remains getting defiled by sickos."

The fear that had been building in President Peterson reached a crescendo. The realization of his predicament, trapped between Angelo's cold fury and the terrifying reality of his own exposed secrets, was complete. The trap was sprung, and President Peterson knew there was only one escape. Comply.

"Anything," President Peterson cried, his voice desperate. "I'll do whatever you want. Just...just don't ruin my legacy."

"*That* is the attitude I like to see," Angelo said. "Peterson, we need complete access. To the mission records, transportation, apartments, ward buildings, membership rolls. We want Mauro and his men off our backs, and we want you to shield us. We need pamphlets, proselytizing materials, scriptures. We need two name badges each. One for our shirts, one for our jackets."

President Peterson, still trembling, looked up, confused. "Name badges? Why in the world would you need those?"

Shawn, standing by the door, chuckled. "Because, you silly goose," he said, a wide, innocent grin on his face, "me and my companion need them so our cover isn't blown."

"Your cover?" President Peterson stammered.

"Our cover," Angelo confirmed. "As missionaries in the Church of Jesus Christ of Latter-day Saints. You're going to transfer us to the last area where my brother was serving, and we're going to find everyone responsible for my family's death."

President Peterson swallowed hard, his mind reeling. "What should I have Elder Wendt put on your name tags?"

Shawn raised his hand excitedly, the earlier tension momentarily forgotten in his enthusiasm. "Oh! Oh! I want to be Elder Boobies! You know..." he adopted a mock British accent, "like a British dude would say, 'I 'eld 'er boobies, guvna!'"

"Dammit, Shawn, for the last time, you're not gonna be Elder Boobies!" Angelo said, a huff of exasperation in his voice. He turned back to President Peterson, his expression grim. "Shawn will be Elder Martinez. As for me...call me Elder Rockwell."

Chapter 7

TWO OR THREE WITNESSES

President Peterson trembled in his office chair, his face still ashen from the confrontation.

"Time for you to head home," Angelo said. "Change those pants. They're not quite as clean as they were this morning."

Peterson's eyes darted between Angelo and Shawn. "What happens now?"

Shawn leaned against the doorframe, arms crossed. "Now you keep your head down and your mouth shut."

"You need to understand something," Angelo said, moving closer until he towered over the seated mission president, "We're well-funded. We have eyes everywhere. Consider yourself on house arrest in that cushy apartment of yours."

"But I have responsibilities, meetings with stake presidents, visits to—"

Angelo slammed his palm on the desk. The sound cracked through the office like a gunshot. "You have *one* responsibility now—staying exactly where we tell you to. If you set foot outside that apartment without our permission, every dirty, little secret you've been hiding becomes public knowledge."

Peterson swallowed hard. "The Church would never—"

"The Church?" Angelo laughed. "You think they'll protect you when they find out what you've been doing with those bodies? When they learn how you've been lining your pockets? The Church excommunicates people for a lot less than being a necro pimp."

"And that's just what we already know," Shawn added. "What else are we going to find when we check your browser history?"

President Peterson's shoulders slumped. "What do I tell people about why I'm not available?"

"Food poisoning," Shawn suggested. "Considering the shit you're in, it's not far from the truth."

"We'll be in touch," Angelo said, stepping back. "Now go home. And remember—we're watching."

President Peterson scurried out of his office like a frightened mouse, nearly tripping over his feet in his haste to escape the two men who had just dismantled his safe cocoon. Angelo watched him go with satisfaction before turning his attention back to the mission office's main work area, where their other problem awaited resolution.

Elder Wendt remained secured to the filing cabinet. The young missionary's face had progressed through a kaleidoscope of emotions—from terror when Shawn had pretended demonic possession, to righteous indignation during his attempted exorcism, and now to a resigned, pale dread as Angelo approached.

"Elder Wendt," Angelo said, his voice softer than it had been with Peterson but no less menacing, "let's have a chat about how things are going to work around here."

Wendt's Adam's apple bobbed as he swallowed. "Are you going to kill me?"

Angelo hovered close to the cowering missionary. "If I wanted you dead, it would already be too late to ask that question."

Shawn leaned against a nearby desk, flipping through a stack of missionary weekly planners. "We're actually offering you a promotion."

"A promotion?" Wendt's eyes darted between them in confusion.

"You're about to become President Peterson's executive assistant," Angelo explained. "You'll handle his calls, manage his schedule, and most importantly, you'll be our eyes and ears."

"I don't understand."

"It's simple," Angelo said. "Peterson is going to tell people he's sick. You're going to make sure his story holds up. You'll relay messages between us and report anything suspicious directly to me."

Wendt nodded, sweat beading on his forehead. "I understand."

Angelo cut the zip tie and straightened Elder Wendt's tie for him. "Good. Now finish the transfer paperwork. Me and Elder Martinez are heading to my brother's last area."

While Wendt scrambled to the computer, Angelo turned his attention to Sister Cohen. She sat in a chair by the wall, hugging herself, her face still pale and her hands trembling. The terror from moments ago hadn't faded.

He contemplated the tremor in her hands, the way she hugged her ribs as if trying to hold herself together. It was a posture he recognized with a sickening lurch in his gut. For an unwelcome instant, he wasn't in a mission office in Brazil, he was fourteen again, watching his mother try to make herself small and invisible in the shadow of his father's rage. The image of Sarah, pale and broken, superimposed itself over the young woman in the chair. The cold satisfaction he'd felt moments ago evaporated, replaced by a raw, protective instinct. This woman was a victim, and he had just walked in on the tail end of her abuse.

"Hey," Angelo said, his tone softening as he approached. He didn't get too close, giving her space. "Are you okay?"

She looked up, her eyes red-rimmed and wide with fear and confusion. "I'm Sister Cohen," she whispered, her voice shaky. "What...what's happening? Who are you?" She gestured toward the office, Elder Wendt, the kicked-in door. "And...and thank you. I think."

Shawn pulled up chairs for himself and Angelo, creating a small circle with Sister Cohen while keeping a respectful distance.

Angelo sat, his gaze steady. "We're here because of Elder Barnes," he said, his voice low and serious. "You knew him, didn't you?"

Sister Cohen's eyes widened in recognition. She nodded. "Elder Barnes was my Zone leader. He was..." Her voice caught, a fresh wave of emotion surfacing. "He was kind. Always encouraging us when things got tough. But what about him?"

"We believe what happened to him..." Angelo needed to choose his words carefully. "It wasn't an accident." He paused, letting that sink in. "President Peterson wanted to sweep that under the rug. And we know what he was planning to do with you in there."

Sister Cohen looked down at her hands, twisting them in her lap. The fear was still present, but a flash of something else—determination, maybe—began to surface in her eyes. "He...he was trying to force me to..." Her voice was gaining a little strength. "He said he'd send me home if I wasn't 'fully honest' about impure thoughts. It was a trap."

"We know. He's a wolf," Angelo said. "And we stopped him."

She looked back at them, studying their faces. They were intimidating, yes, but their actions just now had been directed at Peterson and Wendt, not her. And they were talking about Elder Barnes. "You...you think Elder Barnes's death wasn't an accident?"

"We're almost certain," Angelo replied. "And we think it might be connected to things happening right here in this mission. Maybe even things President Peterson is involved in. Elder Barnes, he was my brother. We're going to find out what happened to him. And we're going to get you connected back with your companion."

"President Peterson separated us," Sister Cohen whispered. "Said I needed 'special counseling' after what happened in Morro Diabólico."

Angelo's eyes narrowed. "What do you mean? You were there?"

"Not when it happened. But our area bordered Elder Barnes's. We'd been warned to stay away from favelas." She leaned forward, lowering her voice. "I think Elder Barnes wanted to start teaching families in the favelas. The week before he...before he returned to Heavenly Father, he came to our apartment with his companion. He seemed curious, kept asking if we'd seen anything unusual or too dangerous near the favela. It sounded like he just felt bad that people were being denied the opportunity to hear the Gospel just because they were born into poverty. He said all of Heavenly Father's children deserve the opportunity to hear the Gospel."

Shawn exchanged a glance with Angelo. "What did you tell him?"

"That we'd seen cars. Nice ones. Going in and out at odd hours." The fear in her eyes was being replaced by a fierce resolve. "I want to help you," she said, her voice firm now.

"Whatever you're doing, I want to help find out what really happened to Elder Barnes."

Angelo studied her face. He saw more than just grief or gratitude in her eyes. There was a keen intelligence there, a shrewdness that had likely been assessing them from the moment they intervened. "It could be dangerous."

"I don't care. Elder Barnes deserves justice. And after what President Peterson just did...I don't trust him. I trust you two more than him right now." She watched Angelo and Shawn with narrowed eyes, her initial relief giving way to critical assessment. "You two aren't going to last five minutes as missionaries."

Angelo raised an eyebrow. "Excuse me?"

"Look at yourselves." She gestured at them. "Elder Martinez looks about twenty-four and is built like a pro athlete, and you, 'Elder Rockwell,' look like you're pushing thirty."

"Thirty?" Angelo looked flattered "I'm actually—"

"She's right," Shawn cut in. "We stick out. The average missionary is, what, nineteen?"

Sister Cohen nodded. "Mostly. And you two have this...I don't know, hardness about you. Missionaries are usually awkward, earnest boys, not..." she waved her hand, "whatever you two are."

Angelo leaned back, considering her words. "Fair point. So what's our cover story?"

A thoughtful silence settled as Sister Cohen's mind went to work, sifting through mission protocols and precedents. She assessed their ages, their out-of-place demeanors, and the implausibility of their sudden appearance. Then, a clever solution clicked into place.

"Missionaries can leave to serve a mission until they're twenty-five," Sister Cohen explained. "Some serve later when they join the Church as converts. That could explain Elder Martinez, at least."

"And me?" Angelo asked.

"You could pass for younger if you didn't act like you had such a stick up your buns."

Shawn burst out laughing. "She's got you pegged, man."

Angelo shot him a withering look before turning back to Sister Cohen. "Anything else we should know?"

"Why were you transferred together? That's unusual. And why has nobody in the mission seen you before?"

Angelo and Shawn exchanged glances, clearly unprepared for these questions.

"We could say you're from the Rio de Janeiro South Mission," Sister Cohen suggested. "Tell everyone you're here on some assistant-exchange program."

"Assistant-exchange program?" Shawn repeated.

"Say you're both assistants to the president in the South Mission. You've come here for a few weeks to exchange ideas with the North Mission. It explains why you were transferred together, why nobody knows you, and even why you might be older."

Angelo nodded, impressed. "That's actually good. Very good."

"I know," Sister Cohen said. "I've been here long enough to understand how things work."

"What else should we know?" Shawn asked.

"Study your missionary handbooks. Know the rules, even if you break them. And for heaven's sake, learn some hymns. Nothing gives away a fake missionary faster than not knowing the words to 'Called to Serve.'"

Angelo watched Sister Cohen with newfound respect. Her quick thinking and mission knowledge made her a potential asset he hadn't anticipated. "You know this world better than we ever could," he said, keeping his voice low. "Can we count on your help moving forward? Help us navigate the mission culture, avoid obvious mistakes?"

Sister Cohen tilted her head, considering the offer. "What would that involve?"

"Occasional questions, helping us blend in," Shawn explained. "Maybe backing us up on our cover story or vouching as an alibi."

"We'd compensate you very well," Angelo added.

Sister Cohen's expression shifted to one of mild offense. "I'm not doing this for money, Elder...Rockwell." She stumbled slightly over the false name. "I'm doing this because Elder Barnes deserved better than what happened to him."

Angelo nodded, recognizing his misstep. "Of course. I apologize."

"I'll keep my cell phone with me," she said, her tone softening. "Call anytime you need guidance."

Shawn glanced toward the door. "Do you want us to stick around until your companion gets back? Help explain things?"

Sister Cohen shook her head. "I've got this. Having two missionaries here will help sell the story to the other office staff." She gave a small smile. "By the mouth of two or three witnesses, right?"

Shawn raised an eyebrow, not following the reference.

"It's a scripture," she explained. "Doctrine and Covenants 6:28. 'In the mouth of two or three witnesses shall every word be established.'"

"Ah," Angelo said, filing away the information. Religious references would be something he'd need to remaster.

Sister Cohen gave them a confident smile. "I'll make sure everyone gets the right story, including Elder Wendt," she assured them, her gaze glaring toward the still-shaken missionary who was now watching them with wide, terrified eyes.

"Elder Wendt, could you please get the address for the Leblon apartment for Elder Martinez and Elder Rockwell?" she said, her tone leaving no room for argument. As Wendt scrambled to comply, fumbling with the computer, Sister Cohen looked back at her new allies. "You guys should go get settled in your new apartment. You're actually quite lucky; the other elders living there are pretty fun. And it's the only mission apartment with air-conditioning."

Sister Cohen looked over Angelo and Shawn again. "And one more thing. President Peterson isn't the only one who needs fresh clothes; if you want to truly immerse yourselves, you guys are going to have to change your underwear."

Chapter 8

YE ELDERS OF ISRAEL

Angelo surveyed the entrance to the Leblon apartment building with a practiced eye. Six stories of aging concrete and faded charm, three blocks from the beach.

"Home sweet home." Shawn smiled, adjusting his backpack, his brand-new missionary name tag—ELDER MARTINEZ—catching the afternoon sun.

The elevator ride was a nerve-racking experience of metal groaning and doors that barely met in the middle. Angelo kept his hand near the gap, ready to force them open if necessary.

When they reached the sixth floor, laughter spilled from behind their apartment door. Angelo tensed. In his line of work, voices usually meant witnesses, complications, variables he couldn't control.

Shawn knocked on the door, slipping easily into his missionary persona with a broad smile. The door swung open to reveal a young elder with sandy-blond hair and freckles.

"The new guys!" he exclaimed. "Come in, come in! The office called ahead. I'm Elder Marcus."

Angelo stepped inside, taking in every detail of the apartment—the worn parquet flooring, the three study desks arranged in the living area, the sparse decorations consisting mainly of spiritual quotes and Mormon ads.

Two other elders sat tensely in the small living space, fidgeting in their chairs with a look of strained anxiety and grim determination, racked with internal torment.

"Elder Rockwell and Elder Martinez," Marcus announced. "They're assistants from the South Mission here for that exchange program."

"Sweet!" said another elder who was sitting with his journal at his desk, setting it aside. "I'm Elder Lawrence. That's Elder Stein and Elder Parkman who are in a bit of competition right now. You guys are lucky—it's P-Day, so we're just chillin'."

Elder Parkman exclaimed, "You, good sir Lawrence, are chillin'. My opponent and I are locked in a match of wills, a battle of wits. What could be more appropriate for a P-Day?"

Elder Stein joined in. "And not just *any* P-Day, a literal *pee* day, as in pee-pee. Parkman and I chugged a gallon of water two hours and ten—no, eleven—minutes ago. The first one to pee loses and has to clean the toilet and empty the bathroom trash can. I am *not* going to lose." Stein squirmed, squeezing back what must have been immense pressure. "Parkman, I don't think I can hold it much longer."

Shawn, sensing the levity of the situation, but also probing for information about what a P-Day was, chuckled along. "Ah, good old P-Day. Glad I didn't arrive on, say, *poo* day! What would I have seen then?"

The others chuckled, instantly endearing him to the new group.

"Down south, our P-Days were...different," Shawn continued. "Definitely no literal peeing contests. So, what else does a typical P-Day look like around here?"

Elder Marcus laughed, shaking his head at Shawn's joke. "Man, I've never heard of a mission with a poo day! That's hilarious." He gestured toward the kitchenette. "Anyway, typical P-Day is pretty chill. We do laundry in the morning—those buckets on the balcony are Elder Lawrence's shirts soaking—then we handle letters to family, shopping for groceries, and whatever else we need to do before five."

"After five, it's back to proselytizing," Lawrence added, closing his journal. "President Peterson's pretty strict about that. Preparation day is for preparing, not slacking off completely."

Angelo nodded, taking mental notes. P-Day. Preparation day. Emails home. Laundry. Groceries. Proselytizing after five. The structure was clear enough.

"We usually hit the soccer court at the church building," Marcus continued. "Nothing serious, just playing around. Elder Lawrence is pretty good, but the rest of us can't keep up with the locals. The youth in the ward always kick our trash."

Shawn nodded. "South Mission P-Days are more structured. President...uh..."

"Vasquez," Angelo supplied. "President Vasquez believes in community-service P-Days. Once a month, we spend the morning at orphanages or cleaning up parks."

"Right," Shawn caught on. "It's actually pretty cool. Last month we painted an elementary school. Kids loved it."

"That's awesome," Elder Stein said, shifting uncomfortably in his seat. "Maybe we should—oh man—suggest that to President Peterson."

"I'm impressed you can even think about painting schools," Parkman groaned, beads of sweat forming on his forehead. "I can't think of anything but rushing waterfalls and exploding bladders."

Angelo looked at the backpack in his hand. "Which room will we be in?"

Elder Marcus led Angelo and Shawn down the short hallway toward the bedrooms. "We just had two beds open up," Marcus said with a hidden degree of gravity, "so you get the room with the AC." There was something in his tone—a subtle weight—that suggested these vacancies weren't from your average transfer. The beds were last inhabited by Elder Barnes and his companion.

Angelo followed, casing the apartment. The apartment was cramped but serviceable—typical missionary housing from what Rockwell had described in his letters. Angelo noted the window dimensions, the distance to the ground, the thickness of the walls. Old habits from his operational days that had kept him alive more than once.

"This is you," Marcus said, pushing open the door to reveal a room with two bunk beds and a pair of small desks. An ancient air conditioner jutted from the window, humming laboriously as it fought against Rio's heat. The unit rattled with each cycle, threatening to give out.

Shawn bounded toward one of the bunks. "Top bunk! Called it!" He tossed his bag onto the mattress with childlike enthusiasm. Shawn had always preferred high ground, even when they were in the field together, a tactical preference disguised as boyish exuberance.

"Fine by me," Angelo said, setting his bag on the lower bunk. He ran his hand over the thin mattress, assessing its comfort—or lack thereof.

Touching Rockwell's mattress hit Angelo with the force of a sucker punch. An unbidden memory flickered behind his eyes: he was eighteen, his duffel bag packed for boot camp resting by the door. A tiny Rockwell had bounced on his newly vacated mattress, his face alight with joy. "I get a big boy bed now!" he'd squealed. The bitter irony was suffocating. Then, he had left so Rockwell could take his place. Now, Rockwell had left, and he was here to take his. Angelo forced the memory down, his jaw clenched.

Elder Lawrence appeared in the doorway, straightening his already immaculate tie. "We've got a good group here. I'm from Ogden, Utah, currently serving with Elder Parkman in the Jardim Botânico area. He's only been out about three months, so I'm training him."

"Parkman's from Delaware," Marcus added, resting a shoulder against the doorframe. "Interesting background—mom's a Jehovah's Witness, dad's Jewish. He and Stein are thick as thieves. They met in the MTC and are practically inseparable when we do splits. You'll hear them laughing from across the apartment."

"What about you?" Angelo asked, maintaining the friendly curiosity expected of a new missionary while mentally filing away every detail.

"I'm from California," Marcus replied. "Got about two transfers left before I head home. I'm serving in the Gávea area with Elder Stein. He's from Colorado, also pretty new—about three months in. Still working on his Portuguese, but he's a good kid." There was a hint of fondness in his voice, the kind that developed between a trainer and his greenie.

"And you're training him?" Shawn asked, testing the springiness of his mattress with an exaggerated bounce.

Marcus nodded. "Yeah, it's my last assignment before going home. Trying to pass on whatever wisdom I've picked up along the way." He glanced around the room with the look of someone who'd soon be leaving it all behind. "Not always easy but worth it."

Elder Stein hobbled into the room, his legs forced together as he danced on the spot, not wanting to miss the action unfolding among the new missionaries. He flashed a wide grin, eager to join the chatter but clearly struggling with his own pressing need.

Just behind him trailed Elder Parkman, his imposing frame slinking off toward the kitchen with a mischievous glint in his eye.

Angelo's instincts flared as he observed Parkman's movements. Something felt off.

"Where's he going?" Angelo wondered, eyes narrowing.

Moments later, Parkman returned from the kitchen, attempting to conceal a two-liter water bottle behind his back. His eyes widened when they met Angelo's gaze. With a quick gesture of his finger to his lips, he shushed Angelo with an exaggerated grin. He then pointed toward the bathroom and nodded.

Parkman tiptoed into the bathroom and set the bottle down by the toilet before slipping back out, looking innocent.

"Guys," he said dramatically, "I can't hold it anymore! I swear, I'm gonna whiz myself!" He feigned desperation, throwing his hands up as if surrendering.

Stein chuckled. "You better not try anything sneaky! I'll be right here listening at the door."

With that proclamation, Stein pressed his ear against the bathroom door as Parkman shuffled inside. Moments later, the sound of tinkling water filled the air.

"Ha! It's really happening!" Stein exclaimed, listening intently.

Parkman emerged with a defeated look on his face. "Fine! You win this round."

Stein couldn't contain his glee. He let out a whoop of triumph. "I knew it! You have inferior pee-pee muscles, and my pee-pee muscles are pro status!" He practically skipped toward the bathroom, throwing the door half closed behind him. The distinct sound of a long, sustained stream filled the air, seeming to go on for an impossibly long minute and a half. When he finally emerged, Elder Stein was radiating pure, unadulterated relief and victory. He stood tall, chest out, a smug grin.

"That, my friends," he announced, spreading his arms wide, "is the sound of sweet, sweet victory!"

But his triumph was short-lived. Elder Parkman, who had been watching with an expression of anticipation, calmly stepped past the elated Stein, entered the bathroom, and emerged moments later holding something behind his back.

"Actually, Stein," Parkman said, a slow, mischievous smile spreading across his face. He pulled his hand from behind his back, revealing the empty two-liter bottle. "*This* was the sound of victory."

Stein's jaw dropped. His triumphant glow vanished, replaced by utter disbelief and dawning horror. "Wait...what? But...I heard you!"

Parkman chuckled, holding up the empty bottle. "I didn't actually pee, Stein. I emptied *this* into the toilet so you'd think you won!"

Angelo stifled a laugh while Stein's face fell into disbelief mixed with frustration. "Wait! That means you still have to pee worse than ever!"

"I guess that's true," Parkman admitted.

In a flash of competitive spirit, Stein blocked Parkman's path to the bathroom door. "Not so fast!"

Parkman attempted to shove past him but found himself caught in a playful struggle as Stein began tickling him while also trying to push on Parkman's bladder.

"Come on, let the man wee!" Shawn belted between belly laughs. "This is all in good fun!"

Just then Elder Marcus stepped in like an older brother mediating a quarrel between siblings. "All right, all right," he said while trying not to smile. "That was clever, now let Elder Parkman go before he floods the apartment!"

Shawn wiped tears of laughter from his eyes,. "Sister Cohen wasn't kidding when she said this was a fun group. Now I see why!"

Elder Marcus leaned against the wall, his expression turning sheepish. "Man, I feel like such a jerk. Here we are going on about ourselves, and I haven't even asked about you guys. Where are you from?"

Angelo settled onto his lower bunk, adopting the relaxed posture of someone with nothing to hide. "I'm from Utah in a small town outside of Provo." The lie came easily, built from fragments of his own past. "Been on my mission about eighteen months. President Vasquez thought it would be good to see how other missions similar to ours operate, share some best practices."

"Elder Rockwell here is being modest," Shawn interjected, shaking his head. "He baptized an entire family last month—parents and three teenagers. President calls him 'Golden Boy.'"

Angelo shot Shawn a look of amusement and warning. "It wasn't that big a deal."

"Where in Utah, exactly?" Lawrence asked, his interest piqued.

"Pleasant Grove," Angelo replied. "My dad worked construction, handy with a hammer, Mom taught piano lessons from home." The fabricated backstory flowed naturally, built from the remnants of his real childhood.

"And I'm from Arizona," Shawn added. "Chandler, specifically. Family owns a landscaping business. Desert plants, you know? Cactus and stuff." He gestured with his hands. "Elder Rockwell and I met in our first apartment. Been tight ever since."

He paused, his expression turning slightly serious, a vulnerability appearing in his eyes. "We're probably a little older than most of the guys out here, huh? For me, it took a while to figure things out. I actually joined the Church in college because of a girl I liked. Total cliché, I know." He gave a self-deprecating shrug. "She ended up dumping me, I ended up dropping out, but somewhere along the way, I fell in love with God instead. Took me a bit to get my act together and want to serve a mission, but here I am."

Angelo picked up the thread, his voice taking on a reflective tone. "For me, it was similar, in a way. Grew up in the Church, but I think I was just going through the motions for a long time. Didn't really have my own testimony until a few years ago. Had to figure out what I really believed for myself before I felt ready to commit. It's been the best decision I ever made, even if it was a little late."

Lawrence, Marcus, Stein, and Parkman exchanged glances, their earlier competitive energy replaced by genuine warmth and understanding. "Wow," Marcus said. "That's...really inspiring, guys. Thanks for sharing."

Lawrence nodded, a thoughtful look on his face. "Yeah, it's easy to forget everyone's got their own path. That's awesome you guys found your way here."

"Well, we're still getting our bearings," Angelo said. "President Vasquez in the South Mission has noticed how well you guys are doing here in the North Mission, especially with baptisms and convert retention. He thought it would be a great opportunity for us to come observe, exchange ideas, and hopefully pick up on some of your...secrets." Angelo let a hint of curiosity color the last word.

Elder Stein, unable to resist a joke, piped up, "The only secret to our baptism numbers is that we wait for someone to invite us in, roofie their drink, and baptize them while they're passed out. When they wake up, they're full-fledged Mormons!"

Shawn, enamored by these kindred spirits, blurted out with a laugh, "I love these guys! Elder Rockwell, can this be our new mission? Let's just hang with these guys!"

Marcus, however, steered the conversation back to a more serious subject. "Well, this is one of the harder areas of our mission," he said, his tone shifting. "My area hasn't seen a baptism in six months. The missionaries whose spot you're replacing were absolute rock stars, though. Their area was pretty much as dry as mine until Elder Barnes arrived. He showed us that genuine love and affection for the people, and doing whatever it takes to help them, was the key. His area went from having zero baptisms to baptizing an entire family and several others in his time here. He was an amazing missionary."

"That is wonderful," Angelo said, envisioning his brother, emotion welling in his eyes "So heartbreaking though. The president told us of the recent tragedy, Is there anything else that you could tell us about him or his area that you think might help us?"

Elder Marcus looked down, a shadow crossing his face. "Elder Barnes was... Well, he was something special." His voice was thick with emotion. "He wasn't just about the numbers or the rules. He really cared about people, you know? Took time to listen, to understand. He always said the mission wasn't just about converting others but about converting ourselves in the process."

Angelo felt a lump in his throat. He had known Rockwell was good—he had always been good—but hearing it from someone who had served alongside him made it all the more real. He nodded slowly, absorbing Marcus's words.

"Yeah," Lawrence chimed in with a soft smile. "Rockwell had this way of making everyone feel important. Even on the rough days when doors were slammed in our faces or when we were soaked through from rain, he'd keep us going with a joke or a story. Made everything seem lighter."

Stein nodded vigorously. "Totally! And his Portuguese was flawless—like, native-level good. It made such a difference when talking to people here. They trusted him because he took the time to really learn their language and culture."

Parkman stood, arms crossed. "He'd also never let anyone slack off," he added with a chuckle. "I remember once I was feeling down and didn't want to go out. Rockwell sat on my desk during study time and told me uplifting story after uplifting story. Said it was important we keep pushing because every day counts."

Angelo's heart tightened as he imagined Rockwell doing those things, being that kind of person. It stoked the fire of vengeance within him but also reminded him of the pure soul he sought to avenge.

Shawn broke the contemplative silence with his characteristic levity. "Well, Elder Rockwell here is pretty much cut from the same cloth," he said, clapping Angelo on the back. "Except this old cloth right here next to me," he squeezed Angelo's shoulder, "looks badly in need of ironing out those wrinkles." Shawn gestured toward Angelo's eyes.

The room erupted in laughter, breaking some of the tension that had built up.

Lawrence's smile faded as he glanced at Angelo. "If you need anything or have questions about how we do things around here, don't hesitate to ask."

"Yeah," Parkman agreed. "And if you ever want to join in our pranks, let us know."

Shawn's eyes sparkled as he exchanged glances with Angelo, communicating that their cover might be easier than expected.

As they settled into their new environment, Angelo felt a strange sense of peace amid his boiling need for revenge, a brief reprieve granted by these new companions who had so deeply loved and respected his brother.

Elder Marcus looked up from a planner in his hand. "Oh, I almost forgot to mention—we've got Ward Correlation meeting tonight at the church at seven." He looked at Angelo and Shawn. "It's basically where we sync up with the local ward leadership about missionary work. The bishop will be there, along with the ward missionaries."

"And Brett," Elder Lawrence added. "He's our ward mission leader. He's an American who works here in Rio. He can be intimidating at first, like, major military vibes, but he's pretty cool once you get to know him."

Angelo kept his expression neutral, despite the surge of interest at hearing Brett Sawyer's name. This was exactly the connection he'd been hoping to make.

"You guys should definitely come," Marcus continued. "It'd be a great chance to meet everyone and get integrated into the area. Plus, Sawyer always brings refreshments from the bakery."

"Creme puffs, dolce de leite, brigadeiros!" Stein added with a dreamy expression. "Worth sitting through any meeting for."

Shawn nudged Angelo. "What do you think, Elder? Sounds like a good opportunity to learn the ropes around here."

Angelo nodded, the perfect opening. "Absolutely. We'd love to join."

"Great!" Marcus smiled. "We usually walk over together around six thirty. The church is only about ten minutes away."

Angelo smiled back, his mind already racing with possibilities. Brett Sawyer—the mysterious American expat with military connections who had worked closely with Rockwell. The perfect source of information, potentially even an ally.

The evening suddenly held much more promise than just refreshments.

Chapter 9

MEET TOGETHER OFT

After getting to know their new colleagues, Angelo nodded to Shawn. "We should take a walk, get familiar with the area." Once outside in the warm Rio evening, with the sun beginning to hide behind the tall buildings, Angelo loosened his tie as they moved away from the apartment.

"So, what do you think of our new companions?" Shawn asked.

"They're clean. Just kids doing missionary work. No signs of involvement in anything suspicious."

"Agreed. That apartment's got nothing worth investigating either. Oh, and don't take the lid off the trash can in the bathroom. I made that mistake," Shawn said with a grimace. "I guess the toilets in Rio can't handle flushing paper."

They turned a corner, blending into the flow of evening pedestrians.

Angelo kept his voice low. "Leads that lead to more leads, that's what we need from this meeting," Angelo murmured, his eyes always scanning his environment. "We play it humble, hat in hand, like we're relying on *their* local knowledge. If we come on too strong, they'll put their guard up, and we won't have time to win them over. Our first impression has to disarm them, make them like us."

Shawn nodded. "Smart. And what about Ricardo? His name kept coming up in Rockwell's journal."

"I'll make contact ASAP. Set up a meeting for tomorrow morning. If he was as close to Rockwell as the journal suggests, he might have valuable information." Angelo paused at a street vendor, buying two skewers of meat and a couple bottles of juice to maintain their casual appearance.

"What about Sawyer?" Shawn accepted the juice.

"We'll size him up at the meeting tonight. Ex-military means he'll be more perceptive. We need to be careful."

They walked on, the Rio evening pulsing around them, a vibrant symphony of life. Laughter and the rapid-fire cadence of Portuguese spilled from packed outdoor cafés.

Shawn took a long pull from his passion-fruit juice and sighed. "You know, for a city with a bar on every corner, this is a special kind of hell. I'd kill for a cold *cerveja* right now, but no, I'm stuck with glorified fruit punch."

His eyes then followed a group of young women laughing as they passed, their vibrant summer dresses catching the evening breeze. "And don't even get me started on the local talent. I gotta give these missionaries credit. If I had to spend two years here trying to 'lock my heart' while *that* is walking around...man. That's a level of spiritual warfare I'm not equipped for."

Angelo offered no reply. His gaze remained level and unfocused, sweeping methodically over the crowds, the rooftops, and the dark reflections in shop windows.

"Someone in this city has blood on their hands. We find out who, then we make them pay. We have some leads, we just need the path to become clear."

As they rounded back toward the apartment, Angelo added, "Let's clear the apartment tomorrow while they're out. Thorough sweep, just to be certain."

"You got it, Operator." Shawn took a swig of juice. "Those kids seem too genuine to be mixed up in anything dark."

"Sometimes the most dangerous enemies are the ones who look the most innocent."

Angelo and Shawn arrived at the Jardim Botânico Ward Building with the other missionaries from their apartment. The evening air buzzed with energy as they noticed youth from the ward engaged in a spirited soccer match on the outdoor fenced-in court. The rhythmic thud of the ball and shouts of enthusiasm echoed through the streets.

"Looks like they've got some future stars here," Shawn remarked with a smile.

Angelo chuckled, watching a particularly agile kid dribble past two defenders. "Might be worth challenging them one of these days. Could use the workout."

"I don't think that's a good idea, Elder Rockwell. I've seen your dirty slide tackle, and I wouldn't put kneecapping a teenager past you," Shawn ribbed.

Angelo thought about it, realized Shawn was right, and nodded a smile.

As they entered the building, Elder Lawrence led them down the hallway toward the cultural hall. "We usually have our correlation meetings in here," he explained, his tone efficient and welcoming.

The cultural hall had tables and chairs set up in a neat arrangement, ready for the evening's discussions. Angelo and Shawn followed Lawrence's lead, helping to place hymn books at each spot on the tables.

"So, you guys excited to meet Brett Sawyer?" Elder Lawrence asked while carrying way more folding chairs than one man should be allowed to carry.

"Definitely," Angelo replied. "He sounds like an interesting guy."

"Interesting doesn't even begin to cover it," Lawrence said with a grin. "You'll see."

They continued their preparations until the soft creak of the door signaled someone's arrival. A short, skinny man with an earnest smile and a warm demeanor entered, carrying a bicycle helmet under one arm.

"Good evening, elders. I'm Bishop José, but you can call me 'Bicycle Cheese Man.'"

Shawn's eyebrows shot up in amusement. "Bicycle Cheese Man? Do I want to know what 'bicycle cheese' is?"

Bishop José laughed, setting his helmet on one of the tables. "It's because I ride around on my bicycle selling homemade cheese. You have to try it. Fresh cheese, just like I used to make in Minas when I was a kid. Anyway, welcome to our ward."

Angelo extended his hand. "Elder Rockwell. And this is Elder Martinez."

The bishop shook their hands. "It's good to have you both here. We look forward to working together and serving alongside you."

"Likewise," Angelo replied.

The double doors to the cultural hall swung open as Sister Cohen entered, followed by a petite Brazilian woman with warm brown eyes and a shy smile. Angelo recognized Cohen from their meeting at the mission office but kept his expression neutral as she approached.

"Elders, I'd like you to meet my companion, Sister Dos Santos," Sister Cohen announced, gesturing to the young woman beside her. "Sister, these are the new missionaries I was telling you about—Elder Rockwell and Elder Martinez."

Sister Dos Santos offered a small wave. "It's nice to meet you both. Sister Cohen says you're here to help improve our mission. We can use all the help we can get after..." She glanced at the floor.

"After Elder Barnes," Angelo finished for her, careful to maintain his cover.

"Actually, we're the ones who need the help," Shawn said, playing the charm-and-disarm routine with his big smile. "Your mission here is just run so effectively, and the south is falling behind, so we're here to steal the secret."

Angelo noticed Elder Parkman's attention had shifted entirely to Sister Cohen the moment she entered. The missionary's eyes followed her movements with unmistakable admiration, his face softening whenever she spoke. When Sister Cohen adjusted her hair, Parkman straightened his tie and cleared his throat.

"Sister Cohen, we saved you and Sister Dos Santos seats over here," Parkman said, his voice cracking as he pulled out a chair next to his own.

Elder Stein nudged Parkman in the ribs, giving him a pointed look. "Elder, remember to lock your heart," he whispered. "Mission rules."

Parkman's cheeks flushed. "I was just being polite."

"Sure you were," Stein replied with a knowing smirk. "Your politeness has been showing ever since she transferred to our zone."

Sister Cohen seemed oblivious to the exchange as she guided Sister Dos Santos to their seats, though Angelo caught her glancing in Parkman's direction before focusing on Bishop José, who was beginning to organize his notes for the meeting.

The door to the cultural hall swung open with purpose, drawing Angelo's attention. A man with military bearing stepped through, and the energy in the room shifted.

This had to be Brett Sawyer.

Angelo assessed him with a practiced eye. Sawyer wore tan khakis that strained against thighs as thick as tree trunks, evidence of years of disciplined physical training. His loose-fitting polo did little to conceal the powerful frame beneath—Angelo suspected an impressive six-pack, despite the man's age. A leather-bound planner was tucked under one arm, worn but meticulously maintained.

Sawyer's face reminded Angelo of an aging action star—weathered by experience but still commanding. His white flattop haircut added to the impression of a man who maintained standards, regardless of trends. He moved with the fluid confidence of someone who knew exactly who he was and what he was capable of.

The room seemed to orient itself around Sawyer as he strode forward. Even Bishop José straightened in his presence. Angelo noted how the missionaries' demeanor shifted—backs straightening, expressions more attentive.

"Elders," Sawyer greeted them, his voice a controlled baritone that carried without effort. His piercing blue eyes swept the room, landing briefly on each person before moving to the next. When those eyes locked onto Angelo's, he felt a momentary jolt of recognition—not that Sawyer knew him but that Sawyer recognized something in him. The gaze of one predator acknowledging another. Angelo maintained his "Elder Rockwell" persona, offering a respectful nod while mentally cataloging everything about the man.

Sawyer placed his planner on the table, economical and deliberate. Every gesture conveyed intention and discipline. This was not a man who wasted motion or words.

The small gathering arranged themselves around the folding table. The metal chairs scraped against the floor as everyone settled in, creating an informal boardroom atmosphere. Brett Sawyer commanded the space without effort, his presence drawing everyone's attention like a magnet.

"Brother Sawyer, these are our new missionaries." Bishop José gestured toward Angelo and Shawn. "Elder Rockwell and Elder Martinez."

Sawyer extended a hand. "Brett Sawyer. Ward mission leader." His grip was firm but measured as he shook Angelo's hand. "Good to have fresh faces in the ward."

"Pleasure to meet you, sir," Angelo replied, matching Sawyer's grip.

Sawyer released his hand and placed his leatherbound planner on the edge of the table. Elder Stein, buzzing with energy, practically bounced to his side.

"Brother Sawyer! It's so great you could make it!" Stein gestured enthusiastically, his hand catching the edge of the planner and sending it tumbling toward the floor.

There was a collective gasp from the others, but before gravity could claim the object, Sawyer moved. In a blur of motion that seemed impossible for a man his age, his hands shot out. With startling speed, he snatched the planner with his left hand, inches before it hit the floor. He straightened up, the planner securely in his grasp, his expression unfazed.

For a beat, the room was silent, the missionaries staring with wide-eyed awe.

"Whoa..." Stein said, his excitement amplified. He turned to Angelo and Shawn, his eyes practically bugging out. "See? That's what I'm talking about! Brother Sawyer! Can you tell the new elders about your jiu-jitsu training? He trained at the Gracie Dojo before anyone even knew what UFC was," he explained. "Please, tell them about it!"

Sawyer's expression softened at Stein's enthusiasm. "That was a long time ago."

"But you trained with Royce Gracie himself!" Stein persisted. "That's legendary!"

Elder Parkman shouldered his way next to Stein. "Forget jiu-jitsu. Tell them about the SEALs, Brother Sawyer." He turned to Angelo and Shawn. "He was in special operations. He's an Army Ranger but had to do SEAL training too! The real deal."

Sawyer said, "Elder, those stories aren't appropriate for—"

"Which was harder, Brother Sawyer? Special Forces or serving a mission?" Parkman asked, leaning forward.

Sawyer considered the question, his eyes reflecting a distant memory. "SEAL training pushed my body to limits I didn't know existed. But a mission..." He paused, glancing around at the missionaries. "A mission tests your spirit in ways that no physical challenge ever could. You can't muscle through a crisis of faith or a broken heart."

Angelo noted how Sawyer's answer seemed to land with genuine weight among the missionaries. Even the overeager Stein and Parkman grew reflective.

"Have you ever killed a guy?" Elder Parkman, perhaps emboldened by the moment or simply lacking a filter, blurted out.

The question hung in the silence, raw and inappropriate. Several missionaries flinched, their eyes wide with shock.

"Yes," Sawyer answered, devoid of emotion.

The single word was a heavy stone dropped into the quiet room.

"Dude...you can't just ask that when the answer might be *yes*," Stein whispered, his earlier excitement replaced by bewildered horror.

Parkman's face crumpled with regret. "Awww jeez, I'm so sorry. I didn't even think before I said that." He glanced at

Sawyer, then his gaze darted to Sister Cohen, his expression a desperate plea that he hadn't completely disappointed her.

Bishop José cleared his throat and tapped his pen against his planner. "Let's begin our correlation meeting," he announced, redirecting everyone's attention to the agenda.

Angelo settled into the metal folding chair, his posture relaxed but his senses heightened. He watched as the missionaries took turns reporting on their teaching activities. Elder Marcus detailed his progress with the Graca family, who were considering baptism but still had concerns about tithing. Sister Cohen shared her experiences teaching a university student who had questions about the Church's stance on evolution.

Shawn played his part perfectly, asking appropriate questions and offering encouraging nods at the right moments. Angelo noticed how he mirrored the other missionaries' enthusiasm without overdoing it.

Brett Sawyer remained mostly silent, jotting notes in his planner. His eyes, however, missed nothing. Angelo caught him studying the "new missionaries" several times.

Angelo felt the tedium of the meeting washing over him but maintained his attentive facade. Beside him, Shawn suppressed a yawn, disguising it as a thoughtful pause.

As the meeting concluded, the missionaries lingered, breaking into smaller conversations. Angelo saw his opportunity when Brett Sawyer headed toward the exit.

"Brother Sawyer," Angelo called, he and Shawn stepping into the hallway after him. "Do you have a moment?"

Sawyer paused, turning to face them. "What can I help you with, Elders?"

Angelo studied Sawyer with professional admiration. Here was a man who commanded respect without demanding it, a quality Angelo recognized from his years working with elite operatives.

"Brother Sawyer, I've got to say, I'm impressed by how everyone in this ward responds to your leadership," Angelo said, his tone genuine, despite his ulterior motives. "You've clearly built something special here."

Sawyer's expression remained measured, but Angelo caught the subtle softening around his eyes. "The Lord does the building, Elder. I'm just trying to follow the blueprint."

"Well, you're following it better than most," Angelo continued. "Elder Martinez and I were sent from the South Mission to improve our effectiveness. Truth is, we could learn a lot from how things operate in this area." He leaned in. "I'd love to pick your brain, if you're willing."

Shawn nodded enthusiastically. "We've heard great things about your approach to missionary work."

Sawyer studied them, his probing, blue eyes seeming to search for something beneath their words. Whatever he was looking for, he appeared satisfied.

"I appreciate your initiative, Elders," Sawyer said, his voice warming. "I'd be happy to share what I've learned." He glanced at his watch. "Give me about an hour to take care of some business. Then meet me at my apartment." He pulled out a small notepad, wrote down an address, and handed it to Angelo. "Ipanema Beach. Building with the blue awning, top floor. The doorman will be expecting you."

Angelo took the paper, noting the prestigious location. "We'll be there."

"In the meantime," Sawyer added, gesturing back toward the cultural hall, "enjoy the refreshments. I brought some chocolate brigadeiros that'll make you forget every dessert you've ever tasted."

"We won't miss them," Shawn promised with a grin.

Sawyer nodded, then turned to leave, his movements still carrying that military precision as he walked down the hallway.

Angelo and Shawn stepped outside the church building, the evening air providing a welcome contrast to the stuffiness of the correlation meeting. Angelo loosened his tie as they walked toward their apartment, just far enough away from the others to speak freely.

"That went better than expected," Angelo said, satisfaction evident in his voice. "Sawyer practically invited us into his inner circle without us having to push."

Shawn chuckled, slipping his hands into his pockets. "These church folks make this almost too easy. Give them a smile and a scripture, and they hand you the keys to the kingdom."

"And did you see how they all look at Sawyer? Like he's some kind of demigod." Angelo shook his head. "That kind of respect is earned. He's definitely our guy."

"The missionaries were practically falling over themselves for his attention. I thought that Stein kid was going to write Sawyer's biography right there in the cultural hall."

They paused at a street corner, waiting for the light to change. Angelo felt a rare sense of optimism about their mission. Everything was falling into place with remarkable ease.

"We couldn't have planned this better if we tried," Angelo said. "One meeting, and we've got access to Sawyer's home, the missionaries' trust us, and no one's questioning our cover."

"It's like we hit the missionary jackpot," Shawn agreed, grinning. "They're eating out of our hands. Even that Bishop José character, I thought I was going to lose it when he called himself the Bicycle Cheese Man."

Angelo laughed. "And now we've got a direct line to the most connected man in the ward. If anyone knows what happened to Rockwell, it'll be Sawyer."

"You think he suspects anything?" Shawn asked, his tone shifting to professional.

Angelo's confident smile tightened. He recalled a moment Sawyer's eyes had locked onto his—that brief, piercing gaze that felt less like a greeting and more like an assessment.

"Ninety percent of me says no," Angelo said, his voice more measured. "But there was a look. He's not just seeing 'Elder Rockwell.' He's sizing up a threat. It's instinct for men like us." He paused, then shook his head, dismissing the thought. "But in the end, it doesn't matter. He invited us in. We're good. They see what we want them to see—two eager missionaries here to learn their secrets of success."

Chapter 10

IF ANY OF YOU LACK WISDOM

The elevator ascended smoothly toward Brett Sawyer's penthouse overlooking Ipanema Beach. Angelo adjusted his tie, the fake "Elder Rockwell" badge gleaming. Beside him, Shawn, "Elder Martinez," smirked with confidence. The doors opened into a private foyer. Angelo knocked.

The door swung open almost immediately, revealing Brett Sawyer. He was dressed casually now, in a simple T-shirt and shorts that still couldn't quite conceal the powerful physique beneath. His flattop was as immaculate as it had been at the church.

"Elders, right on time," Sawyer said, his voice the same controlled baritone, though perhaps a touch warmer in the confines of his home. He stepped back, ushering them inside. "Come on in. Make yourselves comfortable."

The apartment was stunning, just as Angelo had expected. Floor-to-ceiling windows offered a breathtaking panoramic view of Ipanema Beach and the ocean beyond. The decor was minimalist but expensive, with a clear emphasis on functionality and quality. It was the home of a man who appreciated precision and order. Angelo and Shawn took it all in.

"Have a seat," Sawyer offered, gesturing toward a pair of plush armchairs positioned to take in the view. He moved toward a small, well-stocked snack bar in the corner. "Can I get you anything? Water? A soda?"

"Water would be great, thank you," Angelo replied, settling into an armchair. Shawn echoed the request. Everything felt routine, the kind of polite hospitality one would expect.

Sawyer returned with three glasses of ice water, handing one to each of them before taking a seat on a leather sofa opposite them. He took a slow sip from his glass, his penetrating eyes studying them over the rim. The polite smile remained on his face, but something in his gaze was sharpening, a subtle shift from congenial host to...something else.

The small talk they'd anticipated, the gentle probing about their mission experiences, never came. Angelo was about to launch into their carefully rehearsed inquiry about mission strategies when Sawyer set his glass on the immaculate coffee table with a quiet, deliberate click.

The warmth vanished from his expression as if a switched had been flipped. His jaw set, and those sharp blue eyes, which had seemed merely observant before, now held an intensity that was startling and deeply unsettling. The man who had trained with Royce Gracie and served in special operations was suddenly very present in the room.

"All right," Sawyer stated, his voice dropping to a low, serious tone that brooked no argument, "let's cut the crap."

Angelo and Shawn exchanged a quick, almost imperceptible glance. The air in the room had become electric.

"There's no way in heck you two are missionaries from the Rio de Janeiro South Mission," Sawyer continued, his gaze fixed on Angelo, then darting to Shawn with the same unyielding intensity. The polite facade was gone, replaced by the unwavering focus of a seasoned interrogator. "You haven't fooled me for a second. Not from the moment I laid eyes on you in that cultural hall."

He leaned forward slightly, his powerful frame exuding an undeniable authority. "So, I want to know exactly who you are. And I want to know what you're *really* doing here."

Angelo felt a familiar prickle on his skin, the kind that signaled a shift from a controlled situation to an uncertain one. His mind, honed by years of navigating treacherous encounters, raced to recalibrate. He and Shawn had walked in confident, maybe even a little cocky, believing their ruse was seamless. They were clearly mistaken.

Shawn, ever the quick reactor, let out a short, nervous laugh. "Brother Sawyer, what are you talking about? We're assistants to the president, just like we said. Food poisoning's got President Peterson laid up, but you can call him and ask." He spread his hands in a gesture of bewildered innocence, but his usual easy confidence faltered.

Angelo maintained his composure, his expression neutral, though his internal alarm bells were now blaring. He offered a placid smile. "We understand if we seem a bit...different, Brother Sawyer. The South Mission, well, it has its own unique challenges, its own way of doing things. We're just eager to learn from your success here, anything that might help us back in our area." He tried to project earnestness, the kind he'd been observing.

Sawyer's expression didn't soften. His eyes, like chips of arctic ice, remained fixed on them. He wasn't buying a word. He leaned back, his arms crossing over his powerful chest. "Nice try, elders," he said, the word *elders* now dripping with sarcasm. "But I've spent enough time around real missionaries—and enough time around men trying to blend in. You two don't fit the first category, and your attempt to blend in *as missionaries* is unconvincing. The polish is there, but it's the wrong kind for this role."

Angelo felt a subtle shift in Shawn's posture beside him, a tensing that signaled Shawn recognized the futility of further deception. Angelo's own assessment was stark: Sawyer was not a man to be trifled with. His military background, his evident intelligence, and the sheer force of his presence made him a formidable opponent or a powerful ally. Continuing the lie would be insulting and, more importantly, unproductive. He needed Sawyer; alienating him now would be a critical error.

Angelo let out a slow breath, the "Elder Rockwell" persona visibly dissolving. He met Sawyer's gaze, a silent acknowledgment of the older man's perceptiveness. He gave a small, almost imperceptible shake of his head to Shawn, a signal to stand down.

"All right, Brother Sawyer," Angelo said, his voice losing the slightly forced, deferential tone he'd adopted. It was flatter now, more direct, the voice of the Operator. "You're right. We're not assistants to the president from the Rio de Janeiro South Mission. President Peterson *did* facilitate our arrival but not for the reasons you were told."

He paused, watching for Sawyer's reaction. Shawn's expression remained unchanged.

"But I have to ask," Angelo continued, a note of genuine curiosity, and perhaps a touch of professional respect, entering his voice, "what gave it away?"

Brett Sawyer leaned back with the slight, humorless smile of someone confirming a well-calculated hypothesis. "It wasn't one thing, elders. It was a collection of...inconsistencies. Things that just didn't add up for men claiming to be seasoned missionaries, even ones from a different mission."

He ticked off the points on his fingers, his gaze never leaving them.

"First off, I noticed both of you wearing long-sleeved shirts. It's hot in Rio, especially this time of year. All the other elders in this area, in pretty much every area I've ever lived in, wear short-sleeved, white shirts. I figured you were either new to the climate, which didn't fit your story, or perhaps hiding something. Scars, maybe? Tattoos? I wasn't quite sure, but it was a red flag."

Angelo and Shawn remained silent, the initial shock giving way to a grim acceptance. Sawyer was dissecting them with surgical precision.

"Then there's your demeanor," Sawyer continued, his eyes sweeping over them. "The way you walk with purpose. Your fitness, your physical prowess—it's subtle but it's there. You both remind me of men I've worked with throughout my career. You carry yourselves in a way that screams military...or something worse."

He let that hang in the air for a moment.

"Beyond that, you were far more observant than any missionary I've ever encountered, and that includes a fair number of assistants to the president. APs are usually suck-ups, sure, eager to please, but not with the kind of focused intensity you two displayed. During that meeting, it felt like you weren't just participating, you were cataloging. Either you were trying to keep up, storing information for later, or you're both extraordinarily vigilant. Not typical missionary behavior."

Sawyer's gaze shifted to Shawn. "And Elder Martinez there," he said, a hint of something like pity in his tone, "had a particularly hard time following the opening song in the meeting. It wasn't *just* that he was a bad singer, I was watching your eyes. It looked like you'd never read from a hymnbook before. The words were just...foreign to you."

Shawn shifted uncomfortably.

"I also couldn't help but notice," Sawyer's voice dropped a notch, "that Elder Martinez, or whatever your real name is, is clearly carrying what looks like a wicked knife in his right pocket. The outline is pretty distinct." He then turned his attention back to Angelo. "Elder Rockwell...for now? I assume you're armed as well. You were trying hard to keep a poker face, but your right hand would often drift up, just a slight pat, to what looked like it might be the position of where a shoulder holster would be. Kind of like how most people will pat their pocket to make sure they have their cell phone. It's a subconscious check."

The air in the room thickened. Sawyer's tone remained even, almost academic.

"So," Sawyer said, his gaze unwavering, "given all that, I assume you're both armed. Please, place your weapons on the coffee table—or as I call it, the Diet Dr. Pepper table."

Angelo met Shawn's eyes. There was no point in denying it, no benefit to resisting. With a resigned sigh, Angelo reached inside his backpack, his movements slow and deliberate, and withdrew his handgun. He placed it on the polished surface. Shawn, with a grimace, pulled a formidable combat knife from his pocket and laid it beside Angelo's firearm. Then he, too, reached under his shirt and into his waistband, producing a compact Glock, adding it to the small arsenal on the table.

Sawyer nodded, his expression satisfied. "Thank you." His gaze lingered on the weapons before looking back at them. "But all those things, gentlemen, were just supporting evidence. Strong indicators, certainly. But the most important thing, the biggest clue that gave it all away... I couldn't see your smile."

Shawn looked bewildered. "What? I was genuinely smiling! Especially when that young kid, Elder Parkman, asked you how many people you'd killed or whatever. That was pretty funny, I thought."

Angelo, however, stiffened. A look of dawning, sickening realization crossed his face. He thought back to Sister Cohen's cryptic advice, the hurried instruction he'd dismissed. His mind replayed her words: *You really need to change your underwear if you're going to pull this off.*

"Garments," Angelo muttered, his voice flat with the impact of the oversight. He looked at Shawn. "Elder Martinez, we forgot the LDS garments." His mind flashed to thoughts of missionaries and family members he'd seen over the years, the subtle but distinct line of white fabric visible at the collar of their shirts, sometimes just above the knee. "They call it the 'eternal smile' because you can always see the sweeping neckline of the undergarment beneath the outer clothes. Especially a white dress shirt." He ran a hand over his face. "That's what Sister Cohen meant by 'change your underwear.' We're not wearing the garments. It's a dead giveaway to anyone who knows what to look for." The sheer simplicity of the error, the cultural blind spot, was galling.

Brett Sawyer gave a nod. "Exactly. It's one of the first signals a member, especially someone in a leadership position who deals with missionaries constantly, would unconsciously register. Temple-worthy, endowed missionaries wear them. You two aren't."

He leaned forward again with the focused intensity of a man who knew the score. "So, why don't you get to the point and tell me why in the world you're here."

The weight of Brett Sawyer's accusation, coupled with the irrefutable evidence of the missing garments, settled heavily in the room. Angelo felt a flash of annoyance at the oversight—such a simple cultural detail, yet so significant.

Shawn managed a weak, "Well, damn. You got us there, Brother Sawyer. Guess we should've paid more attention in the MTC...if we'd actually been there." He attempted a sheepish grin.

Angelo silenced him with a subtle gesture. There was no point in further charades. Sawyer was clearly not a man who tolerated foolishness. The direct approach was now their only viable option.

"All right, Sawyer, you're sharper than we anticipated." He paused, choosing his next words carefully. "So, let's be...clearer. We're not missionaries, obviously. President Peterson *did* facilitate our transfer here, but it wasn't for any 'assistant-exchange program.'"

Sawyer's expression remained impassive, arms still crossed. He waited.

"The reason we're here, the reason for this...deception has to do with Elder Barnes." He saw a flicker of something in Sawyer's eyes at the mention of the name, a tightening around his mouth. "Rockwell Barnes. He was my brother."

That admission hung in the air, slightly shifting the dynamic. It wasn't a full confession, but it was a truth, a deeply personal one.

"We found his journals," Angelo explained, "after...after he was killed." The word *killed* was deliberate, not *passed away* or *returned to Heavenly Father*. "And what we read in those journals, combined with the official story of a random gang-violence incident, it didn't add up. It still doesn't. I've got a gut feeling that this was a targeted attack."

Shawn chimed in, his tone now serious, mirroring Angelo's. "That's why we're here. To find out what really happened to him. We figured posing as missionaries was the best way to get access, to talk to people who knew him, people who might have seen something, without tipping off the wrong crowd."

Angelo nodded. "As for our skills, the things you astutely pointed out..." he met Sawyer's gaze, "let's just say Elder Martinez and I have a shared history. We both served. Special Forces." He didn't elaborate further on the specific units, keeping it general. "Now, we're private contractors. When my family was murdered, I called in a marker."

Sawyer listened, absorbing their words. The revelation about Rockwell being Angelo's brother seemed to recalibrate his assessment, though his stern demeanor didn't entirely soften. He uncrossed his arms, a subtle shift.

"Special Forces," Sawyer repeated, eyes narrowing as he appraised them anew. "You may have heard I was an Army Ranger, did SEAL training." He paused with a mirthless smile. "It's a common misconception. People hear 'special operations,' and those are the names that come to mind. I wasn't *exactly* a Navy SEAL, nor *exactly* an Army Ranger, though I've worked alongside the best of both."

He leaned forward again, his voice dropping almost to a murmur, yet carrying an undeniable weight that filled the luxurious apartment. "I was Delta."

The effect on Angelo and Shawn was profound. Their professional composure, already tested, cracked to reveal a raw, almost startled respect. "Delta Force." The words were an unspoken acknowledgment of a level of elite training, secrecy, and operational experience that few achieved and even fewer talked about. In their world, it was a name spoken with a unique mixture of awe and trepidation. Angelo had known Sawyer was formidable; this revelation placed him in a different stratosphere. Shawn, who moments before had been making light of the situation, now sat straighter, his eyes wide with a genuine deference. Their own significant military backgrounds suddenly felt...less significant.

Angelo felt a knot loosen in his chest, a tension he hadn't fully realized he was holding. This wasn't just a sharp ward mission leader, this was one of *them* but from a tier that commanded ultimate respect. The game had changed again, irrevocably. They weren't just caught, they were in the presence of a legend.

Brett Sawyer let the silence stretch, his gaze sweeping over the two men before him. *Delta.* The word still rang through the quiet of his apartment. He seldom revealed that part of his past, but seeing the instant recognition and professional recalibration in their eyes confirmed his assessment. These weren't just slick operators, they were seasoned professionals, likely from a tier just below his but cut from the same Kevlar cloth.

Their story, stripped of the missionary pretense, started clicking into place. Angelo Barnes, the older brother, a former Special Forces operative turned mercenary. Rockwell Barnes, the bright-eyed, earnest missionary, tragically killed alongside his parents. The official story smelling fishy. The brother, utilizing his unique skill set, coming down to Rio under deep cover to find the truth. It had the brutal logic of their shared world.

Sawyer's mind flashed back to Elder Rockwell Barnes. He remembered the young man vividly. A good kid. More than good, actually. He'd had a rare combination of genuine kindness and quiet strength. Sawyer had seen leadership potential in him, a spark that reminded him, in some ways, of the best men he'd served with—the ones who led through empathy, not just orders. Sawyer had taken Elder Barnes under his wing, offering guidance, seeing him as a future leader in the Church, perhaps even beyond.

But he also recalled Elder Barnes's quiet frustrations. The young missionary had chafed, respectfully but persistently, against some of the mission's more rigid protocols. He felt certain rules, certain interpretations of policy, sometimes became obstacles to genuinely serving people, to reaching those who needed Christ's love the most, regardless of their adherence to arbitrary standards. He'd argued, gently, that compassion sometimes required bending the bureaucratic lines. Sawyer, bound by his own calling and vows, had advised adherence but had privately sympathized with the young elder's perspective.

Now, here was the *elder* brother, bending lines—no, shattering them—in the name of justice for that same young man. The irony wasn't lost on him. Angelo Barnes might be a hardened operator, but his motivation stemmed from a fierce loyalty to the brother Sawyer himself had admired. Their methods were worlds apart, but the underlying protective instinct...Sawyer could understand that. The grief, the rage, the need to *know*.

He ran a hand over his flattop, his intense blue eyes fixed on Angelo. They hadn't fooled him, not for a second. Their mistakes were sloppy, proof they hadn't grasped the depth of the culture they were mimicking. But the core narrative—the brother seeking answers—resonated. He remembered Elder Barnes mentioning an older brother, someone in "military then private security," someone he looked up to, though they weren't raised together for long. He'd spoken of him with a mix of awe and a slight distance.

Sawyer knew there was more to the story, more layers beneath the confessed identities and motivations. The mention of President Peterson facilitating their transfer suggested they already possessed significant leverage or information. They weren't just fishing, they were *hunting*.

His initial suspicion began to temper, replaced by a calculated curiosity. These men were dangerous, operating far outside any acceptable bounds within the Church or any government structure. Yet, they were seeking truth about a young man Sawyer had respected, a death that perhaps wasn't as straightforward as reported. And they shared a background, a language of service and sacrifice, that transcended priesthood quorums and mission rules.

He leaned back, his posture relaxing. The intensity remained, but the immediate hostility lessened. "All right, 'Elder Rockwell,'" Sawyer said, his voice even. "Tell me what you think *really* happened to your brother."

Angelo processed the shift. The 'Elder Rockwell' persona he'd reluctantly adopted had crumbled under Sawyer's discerning gaze. It was a rare, unsettling feeling, having a plan implode so completely. His operations were usually seamless. This meeting had been anything but.

As Sawyer's direct question hung in the atmosphere, a different realization dawned on Angelo. This wasn't a total loss. In fact, the failure of his deception might have inadvertently achieved what the deception was designed for: *access*. Sawyer wasn't dismissing them. He wasn't calling security or church officials. He was asking, *really* asking, what Angelo believed had happened. The confrontational intensity remained, but the undercurrent had shifted from hostile suspicion to cautious engagement.

The irony stung. All his lies, his manipulative approach honed over years in the shadows, had proven useless here. He, the Operator, couldn't penetrate Sawyer's defenses with deceit. But the mere mention of *Rockwell*, his honest brother, combined with the stark admission of their true purpose, seemed to have cracked open a door his lies couldn't even find the handle for. It wasn't *his* maneuvering that yielded this potential breakthrough, it was the lingering impression of Rockwell's earnest character, a goodness Sawyer had apparently recognized and respected. Rockwell, even in death, was opening doors Angelo couldn't breach.

Maybe Sawyer *could* be an ally, or at least a source. The direct approach, forced upon him by Sawyer's acuity, might actually be more effective now. No more beating around the bush, no more feigning piety. Just the raw truth of his mission, laid bare before a man who clearly understood the complexities of violence, loyalty, and seeking answers in dangerous places.

He met Sawyer's unwavering eyes. *All right*, Angelo thought, his calculating mind recalibrating rapidly, *let's try it this way*. Plan B: calculated honesty or at least a version of it. He leaned forward, mirroring Sawyer's earlier posture, lowering his voice to match the man's intensity.

"I'm still putting the pieces together," Angelo admitted, the confession feeling surprisingly less like weakness and more like a strategic starting point. "I don't have the whole picture. But there are too many loose threads, too many things that just don't sit right."

He paused, gauging Sawyer's reaction. The former Delta operator remained still, his expression steely, waiting.

"Start with President Peterson," Angelo continued. "We have Rockwell's journals. He mentioned the mission's strict policies about avoiding certain favelas, specifically Morro Diabólico. He'd apparently questioned it, felt they were missing opportunities to serve. Why was Peterson so adamant? It felt...disproportionate. Officially, it's about safety, I get that. But the level of restriction felt off, especially when compared to other high-risk areas missionaries sometimes work in."

He let that hang for a moment before dropping the next piece. "And Peterson... Let's just say he's compromised. We found leverage. Something dirty from his past back in the States, tied to his mortuary business. Something the Church helped cover up years ago. It was enough to make him co-operative. That's how we got the transfer papers, the badges, access to the apartment."

He watched Sawyer closely, looking for any sign of prior knowledge or surprise. Sawyer's jaw remained tight, but his eyes seemed to sharpen further.

"Then there's the official response to my family's deaths," Angelo pressed on. "Captain Mauro, the BOPE leader who briefed us?"

He saw a flash of recognition in Sawyer's eyes.

"He practically had the case wrapped up before we even landed. Fifteen gang members 'neutralized' in a swift oper-ation. Convenient. It felt less like an investigation and more like tying up loose ends. Peterson and Mauro were practically joined at the hip when we met them. Peterson was jumpy, pushing hard for us to just take Rockwell's things and head back to Utah. Let the professionals handle it, leave it alone. Mauro backed him up, all professional courtesy but with an undercurrent of 'get the hell out.' They wanted us gone."

He leaned back, letting the implications settle. "So, you have a compromised mission president with a history of secrets, prohibitive rules about the exact place my family was murdered, and a high-ranking tactical cop involved in a rushed investigation and cover-up, both seemingly working together to push me out of the country."

Angelo shook his head. "I don't know the connection yet. I don't know *why* they were targeted or why Peterson and Mauro are covering *something* up. Is it just Peterson's dirty laundry getting tangled up somehow? Is it something bigger?

I don't know. But my gut, honed by years of dealing with deception and violence, tells me this wasn't just random gang crossfire. It tells me Peterson, maybe even elements within the Church structure facilitating his cover-ups, are hiding something related to why my brother, mother, and stepfather ended up dead in that favela." He met Sawyer's intense gaze again. "And I came here to find out."

Brett Sawyer let the silence stretch for a long moment after Angelo finished, his gaze fixed on the man before him. He saw the raw grief, the steel of a professional killer, and beneath it, the fierce loyalty of a brother. Angelo Barnes was playing a dangerous game, one that could easily get him killed, but Sawyer recognized the unwavering resolve. He also recognized the ring of truth in Angelo's assessment, or at least a significant portion of it.

Sawyer nodded, a decision forming in his mind. He wouldn't—couldn't—reveal the full scope of his own activities, but perhaps a carefully controlled release of information could serve both their interests, or at least steer Angelo's vengeance away from unproductive paths and potentially, unwittingly, toward areas that aligned with Sawyer's own objectives.

"Your brother, Elder Barnes," Sawyer began, "*was* interested in Morro Diabólico. More than interested. He felt a strong calling to take the Gospel there." Sawyer recalled the conversations clearly—Rockwell's earnest idealism clashing with Sawyer's pragmatic warnings. "He brought it up several times. We discussed it at length, he and I, and with his companion. I counseled him against it. Not because I didn't believe in his sincerity or the potential for good but because that place...it's not just about petty crime or turf wars. It's a different kind of darkness."

Angelo and Shawn exchanged a quick glance. This was new information, a confirmation of Rockwell's unusual focus.

"Elder Barnes believed, rightly so, that every soul deserves to hear the message," Sawyer continued, a hint of respect in his voice for the young man's conviction. "His heart was undeniably in the right place. A brave kid. But bravery without understanding the true nature of the threat can be fatal. I warned him about the cartels, the traffickers, the general lawlessness. But there are layers to Morro Diabólico, dangers that go far beyond what most missionaries, or even most locals, comprehend."

Sawyer paused, choosing his next words with the precision of a sniper. He leaned forward, his keen eyes locking onto Angelo's. "You said you and your partner here were Special Forces. You understand that some battles are fought in the shadows, long after the flags are folded and the parades are over."

A beat of silence.

"I might have a nice apartment overlooking Ipanema, and I might spend my Sundays leading ward meetings, but let's just say my retirement isn't as...complete...as it might appear. I'm still in the business, so to speak."

He let that sink in. Angelo and Shawn's expressions remained guarded, but he saw the subtle shift in their posture, the heightened alertness. They understood the implication.

"I'm here *on assignment*, have been for a while," Sawyer stated. "I can't tell you who I work for or the specifics of my mission. That information is above your pay grade, no offense intended."

He saw a flash of understanding, a dawning realization in their eyes. They were connecting the dots—Delta Force past, current "assignment," warnings about a deeper darkness.

"What I *can* tell you," Sawyer continued, "is that there's more going on in Morro Diabólico than just drug deals and human trafficking, as heinous as those things are. There's a malignancy there, something with tendrils that reach far beyond the borders of Rio, with potential implications for global security." His gaze drifted to the window, as if looking out at some unseen threat over the city. "Things that certain...powerful interests...would prefer remained contained, or better yet, eradicated."

He brought his focus back to Angelo and Shawn. He hadn't explicitly stated he was still on the Delta payroll, or working for Uncle Sam, but the breadcrumbs were there, carefully laid to lead them to that conclusion. He needed them to understand the stakes and to recognize that he was operating on a level that demanded discretion and respect.

"Your brother might have stumbled onto something far bigger, far more dangerous, than he ever could have imagined," Sawyer concluded, his voice a somber warning. "And that, 'Elder Rockwell,' might be the real reason he and your family are dead."

Sawyer let that sink in, observing the grim understanding on their faces. "If I were looking for the missing link that connects President Peterson, Officer Mauro, and whatever Rockwell stumbled upon, I would get to the bottom of what's being hidden in the heart of that diabolical hill."

He paused, considering his next words. "Navigating this city, especially its darker corners, requires local knowledge. Have you heard of Ricardo de Aparcido from the ward?"

Angelo nodded.

"Good. That's your next step. Find him. Rockwell helped turn his life around. He *loved* your brother. Ricardo knows the streets, the players, has connections even the BOPE doesn't touch. If you're looking for a friendly face, someone who understands the city's rhythms and secrets, Ricardo can help you."

Sawyer leaned back, the intensity in his eyes remaining. He offered a professional smile, the kind shared between men who understand high stakes. "Your cover story," he said, the 'assistant-exchange program'? It's safe with me. No one will hear otherwise from me."

He stood, signaling the meeting's end. "You boys operate how you need to. But be smart. Be discreet. Rio has enough eyes already, and you don't need more watching you." He extended his hand first to Angelo, then to Shawn. "If you need anything—*anything* at all—call me, day or night. I'm here to help. Oh, and one more thing: change your underwear."

Chapter 11

THE LITTLE FACTORY

Angelo and Shawn walked back to the Leblon apartment. They'd detoured to a small shop after the meeting, purchasing, among other clothes, plain white undershirts and boxer briefs that could, at a cursory glance, pass for the temple garments they were conspicuously lacking.

Back at the apartment, the atmosphere was subdued. Elder Marcus, Elder Lawrence, Elder Stein, and Elder Parkman were all seated at their respective desks, hunched over scriptures and notebooks, the picture of diligent study.

Angelo and Shawn exchanged a glance. Time to blend. Shawn, ever the method actor, pulled out his newly acquired copy of the missionary handbook and attacked it with the fervor of a student cramming for a final exam. He uncapped a cheap ballpoint pen and began underlining passages and scribbling notes in the margins, his brow furrowed in concentration. Angelo knew Shawn's improvisational genius was directly proportional to his preparation; the more he knew the rules, the better he could artfully break them.

Angelo sat at his own desk, opening his quad. He stared at the distantly familiar columns of text in the Book of Mormon, but the words blurred. His mind wasn't on ancient prophets or Nephite wars. Instead, he was breaking down the evening, analyzing Sawyer, dissecting the interactions. Sawyer was formidable, no doubt. Perceptive. But he'd also willingly invited them into his home. The leverage he held over Peterson was a powerful tool, but Sawyer could be a crucial ally or a dangerous obstacle.

A quiet hour passed, punctuated only by the rustling of pages and the occasional sigh. Finally, Elder Marcus stretched, yawning. "All right, elders, time to hit the hay. Big day tomorrow."

A collective murmur of agreement went through the room. One by one, they closed their books. As if by unspoken agreement, they all knelt by their chairs or beds. Angelo followed suit, the motion feeling foreign and familiar all at once. He bowed his head, listening as Elder Lawrence offered a simple, earnest prayer, asking for guidance, for strength, and for the Spirit to be with them in their work. He prayed for the people of Rio, for their investigators, and for the new elders, Rockwell and Martinez, that they might find success and feel welcome.

Angelo didn't pray, not in the way they did. His prayers were silent, cold reckonings, vows of vengeance whispered to the darkness. But as he knelt there, surrounded by these young men, a strange quiet settled over a small corner of his turbulent mind.

After the "amen," the elders rose and began their bedtime routines. Toothbrushes were deployed, pajamas donned. Angelo and Shawn changed into their newly acquired underclothes.

Soon, the apartment was dark and quiet, save for the rhythmic breathing of sleeping missionaries and the ever-present rattle of the blessed air conditioner in the window. Angelo lay on his bunk, staring up at the slats of the bunk above. Sleep wouldn't come easily, not with the faces of his family swimming in his vision, not with the plan churning in his mind. Tomorrow, Ricardo. Tomorrow, they'd start digging into what secrets lay hidden within the Morro Diabólico.

Angelo and Shawn had barely registered the first light filtering through the thin curtains of their Leblon apartment when a sudden, frantic shouting shattered the morning calm. Angelo was instantly awake, every nerve ending firing, his hand instinctively reaching for a weapon that wasn't there. Shawn jolted upright in the bunk above him, eyes wide.

"No, no, no! Get away from there! Just...stop it!" The voice was high-pitched, pleading, and unmistakably Elder Stein's, laced with an acute note of desperation.

Angelo and Shawn exchanged a look. This wasn't the sound of a spiritual debate. This was distress, albeit of a peculiar kind. Angelo swung his legs over the side of his bunk, his mind already cataloging potential threats. Shawn was right behind him, his usual playful demeanor replaced by a look of grim alertness mixed with curiosity.

They moved swiftly down the short hall toward the bedroom shared by Stein and Parkman, where the commotion seemed to be centered. Angelo rounded the corner first, ready to confront whatever emergency was unfolding.

The scene that greeted them was...unexpected.

Elder Stein, clad in his white garment top and...compromised pajama pants, stood beet red in the middle of their small bedroom. He looked like he'd been caught in a spotlight, one hand clutching the front of his pajamas, the other gesturing wildly toward Elder Parkman. Parkman, a triumphant grin plastered across his face, stood with his back to the small shared dresser, arms spread wide like a defensive lineman, blocking Stein's access to his clean clothes. The overflowing laundry basket sat accusingly in the corner.

"Give it a rest, Parkman! It's not funny! I need to shower! I need clean garments!" Stein's voice cracked, his eyes darting toward the bathroom door down the hall, then back to the impassable Parkman. He was clearly trying to get to his clean clothes before facing the world, or at least the bathroom.

"Not funny?" Parkman boomed, his laughter echoing through the small apartment. He gestured toward Stein, then gave a knowing nod toward the laundry basket. "Elder Stein, this is a *miracle*! Behold, elders!" he announced to Angelo and Shawn, who were now standing stunned in the doorway. "The sacred sign! The holy evidence! Our humble abode has been blessed! The Pancake Man has visited our dear Elder Stein, and now he seeks to prevent the joyous proclamation by...*changing his clothes*!"

Stein groaned, burying his face in his hands. "You're the worst! The absolute worst! Can't a guy just deal with...*evidence*...and get washed up in peace?"

Angelo and Shawn's tactical readiness deflated into sheer bewilderment. Angelo's mind, conditioned to analyze threats, struggled to process the scene. A laundry basket? The Pancake Man? Parkman as a human barricade? It was just plain weird. He looked at Shawn, whose expression mirrored his own confusion, though a hint of amusement was beginning to dawn in Shawn's eyes.

"The...Pancake Man?" Shawn ventured, his brow furrowed.

Elder Parkman, clearly relishing the chaos and his role as guardian of the dresser, puffed out his chest. "Indeed, Elder Martinez! A most esteemed nocturnal visitor! And the...*offerings* on Elder Stein's current attire are the ceremonial standard, alerting all to the joyous occasion!" He patted the dresser behind him. "No clean garments shall be procured until the tale is told!"

Elder Stein, his face still crimson, finally managed to look at Angelo and Shawn. "This happens sometimes," he mumbled, his voice thick with shame, his hand still covering the front of his stained pajama pants. "What? You guys don't get visits from the Pancake Man down south?" He looked pleadingly at Angelo and Shawn, as if seeking an intervention.

Angelo blinked slowly. His mission involved infiltrating a criminal conspiracy, avenging his family, and navigating a web of deceit and violence. This...was something else entirely. He had faced down armed combatants, outsmarted intelligence operatives, and stared death in the face, but the dynamics of these antics were beyond his comprehension.

Shawn, his initial tactical alertness replaced by a bemused curiosity, couldn't hold back. "Okay, I gotta ask," he said, a grin spreading across his face as he stepped further into the room, carefully positioning himself out of the direct line of fire between Stein and Parkman. "The Pancake Man? Spill it, Parkman. What's the deal? Is this like a missionary-initiation thing I missed in the MTC?"

Elder Parkman was clearly delighted to have an audience and to prolong Stein's discomfort. He gestured magnanimously toward the mortified Stein.

"Ah, Elder Martinez, a seeker of divine wisdom!" Parkman proclaimed with mock solemnity. "The Pancake Man is a figure of...nocturnal significance. Much like your sandman, or perhaps the tooth fairy, he visits in the quiet hours of slumber." He paused for dramatic effect, his eyes twinkling. "However, instead of dreams or dimes, when you awaken after a visitation from the Pancake Man, you discover...well, let's just say someone has left a bit of pancake batter in your bed. Or, more accurately, *on* your sacred underthings, which then make a hasty pilgrimage to the laundry receptacle! Or, in Elder Stein's current predicament, remain upon his person until certain conditions are met!"

He leaned in conspiratorially, lowering his voice, though it still boomed in the small apartment. "Most of the time, said batter is strategically located, right in the front of your garment bottoms, if you catch my drift." He winked. "You know," he continued, adopting a scholarly tone, "the esteemed Elder Boyd K. Packer, in his infinite wisdom, taught us to keep our thoughts pure and to never, *ever* abuse ourselves, for our bodies, you see, possess a remarkable self-regulating mechanism. A natural...release valve for our little factory that operates on its own. You, in your southern vernacular, may refer to this phenomenon as a 'nocturnal emission.' But here in the sophisticated climes of the north, we, the enlightened, call it a visit from the Pancake Man."

Parkman straightened up, a proud smile on his face, always the type to overshare. "To be perfectly honest, Elder Martinez, I myself had never been graced by the Pancake Man's presence until I *came* on my mission."

At Parkman's phrasing, "came on my mission," Shawn couldn't help it; a snort of laughter escaped, which he tried to cover with a cough, though his shoulders were shaking.

Parkman, oblivious, or perhaps choosing to interpret it as a cough of profound understanding, pressed on. "It was probably," he admitted with a shrug and a sly grin, "because I was, shall we say, spanking the monkey with rather dedicated frequency, which I shall have you know I have fully repented of. But once circumstances...*required* a cessation of said simian spanking, after a few weeks, lo and behold, the Pancake Man made his presence known!"

Shawn, having recovered from his giggle fit, wiped a tear from his eye. "Okay, okay, I get it," he said, his voice still thick with suppressed laughter. "The Pancake Man. Got it." He paused, a mischievous glint in his eyes. "Down south, where we're from," he nodded toward Angelo, "we have a similar...entity. We call it a visit from Elder Rockwell's sister."

A moment of silence, then Elder Parkman let out a hearty, unrestrained roar of laughter. Elder Stein, despite his previous mortification and desperate need to get to the shower and change, dissolved into high-pitched giggles.

Angelo stood in the doorway, a silent observer of this theological and biological discourse. He registered Shawn's barb, the playful jab at his adopted persona. Internally, a small, almost imperceptible ripple of amusement broke through his hardened exterior. It was a childish joke, but in the absurd context of his current undercover operation, surrounded by these earnest, goofy young men, it landed with a strange guilty-pleasure resonance. He didn't smile, not outwardly, but for a moment, his eyes softened.

"All right, all right, Elder Stein," Parkman conceded, still chuckling. He remained firmly planted in front of the dresser. "You can *earn* access to your clean apparel and then proceed with your ablutions. But only on one condition."

Elder Stein, his hand still protectively near his crotch, eyed Parkman with suspicion. "What condition?" he asked warily.

"Entertainment is a scarce commodity here in the Lord's vineyard, my friend," Parkman declared, a mischievous glint in his eye. "Some of the funniest parables I've ever heard have been the sacred tales of other elders' encounters with the esteemed Pancake Man. So, you regale us with the dream, the vision, the nocturnal narrative that accompanied this...visitation. And then, and only then, shall this blockade be lifted and your shame be laundered."

Stein groaned, the sound a mix of acute embarrassment and weary resignation. "You're evil, Parkman. Pure, unadulterated evil." But Angelo could see a flicker in Stein's eyes—a story-teller's spark. He wanted to get to the bathroom, desperately. But the thought of holding court, even with such mortifying subject matter, held a certain appeal.

"Fine." Stein sighed dramatically, running his *clean* hand through his short blonde hair. "All right, all right, I'll share the story. *Then* I can finally go clean these...these sin-soiled undergarments and change." He gave an exaggerated shiver.

Then Stein took a deep breath, glanced at Angelo and Shawn as if to gauge their level of judgment (Angelo offered none, Shawn offered a grin of anticipation), and then launched into his tale, still standing awkwardly in his compromised clothing.

"All right, so, I was back home, right? Before the mission. All the young men and women from the ward, we were sitting in a circle in the cultural hall, playing some stupid party game. And then," he lowered his voice conspiratorially, "I look down, and...well, my...you know." He gestured toward his crotch. "It had fallen off. Just...rolled right out of the bottom of my shorts."

Shawn snorted, trying to stifle a laugh. Parkman, still guarding the dresser, was beaming.

"So, naturally, I picked it up. Tried to put it back on, reattach it. But nothing. It wouldn't stick. And then, some wise guy in the circle, probably McKay Jensen, noticed. And he's like, 'Hey, what's that? Cool! Let's pass it around!'"

The image was so absurd that even Angelo felt the corner of his lip twitch.

"So, they start passing it around the freaking circle!" Stein's voice rose in mock indignation. "Like show-and-tell! Can you imagine? 'Look, kids, it's Elder Stein's disembodied unit!' And then...and then it got to *her*." He paused for dramatic effect. "Becky Sorensen. My ultimate crush since, like, fourth grade.

She's holding it, looking at it all curious, and I just...I lost it. Evidence of the Pancake Man, guys. Everywhere. Like a flash flood in the cultural hall. All over Becky's Sunday best."

Parkman howled with laughter, while maintaining his post. Shawn was practically doubled over.

"But wait!" Stein held up a hand, a manic gleam in his eye. "That's not even the worst part!"

"There's *more?*" Shawn gasped.

"Oh, there's more," Stein assured him. "The worst part is, I woke up from *that* dream...into *another* dream! A dream within a dream! And in this one, there was so much pancake batter. So. Very. Much. It was like...like a biblical plague of pancake batter. And it was dripping, right through the top bunk, where I was, and covering the bottom bunk. Like an entire sludge of gooey, thick pancake batter, seeping through and dripping right onto...Elder Parkman!"

He pointed an accusatory finger at Parkman, whose laughter had stalled in surprise.

"And the worst part," Stein leaned in, his voice dropping to a dramatic whisper, delivering the final, ribbing blow, "the absolute *worst* part...is that Elder Parkman *loved* every second of it! He was swimming in it! Rolling around in it! Because he's just such a weirdo!"

The apartment erupted. Parkman roared with laughter, his big frame shaking so hard he almost stumbled away from the dresser. Stein, his story told, dissolved into relieved giggles, the tension of his embarrassment finally broken.

Shawn, eager to show off what he had been studying, proudly added, "I guess that's why the handbook says to sleep in the same room but *not* the same bed as your companion."

"Let's keep it clean, guys," Elder Lawrence groaned from his bed, clearly annoyed.

"Well played, Elder Stein!" Parkman wheezed, clutching his stomach. "Well played indeed!" He finally stepped away from the dresser. "The path to purification and clean garments is clear. Go forth and launder!"

Stein, with a triumphant grin, made a beeline for the now-unguarded dresser. The Pancake Man had visited, but Elder Stein had gotten the last laugh. Angelo watched them, a silent observer of this bizarre and endearing morning devotional. This mission was proving to be stranger, and perhaps more human, than he could have ever anticipated.

Soon a semblance of missionary morning routine began to take shape. Angelo and Shawn went through the motions, dressing in their white shirts and ties, the unfamiliar fabric of the newly purchased undergarments a constant, awkward reminder of their cover.

They sat with the other elders in the living area as Elder Marcus led a scripture study and a prayer, Angelo bowing his head and closing his eyes, his mind a whirlwind of tactical considerations rather than spiritual reflection. He offered clipped, appropriate responses when questions about scriptural interpretation were posed to "Elder Rockwell."

Time crawled by as they feigned diligent study, Rockwell's quad open before Angelo, the pages a blur. He watched the clock, every tick a slow count toward their arranged meeting with Ricardo de Aparcido. The other missionaries eventually dispersed, leaving Angelo and Shawn with the quiet apartment. Finally, the appointed hour approached. They straightened their ties, grabbed their backpacks, and stepped out into

Rio. The journey to Ricardo's office wasn't long, leading them away from the charm of Leblon and toward the sleek, modern towers of a burgeoning business district, culminating in their arrival at an impressively high-end office building. Time to meet Ricardo.

Chapter 12

SEEK DILIGENTLY

Elder Rockwell and Elder Martinez arrived on a bustling floor of the business high-rise, a drone of activity humming with the low thrum of bureaucracy. Ricardo de Aparcido's office wasn't the opulent suite Angelo had expected from a man of influence but rather a cornerstone of this functional, almost governmental-looking building in Rio's business district. Phones rang incessantly, and people moved with determined strides through corridors lined with filing cabinets and doors bearing official-looking plaques.

Inside Ricardo's personal office, the man himself was a whirlwind, juggling a phone call in rapid-fire Portuguese while simultaneously signing a stack of documents. The space, though not lavish, was clearly the domain of a busy man. Framed certificates of community involvement and photos of Ricardo with various local figures adorned the walls, alongside a large, detailed portrait of Rio with certain districts highlighted. He motioned for Angelo and Shawn to take the worn but comfortable guest chairs, his expression a mixture of apology and harried focus.

Finally, Ricardo slammed down the phone and turned to them, a broad, welcoming smile transforming his face. "Elders! Forgive the chaos. Always a fire to put out, you know how it is." He spoke with authority, but his warmth was unmistakable. "Brother Sawyer called ahead. Elder Rockwell and Elder Martinez, is that right?"

Angelo nodded, offering the polite, deferential smile he'd been practicing. "Yes, sir. Thank you for seeing us on such short notice." He noted the name "Elder Rockwell" seemed to resonate with Ricardo, a flicker of something warm and familiar crossing the man's face.

"Nonsense, nonsense," Ricardo said, waving a dismissive hand. "Anything Brett Sawyer asks, Ricardo delivers. And anything for the Church, for the ward. You tell me what you need, how I can help. More resources for the youth program? Help with the bishop's food drive? My people are your people."

"That's very generous, Brother de Aparcido," Shawn chimed in, his "Elder Martinez" persona radiating earnest enthusiasm. "We're actually here from the South Mission on an exchange. President Peterson sent us to learn from the success here. We heard that this ward is doing remarkable things."

Ricardo's smile softened, a nostalgic look entering his eyes. "Ah, you are here to learn the secrets, eh?" He chuckled, a deep rumbling sound. "The secret is love, elders. Just love the people. That's what *your* Elder Barnes taught me." His gaze lingered on Angelo's name tag. "You...you remind me of him a little. The name, of course, but something in the eyes too."

Angelo felt a slight jolt. He wasn't trying to resemble Rockwell in demeanor, but the name alone was clearly a powerful trigger for Ricardo. "We've heard a lot about Elder Barnes," Angelo said. "He seems to have made a real impact here. We were hoping to understand more about the kind of work he did, the people he connected with."

Ricardo leaned back with a wistful expression. "Elder Barnes..." Ricardo began, his voice growing softer, "he saved my life. Not in a dramatic way, no dashing into a burning building. He saved me from myself."

He paused, gathering his thoughts. "The first time he and his companion knocked on my door, I was a mess. Drunk. Three sheets to the wind, as you say. I brushed them off, told them to come back another time, just to get rid of them. They set a little appointment in their notebook, then I forgot all about it." He shook his head with a rueful smile. "But they came back. Persistent, those two. I was sober that time, a little embarrassed, but I let them in. I don't know why. Maybe it was the look in Elder Barnes's eyes. So much...hope. And genuine care for a stranger like me."

Angelo listened intently, picturing Rockwell, his earnest brother, facing this man.

"He didn't judge me," Ricardo continued, his voice thick with emotion. "He just talked. About his family, about God, about finding peace. And he listened. *Really* listened. To my problems, my excuses, my anger. Week after week, he came back. He shared his light with me, and little by little, it started to chase away my darkness."

Ricardo's eyes glistened. "I stopped drinking. I found my beautiful Maria again, my wife—we had been separated. She saw the change in me. Elder Barnes, he taught us together. After weeks," Ricardo's voice swelled with pride, "I walked into my old bar, the place where I wasted so many years and so much money. I told my old cronies, 'You won't see Ricardo in here anymore, unless it's to bring you to church. And I won't have a beer in my hand, I'll have this!'" He pantomimed holding up a book. "A Book of Mormon!"

He beamed at them. "Elder Barnes. He was a redeeming angel. He saw good in me when I couldn't see it in myself. Anything I can do to honor his memory, to help the work he loved, I will do it."

Shawn, who had been listening with a surprisingly rapt expression, nodded vigorously. "That's...that's an amazing story, Brother de Aparcido. It reminds me of someone we taught back in our old area down south."

Angelo tensed, wondering where Shawn was going with this.

"This fella," Shawn continued, leaning forward, "he was tough. Ex-military, actually. Had a hair-trigger temper and a vocabulary that would make a sailor blush. Everyone else was scared of him. Said he was a lost cause." Shawn shook his head, a theatrical sigh escaping him. "But Elder Rockwell, he saw something else. He kept going back, kept talking, kept showing this guy kindness even when he was cussing us out six ways from Sunday. And slowly, he started to soften. He started asking questions. Next thing you know, he's coming to church. He even started reading his scriptures!" Shawn grinned, a picture of missionary triumph. "Turned his whole life around. Said it was the first time anyone had bothered to see past his rough exterior. Shows you what a little persistence and a lot of love can do, right?"

Ricardo's eyes shone with appreciation. "Exactly, Elder Martinez! Exactly! Your Elder Barnes, he understood this. He shined with the true light of Christ." He looked at Angelo again. "You young men, you have a powerful calling. A sacred duty. Ricardo de Aparcido is at your service."

Ricardo's smile widened, a nostalgic gleam in his eyes as he leaned forward, as if sharing a precious secret. "I remember the day Elder Barnes taught me the Word of Wisdom," he said, his voice filled with a fond amusement. "He told me, very gently, kindly, that if I wanted to be baptized, the caipirinhas, the cachaça, all of it...it had to go. I looked around my house, and saw a monument to my old life, bottles everywhere." He chuckled. "And then, that young man, barely old enough to be out of his mother's sight, he gets this look in his eye, a little bit of mischief, a little bit of holy fire, you know? He says, 'Brother Ricardo, why don't we take every last bottle out to your beautiful garden right now? And we can send them to a better place together.'" Ricardo threw his head back and laughed, a sound of pure, unadulterated joy. "And we did! Oh, Holy Mother...we did! We were like two boys, giggling and smashing bottle after bottle against the garden wall! Pop! Crash! Bang! There was a twenty-five-year-old Macallan, a gift from a client, could have paid for a whole semester of my boy's private school. Crash! Gone! And you know what? I didn't feel a moment's regret. Only freedom. Only joy. That Elder Barnes, he helped me smash my old life to pieces so I could build a new one."

Angelo felt the burn of that raw emotion, the image of his pure, innocent brother, smashing bottles with a reformed drunkard in a sun-drenched garden, almost too much to bear. It was a Rockwell he recognized, a Rockwell whose light was now extinguished. Such beautiful destruction, Ricardo breaking free from his past with Rockwell's guidance. A pang of bitter truth twisted inside Angelo: some men, like Ricardo, sought transformation, actively breaking down the old to build anew. Others, like his father, Oren Barnes, only ever sought to break things—spirits, hands, families—reveling in ruin with no desire for redemption, only destruction. He pushed the feeling down, the Operator taking control. He needed information, not sentiment.

"That's...quite a testament to Elder Barns's spirit, Brother de Aparcido," Angelo said, his voice carefully modulated to sound moved, yet still focused on their supposed purpose. "We're trying to learn from that kind of effectiveness. In the South Mission, where Elder Martinez and I are from, President Vasquez encourages us to go into *all* areas, even the favelas, as long as we're prayerful, with a companion and to exercise caution, of course. We've found some of our most receptive families in those more...challenging communities." He paused, setting the hook. "Here in the north, though, we've heard the restrictions on favelas are much tighter. Particularly one...Morro Diabólico."

Ricardo's smile faded, his expression becoming serious, almost grim. "Ah, elders. Yes, many favelas are dangerous, and you are wise to be cautious everywhere. But Morro Diabóli-co..." He shook his head, a deep sigh escaping him. "That is a different beast. So much violence, so many...many people."

He leaned forward, his voice dropping. "There are es-timates, whispers that say more than a million souls live crowded onto that hill. A million! Can you imagine? But the truth is, no one really knows. The government, the census takers...they can't get anyone up there to count. It's like a sovereign, lawless nation within our city."

Ricardo sat back, a frustrated anger tightening his features. "And this, elders, this lack of numbers...it makes my blood boil." He gestured emphatically. "I work with committees, with the city, trying to get aid, resources, sanitation, education to the people who live in these conditions. But how can we get sufficient funding, how can we allocate help effectively when the official population count for places like Morro Diabólico is practically zero? It's a direct correlation! No official popula-tion means no allocation. It's madness, and the people suffer."

Shawn, playing the part of the concerned, slightly naive missionary, chimed in. "But surely there must be some records? For births, or..."

Ricardo let out a short, sharp laugh. "Records? Elder Mar-tinez, up there," he gestured toward the unseen favela, "it is as if they are ghosts. Birth certificates? Rarely registered, if at all. Death certificates when someone passes? Often, there is no official notice. Marriage licenses?" He threw up his hands. "Nothing! The inhabitants of Morro Diabólico, for all official purposes, might as well be living in another country, undocumented, unseen by the bureaucracy."

He leaned forward again, his eyes intense. "And because of this...this invisible population...the problems, they fester. Crime of every imaginable type. Drugs, obviously, that's the engine. Kidnapping, extortion, you name it." His voice grew even lower. "Even murder, elders. And that is the greatest tragedy of their nonexistence. Not only is it almost impossible to find a body if someone is killed within those twisting streets, but often, we have no official record that the victim even existed in the first place. The paperwork, if ever started, is so screwed up, so incomplete. It's as if their lives and deaths simply don't count."

Angelo leaned forward. "Brother de Aparcido, that's truly terrible. But what about the police? Surely, with problems that severe, they must intervene? We've heard of BOPE, the special-operations units. Don't they go in and...clean things up?" He tried to inject a note of naive hope into his voice, the kind of question a sheltered missionary might ask.

Ricardo let out a mirthless chuckle, a sound heavy with cynicism. He looked from Angelo to Shawn, as if gauging their understanding of the world's harsher realities. "BOPE?" He shook his head. "Ah, elders, the movies make them look like incorruptible knights in shining armor, yes?" He glanced around his office as if the walls might have ears. "The truth is, in Rio, it's harder to find a straight cop than it is to find a straight wall in the favela."

He sighed, the frustration evident. "Think about it. These officers, many of them, they are not paid well. They have families to feed, bills to pay, just like anyone else. Then you have the *traficantes*, the cartels. They have money, elders.

Rivers of it. More money than the government could ever offer in a salary. What's a few thousand reais to ensure a blind eye? A delayed raid? A tip-off about an impending operation? For some, refusing can mean...complications."

Ricardo's gaze hardened. "BOPE, yes, they are supposed to be the elite, the incorruptible. And some are. But even *they* are not immune. The tendrils of the cartels, they reach everywhere. Sometimes, a BOPE operation might go in loud, make a lot of noise, a few arrests that look good for the cameras. But the real powers, the ones pulling the strings? They often get a polite warning beforehand. The major players slip away, the big stashes are moved. It's a show, elders. A performance for the public, while the real business continues in the shadows."

He leaned back, a sense of weariness settling over him. "The drug *banditos*, they can pay far more than the people ever could. The people in Morro Diabólico, they have nothing to offer except their pleas for help. It's a tragic equation, but it's the reality we live with."

Angelo absorbed Ricardo's bleak assessment, the pieces clicking into place. The corruption Ricardo described was the grease that made such cover-ups possible. He kept his expression neutral, nodding with a thoughtful frown, as if processing these heavy truths for the first time.

"That's...a very difficult situation, Brother de Aparcido," Angelo said. "It must be heartbreaking to see so many people trapped in that kind of environment, almost abandoned by the system." He paused, then continued with a hesitant tone. "With the Elder Barnes you knew, the one who was so fearless in sharing his testimony...did he ever...try to take the Gospel into Morro Diabólico? Did he ever mention wanting to reach the people there?"

Ricardo's brow furrowed in thought, eyes distant. "Morro Diabólico," he murmured, tapping a finger against his chin.

"He talked about it, yes. It weighed on him, all those souls. He was always one to go where the need was greatest." Ricardo gave a faint smile. "He used to say, 'The darker the place, the brighter the light needs to shine.'"

Then, Ricardo's eyes lit up with recollection. "Ah! Yes, I remember! He told me a story once. It was quite something." He leaned forward, his voice dropping, as if recounting a daring escapade. "He and his companion at the time, I think it was Elder...Elder Paul, maybe? A young fellow, a bit timid. Anyway, they had been praying about it, feeling that pull. They decided to approach the edge of Morro Diabólico. Not to go deep inside, mind you, Elder Barnes wasn't reckless, but to see if they could perhaps speak to someone near the entrance, offer a pamphlet, plant a seed."

Ricardo shook his head, a mixture of admiration and re-membered anxiety in his expression. "They didn't get very far. Just as they were approaching one of the main access roads, a group of men appeared. *Traficantes*. Young, hard-faced, car-rying machine guns." Ricardo made a gesture with his hands to indicate the size of the weapons. "They surrounded them. Demanded to know who they were, what they wanted."

Angelo felt a knot in his stomach. This was it. This was the kind of courage, the kind of reckless faith that could have gotten Rockwell killed.

"Elder Barnes told me he was very polite, calm, even as these men were shouting, waving their weapons," Ricardo continued, his gaze fixed on Angelo, as if seeing Rockwell in that moment. "They showed their missionary badges, their IDs. The *traficantes* searched their bags, looking for...well, who knows. Drugs, weapons, listening devices."

A smile spread across Ricardo's face. "The only thing the *traficantes* found were scriptures, pass-along cards, and copies of the Book of Mormon. And Elder Barnes, even with a machine gun poking him in the ribs, seized the moment. He said he looked one of the young men, the one who seemed to be the leader, right in the eye. He told me this young man couldn't have been much older than Rockwell himself."

Ricardo chuckled, a warmth returning to his voice. "He said, 'Son, this book can change your life. It talks about peace, about a better way. We have a church nearby, a place of refuge. You would be welcome there.' And then," Ricardo's eyes twinkled, "he handed the armed *traficante* a copy of the Book of Mormon and a little card with the church address."

Angelo blinked, a strange mixture of disbelief and a painful pride warring within him. That was Rockwell, all right. Utterly, impossibly Rockwell.

"The *traficantes* were stunned, I think," Ricardo said, still smiling. "They just...let them go. Told them to get out and never come back. Elder Barnes said his companion, Elder Paul, was white as a sheet and shaking like a leaf the whole way back. But Rockwell? He was proud. Not proud of being reckless but proud that he hadn't backed down, proud that he'd managed to leave a seed of the Gospel, even in such a dangerous place. He told me, 'Brother Ricardo, you never know which heart the Lord is preparing.' He truly believed that."

Ricardo leaned back, a fond, reflective look on his face. "Yes. That was your Elder Barnes. Always looking for an opportunity to share the light, no matter the dark circumstance. It spooked him, though. He admitted that. He said he understood then, truly understood, the kind of darkness they were up against in a place like Morro Diabólico. But it didn't make him want to try any less, just made him more determined to find a way."

Angelo listened, the image of his brave, perhaps foolhardy, younger brother facing down armed *traficantes* with nothing but a Book of Mormon painting a vivid, painful picture. Rockwell's unwavering faith, his almost reckless desire to share his beliefs, was precisely the kind of trait that could have led him into mortal danger, especially if he'd tried to venture back into such a lion's den.

"That's Rockwell, all right," Angelo said, a tremor of raw emotion just beneath the surface of his controlled tone. He met Ricardo's gaze. "Brother de Aparcido, knowing Rockwell, knowing that fire he had...after that first encounter, do you think he might have tried to go back? Perhaps more discreetly? Did he ever mention any other attempts or specific areas within Morro Diabólico he felt drawn to or anyone he might have hoped to connect with there, even peripherally?"

Ricardo's expression grew somber. He shook his head. "He was very shaken by that first encounter. But you are right, that fire...it wasn't easily extinguished. He spoke of the, . . .the lost sheep there, a deep feeling many many souls were in desperate need of the light there. But specific plans to reenter? No, he never shared such details with me. I think he knew it would worry me too much. And, perhaps he understood it was a path he'd have to walk with *extreme* caution, if at all." Ricardo sighed. "He was wise enough to know some burdens are not meant to be shared if they endanger others."

Shawn leaned forward. "Brother de Aparcido, the official report said Elder Barnes, his mother, and stepfather...they died because they took a wrong turn *into* Morro Diabólico. If that's truly where it happened..." He glanced at Angelo. "If Elder Barnes was already known to some elements in there from a previous attempt to, well, proselytize, could that have...complicated things? Could he have been recognized?"

Ricardo winced, the implications clear. "It is possible. In a place like that, memories are long, and outsiders, especially *missionaries*, stand out. If they were seen by the wrong people..." He left the unspoken conclusion hanging heavy in the air.

Angelo pressed gently. "*If* we were to try to understand what *really* happened that day, to find out *if* it truly was just a tragic wrong turn, where would one even begin to ask questions in a place like Morro Diabólico without...ending up like them? Are there less direct ways to gather whispers? People on the fringes who might talk, who might have seen something, if approached correctly?"

Ricardo looked from Angelo to Shawn, his gaze lingering on Angelo. Brett Sawyer's call had likely clued him in that these were not ordinary missionaries. Maybe more. He seemed to wrestle with himself for a moment, the loyalty and affection he felt for the deceased Elder Barnes warring with his innate caution. Finally, he let out a long, troubled sigh.

"Elders...going into Morro Diabólico looking for answers about a death that involved the *traficantes*...it is a death wish. Plain and simple." He paused, his brow furrowed. "However-er...if one were desperate, if one *had* to...you don't approach the *tubarões*, the sharks. They will eat you alive. No, you look for the *peixes limpadores*, the cleaner fish. Or perhaps, more accurately, the little sucker fish that swim around the big predators, making noise, puffing themselves up."

His eyes narrowed thoughtfully. "These types, they are not deep inside the true power structure. They hang around the edges, in the *asfalto*—the paved streets that border the favela—sometimes in the busy markets or the small bars, just outside the main entrances. They hear things because they are always listening, always trying to catch a crumb of information they can use to seem important. They brag. They are visible, sometimes *too* visible for their own good."

Angelo felt a flicker of grim anticipation. This was the kind of opening they needed. "These...sucker fish," Angelo said, "do they have names? Or places they frequent?"

Ricardo rubbed his chin. "Names, they are like the wind in those parts, always changing. But there are always *types*. Look for the loudmouths, the ones trying *too* hard to impress anyone who will listen. There is one I have heard whispers about recently. Not a big fish, no real power, more like a...a fat, little remora, clinging to a much larger shark." He met Angelo's eyes. "They call him Fofinho. He's often seen around the main entry points to Diabólico, in the Vila Isabel side market, trying to act like he's the right hand of a dangerous man named Fogo. Fogo..." Ricardo's voice dropped, a note of fear creeping in. "Now *he* is a shark you do *not* want to attract the attention of. A true killer. But this Fofinho, he's mostly hot air, a suck-up. Sometimes, though, hot air can be useful if you know how to harness it."

Angelo and Shawn exchanged a glance. *Fofinho*. A name. A potential lead to Fogo, the man who imperceptibly haunted Angelo's waking thoughts and nightmare-fueled slumber—the man who had pulled the final trigger on Rockwell.

"Thank you, Brother de Aparcido," Angelo said. "That's very helpful. We appreciate your insight more than you know."

Ricardo nodded, his expression grave. "Be careful, elders. What you are contemplating...it is walking into the fire. Elder Barnes was a light, but even blazing light can be snuffed." His gaze was a silent plea for them to reconsider.

Outside, on the bustling Rio street, the sounds of the city seemed to fade as Angelo looked at Shawn. The sunlight glinted off the passing cars, but all Angelo could see was the path ahead, leading into the shadows of Morro Diabólico.

"Fofinho," Shawn said, breaking the silence, a grim tightness around his mouth. "Sounds like our first dance partner."

Angelo nodded, his jaw set. "He's the appetizer. Fogo's the main course." The hunt had a new, specific target. The path to vengeance was becoming clearer, and it led straight through the heart of Morro Diabólico, starting with a "fat, little parasite."

Chapter 13

FISHERS OF MEN

The aroma of hot bread and sweet fried dough clung to the air around the small *padaria* on the edge of Vila Isabel, a bustling neighborhood that bled into the imposing, chaotic sprawl of Morro Diabólico. Angelo and Shawn sat on a low concrete wall, partially shaded by a faded awning, observing the flow of life at one of the favela's main arteries. People, motorbikes, and dented cars moved with a restless energy, a stark contrast to the quiet, almost reverent conversation they'd just had with Ricardo de Aparcido.

Angelo took a bite of a *coxinha*, the savory chicken filling a welcome counterpoint to the *guaraná* soda he sipped. Shawn, beside him, was methodically decimating a bag of *pão de queijo*, popping the small cheese breads into his mouth one after another.

"So," Shawn said around a mouthful, "Ricardo. Quite the evangelist himself now, eh? Watering his garden by smashing bottles. That's a visual, all that innocent booze," he said with a frown. He wiped his greasy fingers on a napkin. "Gotta say, for a civilian, he's got a decent read on things. The corruption, the favela dynamics...pretty spot on."

Angelo nodded, his gaze fixed on a group of young men about two blocks away loitering near a narrow alleyway that snaked up the hillside. They were swaggering, eyes constantly scanning, the kind of "pilot fish" Ricardo had described. "Ricardo's more than just a convert, Shawn. He's sharp. Savvy." Angelo paused, considering. "He's got a good heart. But there's a shrewdness there. He chose his words carefully when talking about Morro Diabólico, about the police."

"You think he was on to us?" Shawn asked, his eyes watchful, mirroring Angelo's surveillance. "More than just two eager elders from the 'South Mission'?"

"I think he suspected something wasn't entirely kosher, yeah. The way he kept looking at my name tag. He also mentioned I reminded him of Rockwell, 'something in the eyes.' That wasn't just about the name. He picked up on something." Angelo took another bite of his coxinha, chewing thoughtfully. "He's seen real grief, real devotion in Rockwell. Maybe he saw the shadow of that in me, twisted into something else."

"Or maybe Brett gave him a heads-up," Shawn suggested, tossing the empty *pão de queijo* bag into a nearby bin. "Something like, 'These guys aren't your average tract-knockers, but they're on the level about Rockwell. Hear them out.'"

"Could be. Brett's no fool either. He wouldn't have looped in Ricardo if he thought Ricardo couldn't handle it or if he thought Ricardo would spook easily." He finished his *coxinha* and crumpled the napkin. "The interesting thing is, whatever Ricardo suspects, he didn't seem to care *who* we are, as long as our interest in Rockwell, in what happened to him, is genuine. His loyalty to Rockwell, to his memory, overrides everything else. He wants answers, or at least someone to *get* them. He wants justice for the kid who saved his life."

Shawn stretched, his shoulders popping. "So, this Fofinho character. Ricardo seemed pretty certain he's our man, or at least our man's sycophant."

"It's a starting point," Angelo said, his gaze unwavering from the mouth of the favela. "Ricardo armed us with a name and a hunting ground. He also gave us a healthy dose of caution about Fogo. He wasn't exaggerating; you could see it in his eyes. He's heard things, probably seen things, related to Fogo that chilled him to the bone."

The disconnect was jarring: the earnest, heartfelt stories Ricardo shared about Rockwell's gentle perseverance, his bottle-smashing, life-altering joy, contrasted with the cold, brutal reality of the men they were now targeting. Rockwell had tried to bring light into this darkness with faith and love. Angelo was here to bring fire and retribution.

"One thing's for sure," Shawn said, his voice losing its earlier lightness, "Rockwell accidentally kicked a hornet's nest trying to preach to those *traficantes* with a Book of Mormon. Brave as hell, but damn, kid."

Angelo's jaw tightened. "Brave or too innocent to know better. Or both. It doesn't matter now. What matters is Fogo." He thought of the image Ricardo painted: Rockwell, armed with nothing but scripture, facing down men with machine guns. It was the essence of his brother, distilled into one terrifying, beautiful act of faith. An act that may have signed his death warrant.

"Ricardo basically confirmed that if they took a wrong turn into Diabólico, and if Rockwell was recognized from that earlier stunt..." Shawn let the thought hang.

"It wouldn't have been a random act of violence," Angelo finished, his voice flat. "It would have been an execution." And the man who pulled the trigger was still out there. Fofinho was just the gatekeeper.

Angelo pushed himself off the wall. The relative peace of the *padaria*, the taste of the fried dough, it was all a thin veneer over the ugly truth they were peeling back. "Ricardo gave us what we needed. Now it's our turn to do what Rockwell couldn't." He glanced at Shawn. "Let's find our fat, little fish."

The sun, now past its zenith, beat down on a crowded street fair near Vila Isabel, a chaotic symphony of shouted prices, sizzling street food, and the relentless thrum of motorbikes weaving through the throngs of people. Angelo and Shawn, blending into the crowd near a fruit stall, scanned the faces, their casual demeanor masking a hunter's focus. They'd been observing for nearly an hour, letting the rhythm of the market wash over them, waiting for Fofinho to surface.

Then, a voice, loud and grating, cut through the general din. "*Ei, psiu*! Old man! You think this rotten mango is worth *that* much? Are you trying to rob *me*?"

Angelo's gaze snapped toward the sound. A portly man, sweating profusely in a bright-yellow soccer jersey that strained over his considerable gut, was berating a withered fruit vendor. He had a small, scraggly goatee and an air of puffed-up self-importance that was almost cartoonish. Two younger, leaner lackeys flanked him, smirking. This had to be their guy.

"He matches the description," Shawn murmured, almost imperceptibly, his eyes narrowed. "Definitely full of hot air and looks like he enjoys throwing his weight around."

Fofinho jabbed a thick finger at the vendor, who cowered. "I should have you thrown out of this market for trying to cheat me! Do you know who I am? I am Fogo's right hand! He sends *me* to make sure things are...equitable!" He punctuated the last word with a leering grin at his companions, who chuckled obsequiously. He then grabbed two of the choicest mangoes from the vendor's cart, keeping one for himself and tossing the other to one of his toadies. The old vendor said nothing, his face a mask of resignation.

Fofinho, pleased with his minor act of tyranny, swaggered away from the stall, his cronies trailing him like hyenas. He spotted a young boy, no older than ten, struggling to push a cart laden with empty soda crates. With a malicious grin, Fofinho stuck out his foot, tripping the boy. The cart clattered, crates spilling onto the dusty ground. The boy looked up, tears welling in his eyes.

"Watch where you're going, *moleque*!" Fofinho boomed, laughing as his friends joined in. "This is a busy place! Not a playground for little rats!"

Angelo felt a cold knot tighten in his stomach. This wasn't just a loudmouth; this was a petty bully, thriving on the fear of the weak. The sight of Fofinho, puffed up and sneering as he tripped the small boy, ripped a raw nerve from Angelo's own past. He was suddenly ten years old again, small and scared, trying to navigate the minefield of his father's moods. He saw Oren, his massive frame filling their small kitchen doorway, a cruel smirk after he'd casually backhanded a glass of milk from young Angelo's grasp, just to watch it shatter and see the boy flinch. Oren hadn't even needed a reason; the power to cause distress, to humiliate someone smaller, was reason enough. The memory was still sharp, carrying the sting of helplessness and the bitter taste of his mother's hushed words of comfort later on, her own eyes shadowed with fear. Fofinho was a pale imitation, perhaps, but the same rotten core was there. The kind of man who hid behind a more dangerous predator.

Fofinho and his crew settled onto some overturned buckets near a stall selling cheap electronics, the amplified beat of rap music thumping from a nearby speaker. Fofinho, clearly holding court, began to brag, his voice carrying over the market noise.

"Yeah, Fogo, he trusts me with everything," Fofinho declared, gesturing expansively, throwing his arms wide. "Big things are happening, big things. He wouldn't make a move without consulting me. I'm essential, you hear me? *Essential.*"

His companions nodded eagerly, hanging on his every word. The conversation drifted, as barroom boasts often do, to women.

"And the *gatinhas*," Fofinho said, winking, "they can't resist a man of importance. A man connected to Fogo. They know who butters their bread, eh?" He puffed out his chest. "Take that pretty little thing down in Copacabana, that Lucia. Works at the fancy hotel, thinks she's too good for the favela now." He let out a crude laugh. "But she knows I can make her life easy or very, very difficult."

Angelo and Shawn exchanged a glance. This was getting interesting.

"Yeah, Lucia," Fofinho continued, his voice laced with smug satisfaction. "She's got a nice little apartment in that big white building, the 'Princesa do Mar.' Real classy." He chuckled. "She 'pays' her dues to me to keep her job, to keep her little sister safe up here. Tonight, she pays a little extra. I'm heading down there soon, after I collect a few more...*tributes*." He leered at his cronies. "She always puts up a little fight at first; makes it more fun. But she always comes around. They always do when Fofinho comes calling."

Angelo didn't need to say a word. Shawn caught his eye, a nod passing between them. The "Princesa do Mar." Fofinho had just handed them an engraved invitation to a private party they fully intended to crash. Getting Fofinho alone, away from his favela turf and his boss's immediate shadow, was a gift.

"Perfect," Angelo said with a cold smile.

The late-afternoon sun cast long shadows across the mosaic sidewalks of Avenida Atlântica as Angelo and Shawn loitered near a refreshment kiosk, an easy stone's throw from the stately entrance of the Princesa do Mar apartment building. The air, thick with salt and the distant rhythm of samba, did little to cool Angelo's focused patience. They'd been nursing lukewarm *águas de coco* for the better part of an hour, their anodyne appearance belying the predatory stillness within.

"He's cutting it close to his 'tribute' time," Shawn murmured, his gaze sweeping the promenade.

Angelo nodded, eyes fixed on the corner Fofinho was expected to round. "Let him think he's got all the power. Makes them sloppy."

The plan was simple: follow Fofinho into the Princesa do Mar, up to Lucia's apartment, then have a friendly, one-sided chat.

A flash of gaudy yellow, like a banana Laffy Taffy, caught Angelo's eye. Fofinho waddled into view, his cheap gold chains glinting, a greasy empanada in each hand. He paused at the entrance of the Princesa do Mar, slicking back his greasy hair and adjusting the front of his strained soccer jersey. He spoke through the intercom and was buzzed in.

"Showtime," Angelo said, dropping his coconut shell into a bin. He and Shawn moved with unhurried purpose toward the entrance.

They were halfway across the sidewalk when a figure stepped into their path; he looked like a man ready to pick a fight. He was young, earnest, and clean-cut, with equal parts resolve and anger painted on his face.

Angelo's hand, already loose and near his side, twitched. His eyes, accustomed to cataloging threats with chilling speed, narrowed. The boy, likely in his late teens, was dressed in a too-large polo shirt and cheap slacks. His posture was stiff with a righteous tension. No weapon visible, hands clenched at his sides.

Shawn, ever the echo of Angelo's instincts, shifted his weight, his own relaxed demeanor a constructed facade. He caught Angelo's eye for a nanosecond, a silent question.

Before either could fully categorize or dismiss him, the young man launched his offensive. "Worship Jesus, not Joseph Smooch!" he proclaimed, his voice ringing with an earnest fervor that was almost painful to witness. He took another step closer, his gaze fixed on them with unwavering condemnation. "The Bible is the *true* word of God! You are false prophets! Demons leading the flock astray!"

Angelo almost laughed. *This* was the interruption? After all the planning, the tailing, the anticipation of confronting Fofinho, *this* was the hurdle? A street-corner crusader. Annoyance, sharp and immediate, pricked at him.

Shawn let out a low whistle. "Well, shucks, Elder Rockwell," he drawled, his voice dripping with mock concern. "Looks like he's got us there. He knows about Joseph Smooch. Did you tell him? I thought we agreed Smooch was our little secret."

The young evangelist's brow furrowed, his momentum faltering at the unexpected response. "It is no secret! It is an abomination!"

Angelo stepped forward, crowding the young man's personal space just enough to be unsettling. He leaned in, his voice a low, gravelly rasp that was far removed from the benign tone of Elder Rockwell. "Listen, kid, we appreciate your enthusiasm for...pointless bullshit. But right now? We're on our way to a very important meeting about how to best sacrifice a virgin under a blood moon to ensure a bountiful harvest of lost souls. It's complicated, involves a lot of chanting, blood, and...penises."

Shawn chimed in, nodding sagely. "Yeah, and if Joseph Smoochy isn't pleased, the bake sale could be a disaster. You wouldn't want that on your conscience, would ya? All those little heathens going without their brownies?"

The young man's jaw had dropped. His earnest eyes, moments before blazing with conviction, were now wide with a mixture of shock and confusion. He stammered, "B-but...demons...you...you can't..."

"Oh, we *can*," Angelo said, his voice turning colder. He gestured toward the apartment building. "And we *will*. Now, unless you want to be the guest of honor at our next...bloody virgin penis ritual...I suggest you find a different soul to save. We're busy."

With that, Angelo and Shawn walked past him, leaving the young evangelist standing on the sidewalk, mouth agape, his righteous crusade derailed by a level of crass, bewildering depravity he clearly hadn't anticipated.

The duo reached the heavy glass doors of the Princesa do Mar long after the lock clicked shut from the inside. Angelo swore under his breath, pulling on the handle. Locked. The evangelist's ill-timed fervor had cost them their window. Fofinho was inside, and Lucia was alone with him. Angelo clenched his jaw in frustration.

Shawn peered through the polished glass into the empty lobby. "Well, that's just peachy. Jabba the Gut is probably already making himself comfortable."

Angelo's gaze shifted to the polished brass intercom panel beside the doorframe. His mind, a finely tuned instrument for problem-solving, was already discarding the annoyance and focusing on the new obstacle. He had seen Fofinho at the panel before the street preacher intervened. Though Fofinho's bulk had obscured a clear view of the specific buttons pressed, Angelo's hyperawareness sometimes cataloged details his conscious mind hadn't fully processed. He scanned the rows of names and apartment numbers. His eyes, sharp and accustomed to minute details, caught it: a faint, greasy smudge, slightly fresher than the general city grime, beside apartment 6B. *Fofinho's greasy fingerprint*, Angelo thought. *Sloppy.*

"It's 6B," Angelo murmured. That had to be Lucia. He pressed the button.

Shawn moved slightly, angling himself to see Angelo's profile, ready to play his part.

A moment later, a hesitant female voice crackled through the small speaker. "*Sim?*"

Angelo pitched his voice to be smooth, professional, with an undercurrent of urgent authority, the kind that brooked no argument. "Lucia Freitas?"

"*Sim*. Who is speaking?" The voice was strained, wary. Angelo could almost picture her, Fofinho looming nearby.

"This is Jorge from the Majestic Palace Hotel," Angelo improvised, choosing a name that sounded suitable. "Our manager asked me to contact you urgently regarding an incident with a VIP guest in your section today. He needs to speak with you immediately. It's rather serious and requires the highest levels of discretion."

There was a muffled sound, then Lucia's voice, more flustered now. "Majestic Palace? But I'm off duty. Fofinho is here." They could hear her distress.

Then, a loud, booming male voice barged into the audio. "Who is it? Tell them to go away! You're busy with *me*!"

Angelo spoke clearly, ensuring his voice carried. "Senhora Freitas, the manager insisted. He said it could affect your employment. If you can't come to the door, he explicitly asked me to come up."

Fofinho, an idiot driven by ego and a desire to control every aspect of Lucia's life, apparently took the bait. His voice, closer to the intercom now, was laced with bluster. "Affect her employment? What employment? Tell them to come up! I'll sort this out! Nobody messes with my girl from the morro!" He probably imagined a scenario where he could bully a hotel manager, further cementing his "importance."

A sigh, heavy with resignation, came from Lucia. "*Está bem. I will buzz you in.*" A sharp click sounded, and the heavy glass door unlocked.

Angelo pushed it open with a grim smile. "After you, Elder Martinez."

They stepped into the cool marble-floored lobby. A scent of lemons and floor wax hung in the air. An elegant, but slightly dated, brass elevator stood at the far end. They walked toward it, Angelo pressing the call button.

The ride to the sixth floor was silent, the only sound the soft hum of the elevator. As the doors whispered open, they stepped into a quiet, carpeted hallway. The apartment doors were made of dark, polished wood, each with a brass number.

As they approached 6B, Fofinho's voice, loud and obnoxious, could be heard through the door. "So I tell this little punk, you think you can talk to Fofinho like that? Fogo himself would have skinned him alive! But I'm merciful, you know? I just...teach him a lesson he won't forget..."

Angelo and Shawn exchanged a knowing glance. The fat, little remora was making waves, oblivious to the real sharks now circling just outside his dinky pond. Angelo raised his hand and knocked—a sharp, decisive sound that cut short Fofinho's boast.

The door swung open with a sudden jerk. Fofinho filled the frame, his squat figure tensed in what he clearly thought was an intimidating stance. His face was contorted into a tough mad-dog look, nostrils flared and brow furrowed beneath his slicked-back hair. The effect might have been menacing if not for the empanada crumbs dotting his bright yellow shirt.

The instant his eyes registered Angelo and Shawn, his expression transformed. The tough-guy facade crumbled, replaced by wide-eyed surprise. His mouth opened and closed like a fish suddenly finding itself on dry land.

"You're not... You're—" he stammered, confusion overtaking his features as he struggled to process that these weren't hotel employees but in his mind missionaries.

Angelo smoothly stepped forward, closing the distance between them before Fofinho could recover or slam the door. "We're personal representatives of Jesus Christ, that's right," he said with a calm certainty. "And we're here to ask you a couple quick questions about your eternal soul."

Behind Fofinho, Angelo caught a glimpse of Lucia—thin, nervous, her dark hair pulled back in a tight ponytail. Her eyes widened in confusion, darting between the unexpected visitors and Fofinho.

Shawn stepped up beside Angelo, his smile pleasant but his eyes cold. "It's a real short message. Won't take but a minute of your time." He placed a firm hand on the doorframe, eliminating any possibility of Fofinho closing it.

Fofinho's face cycled through expressions—confusion, suspicion, fear. His hand twitched toward his waistband, but Angelo was already moving.

"Inside," Angelo said, his voice dropping to a register that held no pretense of missionary work. He placed a hand firmly on Fofinho's chest and pushed him backward with enough force to make the smaller man stumble.

They entered the apartment, Shawn closing the door behind them with a soft click that somehow sounded final.

Chapter 14

SWEET BIRDS SINGING

The moment Fofinho's clumsy hand twitched toward his waistband, Shawn moved. He was a blur of efficient violence. Before Fofinho could even process the threat these two missionaries posed, Shawn's hand snaked out, clamping onto Fofinho's wrist like a vise. There was a sickening series of cracks, like dry twigs snapping, as Shawn twisted. Fofinho shrieked, a high-pitched sound cut short as Shawn's other hand slammed into his diaphragm, driving the air from his lungs in a wheezing gasp. The cheap pistol Fofinho had been fumbling for clattered to the hardwood floor.

Fofinho crumpled, clutching his mangled hand, his face a mask of agony and disbelief. He landed heavily on his knees, whimpering, his bravado vanishing. The fingers on his injured hand were splayed at unnatural angles, a grotesque parody of a wave.

While Shawn dealt with Fofinho, Angelo's attention had already shifted to Lucia. She stood frozen near a small kitchenette, her eyes wide with terror, knuckles white as she gripped the edge of a countertop.

"Lucia," Angelo said, his voice calm, almost gentle, a stark contrast to the brutal efficiency he'd just witnessed from his partner. He took a half step toward her, hands open and visible. "We're not here for you." He gazed toward the whimpering Fofinho, then back to her. "We're with an American agency. This...*vermin*...has been on our radar for some time. It's in your best interest to forget you saw us, tell no one, and cooperate. Understand?"

Lucia stared at him, her chest heaving. The words "American agency" seemed to resonate. Hope, mixed with a healthy dose of fear, flickered in her eyes. She nodded, a tear tracing a path down her cheek. Her relief that Fofinho was being dealt with was palpable, even through her fear of these new, terrifying men.

"Good," Angelo said. He then jerked his head toward Fofinho. "Get him in that chair. The wooden one."

Shawn hauled Fofinho to his feet. Fofinho stumbled, still cradling his broken hand, his face slick with sweat. He offered no resistance as Shawn shoved him into a simple wooden dining chair with a slatted backrest.

"Now for the pièce de résistance," Shawn flourished, a grim satisfaction in his voice. He grabbed Fofinho's injured hand. Fofinho let out another strangled cry, trying to pull away, but Shawn's grip was iron. With methodical precision, Shawn forced Fofinho's swollen, misshapen fingers through the narrow slats of the chair back. The bones grated. Fofinho screamed, a raw, animalistic sound that Lucia muffled by pressing her hands to her ears.

Shawn worked quickly, manipulating the broken digits until the bulk of Fofinho's hand was on one side of the slats, his wrist on the other. The hand was already beginning to puff up, turning an alarming shade of purple. "There," Shawn said, stepping back. "Try to get up. You'll be dragging your new favorite accessory with you, and I don't think those fingers will straighten out again easily."

Fofinho stared back at his trapped, mangled hand, his body trembling. He couldn't possibly pull it back through the slats without unimaginable pain, and the swelling was making it worse by the second. He was, for all intents and purposes, anchored to the chair.

Angelo walked around the trapped man, his expression calculating. He picked up Fofinho's discarded pistol, checked the magazine, then tucked it into his waistband. The small apartment was filled with Fofinho's ragged breathing and Lucia's quiet, terrified whimpers.

Angelo looked at Shawn. The Operator was back in his element. They were in control. The fat, little remora was hooked, and the interrogation was about to begin.

Angelo continued to pace around Fofinho, who was now whimpering, his eyes darting between the two menacing figures. The Operator stopped in front of him, his expression blank, his voice devoid of malice, carrying the calm, matter-of-fact cadence of a seasoned professional outlining a standard procedure.

"All right, Fofinho," Angelo began, "let's have a little chat about what's going to happen next so there are no misunderstandings. You, me, and my associate here," he inclined his head toward Shawn, who offered Fofinho a razor-sharp grin, "are going to establish a relationship. A relationship built on a clear foundation."

He paused, letting Fofinho absorb the unsettling normalcy of his tone. "My experience has taught me that the most productive relationships of this nature are based on respect. And the quickest way to cultivate that respect, Fofinho, is by inviting a certain...spirit...to be present. A spirit of profound, unadulterated pain, which in turn cultivates an equally profound spirit of bowel-loosening terror." Angelo's gaze was steady, unwavering. "The idea, you see, is that this spirit will move you so deeply, you'll genuinely *want* to volunteer information. You'll be eager to answer our questions. It's a remarkably effective method. My clients have all been very pleased with the results."

He leaned in slightly, his voice dropping a fraction. "So, let's start, shall we? How about a little game? You know the children's song 'Head, Shoulders, Knees, and Toes'?"

Shawn, who had been observing Fofinho's terror with a look of keen professional interest, suddenly lit up, his face splitting into an almost childlike grin. "Head, Shoulders, Knees, and Toes?" he exclaimed, bouncing on the balls of his feet. "Oh, man, I *love* that game! We used to sing that song all the time!" His enthusiasm was genuine, a chilling counterpoint to the cold emanating from Angelo and the palpable fear radiating from Fofinho.

Angelo's calm, precise words hung in the small apartment. Fofinho, trapped and trembling, stared at him, the initial shock of his mangled hand giving way to a stomach-churning terror. The Operator's detached explanation of cultivating pain was far more chilling than any shouted threat.

"I thought you might like this," Angelo said to Shawn, a current of anticipation in his voice. "How about we switch off between the two of us? I'll start."

Shawn, who had been listening with rapt attention, clapped his hands with a disturbing glee. "Oh, this is gonna be great! Teamwork makes the dream work, right, Fofinho?"

Angelo took a step closer to the whimpering man. "Heads!" he declared, and he smacked the back of Fofinho's skull. Fofinho's head snapped forward, a grunt of pain escaping him. The man's eyes, already wide, bulged further.

Before Fofinho could fully register the blow, Shawn was on him. "Shoulders!" he barked, and slammed a balled fist into Fofinho's left shoulder where his arm met his torso. Fofinho cried out, a choked yelp, his body lurching against the chair, the movement sending fresh agony through his trapped broken hand.

Angelo didn't miss a beat. "Knees!" He kicked Fofinho's right kneecap with a sickening thud. Fofinho screamed—a thin, watery sound—as an electric shock of pain shot up his leg. The kneecap felt like it had been dislodged before settling back with an agonizing grind.

"And toes!" Shawn finished the line, his foot coming down hard on Fofinho's left instep. The crunch of small bones was audible. Tears streamed down Fofinho's face, mixing with sweat and snot. They barely gave him a moment to gasp for air, each blow landing with rhythmic precision. Lucia, huddled by the kitchenette, had her eyes squeezed shut, her hands pressed so tightly over her ears that her knuckles were white.

The grim cadence continued along with song. Knees, then toes, in rhythmic blows.

Then, Angelo started the second, more intense sequence. "Head!" His fist connected with Fofinho's nose. There was a wet squelch, and blood gushed forth, painting a grotesque crimson mask on Fofinho's terrified face. Fofinho shrieked, a sound thick with blood and agony.

Shawn produced his wicked-looking knife. "Shoulders!" he announced, almost cheerfully. The blade flickered, and a shallow, bloody line appeared on Fofinho's already inflamed left shoulder.

They fell back into the brutal, rhythmic back-and-forth with swift, punishing blows to Fofinho's knees and toes. Fofinho's body was a symphony of pain, his earlier bravado a distant, laughable memory. He was a broken, blubbering wreck, his yellow soccer jersey stained with sweat, blood, and tears.

On the final beat, Shawn's voice rang out, "And toes!" Instead of a stomp, his arm moved in a swift, practiced arc.

The knife left his hand, a silver blur, and embedded itself into Fofinho's right foot, pinning it to the wooden floor.

Fofinho's scream was primal, a sound of pure, unadulterated agony that seemed to tear from the very depths of his soul. It was cut short as he nearly passed out, his body slumping against the chair, held in place only by his trapped, mangled hand.

Shawn yanked the bloodied knife from Fofinho's foot with a grunt, the ripping sound making Fofinho convulse. He stepped close, grabbed a handful of Fofinho's greasy hair, and jerked his head up. With his other hand, Shawn brought the dripping point of the knife to within a centimeter of Fofinho's twitching eyeball. Fofinho's breath hitched, his eyes wide with a terror that transcended pain.

"What's the next part?" Shawn asked, his voice a silken threat, his face inches from Fofinho's.

Angelo, standing to the side, supplied the answer in a sing-song tone. "Eyes, ears, mouth, and nose."

Shawn grinned with a terrible, predatory expression. "Oh, Fofinho," he cooed, the knife glinting, "you're going to look so much uglier when we're done. Especially that nose. It's already a good start."

That was it. The image of further mutilation, of the knife hovering before his eye, of the calm, methodical destruction of his face, finally shattered the last vestiges of Fofinho's spirit. A choking sob tore from him, a sound of utter surrender.

"*Não! Por favor!*" Fofinho blubbered, snot and tears and blood mixing on his ruined face. "Enough! I'll talk! I'll tell you anything! Anything you want! Just...just make it stop! Please, make the game stop!" He dissolved into body-shaking sobs, a broken man ready to spill every secret he possessed.

Angelo watched with a satisfied expression. The spirit of pain had done its work. Fofinho was compliant. A cold current ran through him, a familiar echo from a powerless past. How many nights had he lain awake, a boy burning with a furious, helpless wish to make his father Oren Barnes pay for every sneer, every blow, every moment of terror inflicted on his mother and him? That youthful impotence had long since curdled, then hardened, channeling itself into the chilling efficiency he now wielded. Oren was gone, unreachable, but the world was full of men who understood only this language. And Angelo had become exceedingly fluent in making them understand the bill always comes due.

Angelo let the silence stretch, punctuated only by Fofinho's ragged, sobbing breaths. He watched Fofinho, a predator observing its wounded prey.

"Good," Angelo said. "The game stops when we have what we need. Start with Fogo. Tell me about him."

Fofinho, his head lolling, managed a weak nod. "Fogo...*Chefe* Fogo...he's...he's the devil, man. *O Diabo.*" His voice was hoarse, raspy. "He runs everything. Everything in Diabólico. No one crosses Fogo. No one."

"We're not interested in his fan club testimonials," Shawn interjected, wiping his knife clean on a stray dishtowel he'd plucked from the counter, his eyes never leaving Fofinho. "We know he's a bad hombre. Details, Fofinho. Specifics."

"He's gonna kill me." Fofinho sobbed.

"We'll make sure *that* doesn't happen, Fofinho," Shawn assured him knowingly.

"The missionaries," Angelo said. "In the car. The American family."

Fofinho flinched. His eyes, bloodshot and terrified, darted to Angelo. "I...I wasn't there for the shooting part. Not really. I was...I was on lookout further down. I just relayed the signal. The blue kite." He was babbling, trying to distance himself.

"The signal for what?" Angelo pressed, his gaze unyielding.

"That a car...a suspicious car was coming up the hill. We thought it was BOPE or rivals. It was dark, tinted windows. We didn't know... We didn't know they were...*those* people."

"But Fogo knew," Angelo stated.

Fofinho shrugged. "Fogo was there. He...he always takes charge when it's important. Or when things get messy." His voice dropped to a near whisper. "After the shooting started, I came up. I saw...I saw him. Fogo. He was the one who pulled the...the last one, the young one, the prayin' one...out of the car." A shudder racked Fofinho's body. "He...finished him. With the shotgun."

Angelo felt a cold stillness spread through him. The brutal image seared itself into his mind alongside the memory of Rockwell's gentle face. It was the confirmation he'd sought, the final nail in Fogo's coffin, though he had already known it deep within his core.

"He say anything?" Angelo asked, his voice dangerously soft.

Fofinho shook his head, then seemed to remember. "The...the praying one, he was saying, 'Forgive them...they don't know...' Fogo...he said somethin' like, 'We know now.' And...and he said, 'Amen.' Before he..." Fofinho couldn't finish, another wave of sobs overtaking him.

"So Fogo executed a praying missionary and his family because of a mistaken identity? And then he just...walks away?" He knew there had to be more. The cover-up by Peterson, the involvement of Officer Mauro, it all pointed to something bigger. Didn't it?

Fofinho sniffled, wiping his ruined nose with the back of his uninjured hand. "It wasn't... Fogo doesn't make mistakes... that he doesn't...handle. After, there were calls. Important people. Not from the *morro*. People outside. They helped...clean it up. Made it go away. Fogo, he has connections. Big ones."

"Connections that help him with, what, his business?" Angelo probed, shifting the focus. "You don't need connections like that for just drugs and thugging. What did they help with? Something secret? something...special?"

Fofinho's eyes widened slightly, a new kind of fear flickering within them. This was clearly a topic he was even more unwilling to discuss than murder. "I don't know much about that. Fogo keeps that stuff quiet. Only for his most trusted."

Shawn took a step closer, resting the point of his cleaned knife on Fofinho's already brutalized knee. Fofinho gasped, his body tensing. "We're all friends here, Fofinho," Shawn said. "And friends share their secrets. Especially when one friend is holding a very sharp thing and the other friend is looking like a piñata after a birthday party."

"Fogo has a fortified plant. It's up high," Fofinho said, his gaze fixed on the knife. "Deep inside. The place...they call it '*Casa Forte*.' It's like a fortress. Walls, guards, more than just for *pó*...for cocaine. He does other things there. Special things."

"What kind of special things?" Angelo asked.

"I only heard whispers," Fofinho insisted, sweat beading on his forehead. "It's...weird stuff. Not drugs. Something to do with...*corpos*. Bodies." He swallowed hard. "And...and gringos. Different ones. Not like you. Doctor types. They come and go. Quietly. Fogo protects them."

Bodies. Doctor-type gringos. Did this have something to do with Embalmadol-Exo, with President Peterson's mortuary background, his strange experiments? This "Casa Forte" wasn't a drug den; it sounded like a processing plant, a laboratory.

"These doctors..." Angelo pressed. "What do they do there? What's Fogo's interest in bodies?"

Fofinho was trembling uncontrollably. "I don't know! I swear! Only Fogo and his closest guys know. They bring people there...not always dead when they arrive. People from the hill, *desaparecidos*, the ones no one will miss. And then...then the doctor does his thing. Fogo...he gets... *something* from it. Something valuable. More valuable than drugs, he says." Fofinho looked pleadingly at Angelo. "That's all I know, I swear! It's...it's ugly. It's wrong. Even for us. But Fogo...he's not just a trafficker anymore. He's into something else. Something...unholy."

Unholy. Angelo looked at Shawn. The remora had coughed up more than just confirmation of murder. He'd pointed them toward the heart of a much larger, more grotesque operation. The "weird stuff" Ricardo had alluded to was far more sinister than just favela crime. It could be a direct line to Peterson's weird experiments, Fogo was the supplier, and Casa Forte was his factory.

It was more information than they'd hoped for. They had enough to make a move, to find the heart of Fogo's grotesque side business. But Fofinho, now, was a loose end, a sniveling liability.

Angelo turned his attention to Lucia, who was still huddled by the counter, trembling. Her fear was clear, but it was no longer just of Fofinho. Now, it was of them and the repercussions that would surely follow once Fogo learned of his toadie's betrayal.

"Lucia," Angelo said, his voice gentle. He walked toward her, slowly, deliberately, keeping his hands open and visible. "He can't hurt you anymore."

She looked up, her eyes wide and haunted. "My...my sister," she choked out, her voice barely a whisper. "She's still in the Morro. And my mother... Fogo...he'll...he'll kill them. He'll know I was here with...with him." Her gaze flickered toward Fofinho, then back to Angelo, terror etched on her face.

Angelo's expression softened. He understood leverage, threats against family, the vise grip of fear. He'd used it himself countless times, but seeing it wielded against this woman, who was clearly just caught in the crossfire, stirred something akin to...not sympathy but a cold, pragmatic recognition of injustice. She was a victim, much like his own family had been, albeit in a different way.

He pulled out his satellite phone. The sleek, anonymous device looked alien in the small, aging apartment. Shawn watched, eyebrows raised, as Angelo dialed a number.

"This is the Operator," he said into the phone, his voice reverting to its usual clipped, professional tone. "I need an immediate extraction-and-relocation package. High priority. Civilian, noncombatant." He listened for a moment, then continued. "Yes, domestic. Brazil. Currently in Rio de Janeiro. Target family is in Morro Diabólico."

He looked at Lucia. "How many family members need to get out?"

Lucia blinked, confused by the abrupt shift, the efficiency. "My...my sister, Isabella. She's sixteen. And my mother, Sofia. Just them. And me," she added, her voice small.

Angelo relayed the information into the phone. "Three individuals. Mother, two daughters. Youngest is a minor." He paused, then said, "You'll need to start over somewhere safe. You'll need some money to find a new place, get settled, disappear, about a hundred thousand should do it, right?"

Lucia looked lost. The question was so far beyond her current reality of just surviving Fofinho's visits. "I...I don't know... That sounds like so much."

Angelo snorted, a dry, humorless sound. "Arrange for one hundred thousand reais, cash. Clean bills. And secure transport out of Rio. Anywhere they want to go in Brazil, as long as it's not here. I want them moving within the hour. Oh, and my partner and I need fresh clothes." He listened, nodded. "Good. Have your team on standby. She'll be waiting for a black sedan at the front of this building, Princesa do Mar, Avenida Atlântica."

He ended the call and pocketed the phone. "Go downstairs, Lucia," he said, his voice firm but not unkind. "Wait out front. A black car will be there shortly. The driver's name is Miller. He'll take you to your family, and then he'll take all of you somewhere safe. He'll have the money. Don't look back."

Lucia stared at him, speechless, tears flowing freely with relief, disbelief, and a fragile hope. She opened her mouth, then closed it, unable to find words. She finally managed a choked, "Thank you. God bless you".

Angelo gave a curt nod. He wasn't interested in blessings. He was interested in results. As Lucia hurried out of the apartment, almost stumbling in her haste and emotion, Fofinho, who had been watching the exchange with wide, incredulous eyes, suddenly found a flicker of hope.

"*Boss*," Fofinho croaked, his voice thick with pain and a desperate eagerness. He tried to sit up straighter, wincing as his mangled hand and crushed foot protested. "You helped her. You can help me too! I can be useful! I know things! I can help you with Fogo! And you...you can protect me! He'll kill me if he finds out I talked! But you...you're powerful men! You can keep me safe!"

Angelo turned slowly, his face devoid of the momentary softness he'd shown Lucia. The cold, calculating mask of the Operator was firmly back in place. Shawn, who had been observing with a detached amusement, let out a low chuckle.

"Protect you, Fofinho?" Angelo said. "Why would we do that?"

The flicker of hope in Fofinho's eyes died, replaced by a fresh wave of terror. "But...I told you everything! About Casa Forte...about Fogo...about the gringo doctors!"

"And we appreciate that," Shawn chimed in, his smile all teeth. "You were very...forthcoming. Eventually." He gestured around the room, at the bloodstains. "Look on the bright side. Once we get our hands on Fogo, he's never hurting anyone again. And after all, we had a pretty fun game, didn't we?"

Angelo walked over until he was standing in front of Fofinho, looking down at the whimpering wreck. "Where were we in our little song?" he mused, almost to himself. "Ah, yes. 'Eyes, ears, mouth, and nose.'"

Chapter 15

Iron Sharpens Iron

The residue of Fofinho's terror and Lucia's fragile hope clung to Angelo and Shawn long after they'd left the Princesa do Mar. The contact Angelo had made via sat phone for Lucia's extraction had also delivered fresh clothes—standard missionary white shirts, dark slacks, and ties—to a discreet pickup point.

Now, impeccably dressed and looking like they were ready for an evening of door-to-door tracting, they stood in the shadow of a flamboyant poinciana tree, the vibrant red blossoms standing out against a background of fluffy clouds.

Fofinho, amid his blubbering and broken bones, had coughed up more than just confirmation of Fogo's role in Rockwell's murder. He'd painted a disturbing picture of Casa Forte, deep within Morro Diabólico.

Angelo looked at Shawn. "Fogo's destroying more than souls in that hellhole. Those 'doctor types' Fofinho mumbled about, it lines up too neatly with Peterson's mortuary experiments. It stinks of Embalmadol-Exo. It can't be a coincidence that the man who covered up my family's murder has a penchant for repurposed corpses, and my brother's killer is supplying 'bodies' for some weird science project up on Devil's Hill."

Shawn adjusted his tie, his expression hard. "So you think Peterson's not just a necro pimp, he's got Fogo on the payroll as his body snatcher? And Rockwell and your folks stumbled into the supply chain?"

"Or the processing plant. Fofinho said people weren't always dead when they arrived at Casa Forte." The thought of it, the implications of Fogo supplying live subjects for whatever ghastly experiments were happening, was a new layer of horror. "We can't go into Morro Diabólico guns blazing without a better understanding of what we're walking into, and we'll need more than these damn white shirts and a Book of Mormon." He paused. "Brett Sawyer. He told us to call if we needed anything. It's time to see what 'anything' includes."

"Think he'll have more than just Diet Dr. Pepper on offer this time?" Shawn joked.

"He's ex-Delta. He'll have whatever we need," Angelo said. "And he might have answers. Or at least point us in the right direction."

The elevator in Brett Sawyer's Ipanema building ascended. When the doors opened into the penthouse foyer, Sawyer was waiting, dressed in casual shorts and a tight-fitting T-shirt. He registered their pristine missionary attire, then looked at their faces, missing nothing of the underlying tension.

"Elders," he said with an edge of knowing. "Or should I say, gentlemen? You look presentable. Water?"

"Thanks, Brett," Angelo said, dispensing with the honorifics. They were past that now. "But we need more than water."

Sawyer led them into the living room, the stunning view of Ipanema Beach a serene backdrop to the brewing storm of their conversation.

"I figured as much," Sawyer said, gesturing for them to sit. "You wouldn't be back just to show me the progress you've made on singing hymns." He settled onto the leather sofa, his gaze unwavering. "What did you find?"

Angelo laid out Fofinho's intel: Fogo's direct role in the murders, the confirmation of a cover-up orchestrated from outside the favela, and the disturbing revelation of Casa Forte. He described the collection of bodies, the presence of "gringo doctor types," and the unsettling detail that victims weren't always dead upon arrival.

As Angelo spoke, Sawyer listened intently, his expression hardening. When Angelo suggested connecting it to President Peterson's known predilections and the Embalmadol-Exo, Sawyer's jaw tighten

"Peterson," Sawyer said, unsurprised. "I've had my suspicions about him for a while. The Church has its own agency that looks into...irregularities. I've been in contact with them. Peterson's name has come up. Nothing concrete enough to *remove* him but enough smoke to suggest a significant fire."

He leaned forward, his voice dropping. "What you're describing, this 'Casa Forte' and the gringo doctors...it sounds like Peterson's found himself a supplier for his...'research int erests.'" Sawyer looked disgusted. "Fogo delivers the raw materials—people. Peterson, or those he's working with, process them. The chemical you mentioned, Embalmadol-Exo, it fits a pattern I've been tracking."

Angelo perceived there was a lot more to Sawyer than he had allowed them to see. Sawyer was working through the pieces like a detective, and he was letting Angelo see this new layer. Angelo was curious why Sawyer had revealed this level, and it made him even more curious about how many more layers lie uncovered.

"A pattern related to whom?" Angelo pressed.

Sawyer hesitated, choosing his words carefully. "There's a faction within the Church, a group that's diverged radically from the core tenets of faith and compassion. They call themselves the 'Holders of the Rod.'" He said the name with distaste. "They're obsessed with a fire-and-brimstone interpretation of doctrine, focused on hastening the Second Coming, and they believe the ends justify *any* means. Including unconventional pursuits."

Sawyer's eyes grew distant, as if looking through the layers of history that had shaped his faith. Angelo recognized that look—a soldier recalling battlefield memories, vivid and haunting.

"The Church has been evolving," Sawyer continued, "growing away from past mistakes, becoming more inclusive, more compassionate. But the Holders—they've created this narrative that the Church never makes mistakes, that it's perfect and unchanging."

He shook his head, disgust evident in the furrow of his brow. "To me, the Church is like a living organism—it breathes, it grows, it learns. But these people..." His hand tightened around his glass. "The Holders want to drag us backward. They're pushing for a return to limiting priesthood authority, making membership more exclusive, even a return to polygamy. They dream of isolationism, of building walls between us and the world."

Sawyer's expression darkened further. "And violence against 'heathens,' not for any crime but for what they believe or who they love. They glorify the destruction and wrath of the Old Testament. They believe in a God of vengeance, not mercy. They twist scripture to justify their own darkest impulses." He looked at Angelo. "They're bullies. Men of privilege, power, and priesthood trying to suppress free will and exert their dominion. And I believe Peterson is one of them."

Angelo sneered as it sunk in, thinking of his first bully, his father. Control was the language of Oren Barnes. It was also the language of the Holders of the Rod.

Shawn whistled softly. "So, like a cult within the Church?"

"More dangerous than that, more like a faction that has its roots in the very foundation," Sawyer corrected, his eyes like ice. "They have influence, powerful backers, even general authorities and mission presidents. They see themselves as the true disciples, the ones charged with purifying the Church. They're zealots and hypocrites." He shook his head. "To them, people like Fogo are disposable assets, tools to acquire what they need for their grand designs, whether it's bodies for experiments or silencing those who get too close."

"And Peterson *is* one of them?" Angelo said, hiding his growing suspicion that Sawyer knew much more than he had been letting on.

"He fits their profile. Ambitious, compromised, and willing to traffic in the darkest aspects of human exploitation for power and protection," Sawyer stated. "If they're involved in something like dark research, corpses, gringo doctors, then Fogo's operation in Morro Diabólico isn't just a favela drug ring anymore. It's a biolab, protected at a high level because it serves their agenda. That's why the cover-up of your family's murder would be so swift and efficient. Officer Mauro is likely on their payroll, or Peterson's, ensuring the supply chain remains uninterrupted."

The pieces slammed into place with horrifying clarity. This wasn't just about Angelo's vengeance anymore or even Peterson's depravity. It was about a shadowy, powerful group using Fogo as a butcher and Peterson as a mad scientist.

The weight of Sawyer's words about the Holders of the Rod settled heavily in the room. Angelo looked at the man before him, the ex-Delta operative with eyes that had seen too much, now calmly revealing a schism within the Church hierarchy that sounded more like a clandestine war than a theological disagreement. The pieces Fofinho had provided, the horrors implied by Peterson's Embalmadol-Exo, and now Sawyer's intel on this shadowy faction—it all began to form a coherent, chilling picture. But something else was slotting into place for Angelo, something about Sawyer himself.

"You know a hell of a lot about this, Brett," Angelo said, his voice low, cutting through the shock. "More than just 'suspicions' about Peterson. You're talking about internal factions, general authority involvement, biolabs... This isn't just casual observation from a concerned ward mission leader." Angelo leaned forward, his gaze as intense as Sawyer's. "You've been tracking this for a while. Who are you *really* working for?"

A microexpression of something—respect or maybe the relief of an unburdened secret—crossed Sawyer's face. He let out a slow breath. "I was wondering when you'd connect those dots. You're right. My involvement goes deeper than I initially let on." He paused, a subtle shift in his posture, like a soldier coming to a different kind of attention. "I work for an American agency based in Salt Lake City. You could say it's one of the oldest in the country." He met Angelo's eyes. "I work for the Church."

Shawn, who had been absorbing the escalating revelations, said, "No kidding? Like...a deacon?"

Sawyer offered a mirthless smile. "Something more specialized. Think of it as spiritual Special Forces, operating under the direct command of the Quorum of the Twelve Apostles. We're called the Nazerites. Our purpose is to ensure the will of God is carried out, to protect the Church from threats both internal and external. Especially internal."

"I grew up in the Church, Sawyer," Angelo said, a skeptical note in his voice, "and I don't remember hearing anything about this. A Nazerite? Spiritual Special Forces?"

"The fact that you haven't heard about us just means we're doing our job well," Sawyer reassured. "It's a sacred duty. Some callings, some blessings, some experiences...they're so sacred that we're actually told to only reveal our calling when the Spirit prompts us. So while you might not have heard of *us* directly, I'm sure you've heard someone at the pulpit explain they had an experience so spiritual it wouldn't be appropriate to talk about publicly. Chances are good a Nazerite was involved."

Angelo softened. Sawyer's claim seemed outlandish but also believable. The way he spoke, the conviction, it felt...familiar.

Sawyer's expression revealed a depth of conviction that ran far beyond mere duty.

"Throughout history, the Gospel has always needed protectors. Men like David and Moses, who stood against overwhelming odds to safeguard their people. Think of Samson, who fought for freedom despite his tragic flaws. Even in the early Church, right after Christ's death, the Knights Templar emerged as guardians of faith during perilous times."

Angelo and Shawn leaned in, captivated by Sawyer's fervor.

"After the Restoration, figures like Porter Rockwell took up that mantle again. Even Donny Osmond openly—fighting against cultural tides with the same spirit of devotion—but secretly, he's pretty handy with a sniper rifle, when he's activated. We're the ones who try to ensure that the Church remains untarnished by corruption and that its members are shielded from those who would exploit their faith for dark purposes."

He paused, looking Angelo in the eye.

"And now it's our turn to protect it from within. You have a unique opportunity here; not just avenge your brother, but to root out this evil."

Angelo absorbed this. It made a terrifying kind of sense. The Church, a global institution with immense resources and influence, would undoubtedly have its own mechanisms for dealing with serious threats, mechanisms the general membership would never hear about. "So your 'consulting' gig here in Rio..."

"Is a cover," Sawyer confirmed. "I was stationed here to observe Peterson. We've known for some time he was...problematic. Compromised. The rumors about his past, his connections, they raised red flags. The Holders of the Rod have been trying to gain more influence, and Peterson seemed like a key player, or at least a useful pawn for them here in Brazil. My mission was to gather enough concrete evidence to expose him and, by extension, shed additional light on this faction's activities."

"And Morro Diabólico?" Angelo pressed, the image of Casa Forte searing in his mind. "Fogo's operation?"

A look of frustration crossed Sawyer's face. "That's where I hit a wall. Peterson is one thing; he operates in our world, within structures I can navigate. But Morro Diabólico...that's Fogo's kingdom. It's a fortress. I have resources, training, even a few Nazerites here at my disposal, but going in there without a solid plan is a suicide mission. I've never been able to get reliable intel from inside, let alone infiltrate it. My mandate is to observe and gather intelligence, not start a war with the cartels that could expose our entire operation and put the Church at greater risk."

Angelo felt a surge of irritation, a residual sting from being played, even if Sawyer's motives were clearer. "You could have told us this from the start, Brett. When we first walked in here playing missionaries."

Sawyer nodded. "I could have. But I needed to see who you were, Angelo. What you were capable of. Dropping something like this on two strangers, even if one was Rockwell's brother, would have been reckless. I needed to know if you were just looking for blind revenge or if you could handle the truth. And, frankly, I was hoping you'd dig up something I couldn't that would give me an angle on Peterson or the favela. It seems you have."

Despite the earlier withholding of information, Angelo still trusted Sawyer. The man's competence was undeniable, and his explanation, crazy as it sounded, fit the bizarre realities they were uncovering. More importantly, Sawyer had a vested interest in Fogo and Peterson, an interest that now aligned with Angelo's. They needed each other.

Sawyer leaned back, the initial tension of his revelation easing, replaced by the grim determination of a soldier outlining a difficult campaign. Angelo watched him, processing the bombshell of Sawyer's true role. It was a paradigm shift but one that, paradoxically, made their path forward clearer. They weren't just two vengeful operatives anymore; they were now linked, however informally, to a clandestine arm of the Church itself.

"All right, Brett," Angelo said, "tell me everything."

Sawyer nodded. "We've been tracking Peterson's movements, communications, finances as much as we can without tipping our hand. What we've confirmed is this: Peterson is deeply entangled with Officer Mauro. Mauro isn't just Peterson's muscle. He runs Petersons security and logistics team. Our surveillance and some...discreet inquiries have shown a consistent pattern. Roughly once a week, Mauro facilitates couriers of small, insulated packages. Each one is about a quart in size. These packages originate from within Morro Diabólico, specifically from the vicinity of Casa Forte." Sawyer's eyes hardened at the mention of the favela. "Peterson never sets foot in the favela. He's too cautious, too insulated. The 'gringo doctor types' Fofinho mentioned? We've managed to identify a few of them. They're all connected to, or known members of, the Holders of the Rod. They're the ones on the ground, overseeing whatever 'processing' is happening inside Casa Forte."

"And these packages?" Shawn asked. "Where are they going?"

"Salt Lake City," Sawyer said, the name of the Church's headquarters hanging heavy. "Every week, like clockwork, through Peterson's channels he's established. He ensures they get shipped out, no questions asked."

"What's in them?" Angelo asked.

"That's the million-dollar question," Sawyer said, a flicker of frustration in his eyes. "We haven't been able to intercept one without risking exposure. Our best guess, based on Peterson's known research with Embalmadol-Exo, is that the packages contain the chemical itself or some derivative of it. But why it needs to come specifically from Morro Diabólico, processed by these faction members in a place like Casa Forte...that's where it gets murky."

He tapped his fingers on the armrest of the sofa in a thoughtful, troubled rhythm. "It doesn't make complete sense. Embalmadol-Exo, from what we understand, is a complex compound. If it's just the chemical, why source it from a violent favela? Why not produce it in a controlled lab, especially if it's for something as critical as their pursuit of...whatever they're chasing?"

Angelo considered this. "Maybe it needs a biological component. Something fresh. Fofinho said people weren't always dead when they arrived. What if it's not just the embalming fluid but something *from* the corpses?" The pieces Fofinho had given them—"fresh product," "bodies," "unholy"—took on an even more sinister meaning.

Sawyer nodded. "That's one theory we've been exploring. There must be some kind of special ingredient that can only be sourced in the favela. Which leads to another puzzle. The quantity. A quart a week isn't a massive amount, but for a highly potent substance, it's significant. What are they doing with that much of it in Salt Lake? Are they stockpiling it? Using it for widespread experimentation within their faction? We don't know. Only that there's a steady, protected supply chain running from the depths of Morro Diabólico straight to the heart of the Church's power base."

The scale of it was unnerving. Angelo's personal vendetta had just intersected with something far larger, and more dangerous, than he could have ever imagined. He now understood why Sawyer had been so reluctant to bring them in. He had just described a war within the faith, a holy war for the soul of Mormonism, and it seemed that their actions in Rio and beyond would become a front in that war. While Angelo had no deep love for Mormonism in general, he had a loathing for bullies, especially self-righteous ones.

"So, Casa Forte," Angelo said. "That's where Fogo processes these deliveries for Peterson and his Holders of the Rod."

Sawyer nodded. "It would seem so. And it's likely fortified if it's as critical to their operation as it sounds." He looked from Angelo to Shawn. "Going in there isn't a missionary-companionship activity. It's a full-blown assault. Even for men of your caliber, going in blind and underequipped against a cartel fortification run by someone like Fogo, backed by this kind of shadowy power...that's a suicide mission."

Angelo met Sawyer's gaze. "We're not going in blind. And we don't intend to go in underequipped." He paused. "You said to call if we needed anything."

A smile crossed Sawyer's face. "I did." He stood up and walked toward a heavily reinforced door at the far end of the living room. Sawyer pressed his thumb to a nearly invisible panel, then entered a code. There was a soft hiss of hydraulics and the distinct thunk of heavy bolts retracting.

The door swung inward, revealing a small climate-controlled room. The walls were lined with weapons. Handguns, assault rifles, shotguns, sniper systems. Stacked boxes of ammunition. Body armor, tactical gear, and communications equipment hung from hooks.

"The Lord provides," Sawyer said, gesturing toward the room. "And sometimes, he provides through off-the-books contingency budgets." He turned back to Angelo and Shawn. "Fogo and Casa Forte are the tip of a very ugly spear. Taking them down won't be easy, and it will have repercussions. But if you're determined to go through with this..." He gazed at the tools of their deadly trade. "Choose what you need, then we'll talk strategy."

The heavy steel door of Brett Sawyer's arsenal stood open, a gateway to lethal possibilities. The air inside was cool and dry, smelling of gun oil and potential. Angelo moved with a practiced eye, his gaze sweeping over the racks of weapons—a curated selection of death-dealing instruments, meticulously maintained.

Shawn, on the other hand, was practically vibrating. His eyes, wide and alight, darted from the suppressed submachine guns to the compact Rattlers, then lingered with affection on a row of breaching shotguns and a collection of what looked like military-grade electronics and demolitions equipment. "Holy mother of all things that go boom," Shawn said, his voice a reverent whisper. "Brett, you beautiful, overprepared bastard. Is that C-4 over there?"

Sawyer, leaning against the doorframe, gave a knowing smile. "Composition B, mostly. More stable for long-term storage in this climate. But just as persuasive."

Angelo focused on practicalities. He picked up a sleek, matte-black carbine, short-barreled and adaptable. He worked the action, the sound crisp and precise. "We need quiet precision," Angelo said. "That favela's a crowded place. Collateral damage is a liability we don't need." He selected a suppressor and a red-dot sight, his movements economical.

"Quiet for entry, sure," Shawn agreed, reluctantly tearing his eyes away from the explosives. He grabbed a similar carbine, his movements mirroring Angelo's efficiency. "But if Fogo's in Casa Forte..." He didn't need to finish the thought. His gaze drifted back to the demolition kits.

"One step at a time," Sawyer cautioned, though his eyes held no disapproval of Shawn's pyrotechnic inclinations. "Getting to Casa Forte is the first mountain. Getting *inside* is the second." He gestured them back into the main living area, where he laid out a large satellite map of the Morro and circled the area of Casa Forte in red.

"Here's the broad stroke," Angelo began, picking up a pen and tracing a route on the map. "We go in quiet, low profile. Night approach would be best. But we may have to adapt, especially if we want to find Fogo inside. Standard missionary attire, armor underneath, we clear any street-level surveillance. We observed a few blind spots on the perimeter near Vila Isabel during our recon for Fofinho."

Sawyer nodded. "The western edge, near the ravine. It's steep, less patrolled. More difficult terrain but fewer eyes. It would require climbing gear and a high level of effort." He tapped the map. "Drainage tunnels run under parts of the lower favela. Risky, tight, dirty, but they could get you closer to the midlevels without exposing yourselves on the main paths. Once you emerge, though, there's no hiding that you basically came out of a sewer. Hmmm... Those may be handier for exfiltration."

"Once we're past the initial sprawl, how do we approach Casa Forte itself?" Shawn asked, leaning over the map. "Fofinho said it's a fortress."

"It is," Sawyer confirmed. "Fogo controls the high ground. The approaches are likely watched, possibly mined or booby-trapped. Unless we're extremely lucky, we can't just walk up to the front door."

"I vote for getting lucky," Shawn chimed in with a smile.

Angelo zoomed in on the area around Casa Forte. "Fofinho mentioned 'gringo doctor types' coming and going quietly. That implies a discreet entry point, or at least regular, predictable movements we could exploit." He looked at Sawyer. "You said your agency identified some of these Holders of the Rod operatives. Do we have a name, a face, a schedule for any of them?"

Sawyer pursed his lips. "We have a partial—a Dr. Theodore Neiman. British. Matches the 'gringo' description. He's been flagged entering and leaving Brazil on a specific schedule, usually a three-day rotation. Flies into Galeão, picked up by a car that my fellow Nazerites traced back to one of Mauro's shell companies, and then he disappears toward the favela. According to his known flight schedule, he's due to arrive tomorrow morning and would likely be going up to Casa Forte that day."

"Perfect," Angelo said, a predatory stillness in his eyes. "We intercept this Dr. Neiman. Borrow his credentials, maybe his face if Shawn's feeling artistic with his makeup kit from Sephora. He becomes our Trojan horse."

Shawn grinned. "I do have a knack for prosthetics. Give me a few hours with a good photo, and I can make you look like his uglier brother."

"If the impersonation works, we walk in," Angelo continued. "Gather intel, locate Fogo's personal quarters or command center. Identify structural vulnerabilities." He looked to Shawn. "And if Fogo is confirmed on-site, we bring the house down."

Shawn's eyes lit up. "A structural collapse. Oh, that's poetry, Operator. We can use shaped charges, focus the blast. Make it look like shoddy favela construction finally gave way. Minimal fuss, maximum impact. Lots of boom, boom, badonk-a-donk." He was already mentally calculating charge placements.

Sawyer listened, his expression thoughtful. "It's a high-risk, high-reward plan. If the impersonation fails, you're compromised deep inside. And leveling a building in Morro Diabólico, even if it's Fogo's stronghold, will draw massive heat. BOPE, the federal police, Officer Mauro...they won't just ignore it."

"By the time they figure out what happened, we'll be ghosts," Angelo stated, his confidence absolute. "We exfiltrate the same way we came in or use a contingency. Plan B—use the chaos of the collapse as cover. Plan C—die. And if all that fails, maybe consider that sewer Brett mentioned. We regroup, then we pay President Peterson a visit. A much more...personal visit."

Sawyer nodded. "While you two are playing in Fogo's sandbox, I'll make sure Peterson stays put. I have a contact high up in the local Church administration, someone who owes me a significant favor and isn't aligned with the Holders of the Rod. I'll ensure President Peterson's 'food poisoning' is...severe. Confined to his apartment with no visitors or outside communication that I don't know about. He'll be primed and waiting for your...debrief."

Sawyer walked over to a secure phone, dialing a number. "General strategy is sound," he said, waiting for his call to connect. "But the devil, as they say, is in the details. Neiman's pickup, the route to the favela, the exact layout of Casa Forte...we're still working with too many unknowns."

"We'll adapt," Angelo said. "Neiman is the key. Once we have him, we'll have his access. And if he's talkative, he might fill in some of those blanks before he...retires."

Sawyer spoke quietly into the phone, his voice calm but firm, outlining the need for President Peterson to remain indisposed and isolated. Angelo and Shawn continued to pore over the map, discussing entry vectors for intercepting Neiman, contingency plans, and the specific types of charges Shawn would need for a controlled demolition. The living room, with its luxurious furnishings and breathtaking view, had transformed into a tactical-operations center, the three men a deadly triumvirate plotting an assault on an urban fortress and the dark conspiracy it protected. The taste of vengeance was a coppery tang in Angelo's mouth, sharper and more focused than ever. This wasn't just about Rockwell anymore, it was about burning out a cancer. And Casa Forte was the primary tumor.

As Sawyer hung up the phone, he looked at Angelo and Shawn, his expression set. "Peterson is locked down. My contact will ensure he receives 'attentive care' that keeps him isolated until further notice." He returned to the table. "Right. Let's talk about setting up your appointment with Dr. Neiman."

Chapter 16

DOCTOR HEAL THYSELF

The door to the Leblon apartment clicked open, and Angelo and Shawn stepped inside. It was late. They'd left Sawyer's penthouse armed with a plan and a grim anticipation for the coming days. The faint hum of a fan and the low murmur of voices told them the other elders were still awake.

In the living area, Elder Marcus was engrossed in a letter from home, a faint smile on his face. Elder Lawrence, ever diligent, polished his shoes with meticulous care. Elders Stein and Parkman sat huddled over a worn chess board, their hushed arguments punctuated by the occasional flick of a chess piece.

Parkman looked up first, his normally jovial expression curious. "Hey, Elder Rockwell, Elder Martinez! You guys are back late. How was your day?"

Stein paused his game. "Yeah, did you learn all the secrets to baptizing the entire Barra da Tijuca in one go?"

Angelo shared a fleeting glance with Shawn. The Operator's internal gears shifted from tactical planning to plausible fabrication. "It was...productive," Angelo said.

Shawn, however, beamed his 'Elder Martinez' persona. "Productive? Elder Rockwell is too modest! It was a banner day for the Lord's work, elders! A real spiritual feast!"

Marcus lowered his letter. "Oh yeah? What'd you get up to?"

"Well," Angelo began, unbuttoning his collar as if genuinely tired from a long day of soulful labor, "first, we met up with a member, a real pillar of the ward. Brother Ricardo de Aparcido. Just wanted to touch base, ask for some referrals. A truly inspiring man."

"De Aparcido?" Lawrence paused his shoe polishing, looking impressed. "He's a legend. Elder Barnes brought him into the fold. Great dude."

"He certainly is," Shawn said, nodding. "Full of the Spirit. He gave us some great insights. Really got us motivated."

"Then," Angelo continued, "inspired by Brother de Aparcido's example, we felt prompted to do some street contacting. Headed over by Vila Isabel. You know, where the street fair is."

"Street fair, huh?" Stein grinned. "Sell any eternal truths alongside those dodgy empanadas?"

"You'd be surprised, Elder Stein," Shawn said, wagging a finger. "The harvest is ripe, even among the bargain hunters. Made some good connections, planted a few seeds. You can feel the Spirit working when you just open your mouth."

Angelo picked up the narrative. "After that, we decided to do a bit of door knocking in a nearby area. And, you know, sometimes the Lord just guides your feet. We came to this one apartment building, Princesa do Mar, right on the beach."

"Oooh, fancy," Parkman said. "Did they have a golden investigator waiting with cookies and milk?"

"Not exactly cookies," Shawn said, "but we were invited in! A lovely lady named Lucia. She was going through some...struggles in her relationship. Real turmoil. Her partner... Well, let's just say he wasn't treating her with the kind of respect a daughter of God deserves." Angelo thought of Fofinho's broken hand and pinned foot, a grim internal smile.

"We spent a good while with her," Angelo added, his expression empathetic. "Listened, offered counsel from the scriptures. I really feel like we made a breakthrough. She seemed determined to turn her life around, make some positive changes."

Lawrence nodded. "That's what it's all about, elders. Ministering to the one. Helping people overcome their challenges. Excellent work."

"And to cap off a perfect day," Shawn announced, spreading his hands wide, "we finished up at Brother Sawyer's house. He'd invited us over, and you know Brother Sawyer—always hospitable. Offered us some refreshments while we chatted about work in the ward. He's got such a strong testimony."

The other elders nodded, all familiar with Brett Sawyer's imposing presence and spiritual gravitas.

"Wow," Marcus said, shaking his head. "You guys packed it all in. Referrals, street contacting, a discussion, and a visit with the ward mission leader. Sounds like a textbook day of missionary success."

"Just trying to follow our feelings, Elder Marcus," Angelo said with a humble smile. "It leads you to some...unexpected places."

Shawn clapped Angelo on the shoulder. "And people! The Lord truly does prepare people! I tell ya, I haven't felt this invigorated since the MTC!"

As the other elders digested this tale of whirlwind missionary endeavor, some with admiration, others with a touch of bewildered envy, Angelo caught Shawn's eye again with the ludicrous understatement of their day. It was a dangerous game they played, and this was just one more layer of the deception. The real work—the dark and bloody kind—was still ahead.

The aroma of baking, sweet and rich, nudged Angelo from his shallow sleep. It was a jarringly domestic scent in the middle of their covert operation. Shawn stirred in the bunk above, a groan escaping his lips before he, too, sniffed the air. "Bruh, is that...muffins?"

They emerged from their room to find Elder Stein, a triumphant grin on his face, pulling a tray of golden-brown mounds from the small oven. "Morning, elders! Hope you're hungry. Special delivery from home!" He gestured proudly to a box of chocolate chip muffin mix on the counter. "Mom sent a care package. You know, it's crazy, but chocolate chip cookies just aren't a *thing* here in Brazil. I mean, how does an entire nation survive without proper chocolate chip cookies? It's a culinary tragedy, I tell ya. No chocolate chip muffins either!" He winked, then began distributing the warm muffins onto plates.

The other elders, Marcus and Lawrence, were already at the small kitchen table, their expressions expectant. Angelo and Shawn joined them, the scent of warm chocolate making Angelo's stomach rumble, despite the tension coiling in his gut about their upcoming rendezvous with "the Doctor."

Lawrence looked up from the breakfast table and said, "Elders, I don't know why, but I feel impressed to share one of my favorite scriptures I crossed in my study today. It was D&C Section 18 verse 15-16. While it specifically speaks about the joy of bringing souls unto the Lord, the gist is the work should be joyous, and today with these muffins and the Spirit in my heart, I genuinely do feel joyous."

The other elders nodded with appreciation and approval.

Stein passed a plate to Angelo, then Shawn, then presented one to Elder Parkman with a flourish. "For you, my friend. May your day be as joyous and delightful as this muffin."

Parkman beamed, his eyes lighting up. "Elder Stein, you're a true artist of the morning baked good!" He didn't hesitate, taking a large, enthusiastic bite. His eyes closed in bliss. "Mmm, perfect," he mumbled, chewing happily. His mouth still full, he took an even bigger second bite, his cheeks puffing out. He chewed for a second, the blissful expression still lingering, then it faltered. His jaw slowed, his eyes opened wide, and a look of profound confusion, rapidly morphing into disgust, washed over his face. He made a gagging sound and spat the half-chewed mouthful onto his plate. "Hot dog!?" he spluttered, crumbs clinging to his lips, his face a bewildered mask of betrayal. "A salty freakin' hot dog!?"

Elder Stein howled with laughter, doubling over. The other elders stared, first at Parkman's rejected muffin, then at Stein's unrestrained glee.

"You didn't!" Elder Marcus gasped, a grin spreading across his face.

Stein, barely able to speak through his laughter, pointed a shaking finger at Parkman. "Payback...for the Pancake Man!" he choked out, wiping a tear from his eye. "I told you, Parkman! I told you I'd get you back!"

Parkman stared at the offending muffin, a large pink hot dog chunk staring back, then at Stein, his expression shifting from disgust to a grudging, bewildered respect. He poked at the muffin, revealing the bite-scarred chunk of steamy hot dog nestled among the chocolate chips. The sheer audacity of it was, even to the prank-master Parkman, impressive.

"Fine, I'm impressed," Parkman said with a smile. "Now, pass the mustard."

The briefing the night before from Brett Sawyer had been precise. Flight BA249 from Heathrow would land at Galeão International at 10:45 a.m. Dr. Theodore Neiman traveled light: carry-on, slim briefcase. Usual pickup was a black sedan, "Brasil Vida Funeral Arrangements"—Peterson's morbid little joke. Driver often rotated. No sign of a standard code phrase for tomorrow's pickup, that we have found so far."

That last detail was the grit in the gears. Angelo, Shawn, and Sawyer had huddled around the gleaming expanse of Sawyer's penthouse living room, which had rapidly transformed into a makeshift tactical center.

"So, no easy snatch at arrivals," Shawn had mused, idly flipping a custom-made Bowie knife Sawyer kept on his bookshelf. "Means we hit the car en route to Devil's Hill?"

"Too messy," Angelo countered, eyes narrowed in thought. "Potential for a firefight he's not meant to survive or collateral that draws every BOPE officer in Rio. We need him intact, his credentials usable. The impersonation for Casa Forte hinges on it."

Sawyer, who'd been reviewing data on a ruggedized laptop, looked up. "Peterson's office communications are encrypted, but we picked up chatter weeks ago about a compromised device. Found a fragmented log. One UK mobile number linked to 'shipment inquiries.' Might be our Dr. Neiman."

"Get it," Angelo said. He turned to Shawn, a predatory gleam in his eye. "Still got that number-spoofing software on your mobile device?"

Shawn produced the untraceable phone. "Ready for its close-up, Elder DeMille."

The plan was audacious, relying on Neiman's presumed paranoia and self-importance. Angelo composed the text: *Dr. Neiman. URGENT. Compromised transport. Primary vehicle unavailable. Secondary extraction protocol active. Await Mr. Silva, black Mercedes S-Class, diplomatic plates, Terminal 2 arrivals. Sign: 'HOLY ROD MEDICAL FIRM.' Maintain silence. Discretion vital. Your safety is priority. - M. Security.*

"Holy Rod." Shawn had snorted when he read it. "I've got a Holy Rod for him."

"He's a zealot with the Holders," Angelo said. "He'll see it as divine intervention or a necessary precaution for a man of his...stature."

The humid air outside Galeão's Terminal 2 was thick enough to chew. Angelo, looking every bit the discreet corporate security man in a dark suit, held the simple placard: *HOLY ROD MEDICAL FIRM*. The black Mercedes S-Class idled at the curb, Shawn a shadowy figure behind the wheel, mirrored sunglasses and a chauffeur's cap obscuring his features.

Passengers from British Airways flight 249 began to emerge. Angelo's gaze, sharp and discerning, found him almost immediately. Dr. Theodore Neiman was a study in nervous energy, his sharp, angular face pale, acne scars standing out against his pasty complexion. Short, dark, curly hair, rumpled linen jacket, a wheeled carry-on, and a slim leather briefcase clutched like a holy relic. He spotted Angelo's sign, and a wave of something akin to relief washed over his tense features. He navigated toward Angelo with jerky, purposeful strides.

"Mr. Silva?" Neiman's voice was clipped, undeniably British, his eyes darting.

Angelo inclined his head. "Dr. Neiman. A pleasure. The car is this way. We need to maintain discretion." He took the carry-on, guiding Neiman toward the Mercedes. Shawn, all silent professionalism, handled the luggage and opened the rear door.

Once they were gliding away from the airport, Neiman leaned forward. "This 'M. Security,' is he a recent appointment? I typically liaise directly with President Peterson for alterations to my itinerary."

"Recent protocols, Doctor," Angelo said. "President Peterson felt more specialized oversight was prudent for key assets, such as yourself."

The doctor seemed mollified, settling back.

Shawn drove with efficiency, not toward the favelas but into the winding, affluent hills of Santa Teresa, toward a secluded colonial house Sawyer used for sensitive meetings.

As they turned onto a quiet cobblestone street, shaded by ancient trees and high garden walls, Neiman's brow furrowed. "This isn't the standard approach. Are we not proceeding directly to the facility?"

"A slight deviation, Doctor," Angelo said, a new, harder edge sharpening his tone. "President Peterson requires a preliminary consultation at a secure, off-site location. New intelligence has come to light."

Neiman's unease was now visible. "New intelligence? He made no mention of this in our last encrypted exchange."

The Mercedes slid into a discreet driveway, ornate iron gates hissing shut behind them, cocooning them in sudden, profound silence. The air in the car grew heavy.

"Mr. Silva, where have you brought me?" Neiman demanded, his voice tight, his knuckles white on his briefcase.

Angelo turned fully in his seat. The bland mask of "Mr. Silva" evaporated, replaced by an unnerving, predatory calm. "Dr. Neiman," he said, his voice soft, yet sharp as obsidian, "let's dispense with formalities. Your meeting with President Peterson has been canceled. As has your immediate visit to your 'facility.'" He paused, letting the implications settle in Neiman's rapidly paling face. "Instead, you'll be having a detailed discussion with us. About your...rather unique contributions to science."

Neiman's pasty complexion paled even further. His mind, accustomed to the clandestine but orderly world of Peterson and the Holders of the Rod, struggled to process this abrupt shift. This wasn't just a deviation, it was a hijacking. Before he could formulate a protest, Shawn exited the driver's seat and opened Neiman's door. His earlier passive demeanor was gone, replaced by an undeniable menace, though his voice was chillingly polite.

"Doctor," Shawn said, his mirrored sunglasses reflecting Neiman's wide-eyed stare. "If you'd be so kind as to join us inside? We have a comfortable setting for our...business chat." His posture, the set of his shoulders, conveyed an absolute lack of negotiation.

Terror, cold and sharp, lanced through Neiman. He looked from Shawn's implacable presence to Angelo's glacial calm in the car. The fight seemed to drain out of him, replaced by a dawning, sickening realization: his world of secret science and fanatical faith had just collided with a far more unpredictable reality. He was a man of test tubes and scripture, not...whatever this was. Was it a hostile takeover? Corporate espionage of the most ruthless kind? His work was groundbreaking, revolutionary. Perhaps there was still a way to navigate this, to leverage his indispensable knowledge. He clutched his briefcase tighter, and with a surge of adrenaline-fueled fear, mixed with a desperate hope, Dr. Neiman allowed himself to be ushered out of the Mercedes toward the imposing colonial house.

The colonial house was cool. Dr. Neiman sat stiffly on an antique velvet armchair, his briefcase resting on his lap like a shield. His earlier terror had subsided into a watchful, resentful suspicion.

Angelo pulled up a straight-backed chair, positioning himself opposite Neiman, while Shawn lounged with deceptive casualness against a heavy mahogany sideboard, seemingly absorbed in a dusty painting of a forgotten patriarch.

"Dr. Neiman," Angelo began, "allow me to offer our sincerest apologies for the unconventional nature of our initial contact. Rest assured, it was a necessary precaution. Your safety, and the integrity of certain proprietary information, is paramount to our employer."

Neiman's thin lips pressed tighter. "Your 'employer'? And who, precisely, might they be? This is highly irregular. President Peterson will hear of this."

"I'm sure he will," Angelo said with a smile. "As for our employers, let's just say they represent one of the largest, most research-intensive pharmaceutical conglomerates on the planet. Perhaps you've heard of...Aegis Life Solutions?"

Shawn chimed in. "Our acquisitions-and-development department has been intrigued by certain advancements originating in this region. Specifically, a compound known as Embalmadol-Exo."

Neiman's head snapped up, his eyes fixed on Shawn with a sharp intensity. "Embalmadol-Exo is not for commercial exploitation."

"Precisely what we understood," Angelo said, nodding gravely. "Which made President Peterson's recent overtures to us rather perplexing. He seemed quite keen to discuss a potential licensing agreement, even a full buyout of the formula. He painted a picture of a revolutionary preservation agent, but frankly, Doctor, his proposed valuation seemed...exorbitant for a glorified embalming fluid, however advanced."

A subtle scowl of indignation, perhaps even betrayal crossed Neiman's face. His pasty skin seemed to flush. "President Peterson...approached *you*? To *sell* Embalmadol-Exo?"

"He did," Angelo confirmed, leaning forward. "Which is why we felt it necessary to consult with someone closer to the actual research and development. Someone who understands its true potential, beyond simple...preservation. We felt perhaps President Peterson wasn't providing the full picture, or worse, was attempting to divest something...sacred...for personal gain."

Angelo let that hang in the air, watching Neiman's internal struggle. The doctor's fingers tightened on his briefcase, wrestling with himself, the zealot battling the cautious scientist, the betrayed subordinate warring with the keeper of secrets. He wouldn't, Angelo knew, speak of the grim realities of the Morro immediately. That was too dark, too damning. But his pride in his work, his contempt for Peterson's perceived greed, that was a lever.

"President Peterson," Neiman began, his voice tight with carefully controlled fury, "is a mortician. A man of practicalities. He understands ledgers and profits. He does not, perhaps, fully grasp the profound spiritual and scientific breakthrough that Embalmadol-Exo represents, particularly with the recent...enhancements."

"Enhancements?" Angelo prompted. "He mentioned a remarkable lifelike quality, reduced desiccation, but nothing beyond that."

Neiman scoffed. "Child's play. The base compound achieves that, yes. But true advancement, the quantum leap, came with the introduction of the catalyst." He paused, savoring the term. "We refer to it as the 'Light of Christ.' A biospiritual additive, if you will."

Shawn pushed himself off the sideboard, taking a step closer. "Light of Christ? That's an unconventional designation for a pharmaceutical component."

A smug smile from Neiman. He was warming to his subject, eager to correct their mundane understanding. "It is no mere chemical, gentlemen. It's...an essence. When properly integrated into the Embalmadol-Exo matrix at a molecular level, it doesn't just preserve, it...elevates. It creates a gain of function far beyond simple stasis."

"Gain of function?" Angelo echoed, keeping his face a mask of professional curiosity. "Could you elaborate, Dr. Neiman? What specific functionalities are we discussing? President Peterson was rather vague on the specifics beyond its cosmetic applications."

Neiman looked from Angelo to Shawn, a crafty light in his eyes. He was on his turf now, the expert enlightening the ignorant. He still wouldn't spill the darkest secrets of the favela, Angelo sensed, but the scientist in him, the true believer in the Holders of the Rod's twisted vision, couldn't resist boasting of their miracle. "Let us just say, gentlemen, that with the Light of Christ, Embalmadol-Exo does more than just keep the flesh intact. It prepares the vessel. It retains...a spark. The potential for something more. Something President Peterson, in his pursuit of earthly profits, could never truly comprehend."

Angelo exchanged a glance with Shawn. Neiman was baited. He was talking.

The air in the colonial house grew chilly with Neiman's pronouncements. Angelo maintained his expression of professional interest, a slight frown of concentration creasing his brow as if he were trying to absorb complex scientific data. Shawn, however, shifted his approach, injecting a note of reverent curiosity.

"Doctor," Shawn began, his voice laced with a newfound respect, "this 'Light of Christ'...it's fascinating. President Peterson spoke of it almost dismissively, as if it were just some...biocatalytic enzyme. He clearly underestimated its significance. You say it creates a 'gain of function,' prepares a 'vessel.' What kind of preparation? For what, exactly?"

Neiman's pale eyes seemed to glow with an inner fervor. He leaned forward. "President Peterson is a simpleton in these matters, driven by base desires and earthly concerns. He sees only the mundane applications. But the true Holders of the Rod, we see the grand design. We understand the...*sacred* purpose."

Angelo nodded. "A sacred purpose. Beyond simple preservation, then? You're implying something...transformative?"

"Transformative?" Neiman's laugh was thin, brittle. "My dear sir, we are on the cusp of fulfilling prophecy! Do you not see the signs? The world, even the Church, descends further into darkness each day. Permissiveness, enablement, all cloaked under the guise of 'love' and 'kindness.' It is the pathway to hell, paved with good intentions!" His voice rose in intensity, his bony hands clutching his briefcase. "But the true warriors, the *chosen*," he thumped his chest, "we move forward. We advance the Lord's timetable. The Second Coming is nigh, gentlemen, and we, the Holders of the Rod, have been called as special disciples to aid God in His ultimate mission!"

Shawn leaned in with an expression of wide-eyed fascination. "His ultimate mission, Doctor? What exactly is it?"

Neiman's face took on a beatific, almost smug expression. He quoted, his voice ringing with conviction, "For behold, this is my work and my glory—to bring to pass the immortality and eternal life of man." He paused, letting the words from Moses 1:39 resonate. "The plan of salvation must be completed! And my department, our sacred charge, is to ensure the crowning jewel: immortality, the resurrection, life eternal!" He was practically incandescent with self-righteous zeal. "As it is written in First Corinthians, chapter fifteen, verse twenty-two: 'For as in Adam all die, even so in Christ shall all be made alive!'"

"Immortality," Angelo mused. "That's...ambitious, Doctor. Even for Aegis Life Solutions, reanimation is considered purely theoretical. How do you propose to achieve this...on a practical level?"

"Practical level?" Neiman scoffed, waving a dismissive hand. "We are not limited by the shortsighted 'practicalities' of secular science! We operate under divine mandate! It may be through unconventional means, yes." His eyes gleamed with a disturbing light. "Did not Matthew himself record in chapter twenty-seven, verse fifty-two, 'And the graves were opened; and many bodies of the saints who had fallen asleep were raised'? The Light of Christ, that precious essence we raise and *harvest* in places like Morro Diabólico, brings us closer with each consecrated vessel. Closer to overcoming death, to initiating the glorious resurrection!"

Angelo felt sick. *Harvest.* The word, spoken with such religious fervor, painted a sickening picture when juxtaposed with Fofinho's terrified descriptions of Fogo's operations and

Sawyer's intel about the insulated packages shipped from the favela.

Shawn furrowed his brow. "But, Doctor, if this resurrection is God's will, why the complex methodology? The harvesting, the Embalmadol-Exo... Why doesn't God just, you know, use His spirit magic to bring people back? Seems a lot simpler."

Neiman looked at Shawn with a mixture of pity and condescension. "My son," he said, his tone patronizing, "God *can* do anything. But to simply intervene, to wave His hand and make it so, would be to rob His children of the opportunity to serve Him, to learn, to grow in His likeness. He will not stifle our intelligence, our agency by intervening in matters He has equipped His able servants on earth to handle. The Holders of the Rod, we are His hands! We are effective tools in the hands of the Lord!"

He puffed out his chest, the zealot now fully ascendant over the scientist. "The prophets themselves have testified to this principle! The great Thomas S. Monson declared, 'We are the Lord's hands here upon the earth, with the mandate to serve and to lift His children.' And Spencer W. Kimball, a prophet of profound vision, taught us, 'God does notice us, and he watches over us. But it is usually through another person that he meets our needs.'"

Neiman's gaze swept over Angelo and Shawn, as if anointing them with his enlightened understanding. "We, gentlemen, are those 'other persons' fulfilling the Lord's work, engaging in the sacred science that will usher in the millennial reign. President Peterson, with his grubby deals and necro-commerce, he is but a means to an end. A flawed instrument, yes, but one the Lord, in His infinite wisdom, allows us to utilize for a far greater, holier purpose."

Angelo listened, his mind racing, connecting the horrifying dots between Neiman's fanatical pronouncements and the brutal reality of his family's murder. Rockwell, Sarah, Jason...they weren't just victims of random favela violence, they were obstacles, or worse, potential "vessels," caught in the gears of this monstrous, blasphemous machine. The "Light of Christ" harvested from the favelas. Embalmadol-Exo, preparing bodies. All in the name of a twisted, unholy resurrection. The Operator's cold fury began to simmer beneath his calm exterior. Neiman, in his sanctimonious delusion, had just signed his own death warrant.

With a self-satisfied smile, Nieman leaned back, steepling his fingers, clearly believing he had not only impressed but perhaps even *enlightened* these representatives of Aegis Life Solutions. "You see," he continued, his voice now carrying a confidential, almost inviting tone, "Aegis Life Solutions, with its vast resources, its global reach...it could be more than just a commercial enterprise. It could be...a *conduit*. A powerful instrument in this divine work, should its leadership possess the necessary vision, the spiritual fortitude to look beyond mere profit." He eyed them shrewdly. "Men like yourselves, with your evident understanding of delicate operations and the need for discretion, you grasp the monumental stakes, far more than a man like Peterson ever could."

Shawn, playing his part to perfection, leaned forward, his voice full of intrigue. "Are you suggesting, Doctor, that there might be a...a role for an organization like ours? Beyond a simple acquisition of Embalmadol-Exo? A more...collaborative venture, perhaps, on this sacred purpose?"

Neiman's eyes lit up, the zealot recognizing what he perceived as kindred spirits, or at least, influential individuals awakening to a higher calling. "Precisely!" he exclaimed, his voice regaining some of its earlier fervor. "The Holders of the Rod are not without resources, but the challenges are immense, the opposition, both seen and unseen, formidable.

Imagine what could be achieved with the backing of a global power like Aegis! The acceleration of the Lord's timetable! The expansion of the...preparation. We're always watchful for those whom the Spirit designates as potential allies, those with the capacity to understand and the will to act."

He was no longer merely answering questions, he was actively probing, testing if these powerful men could be drawn into his holy war. His ego, stroked by their deference and understanding, blinded him to the cold, analytical eyes of the predators before him. He believed he was on the verge of a significant coup, bringing influential players to his side, while in reality, every word he uttered was another nail in his coffin.

Inside Angelo, the ice was spreading through his veins. Neiman wasn't just a cog, he was an active, willing recruiter for this horror. The man's intellectual vanity and messianic delusion were making him eagerly offer up the very information they'd come to extract, all while believing he was masterfully guiding the conversation toward a grand alliance.

Angelo maintained his mask of thoughtful consideration. "A fascinating prospect, Doctor Neiman. Truly...profound implications." He paused, letting a beat of silence stretch. "Just a couple of logistical concerns to consider before...deeper engagement."

Neiman waved a magnanimous hand. "Of course, of course. Transparency is key among true collaborators."

"The recent unfortunate incident," Angelo said, "involving the American missionary, Elder Barnes, and his family. Aegis, as you can imagine, is extremely sensitive to any potential negative publicity. Any hint of a connection between such a tragedy and a...proprietary compound like Embalmadol-Exo could be catastrophic for our brand. We need assurances that this was an isolated event, entirely unrelated."

Neiman nodded vigorously, his expression slightly dismissive. "A tragic and unfortunate accident, indeed. Utterly unrelated to our work. It brought unwanted attention, a flurry of police activity, but nothing more. President Peterson assured me the missionary...well, from what he implied, the young man was somewhat...soft. Lacked the true fire, the zeal required of a dedicated saint. A pity, but hardly a martyr in the cause, if you understand my meaning. Wrong place, wrong time. The matter is entirely contained."

Soft? Angelo's jaw tightened. The casual disrespect for Rockwell, parroted from that swine Peterson, stoked the cold fire within him. He filed it away.

"And these weekly deliveries you manage from the Morro," Angelo continued, his gaze drifting over Neiman, his voice dropping, as if stating an obvious but dark unspoken truth, "the Light of Christ...you're harvesting it. From the recently deceased in the favela. Correct?"

Neiman straightened slightly, the clinician taking over from the evangelist. "Correct," he affirmed, almost detached. "The Light of Christ is indeed an actual substance. A complex neuropeptide with trace elements that we're still categorizing, developed through our research and, frankly, divine inspiration. It's concentrated deep within the brain, near the pituitary gland. Very shortly after systemic biological cessation, the gland can be...'milked,' for lack of a more elegant term, of this vital essence. It appears to be uniquely present in human subjects. All attempts to find an animal analog have proven fruitless."

Shawn, who had been listening with an air of almost boyish curiosity, piped up. "So, Doctor, the refrigerated packages you bring out of the Morro...are they specimens? Like, a brain in a jar? Or a couple of brains? Or...?"

Neiman gave a dry chuckle. "Good heavens, no. Far too crude, and the transport logistics would be a nightmare. No, the packages contain pure, concentrated secretions of the Light of Christ. The extraction, the 'milking,' as I termed it, is performed at Casa Forte. We then carefully process and package the raw material into sterile, temperature-controlled vials for immediate transport. The yield has been significant. We can extract approximately one teaspoon of LoC per subject. My weekly recovery quota is roughly one quart. That translates to...let me see..." He did a quick mental calculation. "Approximately one hundred and ninety-two subjects per delivery."

One hundred and ninety-two, Angelo thought, his stomach churning. *One hundred and ninety-two bodies. Every. Single. Week. Just for this one ghoul.* "And in a year?"

Neiman beamed. "Around ten thousand subjects for my collections alone. Of course, there are other doctors contributing to the effort. This year, collectively, we're on track to produce nearly two hundred quarts of LoC. It is, by any measure, quite the miracle of an operation. A testament to the Lord's guiding hand and the dedication of His servants."

Angelo felt the last vestiges of professional detachment shatter. The numbers were staggering, the callousness monumental. He had one final question, one he had to ask, even though he dreaded the answer. "And the missionary, Rockwell Barnes? His mother, his stepfather? Did you harvest them?"

Neiman looked aghast. "Goodness, no! They were respected American citizens, a family. The scrutiny would have been unbearable, potentially jeopardizing the entire operation. As I said, a terrible, tragic accident. Wrong place, wrong time. The local authorities, through President Peterson's influence, dealt with it swiftly. You have absolutely no reason to worry on that account. It's a closed matter."

He smiled reassuringly, the condescending zealot once more.

Angelo held it together, his face a mask of placid agreement. He rose slowly, extending a hand toward Neiman. "Doctor, this has been...illuminating."

Neiman stood, accepting the implied gesture of farewell, a pleased expression on his face, assuming this bizarre but ultimately fruitful meeting was concluding.

Angelo walked him toward the heavy wooden door of the colonial house, his hand falling onto Neiman's shoulder. "You know, Doctor, I heard an interesting thing this morning at the breakfast table. A scripture, I believe. I think Jesus was talking, and He said something like, 'if your joy will be great with one soul that you have brought unto me into the kingdom of my Father, how great will be your joy if you should bring many souls unto me!'" He squeezed Neiman's shoulder. "This is shaping up to be a very joyous occasion for my friend and me. I have a feeling we're going to *send* many, many souls back to God today."

In a quick, fluid motion, Angelo slipped his arm down and around Neiman's neck. He pivoted behind the slighter man, cinching his bicep and forearm into a brutally efficient blood choke. Neiman let out a gasp, his eyes bulging as Angelo dragged him backward and down, his own legs scissoring around Neiman's torso in a textbook rear-naked choke. The fight was brief, a desperate flailing struggle that only tightened the vise.

Just as the pinpricks of unconsciousness were about to engulf Neiman's vision, Angelo released the pressure a tad. The doctor spluttered, a ragged, desperate gasp for air, his eyes wide with terror and dawning comprehension. Angelo savored the moment, the up-close-and-personal sensation of strangling this Mormon Dr. Mengele, this man who had so casually dismissed his brother's life and spirit.

Shawn watched, one eye on the struggle, the other scanning the windows. "Finish the job, Operator."

Angelo tightened the choke again, relentlessly. Neiman's struggles weakened, his body going limp after a final shuddering exhalation. Angelo held on for a long, silent count before releasing his grip.

He got to his feet, breathing a little heavily. Shawn walked over, nudging Neiman's still form with his foot. "Remember that time we garroted that Russian GRU operative in Odessa? Thought he was dead in the trunk, but when we went to dump him by the Black Sea, he popped out and clocked you with a rusty beach shovel."

Angelo grunted. Yeah, he remembered. The throbbing headache had lasted for days.

"Point is," Shawn continued, "you want to be absolutely sure with strangulation. Make sure the job's done."

Angelo looked down at the crumpled form of Dr. Theodore Neiman, his sharp, angular face slack, his pasty complexion tinged with a bruised purple. The zeal was gone, replaced by the vacant stare of the dead. Angelo felt nothing but a cold, grim satisfaction. He gestured with his chin toward Neiman. "You can finish it."

Shawn nodded. His gaze fell on a tall stone obelisk sculpture standing in a corner of the room, some abstract piece of art. He walked over to it, tested its weight, then got a solid grip. With a grunt, he lined up the landing zone, then heaved, toppling the sculpture. It crashed down with a sickening, wet thud onto Dr. Neiman's head. A sound like a dropped melon.

Shawn stepped back, surveying the gruesome tableau.

"Lights out."

Chapter 17

ALREADY TO HARVEST

Angelo stared down at the mangled remains of Dr. Theodore Neiman. The man's pale, acne-scarred face was now a grotesque ruin of squish, the fanatical light in his eyes permanently snuffed. So much for the Holders' grand resurrection plans for this particular specimen.

The initial plan, sketched out in Sawyer's penthouse, had hinged on Neiman: disabling him, extracting every piece of intel about Casa Forte and Fogo's operation, and then Angelo impersonating him to gain access to the favela stronghold.

"All right," Angelo said, the words scraping from his throat. He rolled his shoulders, the adrenaline from the kill beginning to ebb, leaving behind a cold pragmatism. "Let's see what our good doctor brought for his trip."

Shawn knelt by Neiman's discarded briefcase and carry-on. He rifled through them, pulling out neatly folded linen shirts, a pair of pants, a small toiletries bag, and a disturbing number of religious pamphlets interspersed with scientific journals. "Standard travel stuff, mostly. Smells like mothballs and zealotry." He held up one of Neiman's white lab coats. "Doesn't look like he packed his 'World's Best Mormon' mug."

Angelo looked at the lab coat, then at Neiman's slight build, then down at his own frame. Even without the Special Forces muscle he'd packed on, he'd always been a larger man than the wiry, almost gaunt doctor. "No way I'm fitting into his clothes. He was built like a praying mantis."

Shawn snorted. "Yeah, you going as Dr. Neiman would be like a rhino trying to pass itself off as a...baby rhino. Pretty sure they'd notice the extra two hundred pounds and distinct lack of a self-righteous sneer." He paused, tapping a finger to his chin. Suddenly, a mischievous glint flashed in Shawn's eye. "But me, on the other hand..."

Angelo raised an eyebrow. "You think *you* can pull off the look any better?"

"Hey, I'm a method actor, remember?" Shawn grinned, grabbing the lab coat. He slipped it on. It was a little short in the sleeves and snug across the shoulders, but not entirely ridiculous. The problem was his face. Shawn's complexion was darker from the Texas sun, his features broader, his dark hair cropped short, nothing like Neiman's pale, curly haired fanaticism. "Okay, so the bone structure's a bit off." Shawn pulled out a small tube of what looked like concealer. "But with a little theatrical magic..."

Shawn attempted to smear the pale concealer onto his own face. It just made him look like he'd had a bad run-in with a bag of flour. Then Shawn found a travel-sized tub of hair gel in Neiman's bag and tried to muss his short hair into something resembling Neiman's unkempt curls. The effect was less "mad scientist" and more "startled badger."

"You know," Angelo said, "for someone who fancies himself a master of disguise, you look like you're preparing to audition for a mime troupe at a school for the tragically brain-damaged."

Shawn scowled, looking at his reflection in a darkened windowpane. "It's the lighting in here! And your negative attitude. I need proper materials. A wig, maybe some spirit gum for...

for..." He trailed off, seeing Angelo's unimpressed expression. "Okay, fine, maybe the curly hair's a stretch."

"A stretch?" Angelo gave a dry chuckle. "Martinez, you look less like Dr. Neiman and more like a disgraced gyno who lost a fight with a tube of Vagisil."

"Well, whose fault is that?" Shawn retorted, gesturing toward Neiman's corpse. "If somebody," he said, his voice rising with theatrical indignation, "hadn't been in such a rush to play Grim Reaper and send Professor Pasty here to his eternal reward, we might have had time to, you know, get his measurements! Ask about his preferred brand of anemic-looking foundation! Maybe even snag a lock of his precious holy-roller hair for a custom wig!" He threw up his hands. "But noooo, 'the Operator' had to operate. Choke first, maybe ask questions later if the corpse is still warm enough to talk!"

Angelo's eyes narrowed. "First off, he was a clear threat who just admitted to enabling the weekly murder of nearly two hundred people a week for his 'Light of Christ' body-snatching cult. Neutralizing him was essential. Second, even if we'd given him a spa day and a questionnaire, you trying to look like him is *still* a biological impossibility. It's not about the makeup, Shawn, it's about the fact that you have the charisma of a golden retriever, and he had all the charm of a damp sock puppet."

"Oh, I see!" Shawn clapped his hands together sarcastically. "So it's my fault I don't look like I subsist on communion wafers and the tears of the unworthy? Maybe if you weren't built like a brick shithouse, you could have tried squeezing into his little choirboy outfit!"

"I'll take being built like a brick shithouse over looking like a jackass."

Shawn sighed, kicking at the leg of an antique armchair. "Okay, fine. So the 'Elder Neiman surprise visit' is a bust. He did give us Casa Forte, though. And the Light of Christ harvesting. That's gold." He looked at Angelo. "So, new plan? Because I'm pretty sure showing up at the murder favela looking like a clown in a borrowed lab coat isn't going to inspire confidence in Fogo's goons."

Angelo looked from Neiman's body to Shawn, who was now forlornly wiping streaks of makeup from his face with the back of his hand. "No," Angelo said, a new resolve hardening his gaze. "We're not going in as Neiman...we're going in as missionaries."

"Sexy missionaries," Shawn added.

"No." Angelo smiled. "Well-armed, bad-ass-mother-fuckin' missionaries."

They walked back to their sedan. The vehicle, unassuming on the outside, was now a mobile armory, courtesy of Brett Sawyer. Angelo popped the trunk. Inside, nestled among innocuous travel bags, lay the bounty from Sawyer's well-stocked arsenal.

"First things first," Angelo said, pulling out two sets of missionary attire Sawyer had provided—white shirts, dark slacks, conservative ties, and name tags. He tossed a set to Shawn.

"Sexy missionaries 2.0," Shawn said, adjusting his tie. "This time with more banging!"

Angelo ignored him, his attention focused on the weapons. He selected his preferred carbine, checking the suppressor.

Shawn mirrored him with focused intensity as he handled the firearms.

They began to meticulously transfer gear from the larger gun cases into their standard-issue missionary backpacks—extra magazines, suppressed pistols, tactical medical kits, cash for bribes, and a few of Shawn's smaller, more specialized explosive charges. They put in some pass-along cards and scriptures in one of the compartments to maintain the innocent facade of the backpacks.

"All right," Angelo said, once their bags were packed, looking more like they were ready for a scripture study than an assault. "Neiman's credentials should still be useful." He held up the slim leather briefcase they'd taken from the dead doctor. "He was expected at Casa Forte. They're waiting for a doctor, a gringo specialist."

Shawn looked up from configuring a compact comm unit. "So, what, we walk up, flash his ID, and hope they don't notice we're not pale, pasty, and British?"

"No. We go as our missionary alter egos on our way to teach a family." He paused, thinking of the grim irony. "Lucia Freitas's family. They lived at the top of Morro Diabólico, near Casa Forte, remember? We're just two dedicated servants of the Lord, concerned for the spiritual welfare of her mother and sister."

Shawn's eyebrows shot up. "Ballsy. You think Fogo's henchmen are just going to wave us through after what happened to your family? After Mauro went scorched earth and bagged fifteen 'suspects' to close the case?"

"Exactly. The bad press from those killings, Mauro's heavy-handed response...it caused a storm. Fogo knows that. The last thing he needs is another international incident involving dead missionaries, especially if they're clearly identifiable and acting within their supposed calling. Fogo's gang will be cautious. They'll want to verify. They might even want to get a green light from Fogo before they let two gringo missionaries wander too deep into his territory, especially near his prized 'Strong House.'"

Angelo hefted his backpack, the weight of the hidden gear a familiar comfort. "We act like we're oblivious, just doing our job. We make it clear we're expected by Lucia's family. We force *them* to make the call. If we can get them to radio Fogo about two missionaries wanting passage, that's our opening. Neiman's credentials," he tapped the briefcase, "might just be the extra push we need if they're hesitant, a reason for Fogo to let 'the new doctor's associates' pass—under escort, of course. If that doesn't work, we improvise."

Shawn considered it, a slow, predatory grin spreading across his face. "So, we're using their own paranoia against them. I like it. It's devious. And if they do escort us up to Lucia's family near Casa Forte..."

"Then we're exactly where we need to be. With a guided tour, practically." Angelo cinched the backpack straps tight over his shoulders. "Let's go bring some souls unto the Lord."

The narrow entrance to Morro Diabólico loomed before them, a claustrophobic funnel between crumbling brick structures. Angelo felt the weight of his backpack—heavier with weapons than scripture—as they approached. The favela's mouth was a living entity, breathing poverty and danger in equal measure.

They hadn't taken three steps into the favela when two small figures dropped from a low wall to block their path.

The boys couldn't have been older than eleven—skinny, dark-eyed children with the hardened expressions of veterans. Each clutched a 9mm handgun that looked oversized in their small hands.

"Who are you?" the taller boy demanded, waving his weapon with casual menace. "What you want? Show us the bag."

Angelo tensed, calculating angles and timing. Shawn stepped forward with a beaming smile that seemed to brighten the dim alleyway.

"Hello, friends! I'm Elder Martinez, and this is Elder Rockwell," Shawn said, his voice pitched with artificial cheer. "We're missionaries from the Church of Jesus Christ of Latter-day Saints!"

The boys exchanged confused glances, their weapons still pointed toward the missionaries.

"We're here to visit Sofia and Isabella Freitas," Angelo added. "Lucia's family."

The shorter boy frowned. "Freitas? Up on the hill."

Shawn nodded and swung his backpack around. Angelo watched the boys' hands tighten on their weapons as the bag moved. With deliberate slowness, Shawn unzipped the front compartment, revealing a couple copies of the Book of Mormon.

"Would you boys like to learn about Jesus Christ?" Shawn asked, offering a copy to the taller boy. "This book has the answers to life's most important questions!"

The boy lowered his gun slightly, looking at the book with suspicion. "I don't read."

Shawn's smile never faltered. "That doesn't matter! There are some cool pictures in here too." He flipped to an illustrated page showing Christ visiting the Americas. "See? Jesus came to this continent too. Pretty awesome, right?"

Angelo watched this surreal exchange, maintaining his bland missionary smile while scanning their surroundings. Other eyes were on them—from windows, doorways, shadows.

The boy reached out with his free hand and took the book, tucking it under his arm. After a moment, he jerked his head toward the path leading deeper into the favela.

"You go quick."

As they passed between the young sentries, Angelo noticed a subtle movement on a rooftop three buildings ahead. A moment later, a blue kite soared into the air, dancing against the cloudless sky. The simple beauty of it seemed out of place in this environment, but Angelo recognized it for what it was—a signal.

"Heads up," Angelo muttered. "Blue kite. They're tracking us."

Shawn nodded. "Praise the Lord for such a beautiful day," he said loudly, his eyes flicking to the kite. "I feel blessed already."

They continued deeper into the favela, the blue kite floating above them.

Angelo's muscles tensed with each step. The narrow, winding path through Morro Diabólico seemed designed to disorient visitors, with sudden turns and steep concrete stairs crumbling at the edges. The stench of uncollected garbage and sewage hung in the humid air, occasionally punctuated by the acrid smell of burning tires.

"Two o'clock," Shawn muttered.

Angelo glanced up casually. A red kite joined the blue one in the sky. A moment later, a yellow one appeared. The colorful sentinels tracked their progress through the favela, a beautiful yet ominous surveillance system.

"They're not even trying to be subtle," Angelo whispered.

"Why would they? This is their territory," Shawn whispered through his fake smile.

Children peered at them from doorways, their expressions a mixture of curiosity and wariness. Women paused in their tasks to watch the strangers pass, some clutching toddlers to their bodies. Young men lounged in clusters at corners, their eyes hard and evaluating beneath the brims of soccer team caps. Angelo noted the subtle bulges under shirts, the casual way hands rested near waistbands.

The sensation of being watched crawled across Angelo's skin. His peripheral vision caught shadows moving parallel to their path, figures ducking between buildings to maintain pace with them. Not an ambush—at least not yet—but definitely reconnaissance.

"Elders! Elders!"

The shout came from behind them, the voice cracking with age. Angelo turned, his hand instinctively shifting toward his concealed weapon.

An elderly man hurried toward them, his thin frame moving with surprising agility. Deep wrinkles mapped his dark face, and his sparse white hair caught the sunlight. His clothes were worn but clean, and unlike many they'd passed, his eyes held no suspicion, only excitement.

"Elders! It *is* you! The missionaries have returned!" The old man clasped his hands together, his face breaking into a wide, genuine smile that revealed several missing teeth.

"Hello, friend," Shawn greeted warmly, extending his hand. "I'm Elder Martinez, and this is Elder Rockwell."

The old man took Shawn's hand in both of his, shaking it vigorously. "I am Paulo Oliveira. I was baptized, you know! Many years ago. The elders came, they taught me about Jesus Christ and Joseph Smith." He made the sign of the cross, then pointed upward—a curious blend of Catholic and Mormon gestures. "I have been waiting for you to return!"

Angelo noticed that some of the watchful eyes around them had softened at the sight of Paulo's enthusiastic greeting.

"It's wonderful to meet you, Brother Oliveira," Angelo said. "How long has it been since missionaries visited?"

A cloud came over Paulo's expression. "Too many. They just stopped coming." He leaned closer, lowering his voice. "Are you here to help? Many people suffer here. Children without food, the sick without medicine."

Angelo felt a twinge of shame. This man's hope was genuine, his faith somehow preserved in this hellish environment. And they were using that faith as a disguise to pursue vengeance.

"Brother Oliveira," Shawn said, "we know someone who can help. A member named Ricardo de Aparcido. He has resources and wants to support the members here."

Paulo's eyes widened. "Ricardo? The businessman? He brings donations to the base of the hill."

Angelo nodded, pulling out a small pass-along card and writing down Ricardo's contact information. "Call him. Tell him Elder Rockwell sent you. He'll arrange for food, medicine, whatever your community needs."

Paulo took the card as if it were a sacred object. "Bless you, elders. But why are you here today? It is dangerous for outsiders."

"We're visiting a family," Angelo explained. "The Freitas family—Sofia and Isabella. They're relatives of a woman we've been teaching."

"Ah, the Freitas women. Yes, I know them. They live near the top, close to..." His eyes darting toward the summit of the favela.

"Close to what, Brother Oliveira?" Shawn prompted.

Paulo lowered his voice. "Close to the place where the bad men do their business—Casa Forte." He made the sign of the cross. "Strange things happen there."

Angelo felt his pulse quicken. "We need to visit the Freitas family. Would you be willing to guide us? We're not familiar with the paths here."

Paulo straightened his shoulders, pride evident in his bearing. "Of course! Paulo will be your guide. No one will bother you if you're with me." He thumped his chest. "I am respected here. Even the bandidos know not to trouble an old man who has lived in Morro Diabólico all his life."

As they continued their ascent, with Paulo leading the way, Angelo noticed the difference in how they were received. The hard stares softened, the shadowy figures keeping their distance. Paulo greeted neighbors by name, occasionally explaining in rapid Portuguese that these were missionaries, here to help.

The kites still tracked them from above, but Paulo seemed oblivious to their significance. He chattered continuously, pointing out landmarks—a concrete pad where children played soccer, a community water tap installed by some forgotten charity.

"That building there," Paulo said, pointing to a shabby structure with dirty windows, "that is where Isabella Freitas lives with her mother. Sofia is very sick now, you know. The doctors in the city won't come here, and the medicine is too expensive."

Angelo nodded, his eyes scanning beyond the home to a larger, more substantial building. Unlike the haphazard construction of the favela, this building had strategic fortifications—concrete walls topped with broken glass, metal shutters over the windows, a heavy door with patrolling guards.

Casa Forte. The Strong House.

"Brother Oliveira," Angelo said quietly, "what can you tell us about that *great and spacious building* over there?"

Paulo's face darkened, and he crossed himself again. "Nothing good happens there, Elder. Nothing good at all."

Fogo stood at the window on Casa Forte's third floor, watching the kites dance across the sky. His fingers drummed against the concrete windowsill, each tap betraying his growing agitation. The colorful specks shifted positions—blue, then red, then yellow—moving steadily closer to the compound.

Someone was coming. Outsiders.

The door behind him opened. Fogo didn't turn around.

"Speak."

"Two missionaries, boss. Gringos. They're with old Paulo, heading toward the Freitas place."

Fogo's jaw clenched. Missionaries. Again. He thought of the last ones—the boy and his family. The mess. The cleanup. The attention it had brought.

"Show me."

His lieutenant passed him a pair of binoculars. Fogo trained them on the winding path below, quickly locating the trio making their way up the hill. Two young men in white shirts and ties, backpacks slung over their shoulders. Paulo gesticulating wildly as he led them through the narrow passages.

"Missionaries looking for the Freitas family?" Fogo lowered the binoculars. "Sofia and Isabella seem to have disappeared."

"Yes, boss."

"And they're asking for them specifically?"

"That's what the boys said."

Fogo turned from the window, crossing to a table with a satellite phone. He punched in a number and waited. Nothing. Voicemail again.

"Peterson isn't answering." He hurled the phone against the wall. "Third time today. I'm gonna have to call that pig-for-hire Mauro."

The lieutenant shifted uncomfortably. "Should we just—"

"Just what? Kill them? Like the last ones? That worked out so well, didn't it? BOPE crawling all over the Morro. Our shipments delayed. And for what?"

He returned to the window, watching the white shirts weave through the favela. Something wasn't right. First Fofinho disappeared after visiting Lucia. Then Lucia vanished. Now her family was gone too, and missionaries were asking for them.

"Where's Neiman? The doctor should have been here by now."

"No word, boss. The pickup team is still waiting at the airport."

Fogo cursed under his breath. Nothing was going according to plan. The doctor was late, Peterson wasn't answering, and now missionaries were in his territory.

"Get me everything on these two. Names, where they're staying, when they arrived in Rio. Everything."

The lieutenant nodded and left. Fogo's mind raced. The timing was too convenient. These missionaries appearing just as they were preparing for a major extraction cycle.

He pulled out his phone and scrolled to a photo of Fofinho and Lucia taken during one of Fofinho's "visits" to her apartment. Fofinho's obsession with the hotel worker had always been a liability. Had he talked? Had she somehow reached out to these missionaries?

Through the window, Fogo watched as Paulo led the two men closer to Casa Forte. He could see their faces now—one larger with a controlled stillness about him, the other more animated, engaging with Paulo. They didn't move like missionaries. There was something in their posture, their awareness.

"What are you really doing here?" he muttered.

Another lieutenant burst in, his face flushed. "Boss, problem at the checkpoint. Young Tiago was on duty. He says the missionaries gave him a picture book, and he...well, he didn't search their bags properly. Just waved them through after a glance."

Fogo felt a chill run down his spine. "Lock down Casa Forte. Now. Full security protocol."

"And the missionaries?"

Fogo considered his options. A direct confrontation would draw attention. More dead missionaries would bring heat they couldn't afford, not with a delivery so close.

"Watch them. If they approach Casa Forte, detain them. Quietly. I want to know who they are and what they want before we decide what to do with them."

The lieutenant left, and Fogo returned to the window. The colorful kites still tracked the missionaries' progress. In the narrow confines of the favela, those kites were his eyes—a warning system built on the innocent play of children.

"No more dead missionaries. Not until I know what game they're playing."

Fogo pulled out his gun, checked the magazine, and slid the gun back into his hip holster. Whatever these missionaries wanted, they had picked the wrong day and the wrong place to come looking.

As they approached the Freitas' home, Angelo's attention remained fixed on Casa Forte looming nearby. The compound stood apart from the favela's chaotic architecture—its walls too straight, windows too few, security too obvious. Men with bulges beneath their shirts patrolled its perimeter, their movements precise and coordinated.

"You notice the activity?" Shawn murmured, leaning close as if sharing a scripture.

Angelo nodded. The compound had shifted to heightened security. Guards had doubled, communications increased. Someone was nervous.

"We've been made," Angelo whispered back.

Paulo knocked on the Freitas' door. Silence. He tried again, calling out Sofia's name.

"Strange," Paulo said, peering through a window. "Their things are here."

Angelo stepped forward. "Perhaps we should pray for their safe return."

As they bowed their heads in mock prayer, Angelo scanned the rooftops. More men had appeared, their attention fixed on the missionaries. A radio crackled nearby.

"Brother Paulo," Angelo said, straightening up. "Do you know anything about that building?" He nodded toward Casa Forte.

Paulo's expression darkened. "That is not a place good people go, Elder. They say...terrible things happen there."

"What kinds of things?"

Paulo hesitated, lowering his voice. "People enter, but they don't always leave. At night, sometimes there are screams." He crossed himself. "The children are forbidden to play near it."

A young boy ran up to Paulo, whispering in his ear. Paulo's face paled.

"Elders, we must go. Now." His voice trembled. "Fogo's men are coming. They're asking about you."

Angelo felt a surge of satisfaction. Fogo—the man who had murdered his family—was finally within reach.

"Who's Fogo?" he asked, feigning ignorance.

"A devil," Paulo hissed. "He runs the Morro. Please, we must leave before—"

Four men rounded the corner, weapons visible beneath loose soccer jerseys, eyes locked on the missionaries.

"Too late," Shawn muttered.

The lead man approached, his hand resting on a gun in his waistband. "You there! Fogo would like to speak with you about the Freitas family."

"We'd be happy to help," Angelo replied, the perfect picture of missionary eagerness.

The man smiled but it looked plastic. "Then come with us."

Shawn's eyes lit up, focusing on the window as if seeing someone Angelo couldn't.

"Sister Freitas! There you are!" Shawn waved enthusiastically, his smile wide and genuine. "Yes, we received your message. So wonderful to meet you!"

The armed men exchanged confused glances as Shawn stepped toward the door, ignoring their demand.

"One moment, please," Shawn called to the men, turning the unlocked doorknob with practiced confidence. "Sister Freitas has invited us in for refreshments. Such hospitality!"

Angelo caught on, following Shawn's lead with a nod to the bewildered gunmen.

"We appreciate your invitation," Angelo said to the lead man, "but we have important work to do with the Freitas family. Church business, you understand."

Paulo stood frozen until Angelo guided him forward with a hand on his shoulder.

"Come, Brother Paulo. Sister Freitas is waiting."

They slipped inside the modest home, Shawn still chattering to the empty air as if deep in conversation with an invisible woman. The door clicked shut behind them, leaving Fogo's men stunned on the doorstep.

The cramped living room fell silent. Angelo scanned the modest space—worn furniture, a small shrine with a Virgin Mary statue, faded family photos on the walls. His tactician's mind assessed the tight quarters, noting potential cover, weapons, and exit routes.

"Paulo," Angelo whispered, "is there a back room? Somewhere safe?"

The old man nodded, his eyes wide with fear. "There is a small bedroom, through there." He pointed to a narrow doorway.

"Go," Angelo instructed, guiding Paulo with a firm hand. "Stay down, stay quiet."

Paulo hesitated. "But the men—"

"We'll handle them," Shawn cut in, already moving furniture. "Just stay out of sight."

As Paulo disappeared into the bedroom, Angelo and Shawn exchanged a nod. They had maybe ten more seconds before Fogo's men grew impatient.

"Four of them. No gunfire if possible," Angelo whispered.

Shawn nodded, pulling a length of piano wire from his pocket. "Like old times in Kandahar?"

"Just like old times."

They positioned themselves on either side of the door—Angelo behind it, Shawn crouched low beside an old television stand.

Outside, muffled voices grew louder, more agitated.

"Four against two," Shawn whispered with a grim smile. "Hardly seems fair."

"For them," Angelo finished.

The door burst open. Two men entered, weapons visible beneath their shirts. The leader, a tall man with a neck tattoo, scanned the seemingly empty room.

"Where did they go?" he demanded, taking another step inside.

The second man followed, then the third, crowding the small space. Angelo remained still behind the door, waiting for the last man to clear the threshold.

"We know you're in here, gringos," the leader called out. "No more games."

When the fourth man entered, Angelo kicked the door shut with a heavy thud. The sound made all four men turn, giving Shawn his opening.

In one fluid motion, Shawn launched himself from his hiding place, wrapping the piano wire around the neck of the fourth man. He yanked backward, cutting off any chance of a scream. The man's hands clawed desperately at his throat as Shawn dragged him to the ground.

The distraction gave Angelo his moment. He surged forward, driving his elbow into the third man's throat with crushing force. The man dropped to his knees, gasping, eyes bulging. Angelo followed through with a precise strike to the temple that left him sprawled unconscious on the floor.

The leader spun around, reaching for his weapon, but Angelo was already on him. He grabbed the man's gun hand, twisting it backward until something snapped. The leader opened his mouth to scream, but Angelo's other hand clamped over his face, fingers digging into pressure points that sent waves of paralyzing pain through the man's nervous system.

"Sleep," Angelo whispered as the leader went limp. Angelo sent him to the ground with a violent elbow strike to the base of his skull.

The second man managed to pull his gun, but before he could aim, Shawn's foot connected with his knee. There was a sickening crack as the joint bent backward. The man toppled forward, and Shawn met him with an uppercut that snapped his head back. He crumpled to the floor without a sound.

Four bodies lay scattered across the small living room. The entire confrontation had lasted less than a few seconds.

Angelo checked each man, ensuring none would regain consciousness soon. Satisfied, he retrieved zip ties from his backpack and secured their wrists and ankles.

"Clean," Shawn said, breathing slightly heavier than normal. He glanced down at his white shirt, miraculously free of blood. "Guess I haven't lost my touch."

Angelo nodded, dragging the unconscious bodies into a neat pile in the corner. "Paulo," he called, "it's safe now."

The old man emerged from the bedroom, his eyes widening at the sight of Fogo's men incapacitated on the floor. He crossed himself. "*Meu Deus*... How did you...?"

"Special training," Angelo said. "MTC."

Paulo looked from the men to Angelo and Shawn, understanding dawning on his weathered face. "You are not missionaries, are you?"

"Not exactly," Shawn admitted, straightening his tie. "But we are here to help."

Angelo knelt beside the leader, searching his pockets. He found a radio, a switchblade, and a set of keys. "These men were sent to bring us to Fogo," he said, examining the radio. "Which means he's interested in us."

"That's good, right?" Shawn asked. "Gets us closer to Casa Forte."

Angelo nodded, his mind racing through scenarios. "Paulo, is there another way to reach Casa Forte? A back entrance, maybe?"

Paulo hesitated, then nodded. "There is...another way. Not for people like us. Around the back, there's a cleaner entrance. For the clinic, they say." He lowered his voice. "I've seen the gringo doctors use it. They don't like to walk through the entrance with the people. It's guarded. Cameras, a door that needs a card."

Angelo pocketed the radio and keys. "Then we'll find a way." He turned to Paulo. "Some of these men will wake up eventually. You should leave. It's not safe for you here."

The old man hesitated. "But where will I go?"

Shawn pulled out a wad of bills from his backpack. "Here. This should help you disappear for a while. Maybe visit relatives outside Rio?"

Paulo accepted the money with trembling hands. "My sister in São Paulo...I could stay with her."

"Good," Angelo said. "Go now, quickly. And Paulo...thank you for your help."

Paulo slipped out the back door, and Angelo turned to Shawn. "We need to move fast. Fogo will send more men when these four don't report back."

Shawn gestured to the pile of unconscious bodies. "What about them? Should we make sure they don't wake up? I could smash their melons or something." He shrugged.

Angelo's expression hardened. "Leave them. We need to get to Casa Forte."

Angelo and Shawn slipped out the back of the house, the urgency of their situation pressing down on them. They needed to move fast.

As they scanned the narrow alleyway, a familiar figure on a bicycle laden with a large wicker basket rounded the corner. It was Bishop José, the local purveyor of artisanal cheeses.

"Elders!" he exclaimed, his expression a mixture of surprise and delight. "What a joy to see you again! Are you here for my heavenly *queijo?*"

Angelo held up a hand. "Bishop, it's good to see you too, but we're in a bit of a hurry. We need a favor. A big one."

Shawn stepped forward, pulling out another thick wad of reais. "We want to buy all your cheese! And we need you to create a diversion at the main entrance of Casa Forte. Something...memorable." He pressed the money into the bishop's hand. "This is for all the cheese in your basket and for your trouble."

Bishop José's eyes widened at the amount of cash, then narrowed in thought as he glanced toward the imposing structure of Casa Forte. He was a man of God but also a man raised in desperate circumstances; he understood the unspoken currents of danger and opportunity. "A diversion, you say? For the servants of the Lord?" A grin spread across his face. "Consider it done, elders. For the glory of God...and a little bit for the money."

With a newfound spring in his pedaling, Bishop José steered his bicycle toward the main entrance of Casa Forte. Angelo and Shawn watched from the shadows as he approached the heavily guarded gate. Then, with a theatrical wobble and a loud cry, the bishop executed a spectacular crash. The bicycle went one way, he went the other, and the wicker basket flew open, sending wheels of cheese cascading across the cobblestone street.

"My cheese! My precious cheese!" the bishop wailed, clutching his knee in mock agony.

The effect was instantaneous. Children, materializing from the labyrinthine alleyways, swarmed the street, scrambling for the scattered cheese. The guards at the Casa Forte entrance, initially startled, now found themselves overwhelmed by the chaotic scene. They shouted, trying to restore order, to push back the tide of laughing, cheese-grabbing children, their attention drawn away from their posts.

"That's our cue," Angelo muttered with an amused smile.

Under the cover of the cheesy pandemonium, Angelo and Shawn moved swiftly and along the side of Casa Forte, heading for the clinic entrance Paulo had described. It was less conspicuous than the main gate but still monitored. A security camera swiveled above a steel door equipped with a badge reader.

Shawn made quick work of the camera with a small device that emitted a pulse that temporarily looped the camera's feed. Angelo, meanwhile, pulled out Dr. Neiman's ID badge and swiped it through the reader. A green light flashed, and the heavy door clicked open.

They slipped inside, the sounds of the cheese riot fading behind them, replaced by the sterile hum of the clinic.

Angelo pulled out his weapon "Let's find the processing area. Neiman said they 'milk' the subjects here."

They crept toward a stairwell, pausing at each landing to listen for movement. The building's interior was clinical—white-tile walls, fluorescent lighting, nothing like the favela architecture surrounding it. On the second floor, they heard voices and ducked into an empty room. Through a small window in the door, they watched as two men in lab coats wheeled a gurney past. The sheet-covered form beneath was unmistakably human.

"Follow them," Angelo whispered.

They trailed the gurney at a safe distance, using the twisting corridors for cover. The men eventually wheeled their cargo through double doors marked *Processamento*.

Angelo and Shawn exchanged glances. *Processing*.

Finding an observation window, they peered into a scene straight from a nightmare. The room was arranged like a macabre assembly line. Bodies—some clearly dead, others disturbingly alive but near death and sedated—lay on gurneys. Workers in masks and gloves moved between them with mechanical efficiency. At the center of the room stood a large machine with tubes and collection containers.

"Holy shit," Shawn said.

They watched in horror as a technician positioned a thin metal instrument at the base of a sedated man's skull. With practiced precision, he inserted it, twisted, and connected a tube to the protruding end. A pale, viscous fluid began to flow through the tube into a collection container labeled "LoC." A heart-rate monitor attached to the subject let out a continuous flatline beep.

"The Light of Christ," Angelo whispered, his voice tight with disgust. "They're harvesting it. Just like Neiman said."

In another corner of the large room, bodies that had already been "processed" were being prepared for disposal. Angelo watched with continuing horror as workers in masks and gloves methodically transferred the empty husks onto metal gurneys.

"Fuck me," Shawn whispered, his face pale. "They're running a goddamn assembly line."

Angelo's gaze swept across the room, counting at least four dozen bodies in various stages of processing. Men, women, some barely more than teenagers. Their faces slack, eyes vacant—souls harvested and reduced to a teaspoon of fluid in a vial.

Through a glass partition, they could see another room where several large industrial furnaces glowed with hellish light. The smell of burning flesh, masked by toxic chemicals, seeped through the ventilation system.

"Cremation," Angelo murmured. "No evidence. No trace."

A worker pushed a gurney toward the crematorium, the body on it still warm. The cruel efficiency of it all made Angelo's hair stand on end. These people had disappeared into the favela's chaos, their existence erased as thoroughly as if they'd never been born.

"The perfect cover," Shawn said, his voice tight with disgust. "No birth certificates, no death certificates, no questions asked. The world never even knew they existed."

Angelo thought of Rockwell's journals, his brother's words about the forgotten people of the favelas. Had Rockwell stumbled upon this horror? Had he died because he'd discovered what was happening to these defenseless souls?

Below, a new group of sedated victims was being wheeled in. Their chests still rose and fell with shallow breaths. They would be awake for the harvesting—conscious enough for the "Light of Christ" to be at its peak potency at the moment of death.

"This isn't just murder," Angelo said, his voice barely audible. "It's a concentration camp hiding in paradise city."

The ruthlessness of the favela provided the perfect smokescreen—bodies could disappear daily, and the world would simply attribute it to gang violence or poverty. Meanwhile, the Holders of the Rod harvested souls for their twisted vision of resurrection, treating human beings like cattle.

Angelo's hand tightened around his weapon. The cold fury of the Operator crystallized into something harder, more focused. This wasn't just about avenging his family anymore. This was about ending an atrocity.

"We're blowing this place to hell," he said, his decision made. "Every last inch of it."

Chapter 18

REAPING THE WHIRLWIND

Angelo surveyed the horror before them. "We need to move. Start placing the charges. I'll look for Fogo."

Shawn nodded, his expression hardening as he unzipped his backpack and pulled out several compact explosive devices. "I'll set them at structural weak points—support columns, load-bearing walls. This whole place is coming down."

"Be quick but thorough," Angelo said. "I want nothing left standing."

They separated, moving with practiced stealth. Angelo slipped down a narrow corridor, his weapon drawn but held close to his body. The sound of machinery and low voices guided him toward what appeared to be an administrative section of the facility. Through a partially open door, he caught sight of a well-dressed man speaking into a cracked satellite phone—his back was turned, but his posture was unmistakable.

Fogo.

Angelo's pulse quickened. The man who had murdered his family was mere feet away, completely unaware of his presence. He could end it now with a clean shot. But the intelligence Fogo possessed about the operation was too valuable to waste. Angelo needed him alive, at least temporarily. He needed Fogo to know fear. He needed Fogo to suffer.

Meanwhile, Shawn worked methodically, placing explosive charges at critical junctures throughout the building. Each device was compact but powerful, designed to collapse the structure inward, minimizing external damage but ensuring complete destruction of the facility and its gruesome contents.

"First floor clear," Shawn muttered into his comm device. "Moving to basement level. Six charges placed."

Angelo positioned himself outside Fogo's office, listening intently to the one-sided conversation.

"The shipment must go out tonight," Fogo said. "I don't care what Mauro says. We have quotas to meet. The Light of Christ doesn't deliver itself."

Angelo tensed, his finger hovering near the trigger. Just as he prepared to enter, a shrill alarm pierced the air.

"Perimeter breach! Intruders in sector four!" a voice blared over the intercom system.

Inside the office, Fogo slammed down the phone. "What the fuck is happening?" he shouted.

Angelo's comm crackled. "We've been made," Shawn hissed. "Security system tripped in the basement. I've got three more charges to place."

"Finish it," Angelo commanded. "I've found Fogo. Head for the roof next." He put down his backpack and stretched his shoulders.

Angelo didn't waste another second. He donkey kicked the office door inward, the wood splintering around the lock.

Fogo whirled, his hand dropping to the ornate pistol at his hip. He was fast, but Angelo was a phantom.

Before Fogo's fingers could close around the grip, Angelo was on him, a blur of controlled violence. He slammed into Fogo like a freight train, driving him back against a massive desk. Papers and a crystal ashtray went flying. Fogo, though surprised, was a bull of a man, corded muscle under his expensive silk shirt. He roared, a guttural sound, and threw a wild right hook. Angelo ducked, the punch whistling past his ear, and drove his own fist hard into Fogo's kidney. Fogo grunted, the air forced from his lungs, but he didn't go down.

Fogo twisted, trying to bring his knee up into Angelo's groin. Angelo blocked, their bodies crashing together. Fogo was strong, fueled by rage and desperation, his tattooed arms like steel bands as he tried to grapple. Angelo felt a sharp pain as Fogo's head connected with his cheekbone. For a moment, stars danced in his vision, but his training took over. He pivoted, using Fogo's momentum against him, hip-checking him off balance. Fogo stumbled, giving Angelo the smallest opening.

Angelo seized it, delivering a rapid series of hammer fists to Fogo's collarbone, causing Fogo's arm to fall limp, then a brutal elbow strike to the side of his jaw. Fogo staggered, dazed, his expensive shirt tearing at the shoulder. He lashed out blindly, catching Angelo with a blow to the ribs. Angelo absorbed it, his focus unwavering. He saw the momentary weakness in Fogo's eyes, the flicker of pain.

With a grunt, Angelo hooked his leg behind Fogo's, sweeping him to the ground. Fogo landed hard, the breath knocked out of him again. Before he could recover, Angelo was on top of him, one knee pressed into his chest, his forearm crushing Fogo's throat.

"Don't...move," Angelo hissed, the cold muzzle of his pistol now pressed against Fogo's temple.

Fogo gasped, his eyes wide with a mixture of fury and a dawning, sickening fear. He could feel the icy resolve in the man kneeling on him, the absence of hesitation. He tried to buck, to throw Angelo off, but the pressure on his throat increased, choking off his air.

Angelo pulled a pair of zip ties from his pocket with his free hand. He wrenched Fogo's hands behind his back, the cartel leader cursing and struggling against the iron grip. The plastic bit into Fogo's wrists as Angelo cinched them tight, the ratcheting sound a punctuation mark to Fogo's defeat.

Angelo yanked Fogo up by his hair and the collar of his ruined shirt. He shoved his pistol hard into the small of Fogo's back. "Move."

As Angelo propelled Fogo toward the office door like a human shield, Fogo found his voice again. It cracked with a mixture of bravado and terror. "You hear me out there?" he screamed, his voice echoing down the corridor where the sounds of approaching footsteps and shouted commands grew louder. "Kill these goddamn Americans! Shoot them! Don't let them escape!"

Angelo shoved Fogo through the doorway. Armed men converged at the end of the hall.

"Fogo!" one of the men yelled, raising his rifle.

Fogo twisted in Angelo's grasp, his eyes darting between his men and the unwavering American. "Aim carefully, you dogs! Kill him, but don't you dare scratch me!"

His commands were a pathetic blend of ingrained authority and raw, cowardly fear. Angelo felt a grim satisfaction. The formidable Fogo was terrified, and his terror was a weapon in Angelo's hand.

Angelo wasn't there to negotiate. He pressed the cold muzzle of his handgun uncomfortably close to Fogo's ear, the cartel leader flinching and sputtering incoherently. Fogo's orders died in his throat as Angelo's weapon barked, a staccato rhythm of death echoing down the corridor.

The guards at the end of the hall, caught between their leader's conflicting commands and the immediate threat, hesitated for a fatal fraction of a second. Angelo didn't. He fired with cold precision, each shot aimed to neutralize. One man clutched his chest, another spun, his rifle clattering to the floor. They were all going to die in the coming explosion anyway; there was no need for careful, incapacitating shots. Blood bloomed on their chests and heads, their surprise quickly replaced by the vacant stare of death.

Fogo screamed, "My ear! My fucking ear!" Blood streamed from the exploded eardrum. Angelo's shots not only found their mark down the hall, but the blast had hurt Fogo. Maimed Fogo.

A cacophony of gunfire erupted from deeper within Casa Forte, a distinct, heavier caliber. *Shawn*, Angelo thought, a grimace on his face. He hoped his partner was making progress, or at least drawing some of the heat. More of Fogo's henchmen dashed into the hallway and raised their weapons to shoot. Angelo advanced, shoving Fogo before him, the cartel leader stumbling and whimpering as bullets from his men zipped dangerously close.

"He's using me!" Fogo shrieked, his voice cracking. "Stop shooting, you morons!"

Angelo ignored him, continuing his relentless advance, his finger working the trigger with brutal efficiency. He nearly emptied the magazine, each muzzle flash illuminating Fogo's terrified face. The hallway became a slaughterhouse, bodies littering the tiled floor. He'd taken down nearly as many men as bullets he'd fired, a testament to his deadly accuracy, even in the chaotic press.

Angelo held back the last couple rounds, a strategic reserve. The immediate threat in the corridor was silenced but more would come. The sounds of Shawn's firefight grew louder, closer.

Keeping one hand on Fogo and the pistol pressed against his captive's skull, Angelo reached back, his fingers fumbling for the backpack he'd dropped near the office door. He needed more firepower, more options. His fingers brushed against the canvas strap.

"Elder Rockwell, you magnificent bastard!" Shawn's voice, strained but exultant, crackled over the comms, punctuated by another burst of fire that sounded like it was just around the next corner. "Just mopping up the welcoming committee! Advancing on your position! Be there in a flash!"

Angelo grunted, his focus on the approaching wave of reinforcements he could hear thundering down a connecting hallway.

Angelo barely registered Fogo's blubbering. Blood, thick and dark, streamed from the cartel leader's ear, a grotesque ribbon against his tanned skin where Angelo's pistol had roared deafeningly close. "You...you made me deaf, you son of a bitch!" Fogo wailed. "I can't hear a thing on this side!"

A cold smile spread across Angelo's face.

"Looks like I'm almost to your position, Elder Rockwell," Shawn's voice crackled in Angelo's earpiece. "Sending a couple scared pigeons your way. We've got 'em surrounded. Time to hotbox these clowns like a runner caught between first and second."

Angelo grunted, shoving Fogo forward. He reached down, his fingers touching the strap of his discarded backpack, then drawing away after a change of thought. With a practiced motion, he holstered his nearly empty pistol. Time to have some fun.

Just as Shawn had predicted, panicked shouts and the clicks of useless, empty weapons heralded the arrival of four terrified guards. They skidded to a halt in the middle of the corridor, wild-eyed, finding themselves trapped. At one end stood Angelo, a menacing silhouette with the bleeding, whimpering Fogo held firmly in his grip. At the other, advancing steadily with a predatory calm, was Shawn, his wicked combat knife already gleaming in his hand. The guards, their weapons evidently dry, looked like cornered rats.

Angelo didn't give them time to think. With a roar, he surged forward, not releasing Fogo but instead *using* him. He pushed the heavy cartel boss like a human battering ram, Fogo's designer shoes jittering uselessly on the tiled floor as he yelped in terror and pain. The first guard, surprised by the unexpected and brutal tactic, went down as Fogo's considerable bulk slammed into him.

The remaining three, desperate and out of options, tried to fight back. One swung his empty rifle like a club. Angelo, a master of close-quarters combat, sidestepped with fluid grace. The rifle butt, intended for Angelo's head, connected with Fogo's shoulder. Fogo shrieked, a new wave of agony washing over him. Another guard threw a wild punch; Angelo ducked, and the fist crashed into Fogo's already battered face. The third tried a clumsy pistol-whip with his empty sidearm, which Angelo deflected, the heavy steel cracking against Fogo's ribs. The cartel leader was now being systematically pummeled by his own men, each blow aimed at Angelo finding Fogo instead.

Shawn, meanwhile, had closed the distance, a grimly amused expression on his face as he watched the spectacle. He moved with the lethal grace of a panther. One guard, spinning away from Angelo's assault, found himself face-to-face with Shawn. Before he could even register the new threat,

Shawn's knife, the one he'd been itching to use, flashed. A quick, brutal thrust to the throat, a sharp pull, and the man gurgled, collapsing. Shawn moved to the next in a blur of deadly motion. Another swift, precise strike, then another. It was over in seconds. The remaining guards crumpled, their desperate struggle ending in crimson stains on the corridor floor, joining the growing pile of carrion that now choked the hallway.

Angelo slung his backpack over one shoulder, adrenaline coursing through him as he scanned the chaotic hallway. Shawn nodded, his knife glinting in the flickering overhead lights.

"Let's move," Angelo urged, shoving Fogo forward again. The cartel leader stumbled, fear etched on his face.

They hustled through the compound, footsteps echoing ominously. At the stairwell, Shawn kicked open the door, leading them up to the roof.

Fogo gasped for breath.

"Please," he begged, desperation seeping into his voice. "You don't have to do this! Whatever I did, forgive me."

Angelo's expression hardened. "I'll never forgive you. I *can't* forgive you. But I'd be happy to make an introduction to someone who can."

The heavy metal door banged against the concrete wall as Angelo, Shawn, and their captive burst onto the roof of Casa Forte.

The air, thick and stuffy moments before in the stairwell, now felt surprisingly crisp, carrying the faintest scent of salt from the distant ocean. Rio de Janeiro sprawled below them, a breathtaking panorama painted in the fiery hues of a sun beginning its descent behind the jagged peaks of Dois Irmãos. The Christ the Redeemer statue, a distant, pale silhouette against the purple sky, seemed to watch over the city, oblivious to the brutality unfolding atop the Morro Diabólico. From this vantage point, the sprawling favela looked almost serene, its tightly packed structures clinging to the hillside like barnacles, the vibrant colors of its red brick walls softened by the twilight.

The roof itself was a chaotic testament to utility and neglect. Piles of discarded construction materials—broken cinder blocks, rusting rebar, and splintered wooden pallets— lay haphazardly alongside stacks of old tires, their rubber worn smooth and cracked from exposure. Empty fuel drums, some still reeking of gasoline, stood like metal sentinels near a collection of defunct machinery covered in tarps. Along the perimeter, four light posts, each about ten feet high, flickered to life, casting an increasingly stark, artificial glow that fought with the dying natural light, illuminating the impromptu junkyard.

Fogo, his face a mask of terror, stumbled as Angelo shoved him forward. His expensive clothes were torn and bloodstained, his bravado long since extinguished, replaced by a pathetic whimper that was barely audible over the distant city sounds.

"I didn't do anything. You can't do this," Fogo demanded. "This is a case of mistaken identity. Who's paying you? I can pay more!"

Angelo scanned the rooftop, his eyes landing on a particularly burly tire leaning against a stack of others near a collection of discarded medical equipment. "Shawn," Angelo said, his voice devoid of emotion, "hang out with our friend here." He nodded toward Fogo, who flinched at the attention. "Don't let him get any bright ideas."

Shawn, ever prepared, rummaged in his backpack and produced a length of sturdy nylon cord. He approached Fogo with a grim efficiency, looping the cord around Fogo's ankles. Angelo watched, his expression stoic, as Shawn, with a grunt of effort, hoisted Fogo. The cartel leader yelped as he was strung upside down from one of the light posts like a dead shark hung for display on a fishing dock. His zip-tied hands hung awkwardly, his expensive watch glinting in the flickering lamplight.

Angelo walked over to the pile of tires, selected the largest one, and rolled it with a hollow thud across the gritty rooftop. He laid it down and positioned it beneath Fogo's dangling head. If Fogo were lowered just a foot, his head would be swallowed by the dark, grimy interior of the tire. Fogo flapped like a fish, his body contorting in a desperate, futile struggle. But his injuries and sheer exhaustion soon took their toll; he sagged, his movements becoming little more than weak twitches, blood dripping from his nose into his eyes and a cut on his forehead, painting dark, glistening streaks on the rooftop below.

Angelo stepped closer, his shadow falling over Fogo. "Let's talk, Fogo," Angelo began, his voice a low, dangerous rumble. "About my brother. About my family. About this whole filthy business you're in."

"What do you want?" Fogo's eyes, wide and bloodshot, darted between Angelo and the tire beneath him. He attempted one more denial, although his resolve was weakening. "You've got the wrong guy. I was just in the wrong place at the wrong time."

"Cut the shit, Fogo! The longer you hold out the more body parts you lose. Confession is the only way you might come out of this intact," Angelo barked.

Fogo's words came out in ragged gasps, punctuated by whimpers. "Sim...sim...whatever you want." He relented, now resigned to defeat.

"Start with the Americans," Angelo commanded. "The good President Peterson. The good Dr. Neiman. How did you get tangled up with those shining examples of piety?"

"Money," Fogo sputtered, saliva and blood flecking his lips. "Always the money. They paid...paid well. For the product. And protection. Peterson...he had connections. Neiman was the...the scientist. He made promises. Promised me power. It was a good arrangement. I don't care about that immortality bullshit." He coughed, a racking sound. "For me, it was...it was kill or be killed. You understand? In this life—"

"I understand killing," Angelo said. "What I don't understand is why my family had to die. Tell me about that, Fogo. Tell me why a missionary, his mother, his stepfather, ended up in a ditch in *your* favela."

Fogo squeezed his eyes shut, a fresh wave of terror washing over his face. "It was...a mistake," he choked out. "A terrible accident. Idiots! My men...they were supposed to keep out the cops." He sucked in a desperate breath. "The missionaries...your brother...they were never the target. They...they just drove into the wrong place at the wrong time. It was...*estúpido*! It caused me nothing but problems. Headaches. I wish I never heard of your damn church, of any of you!"

Angelo stared at Fogo, his gaze cold and unwavering. The man's story, full of self-preservation and blame, felt too convenient, too neat. He didn't buy it. "An accident?" Angelo repeated, his voice dropping to a lethal whisper. "You expect me to believe that the man who gave the order, the man who fired the last shots into my dying brother, just stumbled into it?" He saw the flicker of recognition in Fogo's eyes at the mention of the final shots, the detail Fofinho had so helpfully, and fatally, provided. "No, Fogo. That's not how accidents happen."

Angelo turned away from Fogo, his gaze sweeping across the rooftop junkyard. His eyes settled on the row of empty fuel cans. He walked over to one, its metal sides dented and streaked with rust. He grabbed it by the rim and gave it a shake. The slosh of liquid inside was unmistakable; by the heft and sound, he guessed there was probably a gallon or so of gasoline remaining.

Calmly, as if tending a garden, Angelo carried the can back toward the light post where Fogo hung. He tipped the container, and a stream of gasoline, rank and pungent, gurgled into the dark maw of the tire beneath Fogo's head. He poured steadily, the gasoline soaking into the grimy rubber, then pooling at the bottom, the fumes rising, acrid and sharp. He continued pouring until the dark liquid overflowed the tire's inner rim, spilling onto the roof, creating a glistening, dark stain that spread outward, mixing with Fogo's pooling blood. Fogo, staring down with wide, terror-filled eyes, could see the shimmering surface of the gasoline just inches from his face, the potent smell already making his nostrils burn and his eyes water.

A new, more desperate level of panic seized Fogo. His pleas, already laced with fear, now became a torrent of choked, frantic words. "Please! You have to believe me! It *was* an accident! A terrible, stupid accident! I...I only finished it because...because he was a loose end! He saw too much! He could identify us! It was...it was business! Just business! I swear! I swear on my mother's grave! Let me go! *Fuuuuuck*! I have money! Anything you want! Just don't do this!" His body thrashed again, more violently this time, the nylon cord creaking under the strain as he tried to swing himself away from the gasoline-filled tire, his voice cracking with a sincerity born of pure terror. "No! Not like this! No, no, no. Shit. You can't... You can't do this. I'm fucking untouchable. You *can't* kill me."

Angelo remained unmoved as Fogo's pleas grew more frantic. He exchanged a glance with Shawn, who nodded in understanding.

"Lower him," Angelo ordered.

Shawn gripped the rope and began to lower Fogo's head toward the tire, the slick gasoline glistening ominously beneath. Fogo's eyes widened in terror, his desperate words spilling out faster than ever.

"Please! You don't have to do this! I was supposed to live forever! I can help you! I swear—"

Angelo stepped closer. "Enough."

With a swift motion, Shawn tied off the rope, securing Fogo's fate with an unforgiving finality.

Then, Angelo spoke, his voice calm, almost conversational. "Shawn," he said, not taking his eyes off Fogo, "get the book."

Shawn reached into his missionary backpack, pushed aside a couple spare magazines for his Glock, and retrieved a copy of the Book of Mormon. Its blue cover was new and bright the gold lettering gleamed in the lamplight.

"Mosiah," Angelo instructed, his gaze fixed on Fogo's blood-slicked face. "Chapter seventeen. Verses eighteen and nineteen."

Shawn thumbed through the thin pages, his fingers, accustomed to the cold steel of weaponry, surprisingly adept at navigating the delicate paper until he found the passage.

Fogo's eyes darted between Angelo and Shawn, his pleas choked off by a new, colder dread. He didn't understand what was happening, but the grim formality of it chilled him.

"Read it," Angelo commanded, his voice resonating with an almost priestly authority.

Shawn cleared his throat, the sound oddly loud in the sudden stillness. He began to read, his voice steady and clear, carrying the words like a pronouncement.

"'And in that day ye shall be hunted, and ye shall be taken by the hand of your enemies, and then ye shall suffer, as I suffer, the pains of death by fire.'"

Fogo's breath hitched. He didn't comprehend the old-fashioned words, but "death by fire" resonated with a terrifying clarity.

Shawn continued, his tone unwavering. "'Thus God executeth vengeance upon those that destroy his people.'"

Angelo's hand slid into his pocket and emerged with a Zippo lighter. The metallic *click* as he flicked open the lid was sharp and distinct. With a practiced flick of his thumb, a small, steady flame sprang to life, casting a warm, dancing light on Angelo's impassive face.

"I am not God's servant, Fogo," Angelo stated, his voice a low, chilling monotone that cut through the night, "I am his executioner."

An animalistic scream tore from Fogo's throat, a raw horror that was cut short.

Angelo tilted his hand. The lighter, still burning, tumbled from his fingers, a tiny spark of doom arcing through the small space between his hand and the gasoline-soaked tire. It landed with a soft *whoomph*.

The gasoline ignited. A wall of orange and yellow flame erupted upward, engulfing Fogo's head and shoulders. The sudden inferno sucked the air from around him, stealing the breath from his lungs. He thrashed wildly, a silent, grotesque dance against the backdrop of the marvelous city. No sound escaped him now, only the sickening sizzle and crackle of the fire consuming flesh and hair. The smell of burning rubber, gasoline, and something far more gruesome filled the rooftop.

The flames climbed higher, fierce and hungry, feeding on the fuel, the unfortunate man trapped within their embrace. Fogo's struggles became weaker, his movements more spastic, until he hung limply, a human torch suspended from the light post. The tire, now a blazing pyre, could burn for hours, a gruesome, flickering monument to the night's events.

Angelo watched for a moment, his face blank in the flickering firelight, then turned. Shawn was already shouldering his backpack, his expression resolute.

Without a word, they gathered their remaining gear. The heavy metal door leading back into the stairwell beckoned. They walked toward it, the heat of the blaze warming their backs. Behind them, Fogo was now a burning beacon, a macabre signal fire atop a temple of evil, his silhouette a grotesque, twisting shadow against the night sky of Rio de Janeiro.

Chapter 19

MOBS MAY COMBINE

Angelo and Shawn walked out of the main entrance of Casa Forte, the gruesome beacon of Fogo's burning body still flickering on the rooftop. The night air, usually alive with the sounds of the favela, was eerily still for a moment before the murmur of a crowd hit them. A significant gathering had materialized, drawn by the sounds of gunfire and the unmistakable smell of burning flesh and fuel. The glow from the rooftop pyre cast long, dancing shadows across the assembled faces, painting them in hues of orange and red.

At the forefront of the crowd, looking both terrified and bewildered, stood Paulo Oliveira and, to Angelo's mild surprise, Bishop José. The Bicycle Cheese Man, his eyes wide as saucers as he stared up at the burning effigy, then at the two missionaries emerging from the heart of the notorious stronghold. As Angelo and Shawn stepped clear of the doorway, a wave of something akin to awestruck wonder, mixed with a healthy dose of fear and an undercurrent of gratitude, rippled through the onlookers. This place, Casa Forte, had been a cancer in the bones of their community, a source of fear and whispered horrors, and now...now it was being cleansed by fire.

Paulo, his face a mask of disbelief, pointed a trembling finger at the burning pyre, then at the two men. "They...they did this." he stammered to Bishop José.

Bishop José, usually so boisterous, could only nod, his jaw slack. He'd seen his share of strange things in the Morro, but nothing like this. American missionaries, dispensing not pamphlets but divine, fiery judgment.

Not everyone in the crowd shared the sentiment of liberation. Sprinkled among the ordinary residents were men whose faces Angelo recognized from his earlier walk through the favela, men who carried themselves with the swagger of banditos. Their expressions were not of awe but of barely suppressed rage. Fogo had been *their* devil. He'd been their provider, their protector in the favela's brutal ecosystem.

Shawn, however, seemed to feed off their hostility. He beamed, the adrenaline of the assault and the satisfaction of a job well done making him almost giddy. He stepped forward, puffing out his chest, his missionary name tag gleaming in the lamplight.

"Something on your minds, amigos?" Shawn called out, his voice laced with a taunting amusement. "You wanna mess with the messengers of the Lord?" He took another step, his smile widening. "Better watch yourselves. You don't want to end up like your *capo* up there." He gestured with a thumb toward the burning silhouette. "Stay in line or you're next. You have *no idea* the power we possess."

An idea, bright and mischievous, sparked in Shawn's eyes. He raised his scuffed copy of the Book of Mormon high above his head like a talisman. "The Lord God Almighty will smite down any who dare lay a hand upon His chosen servants!"

One bold bandito, a thickly muscled man with a spiderweb tattoo crawling up his face, took a hesitant step forward, gripping the butt of a pistol tucked into his waistband.

Shawn's smile didn't falter. He pointed the Book of Mormon at the man like a weapon. "Stay back, asshole!" he rebuked, his voice booming. "Or I'll be forced to show you the righteous power of Jehovah!"

The bandito, fueled by a mixture of bravado and disbelief, took one more defiant step.

Angelo watched, amusement flashing in his eyes.

Shawn was in his element. He reached into his pocket, putting his thumb on the small, unassuming detonator. Then, with a wink at the incredulous bandido, he pressed the button.

There wasn't a deafening roar. Instead, there was a deep, guttural *whoomph*, a rapid series of concussive thuds from deep within Casa Forte. The ground trembled violently. With a sickening groan of tortured metal and collapsing concrete, the stronghold imploded. A massive plume of dust and debris erupted, billowing like a monstrous, angry phantom. The burning pyre on the roof now just another piece of rubble and flame in the pile.

The effect on the crowd was instantaneous. The bold bandito stumbled backward in terror. His companions, along with most of the onlookers, screamed and scattered, desperately trying to escape the choking cloud of dust and terrifying display of power. They ran, stumbling over each other, disappearing back into the winding alleys of the Morro.

Shawn just grinned, stroking the detonator as the dust began to settle.

Angelo and Shawn walked away from the collapsing ruin of Casa Forte. The remaining residents, those who hadn't bolted, stood frozen. Paulo and Bishop José remained, mouths agape. As Angelo and Shawn passed, Paulo stepped aside, bowing his head as if in the presence of avenging angels. Others followed his lead, forming an impromptu escort out of the heart of the blighted hill. Their path was clear.

The remaining banditos, paralyzed by fear after Shawn's fiery speech and the building's collapse, stared wide-eyed at the missionaries. Their earlier aggression was gone, their faces gaunt in the fading light. The devil's angels had turned their domain to ashes.

Angelo shifted his focus to navigating the twisting alleyways. The narrow passages, usually teeming with life, were now eerily deserted or clogged with panicked residents trying to get away from the destruction. Shouts and cries echoed off the corrugated tin and crumbling brick. Fogo's organization, headless and terrified, was no longer a cohesive force. They were rats scurrying from a burning ship, looking for safety before BOPE arrived.

The air was thick with dust, making their eyes water. Angelo tasted grit on his teeth. He felt the dull ache of bruises form-ing, the sting of minor cuts, the metallic smell of Fogo's blood on his hands. The primary target was gone, incinerated in a blaze of righteous fury. There was a hard knot of satisfaction deep within him. Rockwell, Sarah, Jason...they were avenged, at least in part. But the taste was complicated, tainted by the knowledge of Peterson, Neiman, and the deeper rot they represented.

"Sirens," Shawn muttered, the adrenaline beginning to fade, replaced by a pragmatic urgency. "We need to melt—fast."

Angelo nodded, his gaze sweeping the periphery of the favela. Their immediate cover was blown. He pulled out the burner phone Sawyer had provided. Sawyer, ever thorough, had insisted on multiple layers. He'd also provided a contact number with a terse instruction: "Local missionary network. Use only for *dire* extraction. Code: 'Urgent Transfer.'" Sawyer had, through his planning sessions with Angelo and Shawn, identified Sister Cohen as a potential, emergency asset after Angelo's earlier interactions with her. This was that dire moment.

Angleo quickly typed the coded text: *Urgent Transfer needed. Two APs. Compromised area. Morro Diabólico, east perimeter access road. ASAP.* He added a map pin. He hoped Sister Cohen was monitoring it. Her area bordered this hellhole.

"Let's move to the edge," Angelo said, "and hope our sweet sister is quick on her feet."

The stench of fire, and concrete dust clung to Angelo and Shawn as they navigated the outer fringes of Morro Diabólico. The cacophony of distant sirens grew, a tightening noose.

Shawn glanced back, his face grim. "Cutting it close, Angelo. If she doesn't show..."

"She'll show," Angelo said with more confidence than he felt. He was relying on her courage, her recent disillusionment with Peterson, and the bond forged over their shared desire to find justice for Rockwell.

They reached the designated access road, a poorly lit track skirting the favela. Minutes stretched, each siren wail drawing closer. Just as Angelo was considering a more disruptive plan, a pair of headlights rounded a bend. It wasn't a police car. A battered Volkswagen Gol, the kind ubiquitous throughout Rio, slowed its approach.

The passenger window rolled down. Sister Cohen peered out, her face pale in the gloom, her eyes determined. "Elders, get in!"

Angelo and Shawn piled into the small car, the back seat cramped. The car smelled of old textbooks and a hint of cinnamon, like someone had recently transported baked goods.

"Where'd you get the car, Sister?" Shawn asked as she pulled away with a squeal of tires.

"Called in a favor," she said, her knuckles white on the steering wheel. "Brother Ferreira from the Vila Kennedy Ward owes me one. He thinks I'm picking up my companion from a late study. He also thinks I'm a much better driver than I am." She shot a nervous glance in the rearview mirror. "The sirens...are they for...?"

"They're for the campfire we started," Angelo said. He watched her reactions. She was scared but she was here.

"Elder Barnes...Rockwell...you did this for him?" she asked, her voice a whisper.

"Partly," Angelo admitted. "He wouldn't have approved of the methods."

"No," she agreed. "But he wouldn't have approved of what they did to him, either. Change your shirts, you're filthy. Brother Sawyer gave me a couple bags of...supplies for you. Those bags are pretty heavy. You should have everything you need back there."

Ahead, flashing blue lights. A police checkpoint, hastily thrown up to catch anyone fleeing the Morro. Sister Cohen tensed.

"Okay, elders," she said, her voice regaining some of its usual composure, though a tremor ran beneath it. "Look pious. And let me do the talking. We're lost missionaries."

As they neared, a uniformed officer flagged them down. Sister Cohen rolled down her window, offering a polite smile. "*Boa noite*, Officer. Is there a problem?"

"Just a routine check, ma'am," the officer said, his eyes sweeping over Angelo and Shawn in the back. They adopted looks of mild, travel-weary confusion. "Bit late for you and your...friends to be out, isn't it? Especially near here."

"Oh, heavens, I know!" Sister Cohen said, her voice full of exasperation. "My companion and I were supposed to connect with these missionaries from our church for a service project, but we got our wires crossed on the location. Ended up a bit turned around. This area can be so confusing at night." She gestured back toward the Morro. "We heard some commotion; are things all right?"

The officer's suspicion seemed to soften at the mention of "service project" and her innocent, disarming smile. He glanced at their white shirts and name tags. "There was a major incident in the favela. Gang-related. Best you stay clear. Where are you headed?"

"Straight to our apartment building near the Lagoa."

The officer grunted. "All right. Be careful. These aren't safe streets tonight."

As they drove away, Shawn let out a low whistle. "Nice work, Sister. You could've given him a shit sandwich, and he would have eaten it."

Sister Cohen didn't smile. "I just hope Heavenly Father forgives that many lies in one breath. What *really* happened back there? You said something about a campfire..."

Angelo decided a little more honesty was due. "Fogo, the head of the *traficantes*. He was responsible for my brother's death. He's no longer a problem. Neither is his stronghold."

Her eyes widened. "You...took on Fogo? And *won?*"

Before Angelo could elaborate, the burner phone in his pocket vibrated. He answered.

"Go," Sawyer said.

"The contract is signed," Angelo stated, using their pre-arranged code. "The facility is decommissioned. Heavy municipal interest."

"Understood. Your primary target is still at the penthouse. Our eyes at the entrance, the doorman, confirmed he's there.

Heartfelt-friend status confirmed." A pause. "However, bad news. Captain Mauro is likely en route. He won't be ringing the bell. With Fogo gone, Peterson is his golden goose. Expect him to be agitated. Beat him to the penthouse. Peterson's ledger and penance are paramount. Mauro's a gatekeeper, not the prize."

"Understood," Angelo said and ended the call. He looked at Shawn, then at Sister Cohen. "New problem. We need to get to Peterson's building. Now. And a BOPE captain, a dirty one, is probably heading there too."

Sister Cohen's grip tightened on the wheel. The earlier fear was replaced by a steely resolve. "Peterson's. Got it." She pressed down on the accelerator, the little Gol surging forward with surprising spirit. "He has a lot to answer for."

The city glittered around them, oblivious to the silent war being waged in its shadows. Sister Cohen navigated the streets with a newfound efficiency.

"I can get you close," she said as they neared the affluent district where Peterson lived. "But I can't be seen with you when you go in, especially if this BOPE captain is coming. I'll drop you a block or two away."

"Perfect," Angelo said. "Sister Cohen, you've done more than enough. Thank you."

"For Rockwell," she said. She pulled over on a quieter side street, a block from Peterson's luxury high-rise. "Good luck, elders. Be careful. And give 'em...why not, sure, give 'em hell...respectfully." A tiny, determined smile crossed her face.

Angelo and Shawn got out. "We will," Shawn said, offering a nod. "Stay safe, Sister. And if I ever see you again, I'm teaching you how to swear," he said with a smile.

She nodded, then pulled away, disappearing into the traffic. Angelo watched her go, a glisten of something soft in his eyes.

Then he turned to Shawn. "All right. Peterson's penthouse. Let's go have a chat with the president before his guard dog arrives."

"There." Angelo pointed to a gleaming high-rise, its glass facade reflecting the moon.

They scurried to the building and approached the entrance. Angelo had expected resistance, perhaps even a confrontation, but instead found a middle-aged doorman who straightened as they approached. Recognition beamed across his face.

"Elders," he said with a nod, stepping forward to open the door. "It's good to see you. Brother Sawyer said you were friends of the Heartfelt." His eyes darted nervously to the street behind them. "The president is in the penthouse."

Angelo nodded. "Thank you, brother."

In the elevator, Angelo checked his weapon one last time before concealing it beneath his missionary attire. The polished brass doors reflected their disheveled appearance—white shirts, dirty faces, loosened ties, and the unmistakable look of men who'd just escaped a firefight.

"We don't have much time," Angelo said, watching the floor numbers tick upward. "Mauro's probably nearby. Peterson's going to be our only shot at confirming the full extent of who else might be involved."

Shawn leaned against the elevator wall, fatigue evident in the lines of his face. "What if Mauro doesn't come alone? Could be just him, could be a platoon. Hell, might be the whole damn police force."

The elevator slowed as it approached the penthouse level. Angelo's expression hardened, his eyes reflecting cold purpose. "Doesn't matter," he said, his voice dropping to a dangerous whisper. "Peterson's going to need more than all the dirty cops in Brazil to protect him from what I plan on doing."

Chapter 20

Earth and Hell Combine

The luxurious penthouse apartment, usually a bastion of polished calm and stunning views of Lagoa de Freitas, was now a scene of barely controlled chaos, at least in President Peterson's mind. He was a wreck, his normally composed, soft features twisted into a mask of frantic anxiety. Suitcases lay open on the grand marble of the master bedroom, clothes spilling out in a haphazard jumble as he packed items, his hands trembling.

"They'll come for me... The Holders of the Rod...they'll know. They'll know something's wrong." He glanced nervously at the phone, then back at the suitcase. "Fogo's men...if they find out what happened...if they think I'm involved..." His breath hitched. "And Mauro...where the hell is he? He should have been here by now. He was supposed to protect me, to get me out of here if things went south."

The city lights twinkled, oblivious to his personal apocalypse. His hair was slick with sweat, his white shirt rumpled and stained. He was a man teetering on the edge, his world crumbling around him.

In stark contrast, Sister Peterson sat in a comfortable armchair in the grand salon, bathed in the soft glow of a reading lamp. A large, colorful book titled *Really Big Word Searches* lay open in her lap. Her brow was furrowed in concentration, a cheap ballpoint pen poised over a grid of letters. The distant sounds of her husband's panicked movements in the bedroom didn't seem to register, or if they did, she gave no indication. She circled a word with a small, satisfied hum. "Oh, *fire truck*, that's a good one."

President Peterson burst out of the bedroom, clutching a fistful of ties, his eyes wild. "Dear, shouldn't you be helping? Packing? We need to leave! Tonight!"

Sister Peterson looked up with an expression of mild surprise, like a child interrupted from an engaging game. "Leave, dear? But we just had those lovely little shrimp puffs. Are we going out for ice cream?" Her high-pitched voice, usually cheerful, now sounded jarringly out of place.

"Ice cream?" Peterson shrieked, his voice cracking. "The world is ending, and you're talking about ice cream!" He threw the ties onto a nearby sofa. He was trapped. His protectors were gone, his enemies closing in, and his wife was searching for words.

Just then, the silent click of the penthouse elevator arriving into their private foyer went unnoticed by the agitated mission president and his oblivious wife.

Angelo Barnes and Shawn Martinez stepped into the opulent space as if they owned it. They moved with a quiet confidence that was far more terrifying than any loud intrusion. Sawyer's "heartfelt friend," the doorman, had proven to be exceptionally cooperative, ensuring their unannounced arrival was smooth and undisturbed.

Shawn, a small smile on his face, leaned against the ornate doorframe of the salon, casually observing Sister Peterson's word search. Sister Peterson looked up with an unsettling vacancy in her eyes, then returned to her word search. Angelo, however, walked toward the sound of President Peterson's frantic pacing in the bedroom.

He found Peterson near the open suitcases, his face ashen, muttering incoherently. Peterson looked up, his eyes widening in terror as he saw Angelo fill the doorway.

There were no games this time, no theatrical demonic possessions. Angelo's demeanor was cold, hard, and devoid of patience.

"Packing, President? I wouldn't bother. You're not going anywhere just yet. Except maybe to a very unpleasant place if you don't cooperate."

President Peterson recoiled. "You! How...how did you get in here? Mauro was supposed to—"

"I wouldn't count on Mauro," Angelo said, taking a step into the room, his presence radiating an icy menace. "But he could pop-in any second. Let's cut to it, Peterson. I know what you've been doing. I know about the Holders of the Rod. I know about your special deliveries."

Peterson's face, already pale, turned a ghastly shade of gray. He stumbled back, tripping over a half-packed suitcase and landing heavily on the edge of the bed.

Angelo advanced, his voice a relentless current. "I've had a very...illuminating few days. You could say I've been called to serve, in my own way." He paused, letting his words sink in. "Fogo's dead."

The name, the finality of the statement, hit Peterson like a physical blow. He gasped, his eyes bulging.

"And Casa Forte, your little lab in Morro Diabólico? It's been...decommissioned. Permanently." He saw the comprehension, the utter devastation dawning in Peterson's eyes. "And Dr. Neiman," Angelo added, his voice dropping to a near whisper, a chilling finality in his tone, "let's just say he won't be making his return flight."

President Peterson stared, mouth agape, his web of secrets and depravity crumbling around him. The fear he'd felt earlier was nothing compared to the stark, soul-crushing terror that now gripped him. His troubles had indeed become very, very real. The Operator was here, and the bill had come due.

"Fogo, Neiman, Casa Forte...all gone. That's quite a disruption to your...supply chain." He let the words hang, watching the mission president. "The Light of Christ. Neiman was quite enthusiastic about its...properties."

Peterson flinched at the mention of the Light of Christ. His head, which had been bowed in defeat, snapped up. A new, raw emotion, more profound than simple fear for his own life, contorted his features. "The Light...Casa Forte...it's...it's really gone?" he stammered, his eyes wide and pleading with an unbearable dread.

"Yes," Angelo confirmed. "No more 'Light of Christ' coming from Devil's Hill."

The impact of this finality seemed to punch the air from Peterson's lungs. He gasped with a strangled, choked sound. His gaze became unfocused, darting wildly around the room as if searching for an escape. The meticulously planned operation, the secrets, his reputation—all of that was secondary now.

"*She* needs it," Peterson blurted out, the words a raw, desperate whisper. His eyes, wild and bloodshot, fixed on Angelo. "My wife...Sister Peterson...the Light... It's the only thing...the only thing keeping her..." He couldn't finish, his voice breaking into a sob.

Angelo watched curiously. He'd seen Sister Peterson in the other room, her childlike focus on the word search, her strange, disconnected sweetness. He'd assumed it was just...her. But Peterson's words hinted at something far more complex, something tied directly to the horrors of Morro Diabólico.

"Your wife?" Angelo prompted, his voice a shade softer.

Peterson's composure shattered. The dam of denial and self-preservation burst, and a torrent of desperate confession poured out. "A year ago...more than a year, she had a stroke. Massive. The doctors...they said there was no hope. A vegetative state, at best." His words tumbled out, laced with an agonizing guilt. "But Embalmadol-Exo...we'd seen—*I'd* seen the rudimentary function in the...the subjects. Warmth, even small movements, long after they should have been cold and stiff."

He buried his face in his hands, his shoulders shaking. "I was desperate. She was...gone. I couldn't lose her. Neiman...he suggested an experimental application. The Light of Christ. Not just to preserve but to...to *restore* something." He looked up, his face a mess of tears and despair. "And it worked. A little. She...she came back. Not all of her, but...she knew me. She smiled. The childlike innocence...the confusion...those were the side effects, Neiman said. But she was *there*."

The full horror of Peterson's situation settled upon him; with Casa Forte gone, the source of the Light of Christ was gone too. And without her daily, illicitly sourced dose...

"Oh gosh," he whispered, his voice cracking. "Even one missed dose...she'll...she'll slip away again. For good this time." He stared at Angelo, the terror in his eyes absolute. "You don't understand. Every day she lived, every smile, every simple word...someone in Morro Diabólico had to die for it. I...I pushed it out of my mind, told myself I was doing God's work, helping her...but it was murder. It was all murder to keep her here."

Angelo remained silent, letting Peterson's confession fester in the opulent air of the penthouse. The necro pimp's dark secret was far more twisted than just profiting from the dead;

he'd been sacrificing the living to maintain a semblance of life within his wife.

Peterson's confession, once started, became a deluge. He had nothing left to defend, to hide. He had imploded, and the only thing that had mattered, his wife's fragile hold on coherence, was about to be extinguished.

"The Light of Christ, it was just the beginning," Peterson babbled, his voice hoarse. "Embalmadol-Exo, with the Light...we were so close. Closer than anyone knows. To truly open the grave, to overcome death itself. Not just...reanimation but true resurrection. It was God's purpose, His plan for the final days! We were making vessels ready for the Second Coming!"

"The Holders of the Rod," Angelo stated, the name heavy with the damnation Neiman had embodied. "Who are they? Who's above you? Tell me, Peterson, who did those insulated packages go to after they were picked up from you each week?"

"Most of the Church...they have no idea," Peterson choked out. "They preach love and kindness, ignorant of the true work, the hard choices needed to prepare the world." His gaze was alight with a ghost of his former zealotry. "My duty...it came from a higher place. An apostle. He...he's one of the true visionaries. He sees what must be done." Peterson sagged further, the brief strike of conviction extinguished. "And he's not alone. There are others in high positions. They believe. They ...supported the work."

The supply routes were simple, he explained. Fogo delivered the raw product—the harvested Light of Christ—to Holders of the Rod, like Neiman or Mauro. Neiman, under Peterson's direction, ensured its swift, discreet passage to Salt Lake City through established shipping channels Peterson influenced through his business and Church connections. It went directly to a secure facility, a research annex few knew existed, controlled by the Holders of the Rod within the very heart of the Church's power structure.

Casa Forte was the only operational processing platform. The only place where the "Light" was being extracted and refined on such a large scale. It required such specialized equipment. There were plans for more, whispers of expansion, but for now, its destruction meant the wellspring had run dry.

Angelo processed this, a cold understanding dawning. "When we first met, you mentioned Dubai. We flew directly from Texas. How did you know?"

Peterson managed a weak, dismissive wave of his hand, as if it were a trivial detail in the grand scheme of his destroyed world. "The Holders of the Rod...they have eyes and ears everywhere. Especially when it concerns those who might interfere or those...connected to their assets. They noted your arrival in the country, your name flagged because of your financial contributions to Rockwell's service." He gave a watery, weary smile. "They informed me you were an individual of substantial means, likely residing in Dubai based on some of your financial activities. A wealthy expatriate, perhaps a disgruntled, well-to-do ex-Mormon with deep pockets. It was assumed you were merely coming to collect your brother's things, maybe make a fuss. A massive underestimation, clearly." A nibble of something—perhaps rueful respect for the predator he hadn't recognized—passed through his eyes. "They monitor many things, Mr. Barnes. Many people. That's how they maintain control and secure their 'investments.'"

Angelo listened, the pieces of the monstrous puzzle falling into place. An apostle. Others in high command. The secret cult within the Church, fueled by murder and a blasphemous ambition to usurp God's domain. And his family, innocent casualties in their unholy war. The scope of it was staggering, but so was the clarity of his new targets. Peterson had given him routes and a clear understanding of the enemy. The Operator almost had what he needed. All that was left was a little bit of closure and the names of those above Peterson.

Angelo's composure offered no hint of sympathy for the broken man before him. President Peterson's confessions, his grief, his pathetic attempts at justification—they were just noise, the death rattle of a corrupt enterprise. "You're going to tell me who's at the top, Peterson. You're going to tell me which ass I need to kick next. But first," he leaned in, his eyes like a weapon, "you're going to tell me everything about my brother."

Peterson, slumped and defeated, had no fight left. The truth, or at least his version of it, trickled out. "Elder Barnes...Rockwell..." He shook his head, genuine sorrow in his red-rimmed eyes. "It truly was a mistake, a terrible, tragic accident. I...I genuinely cared for him. He was a good missionary, so sweet, so dedicated. He kept all the rules, always. Successful, in his own gentle way. I...I loved him like a son."

The words, unexpected in their sincerity, landed like a blow in Angelo's gut. It was the one thing he hadn't been prepared for, this admission of affection from the man responsible for so much pain. He didn't want to believe it, but Peterson's broken demeanor, the raw grief in his voice when he spoke Rockwell's name, felt sickeningly genuine. Still, the cold anger in Angelo's core remained. "Neiman told us you said Elder Barnes was too soft, not made of strong-enough stuff."

A faint, sad smile touched Peterson's lips. "In many ways, that was a compliment. He had a soft heart, a sensitive soul. But his heart...it sometimes got in the way of doing what was necessary. The right thing, the *hard* thing. Sometimes people *have* to suffer, Mr. Barnes. Sometimes people have to die.

Sometimes entire nations must fall so the Lord's kingdom can be built. It's been that way since the Old Testament."

Peterson rallied slightly, a ghost of his former conviction escaping. "Some people nowadays...they cannot see the terrible disease that tolerance can become. The Lord does not suffer fools, Mr. Barnes. The Lord does not suffer filth. But Elder Barnes...he was the type of missionary who would surround himself with fools, with filth, in the desperate hope, the off chance, that he could enlighten them, clean the dark and dirty stenches of this world." Peterson shook his head, a weary sigh escaping. "Sometimes, fire is the right tool for the job. Warmth from the heart, however sincere, just makes the pathogen grow. Evil needs to burn. It *is* the enemy. And those who knowingly side with it, they are the enemy too."

Angelo's lip curled in disgust. "I can see just how terrible the Holders of the Rod really are," he said with contempt, "if your answer is to destroy a soul rather than fix it."

Peterson seemed to have given up on trying to convince him. He glanced toward the elevator doors, hoping the hum of machinery he heard whirring in the background was more than just the climate control kicking on. He looked at Angelo with a distant, almost pitying expression. "You'll see," he said, his voice barely a whisper. "When you meet your end in the fire, you'll see that I was right. The pathway to hell is paved with good intentions, Mr. Barnes. The pathway to heaven...it doesn't have anyone holding the door open for you. It's not a moving sidewalk. The path is narrow and straight, and it requires constant, unwavering guidance to not stray. Introducing wiggle room, what you call 'fixing,' does nothing but introduce the infinite ability to stray from that path." He sighed again. "I was only ever trying to help the most people stay on that path."

Angelo had heard enough of Peterson's twisted justifications. "Enough. Who do you report to, Peterson? Start laying out the power structure of the Holders of the Rod—now."

The *click* of the elevator arriving in the foyer cut off the president. Angelo, who had been pressing Peterson for the name of the apostle, snapped his head toward the sound.

Relief, pure and overwhelming, flooded Peterson's face. He practically sagged against Angelo, not in defeat but in the sudden, joyous expectation of rescue. "Mauro!" he gasped, his eyes alight. "He's here! They're here!"

Angelo had no time for Peterson's misplaced optimism. Shawn was already a blur of motion. He'd heard the elevator, the unspoken signal of uninvited, heavily armed guests. With lethal efficiency, he yanked his submachine gun from his unassuming missionary backpack, the metallic click of the stock extending echoing in the sudden tension. He flicked off the safety, checked the chamber, then his sidearms, all in a seamless, practiced sequence. Shawn took cover behind a heavy marble-topped console table near the salon entrance, his eyes laser focused on the foyer.

President Peterson tried to scramble away, but Angelo's hand shot out, grabbing a fistful of Peterson's expensive shirt. He hauled up the mission president, spinning him around to face the oncoming threat, Peterson's soft, rotund body now a reluctant shield.

The elevator doors slid open revealing Officer Mauro, flanked by five other men, all clad in the intimidating black tactical gear of BOPE, assault rifles at the ready. They fanned out, their movements precise, disciplined, and menacing.

Peterson, still clutched by Angelo, beamed at the sight of his cavalry. "Officer Mauro! Boy, am I glad to see you! It's about time you got here!"

Mauro advanced, his gaze unwavering. He didn't acknowledge Peterson's greeting. He didn't even glance at him. His focus was entirely on Angelo. As he drew level with Peterson, who was still babbling, Mauro raised his sidearm.

Without a word, without a moment of hesitation, he fired.

The shot was deafening in the confines of the luxurious penthouse. President Peterson's eyes went wide with disbelief, a small, dark hole appearing on his forehead. A gaping cavity opened in the back of his head as blood sloshed out. Peterson slumped against Angelo—dead weight—his last expression one of utter, incomprehensible betrayal.

Angelo, shocked by the sudden, brutal execution of his hostage and primary source of intel, shoved Peterson's body away, where it thudded to the polished floor, blood still gushing from the exit wound.

"Grenade!" Shawn's voice barked from behind the console. He held up a fragmentation grenade, the pin already pulled, his thumb depressing the spoon. His submachine gun was trained on the BOPE platoon. "This penthouse is nice, but I think it's a little small for eight big boys, and one big boom! Anyone makes a sudden move, we all find out what the afterlife's like, real quick!"

The BOPE officers froze, their weapons still trained but their advance halted by the undeniable threat.

Angelo brought his own weapon up, leveling it at Mauro. The corrupt BOPE officer's sidearm was still smoking, now aimed at Angelo's chest. They stood locked in a deadly standoff, the penthouse transformed into a battlefield.

Chapter 21

ARMIES MAY ASSEMBLE

Angelo kept his weapon leveled at Mauro, whose sidearm remained trained on Angelo's chest. The corpse of the mission president lay between them.

Shawn, from his cover behind the marble console table, exuded a terrifying calm. A slight, almost joyful smirk on his face. Angelo knew that look. Shawn thrived in these moments of life-or-death chaos. If he went down, he'd take everyone with him, a final punchline.

"That's right, fellas," Shawn drawled, his voice dangerously light. "One twitch from your fearless leader, and I drop this little *pineapple*. Or maybe I just spray the room first. Then drop it. Either way, we all get to meet the Big Guy upstairs. Or downstairs, depending on your life choices."

The BOPE operatives, disciplined as they were, shifted uneasily. Their eyes vacillated between Shawn, the grenade, and Mauro, awaiting orders, their training battling the primal instinct to not be blown to smithereens.

Mauro's face, was tight. His pistol didn't waver, but Angelo detected a subtle shift in his posture, a minute tightening around his jaw. The corrupt officer was a professional killer, but he was also a pragmatist. He hadn't expected this. Not here, not now. Until about an hour ago, all intelligence had indicated that the two Americans, these disruptive business-men, had been sent safely on a plane back to Utah, their meddling neutralized. Now, they were here, armed, and one of them was holding a live grenade with the cheerful demeanor of a man about to serve party snacks.

A muscle twitched in Mauro's cheek. He didn't want diplomatic issues with the United States. And Mauro, for all his connections, had no solid intel on who Angelo and Shawn truly worked for. The people who signed his paychecks needed to know who these men were and why they had destroyed Fogo's operation.

"You kill us, Officer Mauro," Angelo said, his voice low and steady, "and your employers in Salt Lake will never know what we've learned. They'll never know who's coming for them next."

Mauro's eyes narrowed. He needed to identify them. Killing them solved one problem but created a host of others, the most pressing being the void of information.

"Who are you?" Mauro finally growled, his voice raspy. "Who do you work for?"

Shawn chuckled. "We're missionaries, just spreading the good word." He gave the grenade a little pat with his thumb. "And sometimes, the word is *boom*."

The air remained taut, stretched to its breaking point. Sister Peterson, from the grand salon, hummed a cheerful, off-key tune, the sound of a page turning a stark counterpoint to the deadly stillness gripping the room. Every man present knew that the next breath, the next heartbeat, could be their last.

Angelo knew this fragile standoff wouldn't last. Men like Mauro didn't negotiate when they held the tactical advantage; they pressed or they eliminated. The question was a stalling tactic, a bid for information he could relay before the inevitable bloodshed.

Angelo used the precious seconds, his mind a whirlwind of calculation. His gaze swept the opulent room, cataloging.

Cover: The grand piano, heavy antique credenzas, the thick marble pillars. *Escape:* Sliding glass doors to the expansive balcony, but that was a deathtrap, a thirty-story drop. The main foyer and elevator were blocked by BOPE. *Improvised Weapons:* Heavy crystal decorations, statues, knickknacks, fireplace tools—all secondary. *Strategic Advantages:* The spreading pool of blood from Peterson's body was inching closer to where Mauro stood. The slick marble floor beneath it would be treacherous. Angelo tensed, ready to exploit any nanosecond of distraction, any shift in the balance. He needed an opening, a single heartbeat of chaos.

Simultaneously, Shawn, still a coiled spring behind the console table, was running his own threat assessment. Five BOPE officers, plus Mauro. All heavily armored, visored helmets obscuring their faces, carrying shields and long rifles. Overkill for close-quarters work. Clumsy. Their body armor would stop most pistol rounds, but not all, and certainly not at point-blank range or if he could get a bead on a joint or the face. Angelo was pinned under Mauro's gun, fewer firearms at his immediate disposal. Shawn, despite facing five, felt he had the slightly better tactical position, the grenade his ultimate trump card. He registered the wide expanse of the window behind the sofa, the balcony beyond, Sister Peterson still muttering in his peripheral vision. He could even make out a word in her oversized word-search book—*serendipity*—before a new one was mumbled. His own focus, however, was on the five men whose trigger fingers were sweaty and twitching.

Suddenly, Sister Peterson shot to her feet, her *Really Big Word Searches* book held tight to her chest. Her face was alight with childish glee, her high-pitched voice slicing through the tension. "Oh goody, company! Who wants mini corn dogs?"

The unexpected outburst startled everyone. One of the younger BOPE officers, his knuckles white around the grip of his rifle, flinched. His weapon, already pointed in the general direction of where Sister Peterson had been sitting, discharged with a deafening crack.

The round tore through the air. Sister Peterson, who had turned slightly toward the kitchen as if to procure the promised snacks, gave a small, surprised "Oh!" as the bullet ripped through the *o* in the title of her fallen book, then through her flowery dress, entering her chest. She crumpled to the floor like a discarded doll, a small, dark stain blossoming on the pastel fabric.

Mauro, momentarily distracted by the accidental discharge, flinched. It was the only opening Angelo needed. He kicked Peterson's lifeless corpse aside and threw himself sideways, firing two quick shots at Mauro as he dove. The bullets sparked off the wall near Mauro's head, forcing the BOPE commander to duck. Angelo rolled behind a massive, ornately carved credenza, the heavy wood offering decent cover. He was out of Mauro's direct line of fire, his mind already racing.

Shawn, on the other hand, knew the live grenade in his hand had just become his biggest liability. He couldn't engage in a protracted firefight while juggling a pineapple of doom. The young BOPE officer who'd fired, still looking shocked at his own catastrophic mistake, was his immediate priority.

Exploiting the momentary disarray, Shawn surged forward from behind the console table. He went for the stunned officer, moving with speed. Before the kid could properly react or bring his cumbersome rifle to bear, Shawn was on him. He slammed the barrel of the assault rifle upward with his forearm, deflecting it toward the ceiling. With his right hand, he grabbed the front of the officer's body armor, yanking him off balance and spinning him around to serve as a human shield.

Shawn's right fist, hard as a concrete block, grenade still clutched as an equalizer, connected with the young officer's jaw with sickening force. The impact snapped the kid's head back, his eyes rolling; a pained grunt escaped him as stars exploded behind his eyelids. His knees buckled, and Shawn, still holding the grenade, dragged the now wobbly, semiconscious officer toward the sliding glass doors that led to the expansive balcony. The other BOPE troopers hesitated, unwilling to fire on their comrade.

"All right, fellas!" Shawn barked at the remaining four BOPE officers, who cautiously advanced, their weapons trained on him and his captive. "Let's talk about this! Nobody else needs to get hurt! We just want to walk out of here!"

It was a classic stall tactic, a feint. He had no intention of negotiating. His eyes darted to the grenade in his hand, then to the struggling officer. There was only one way to safely dispose of the explosive and even the odds.

With a sudden, brutal motion, Shawn shoved the live grenade down the back of the young officer's body armor, wedging it between the ceramic plate and the kid's spine. Before the officer could even register the cold steel pressed against his back, Shawn hooked a leg around his captive's, executing a swift, powerful hip toss. The young BOPE operative, his eyes wide with terror, sailed over the ornate balcony railing.

He never hit the ground.

A muffled, meaty *thump* followed by a bright flash and a concussive roar ripped through the air high above the Rio streets. Bits of tactical gear and what was once a BOPE officer rained down onto the city below.

The force of the explosion, even at that distance, rattled the penthouse windows. Shawn had already dropped, scrambling behind a heavy marble coffee table that he flipped on its side. Bullets from the remaining four BOPE officers stitched a pattern across its surface, chipping off shards of stone that flew like shrapnel.

Angelo, still behind the credenza, risked a glance. Mauro was now focused entirely on him, Mauro's rounds impacting the heavy wood, splintering it dangerously close to Angelo's head. Across the room, Shawn was in a similar predicament, pinned down by the coordinated fire of the remaining BOPE troopers.

Angelo knew, with chilling certainty, that the heavy mahogany credenza wouldn't hold forever. Splinters flew with each impact, the wood groaning under the assault of Mauro's relentless gunfire. Angelo was pinned, outgunned. He needed to change the equation, fast. His gaze was drawn to the crimson pool around Peterson's body, then to Mauro. An audacious plan sparked in Angelo's mind. He had to get to Mauro, disarm him, or at least disrupt him enough to close the distance. He couldn't win a shootout from here.

Just as he tensed, preparing to move, Shawn's voice, laced with that familiar, manic energy, cut through the gunfire. "Pineapple!"

Across the room, a large, spiky fruit—an actual pineapple from a decorative platter Shawn had overturned in the chaos—arced through the air. The four remaining BOPE officers, their nerves already frayed, flinched. Their training screamed "grenade" at the unexpected projectile. Some ducked, others raised their shields, their eyes drawn upward.

It was the briefest of hesitations, but Shawn was already in motion. In the same fluid movement he'd used to launch the tropical decoy, he slid something small and cylindrical across the polished marble floor. It skittered toward the BOPE troopers' boots—a flashbang, a parting gift he'd deftly lifted from the vest of the young officer who'd taken the explosive dive off the balcony.

The BOPE operatives, their attention snapping back down from the harmless fruit, registered the flash-bang at their feet a split second before it detonated. A blinding white light seared their vision, and a deafening, disorienting concussion pulsed through the room.

This was Angelo's cue.

With the BOPE squad momentarily stunned and Mauro's attention diverted by the flash-bang's roar, Angelo exploded from behind the splintering credenza. He sprinted full force toward Mauro, aiming for the slick pool of Peterson's blood. As he hit the gore-slicked marble, he dropped into a baseball slide, shooting across the floor with astonishing speed, a human torpedo aimed at Mauro's legs, the blood a gruesome lubricant.

Mauro, caught off guard by the unconventional assault from his flank, barely had time to register the blur of motion before Angelo slammed into his shins. The impact, combined with the treacherous footing, sent Mauro staggering. His pistol barked once, the shot going wide, punching a hole in the expensive silk wallpaper. He stumbled backward, arms flailing for balance, sending him crashing into a heavy glass table laden with decorations. The table broke into chunks of safety glass, and figurines shattered around him.

Angelo was on him in an instant. They struggled on the ground, a tangle of limbs, the fight now brutally intimate.

Meanwhile, capitalizing on the momentary chaos he'd sown, Shawn was up and moving. The bitter smoke from the flash-bang still hung in the air as he leaped from behind the overturned coffee table, his submachine gun already spitting flame. Two of the BOPE officers, still blinking away the flash-bang's aftereffects and trying to regain their bearings, were cut down before they could react. Rounds thudded into their body armor, but Shawn, aiming low and a little to the side, found gaps, sending one sprawling with a shattered knee and the other collapsing with a choked cry as bullets found their mark high in his chest, above his plate.

The remaining two BOPE troopers, more seasoned, or perhaps just luckier, scrambled for better cover, one diving behind a love seat, the other taking refuge behind a thick marble pillar, returning fire in Shawn's direction. The luxurious penthouse was now a war zone, the air thick with the smell of gunpowder, and blood.

Both Angelo and Mauro were on the ground, a tangled mess of limbs in the rapidly congealing pool of President Peterson's blood, shards of shattered crystal from the demolished table digging into their skin. Mauro, dazed, scrambled desperately with his right hand, trying to reach for his fallen sidearm, which lay tantalizingly close.

Angelo saw the movement. His own weapon was pinned awkwardly behind him. His eyes darted around, searching for any advantage. Amid the wreckage of the console table, half covered in blood and glittering crystal fragments, lay a small, heavy object—a marble Christus statue, perhaps eight inches tall, one of the many religious knickknacks Peterson had favored. It was within reach.

With a grunt, Angelo lunged for it, his fingers closing around the cool stone just as Mauro's hand made contact with the grip of his pistol. Angelo violently brought the heavy base of the statue down with all his force onto the back of Mauro's outstretched hand.

A sickening crunch echoed through the penthouse, followed by Mauro's sharp cry of pain. The pistol skittered away, far out of reach. Mauro's left hand, now misshapen, spasmed.

Across the room, the gunfire intensified. Shawn, back behind his overturned marble coffee table, heard the distinct, clipped Portuguese commands of the two remaining BOPE officers. *"Supressão! Avança pela esquerda!"* Suppressing fire. Advance from the left. Their coordination was textbook. A hail of bullets hammered into Shawn's cover, chipping away at the marble, sending stinging fragments flying. He kept his head down, listening intently. He could hear the scrape of boots on the marble floor, the sound uncomfortably close. The flanking maneuver was underway.

Back in the bloody embrace near the shattered table, Mauro, despite the agonizing pain radiating from his broken hand, was far from finished. He was a product of Rio's brutal streets and BOPE's unforgiving training, a master of close-quarters combat. Ignoring the searing pain, he transitioned with frightening speed. His legs, powerful and coiled, snaked around Angelo's torso, seeking purchase in the slippery mess. Brazilian jiujitsu. Angelo recognized the suffocating pressure, the relentless, methodical advance of a skilled grappler.

Mauro, using his uninjured arm and leveraging his hips, began to work his way up Angelo's body, a vise constricting around him. He isolated Angelo's left arm, his movements fluid and economical despite the slick conditions. With a grunt of effort, Mauro trapped Angelo's arm between his thighs and began to hyperextend it, aiming for an armbar.

Angelo reacted, his own training kicking in. He clasped his hands together, forming a defensive grip, trying to prevent Mauro from straightening the limb. But his own wrist, slick with a mixture of sweat and Peterson's blood, offered little grip against Mauro's assault. Angelo could feel his elbow joint screaming in protest as Mauro relentlessly applied leverage. The slippery conditions made it nearly impossible for Mauro to fully lock in the hold, but he was perilously close. If Mauro managed to secure his grip and apply full force, Angelo's elbow would snap backward with horrifying finality.

The staccato rhythm of automatic fire hammered against Shawn's cover, the overturned marble coffee table protesting with sprays of stone dust. He kept his head down, listening to the whine of ricochets and the thud of impacts. One BOPE trooper was behind that thick marble pillar to his left, laying down a steady, disciplined fusillade. The other, he knew from the shifting sound of their fire and the clipped commands he'd overheard, was advancing on his right flank. Classic pincer. They were trying to box him in.

Shawn risked a glance over the top of the table. Sparks flew as another burst from the pillar position stitched across the marble. He ducked back down, his mind racing. He was pinned but not out. Soon they would have to reload. He listened intently, trying to pick out the cadence of the suppressing fire, waiting for that telltale pause, that momentary lull.

Shawn scanned the chaos of the salon. His gaze snagged on a large bronze planter suspended by heavy chains from the high ceiling. It was positioned almost directly above and slightly behind where the officer at the pillar was hunkered down. An idea sparked in Shawn's mind. A ricochet kill off that pot would be a one-in-a-million shot, pure Hollywood bullshit. But he didn't need a kill. He just needed a distraction, something to break their rhythm, to make the suppressing bastard duck. Bullet fragments, even small ones, hitting exposed flesh, especially around the face...yeah, that'd do it.

The suppressing fire paused—a reload. *Now!*

Shawn popped up, just his head and the muzzle of his SMG clearing the table. He didn't aim for the officer, he aimed for the bottom curve of the heavy planter. He squeezed the trigger, sending a short, controlled burst into the bronze.

Sparks erupted as the bullets slammed into the metal. Instead of clean penetrations, the rounds partially fragmented on the thick, curved surface. A shower of razor-sharp copper and lead shards sprayed downward and outward, right into the kill zone where the BOPE officer at the pillar was taking cover.

A muffled yelp and a string of curses confirmed the hit. The suppressing fire choked off. The officer, clutching at his face and neck where the hot, stinging fragments had found exposed skin, dropped behind the pillar, trying to assess the damage. It wasn't a kill, but it was just as good. He was out of the fight, at least for a precious few seconds.

That was the opening Shawn needed. He pivoted, popping up on the *other* side of his marble cover, SMG already swinging toward the advancing BOPE officer. The guy was closer than Shawn liked, maybe ten feet away, moving with grim determination, rifle leveled.

Shawn didn't aim for center mass; he didn't have time for a perfect shot against body armor. He aimed low, sweeping his fire across the officer's thighs.

The advancing officer grunted in pain as the rounds tore through muscle and bone. His legs buckled, and he crashed to the polished marble floor, his rifle clattering away. He landed hard, uncomfortably close, his helmeted head just a few feet from Shawn's position. The tinted visor was down, obscuring his face, but Shawn could almost feel the shocked, pain-filled eyes staring out at him.

Shawn stepped out from behind the table, his SMG rock steady. He didn't waste words. He didn't hesitate. He raised the muzzle, aiming at the center of the officer's visor.

Two quick trigger pulls. *Thwack-thwack.*

Two neat starburst cracks appeared in the polycarbonate, centered perfectly over where the officer's eyes would be. The officer's body went rigid, then limp. Neutralized.

The pressure on Angelo's elbow was excruciating, Mauro's powerful legs and uninjured arm a vise. His free hand, submerged in the muck of blood and shattered crystal, swept frantically across the floor, searching for anything—any leverage, any weapon. His fingers brushed against something hard, unmistakably ceramic. He fumbled, his grip closing around it. It was cold, angular, surprisingly heavy. He didn't need to see it to know what it was—one of Peterson's pious trinkets. This one felt particularly jagged, its form punctuated by sharp points. He recognized the iconic spires of the Salt Lake Temple. The very symbol of faith was about to become an instrument of brutal, earthly violence.

With a surge of adrenaline, Angelo twisted his body, using the slippery floor to his advantage. He brought his hand, clutching the ceramic temple, around in a tight arc. He aimed for the side of Mauro's knee. With a guttural roar, fueled by pain and desperation, Angelo drove the sharp, gothic spires of the statuette deep into the flesh and cartilage of Mauro's exposed knee.

An agonized scream ripped from Mauro's throat, a sound distinct from any he'd made before. His body convulsed, the armbar forgotten as a searing pain shot up his leg. The ceramic spires crunched sickeningly as they impacted bone. In that instant of Mauro's reflexive agony, Angelo wrenched his endangered limb free, the slippery skin finally aiding his escape. The tide, momentarily, had turned.

Across the chaotic salon, Shawn advanced on the last conscious BOPE officer, the one who'd taken the spray of bronze and lead shrapnel from the planter. The man was still huddled behind the thick marble pillar, likely dazed and trying to clear his vision, blood trickling from small cuts on his face and neck. Shawn didn't give him the chance to recover. He laid down a short burst from his SMG into the side of the pillar as he approached, the rounds thudding into the marble, kicking up dust and keeping the officer pinned.

Then, with the fluid grace of a predator, Shawn arced to the side, flanking the pillar. He acquired his target—the officer was attempting to raise his rifle, his movements sluggish. Shawn's first rounds struck the man center mass, punching his tactical vest. The officer gasped, his body jerking from the impact. Shawn didn't stop there. He walked the rounds up the man's torso, a clinically precise stream of lead, climbing from chest to neck. The officer's head snapped back as the final bullets found their mark, the magazine on Shawn's SMG clicking empty on the last shot. The BOPE trooper collapsed, a lifeless heap at the base of the ornate pillar. The last immediate threat was silenced.

Across the room, Angelo was locked in a desperate, slippery struggle. Mauro, despite a mangled hand and a knee spiked with shattered ceramic, fought with the tenacity of a cornered jaguar. His good arm, slick with blood, worked to maintain a desperate guard, his legs half scissoring, trying to keep Angelo at bay, to prevent the American from gaining a dominant position.

Angelo was surprised. He'd expected Mauro, crippled as he was, to be an easier finish. But the BOPE officer's jiujitsu instincts were deeply ingrained. Even in agony, Mauro protected himself, his movements economical, leveraging what little good limb he had left.

But even an expert couldn't fight forever with such grievous injuries. Mauro's movements, though skilled, were becoming slower, his breath coming in ragged, pain-filled gasps. The fight was a brutal symphony of grunts, slick flesh sliding on marble, and the sickening squelch of movement in the blood. Angelo, relentless, pressed his advantage. He pinned Mauro's good leg with his own knee, trapping it against the floor. He used his superior weight and his two good hands to pry at Mauro's defensive arm, inexorably breaking down the guard.

Finally, with a surge of effort, Angelo passed. He slid his knee across Mauro's torso, establishing a dominant side-control position. Mauro gasped, his eyes widening with a fresh wave of terror as he realized his defenses had been breached. He bucked, trying to bridge, to create space, but it was too late. Angelo was a crushing weight.

Angelo's hand, still clutching a jagged shard of the ceramic Salt Lake Temple, rose to finish the job. He aimed for Mauro's temple, the most vulnerable point of the skull. He saw the fear, the resignation in Mauro's eyes. The fight was over. All that remained was the execution.

The first blow landed with a wet, sickening thud. Mauro's head recoiled against the marble, a choked sound escaping his lips.

Angelo struck again. And again. And again.

Each impact was driven by a cold, methodical fury. He wasn't just killing Mauro; he was erasing him, obliterating the man who had stood as a barrier, a corrupt enforcer protecting a system of depravity. With each brutal crunch, he thought of Rockwell, of his mother, of Jason. The ceramic, once a symbol of faith, became an instrument of Angelo's absolute, unforgiving judgment. He continued striking, long after Mauro's body had gone limp, ignoring the spray of gore, making sure the job was irrevocably done.

Shawn, across the room, had just finished reloading his SMG. He'd seen the last BOPE officer fall and had turned his attention to Angelo's struggle, his weapon ready. He watched as Angelo finished Mauro with brutal finality. The penthouse, once a symbol of Peterson's ill-gotten luxury, was now a mortuary, the silence punctuated only by Angelo's haggard breathing.

Shawn leaned against the remnants of the shattered console table, a grin breaking through the tension that had gripped the penthouse moments before.

"Ew, you look so gross right now," he said. He gestured at Angelo's white shirt, now a horrific canvas of crimson. "You look like a horror movie about a homicidal Slip 'N Slide!"

Angelo couldn't suppress the ghost of a smirk. "Yeah, well," he replied, wiping a hand across his face, "this isn't exactly my idea of Sunday best."

Shawn chuckled and pushed off from the table, moving closer to inspect Mauro's lifeless body sprawled on the floor. "You could always take up painting as a side gig. I hear 'blood splatter' is all the rage in the Salt Lake City contemporary art scene."

Angelo shook his head, shaking off the humor as he took stock of their surroundings. They had won this battle, but it was the first in a war that they never even knew existed.

Chapter 22

FEW ARE CHOSEN

Angelo pulled out his phone. The adrenaline was fading, leaving him with a bone-deep weariness that made each movement deliberate and slow.

He dialed Sawyer's number, pressing the phone to his ear.

"It's done," Angelo said when Sawyer answered. "Peterson's penthouse is secure. Mauro's permanently retired. Peterson was unable to find the complete picture."

"Understood." Sawyer's voice came through, calm and measured. "We need to debrief. Meet me at my apartment in an hour. We'll talk over a bowl of ice cream."

Angelo almost laughed at the thought of ice cream after what they'd just done.

"Ice cream," he repeated.

"Rocky Road," Sawyer confirmed. "Don't clean up too much. Use the service elevator. I'll handle the rest."

Angelo ended the call, catching Shawn's questioning look.

"We're having dessert with Sawyer," he said, pocketing the phone. "Apparently nothing says 'successful bloodbath' like Rocky Road."

Angelo stepped out of Sawyer's en suite bathroom, steam ghosting around him. The hot water had sluiced away the blood, grime, and some of the tension, but the chilling residue of the penthouse assault still clung to him. He ran a hand over his freshly scrubbed face. Sawyer had provided a change of clothes: a pair of too-large BYU Cougars sweatpants and a matching T-shirt. It felt bizarrely mundane, almost sacrilegious, after the day's carnage.

In the expansive living area, Shawn, similarly attired in mismatched university apparel, was draped over one of Sawyer's plush leather armchairs. Laughter, rich and unrestrained, boomed from him. Sawyer, leaning against the polished surface of his wet bar, a tumbler of what looked like Diet Dr. Pepper in hand, was smiling, a genuine, crinkle-eyed smile that Angelo hadn't seen much of since their initial, tense reunion.

"And then, bam! Pineapple surprise for the guy by the elevator!" Shawn said, gesturing expansively with one hand, nearly sloshing his drink. "He looked like he'd seen a ghost that shat a fruit salad!"

Sawyer chuckled, shaking his head. "Classic misdirection, Martinez. Oldest trick, still the best. We pulled something similar in Baghdad once, though it involved a roasted-chicken thigh and a very surprised goat. Different food, same principle." The shared history, the easy camaraderie of men who'd faced death, hung in the air. It was a language Angelo understood, even if he wasn't actively participating.

As Angelo walked further into the room, Sawyer's smile softened, his attention shifting. "Feeling more human, Rockwell?" he asked, his tone still light but with an undercurrent of concern.

"Cleaner, at least," Angelo said, his voice a low rumble. He accepted the glass of Diet Dr. Pepper Sawyer offered. "Thanks for this, Brett. For all of it."

Shawn, still grinning, said, "Yeah, man, your hospitality is five-star. Though your taste in collegiate apparel is questionable." He tugged at the oversized Weber State Wildcats shirt Sawyer had lent him.

Sawyer let out a soft laugh. "Beggars can't be choosers. Besides, it builds character. Or at least offers a convenient disguise if you need to blend in at a pep rally." Sawyer waited for their courtesy laughs before continuing. "By the way, Sister Cohen checked in after dropping you two off. She's safe and sound. She provided a thorough report on the events at the mission office and reported President Peterson's conduct. She's been reassigned to a quiet, safe mission in the interior to finish her service. She sends her thanks."

Angelo's heart clenched at the mention of Sister Cohen. He remembered her expression of relief when they'd intervened in Peterson's office; it was a mix of fear and hope that he would never forget. "She deserved better than what she faced."

"And you two rescued her from that nightmare. You've had a front-row seat to the Holders' little theater of horrors. You've seen what they're capable of." Sawyer focused his gaze on Angelo, then flicked to Shawn before returning. "We need to have a serious talk."

Angelo nodded, the images from Casa Forte, Neiman's fanatical gleam, Peterson's terrified confession, and Mauro's brutal end replaying in his mind. "They're more than just a rogue element."

"Far more," Sawyer confirmed, his voice taking on a grim edge. "What you encountered with Peterson, Neiman, and even Mauro's crew? That's just a regional franchise, albeit a significant one. The Holders of the Rod are a theological cancer within the Church. Think global. They have reach, resources, and adherents in places you wouldn't believe."

He paused, letting the weight of his words sink in.

"Peterson wasn't exaggerating about an apostle being involved. Maybe more than one. There are men in very high places, men who wield immense influence, who believe fervently in this twisted 'Light of Christ' science. They see themselves as righteous crusaders, preparing the world for a new era, and they believe any atrocity is justified if it serves their interpretation of God's will."

Shawn leaned forward, deeply curious. "So, Neiman's talk of 'vessels' and harvesting...that's their core business?"

"A significant part of it," Sawyer confirmed. "Embalmadol-Exo, the Light of Christ—it's not just about some warped idea of resurrection or keeping a loved one in a state of semilucidity, like Peterson did with his wife. From what we've pieced together, it's about control, power, and a perverted sense of divine selection. They're experimenting, refining for something more. Something that could give them an unprecedented edge."

He looked at Angelo. "Casa Forte, the operation Fogo was running, that was sophisticated. The logistics, the security, the 'extraction cycle' Neiman mentioned... That takes organization, funding, and protection from on high. Mauro and his BOPE unit weren't just corrupt cops on a gang payroll, they were an extension of the Holders' enforcement arm, ensuring their operations ran smoothly and were left untouched."

Angelo thought of the sheer number of bodies, the cold efficiency of the processing room. "And they just...get away with it?"

"Largely, yes," Sawyer said, his expression bleak. "They operate in the shadows, cloaked by faith and layers of plausible deniability. They recruit from the devout, the disillusioned, the power hungry. They prey on desperation, like they did with Peterson. The people you've dealt with, Angelo...Fogo,

Neiman, Peterson, Mauro...they were dangerous, yes, but they were also expendable cogs in a much larger machine. You've kicked the beehive, and the swarm is undoubtedly aware they've been disturbed."

Shawns eyes widened, a dawning realization flashing in his expression. "Oh! Is that why they call Utah the Beehive State?"

"No," Sawyer said.

Shawn huffed, crestfallen, but quickly refocused on the story.

Sawyer picked up his glass again, swirling the ice. "You saw how formidable Mauro's unit was, even cornered. That's the kind of asset the Holders can deploy. They have loyalists within law enforcement, intelligence agencies, financial institutions. They're not some street gang you can dismantle by taking out a few leaders. This is a shadow war, and you've just fired some very visible shots." He took a slow sip. "What you did in Morro Diabólico and at Peterson's penthouse...that's not the end. It's barely the beginning of understanding how deep this rot goes."

Shawn leaned his head back against the plush leather of the armchair. He listened to Sawyer lay out the terrifying scope of the Holders of the Rod, and a knot formed in his gut. If he hadn't seen the horrors of Casa Forte with his own eyes, the industrialized genocide happening within shouting distance of Rio's glittering beaches, he'd have dismissed it as bullshit. But he *had* seen it. He'd smelled the death, seen the vacant eyes of the victims, and felt the sickening fervor of Neiman's obsession.

"I just...I can't wrap my head around it," Shawn finally said, his voice rough. He looked from Sawyer to Angelo, then back to Sawyer. "All those people in Morro Diabólico. Thousands of them. How does something like that happen, on that scale, without anybody noticing? With some crazy members of a powerful American institution, the *Church*, behind it? How do these Holders bastards think they can get away with this?"

Sawyer's expression was grim. "They *have* been getting away with it, Shawn. For years. Decades, possibly, in various forms. The higher-ups, the ones pulling the real strings, stay incredibly well insulated. They've mastered the art of fostering secrets, cloaking them in the language of the sacred, making them untouchable, unquestionable. Anyone who gets too close, asks too many inconvenient questions, is branded a doubter, an apostate, or worse."

Angelo began to nod in understanding, as if a sermon were starting to ring true.

Sawyer continued. "And if something *does* go catastrophically wrong, if a light starts to shine where they don't want it? They have an army of willing scapegoats. People so fervent, so utterly convinced of the righteousness of the cause, they'd gladly fall on their swords, become martyrs, or take the fall as a misguided lone wolf. They'd see it as a test of faith, a noble sacrifice."

Shawn envisioned the horrors he had witnessed throughout his career. Horrors done by the hands of religious extremists and in the names of various deities.

Sawyer paused, his gaze hardening. "Worst-case scenario? Let's say an apostle, one of the big fish, actually gets publicly implicated, something undeniable. How hard would it really be to believe that an eighty- or ninety-year-old man, already frail, just happened to pass away 'peacefully in his sleep' at a very convenient time? A heart attack, a stroke...perfectly plausible. Case closed, problem solved, legacy 'protected.'"

Angelo felt a chill down his spine. He saw goosebumps down Shawn's forearms.

"Plus," Sawyer continued, "think about it. Even if some general authority *did* get convicted, what's the real deterrent?

Most of these men are ancient. They've lived long, comfortable lives, revered by millions. A life sentence when you're ninety? It's hardly a meaningful punishment. It's an asterisk at the end of a long chapter."

Sawyer walked over to the window. "The Church has essentially unlimited funds. They own enough land to be considered a small country. They have tendrils in governments across the globe, a significant number of influential officials in the United States government owe them favors or allegiance. They own a university, a prestigious law school where they get first pick of some of the brightest legal minds in the country—minds they can cultivate, indoctrinate, and deploy with a zealous fervor you'd never find in a typical corporate legal department defending a CEO."

He turned back, his eyes finding Shawn's. "An army of loyal subjects worldwide who believe every word spoken from the pulpit is divine revelation. An entire private-education system from kindergarten through doctoral programs, shaping minds from a young age. Unlimited funds, deep political and business connections... You tell me, Shawn. Who *would* stand against them? Who *could*?"

The question hung heavy. Shawn looked at Angelo, whose face was a mask of focused resolve, then back at Sawyer. The sheer, monolithic power Sawyer described was staggering. It wasn't just a criminal enterprise, it was an empire built on faith, shrouded in piety, and defended by legions of the devout and the compromised. The bad guys didn't wear black hats, they wore suits and sat on cushioned chairs in Salt Lake City. The scale of it, the audacity, was beyond anything he'd encountered. It made their bloody work in the favela and Peterson's penthouse feel like swatting at a mosquito while a plague of locusts loomed on the horizon.

Although Angelo was fatigued by the long day, he remained focused, hungry for knowledge. And this wasn't just a debrief, Sawyer was building to something, a reveal he'd likely been orchestrating since Angelo and Shawn had first stumbled into his orbit.

Angelo rose from the plush sofa, the borrowed BYU sweatpants feeling alien against his skin, and walked toward the window, beside Sawyer. The city lights of Rio sprawled below. He took a slow sip of his Diet Dr. Pepper, the bubbles a faint sting on his tongue.

"All right, Brett," Angelo said, his voice quiet but firm, cutting through the lingering echoes of Sawyer's unsettling revelations about the Holders' power. He turned from the cityscape to meet Sawyer's eyes. "You've painted a bleak picture. An empire of faith built on secrets, defended by zealots. Untouchable, almost." He paused, choosing his words carefully. "So, who *does* stand against them? There has to be an opposition. We understand *why* the Holders of the Rod need to be opposed, but what's the *how*? What about you? You stood against them."

An air of something—respect, perhaps, or grim satisfaction—crossed Sawyer's face. He'd laid the bait, and Angelo had taken it, asking the precise question Sawyer had been maneuvering him toward.

Sawyer let out a slow breath. "That's a lot to unpack, Angelo. And it doesn't all need to happen tonight; you boys look like you've been through the wringer and then some." He offered a tired smile. "But, yes, you're right. There *is* an opposition. And I *do* want to share the bigger picture with both of you."

He gestured for them to sit, and they gathered again in the living area, the earlier levity replaced by a heavy anticipation.

Sawyer settled into an armchair opposite them, leaning forward, hands loosely clasped.

"The Church, at its heart, has always been in a battle for its own soul. For every faction like the Holders, driven by a hunger for power and a literal, often brutal, interpretation of doctrine, there's another current. We call ourselves the Heartfelt. We believe in the spirit of the law, not just the letter. In compassion, in the Atonement's reach, in following the Spirit, even when it leads us down uncomfortable paths."

He looked from Angelo to Shawn. "The Holders focus on works, on control, on hastening Zion through any means necessary, including horrific ones. We focus on the heart, on faith, on the belief that God truly does look upon the intent."

"A philosophical difference is one thing," Angelo interjected, "but the Holders are...proactive. Violently aggressive."

"Exactly," Sawyer agreed, "and so must be the counterweight. Within the Heartfelt, there exists a specific calling, an order, if you will. This is the Order of the Nazarites I mentioned the other day."

Angelo's eyebrows lifted.

"The name goes back to ancient times, to men like Samson, set apart, consecrated for a specific purpose. In the context of the restored Gospel, our role became...unique. Think of us as a divine check and balance. A fail-safe. Porter Rockwell, 'the Destroying Angel' of Mormon history, was one of us, sworn to protect Joseph Smith, albeit with a very different understanding of 'protection' than most Sunday school lessons would care to admit."

Sawyer leaned back, his gaze distant as if peering into the past. "The Church has faced existential threats from within since its earliest days. After Joseph's martyrdom, there was a battle for succession—Brigham Young versus Sidney Rigdon. It was a fight for the very survival of the Church. The Nazarites played a role in ensuring the continuity that Brigham represented. That led the Church to where it is today, for better or worse. The struggle over polygamy was another brutal internal war. It tore families and communities apart. The mainstream Church, the one that eventually embraced the Heartfelt principles more openly, shed the more extreme fundamentalist elements. Many factions broke off then, and at other times. Each schism, each near-collapse, often had the unseen hand of the Nazarites working to preserve what we believe to be the true core of the Gospel, even if the methods were unconventional."

"If I were the leader of the Church," Shawn said, "would I be able to use the Nazerites to make a hit on anyone I want? Because I'd be calling my bookie and fixing some fights."

Sawyer smiled, then his eyes met Angelo's again, a profound seriousness in them. "President Harold B. Lee, a prophet of the Church, once said, 'You don't need to worry about the president of the Church ever leading people astray, because the Lord would remove him out of his place before He would ever allow that to happen.'"

He let the quote hang in the air.

"Most members hear that and find comfort, a reassurance of divine guidance. They picture the Lord gently taking a prophet home, a peaceful passing. The Nazarites...we understand it differently. If a Church leader attempts to lead it astray, to turn it into something like what the Holders of the Rod, or our high roller in Shawn's example envision, well, someone has to serve the eviction notice. We're the instruments of that removal. It's a sacred, terrible duty, undertaken only when the very soul of the Church is at stake."

The weight of Sawyer's words settled heavily in the room. It was a history not found in any official Church manual, a theology whispered in the deepest shadows of the institution.

Angelo thought of the raw power wielded by the Holders, then of this ancient, hidden order, equally committed, equally capable of extreme measures but fighting for a different vision of God's will. The battle was far older, far deeper than he could have imagined.

Angelo listened, his mind racing to connect the disparate pieces. This wasn't just a secret society, it was a divinely sanctioned black ops unit, operating outside the bounds of conventional morality and mortal law. The concept was staggering, terrifying, and deeply resonant with his own life lived in the gray areas.

Sawyer watched Angelo's stoic face, then Shawn's stunned expression, and continued. "The calling of a Nazarite comes with certain assurances. Certain gifts. It's a covenant, and like all covenants with the Lord, there are blessings attached, commensurate with the burden."

He paused, choosing his words with the precision of a surgeon. "Each Nazarite is unique. Upon their calling they're blessed with gifts tailored to their strengths and the specific tasks for which they're foreordained. Some are granted gifts of intellect, an ability to see patterns and connections others miss. Some possess a strength, a resilience that borders on the...supernatural. There have been accounts of Nazarites who seemed almost invincible, who walked unscathed through perils that should have claimed them."

Shawn couldn't help but think about the magical family Madrigal from Encanto when he heard about being blessed with special gifts. He knew the timing was bad to bring it up, so he filed it away for later; however, he couldn't file away the fact that "We Don't Talk About Bruno" was now playing in his head on a constant loop.

Angelo was still in the moment. A chill traced its way down his spine. He thought of the supernatural calm Sawyer had displayed when they'd first met, the way he'd dismantled their deception with such quiet certainty.

"With this calling," Sawyer went on, "comes the knowledge of one's place in the eternities. Our calling and election is made sure. It's a profound trust the Lord places in us. It means He knows our hearts, knows that we will use whatever means are necessary to advance His work, to protect His Church from those who would pervert it." He leaned forward, eyes intent. "And because of that trust, because the Lord looks upon the heart, Nazarites aren't always held to the same strict interpretation of laws, whether they be God's or man's. Porter Rockwell, for instance. History records he owned a brewery. He ran a saloon, maybe even a brothel, depending on which accounts you believe. Outwardly, those things would condemn a man in the eyes of the Church. But Porter's heart was fixed on protecting the heart of the Church, on preserving the Restoration. The Lord knew his intent. Men judge the outward appearance, but the Lord...He judges the heart."

Angelo absorbed this, the implications vast. It was a divine carte blanche, a sanctified ruthlessness. He thought of his own life—the violence, the darkness he'd waded through. Could such a path ever be deemed...holy?

Sawyer looked at Angelo, his gaze piercing. "As a Nazarite, I cannot be taken from this world until my time is truly done. It might sound...unbelievable. Arrogant, even. But I testify to you, Angelo, I cannot be killed. I've seen evidence of this on more occasions than I can count, in situations where, by all rights, I should have been a casualty statistic." He said it with a quiet, unshakable conviction, a simple statement of fact.

Angelo didn't doubt him. He'd seen men with similar auras of unyielding certainty, men who seemed to bend reality to their will. Sawyer wasn't just a highly trained operative, he was something more.

Sawyer's expression softened, a hint of wistfulness in his eyes. "Your brother..." A flicker of genuine affection was in his voice. "I came to know him well during his mission. A remarkable young man. So full of light, so purely good. I truly believe he carried Nazarite blood. There was a strength in him, a spiritual depth that was extraordinary."

Nazerite blood. The phrase caught in Angelo's mind.

He sighed. "I had hoped... I had envisioned him as a potential Nazarite. But as I got to know him, I saw his true calling lay elsewhere. He was destined to be a leader among the Heartfelt. I could see him as a general authority one day, maybe even an apostle, a true crusader for the compassionate, Christ-centered Gospel. He had the heart, the spirit, the unwavering faith. But...," Sawyer's gaze met Angelo's, "he didn't have the...skill set for the other side of it. The violence, the fortitude required to carry out the execution part of what a Nazarite must sometimes do. His soul was gentle. His superpower was his empathy. Hurting others, even if they deserved it, would have broken him."

Angelo felt a pang, a familiar ache for the brother whose kindness had been a beacon in his own hardening world. Sawyer was right. Rockwell wouldn't have survived this life, not the one Angelo lived, and not the one Sawyer was describing.

Then, Sawyer's gaze locked onto Angelo with an intensity that was almost palpable. "But that Nazarite blood, I believe it flows just as strongly in you, Angelo. Perhaps even more concentrated, forged in a different fire. All the hardship, the pain, the darkness you've endured...perhaps it wasn't just a series of unfortunate events. Perhaps it was the refiner's fire, shaping you, preparing you to be an instrument, a weapon, for a purpose you never could have foreseen."

The weight of Sawyer's pronouncements settled in the room, thick and heavy as the dusty favela air had been earlier that day. Angelo felt the words like a physical force, reshaping the landscape of his understanding, chiseling away at the certainties he'd clung to. Nazarite blood. A refiner's fire. A purpose he could never have foreseen.

Shawn's shock had long been replaced by a sort of wide-eyed, almost childlike wonder. An idea, bright and absurd, dawned on his face. He leaned forward, his eyes wide with a sudden, enthusiastic realization that he couldn't contain.

"Whoa, hold up," Shawn exclaimed, snapping his fingers. "So, what you're saying, Sawyer... Operator, you hear this?" He turned to Angelo with a grin. "I think you just got recruited to, like, the Mormon Avengers. Or the Justice League, but with, you know, scriptures and less spandex. Probably." He looked back at Sawyer. "So, if this is the team up, are you Wolverine? Or maybe Deadpool with the whole 'can't be killed' thing and the snappy comebacks?"

Sawyer gave a dry smile, a fleeting sparkle in his otherwise serious eyes. "Wolverine," he said.

Angelo, however, remained anchored in the heavier currents of Sawyer's revelations. Shawn's levity bounced off him. "How are Nazarites any different?" Angelo asked, his voice a low rumble. "From the Holders of the Rod, I mean. They believe the ends justify the means. It sounds like you're saying the Nazarites operate on the same principle. Inflicting pain, taking lives, operating outside the law... Where's the line, Brett?"

Sawyer could see the sincerity in Angelo's question, the struggle behind the hardened facade. This wasn't just academic curiosity; Angelo was weighing the offer, perhaps even considering if such a path could somehow redeem the darkness he'd waded through.

Sawyer nodded. "That's the crucial question, Angelo. The one every Nazarite grapples with. The difference lies in two fundamental things: faith and the covenant." He leaned forward again. "First, we operate on the faith that by striving to embody the greatest love for the greatest number of individuals—no matter who they are, where they're from, or what they've done—our actions will ultimately lead to a better outcome, a truer reflection of God's will. But love, in a world as fallen as ours, isn't always gentle. Sometimes it needs a fierce defender. We stand up for the masses, the weak, the needy. We protect the peacemakers from the power hungry. Sometimes, to protect the flock from the wolves, you need men willing to be the sheepdogs that hunt wolves. That's where the Nazarites come in."

"And the second," Sawyer continued, his voice taking on a more somber tone, "is the covenant. When a man is ordained a Nazarite, he's held to the same sacred covenant I mentioned about the prophet of God. President Lee's words about the Lord removing a prophet who leads the people astray? That applies to us with an ironclad certainty. If a Nazarite loses his way, if he allows pride or any corrupting influence to divert him from that principle of greatest love, if he begins to lead the people astray...he *will* be taken out of his place. And not gently."

Sawyer's eyes held a chilling gravity. "It has happened. Rarely, thankfully. But for the good of the Church, and frankly, for the good of the individual Nazarite, there's a...a physical excommunication of the spirit. Enacted by another Nazarite. So, unless you want an army of what you might call 'superhuman spiritual assassins' on your tail, you *always* act in love for the greatest number of God's children. You cannot be a respecter of persons or authority when it conflicts with that higher law. Nazerite justice is meted out equitably to all of His children, saint or sinner, powerful or weak. That's the check. That's the balance. And that's the profound, terrifying difference between us and the Holders of the Rod."

Sawyer let the silence stretch, allowing the weight of his words about Rockwell, the refiner's fire to settle fully on Angelo.

Shawn's earlier excitement was replaced by a stark understanding. The 'Mormon Avengers' suddenly sounded a lot less like a comic book...but maybe a little like Highlander? Either way, Shawn was loving it.

"Think about what brought you here, Angelo," Sawyer said. "You came to Rio seeking vengeance, a raw, understandable human desire. But look at what transpired. Your pursuit of Fogo, of Peterson...it wasn't just about Rockwell, it was about dismantling a system of profound evil. You tore down Casa Forte, a place of unimaginable suffering. You exposed a horrifying conspiracy that preyed on the most vulnerable, all under the guise of faith. Was it brutal? Yes. Unequivocally. Did it conform to any law, earthly or ecclesiastical, as most understand them? No."

Sawyer leaned forward, his gaze intense. "So tell me, Angelo, who else could have done it? Who else *would* have? The authorities were compromised. Some church leaders, at least the parts you encountered, were either blind or complicit. Sometimes, the only way to excise a cancer so deep, so malignant is with a blade sharp enough and a hand steady enough to cut without flinching. You wielded that blade. All those years you spent in the shadows, Angelo, honing your skills, learning the brutal calculus of survival and retribution. You thought you were serving masters of a different kind, driven by your own pain, your own quest for a power that could shield you. But perhaps you were being prepared for something else entirely. That 'Nazarite blood' I spoke of...it doesn't just manifest as faith and righteousness. Sometimes, it manifests as an unyielding will, a capacity to face the abyss and not be consumed by it but to *harness* its darkness to fight an even greater one."

Angelo could feel an emotion welling inside that he hadn't felt in a long time. The closest he could come to describing it would be inspiration, maybe a budding purpose.

Sawyer's eyes seemed to see past Angelo's impassive mask, into the core of the man. "Your life has been anything but easy. You've seen the worst of humanity, you've been a part of it. But in that crucible, something was forged. A resilience. A clarity about the true nature of evil. A refusal to be broken. Those aren't just scars, Angelo. They're armor. They're weapons."

Another unfamiliar feeling was stinging in Angelo's chest and eyes, his lip starting to quiver. He would never let a tear fall, but Sawyer's pitch was striking a raw nerve.

"The Lord needs instruments of all kinds. He needs the gentle shepherds, like your brother was, to guide the flock. But He also needs the dogs. He needs those who can stand on the walls of Zion and not just sound a warning but *fight* the encroaching darkness with its own fire. The Holders of the Rod aren't playing by polite rules, Angelo. To counter them, to protect the true heart of this Church, sometimes...neither can we."

He rose slowly, standing before Angelo as a fellow soldier offering a new, sacred, and perhaps terrible commission.

"This isn't a path one seeks out, it's a burden, a sacred and often terrifying responsibility. It asks everything of you. It will demand your strength, your cunning, every lesson your hard life has taught you. It offers little in the way of power or acclaim. But it offers purpose. A chance to turn all that pain, all that darkness you've carried into a righteous fire against those who truly pervert the things of God."

Sawyer's gaze held Angelo's, unwavering. The question, when it came, was simple, direct, yet heavy with the destiny of worlds.

"Angelo Barnes, the Lord needs a destroying angel in these latter days. Are you willing to accept this calling and fight as a Nazarite?"

Angelo's usual expression, the poker face he'd cultivated over years of navigating dangerous waters, softened. A genuine, almost hesitant smile graced his face as he nodded. The day's events, culminating in Sawyer's incredible revelations, spun in his mind—a whirlwind of violence, conspiracy, and now a calling that defied all earthly logic but rang so true in his heart.

"Brett, I...I respect you very much," Angelo said. He'd built walls around himself so high and thick that few had ever glimpsed the man behind them, but Sawyer, with his quiet conviction and shared history in the shadows, had found a way to peek over. "It's been such a crazy day. Beyond crazy." He ran a hand through his still-damp hair. "And this..." He gestured vaguely, encompassing the penthouse, the lingering scent of Sawyer's Diet Dr. Pepper, the air thick with the gravity of their conversation. "This is a lot to process. I'm going to need some time to think about this."

Before Sawyer could frame a reply, Shawn, who had been vibrating with that childlike energy since the mention of "magic gifts" and "invincibility," piped up. He bounced slightly in the plush armchair. "Think about it? What's there to think about, man?" He grinned, his eyes wide with a mixture of awe and pure, unadulterated excitement. "The guy just asked you if you wanna be an invincible badass, practically a Mormon superhero, and you're gonna *think* about it?"

Shawn then swiveled his attention to Sawyer, his expression a blend of mischief and curiosity. "Hey, can you bless *me* with invisibility powers while this guy gets his head together? Or maybe super strength? I'm not picky. Just, you know, something cool like talking to animals." He paused, then his tone shifted, a spark of genuine inquiry replacing the playful banter. "Seriously, though, what about me? Do I get ancient powers, or am I just the sidekick with cool gadgets and snappy one-liners?"

Sawyer let out a soft chuckle, a warm, genuine sound that momentarily eased the immense weight of the preceding revelations. He regarded Shawn with an amused gaze, acknowledging the younger man's characteristic blend of humor and sincerity. "Your loyalty, quick wit, and skill with…'persuasive devices,' those are formidable powers in themselves, Elder Martinez." He offered a wink. "And the Lord certainly has a plan for all His children, especially those who stand by their brothers. We can certainly discuss your path and purpose when the time is right."

Then, his attention returned to Angelo, his expression softening into one of profound understanding. The earlier intensity was still there, but it was tempered with patience. "Angelo, your response is understandable. This isn't a decision to be made lightly, on the heels of everything you've been through. It's a covenant, a commitment that shapes not just a life but an eternity." He paused, his gaze unwavering, conveying a depth of experience that spoke volumes. "Take all the time you need. Mull it over. Pray about it, if that's your inclination." Sawyer leaned forward, his sincerity palpable. "If any questions come up, anything you want to talk through, or if there's anything I can help you guys with, don't hesitate to call." His voice was firm, carrying the quiet assurance of a promise made and kept many times before. "Even if your answer is no, Angelo, that won't change a thing between us. I'll always be here for you and Shawn. You have my word on that. We've walked through fire together, and that forges a bond."

Angelo met Sawyer's gaze, an acknowledgment passing between them. The offer of unwavering support, regardless of his decision, resonated deeply within him. He nodded, and Sawyer understood the gratitude it conveyed. The path ahead was uncertain, but for the first time in a long, dark while, Angelo didn't feel alone as he peered into the precipice.

As they settled into a reflective silence, the weight of their conversation lingered. Angelo rubbed the bridge of his nose, wrestling with the implications of this offer. Called to be a protector...but of what? An organization he didn't believe should be saved? An organization that had let him down time and again? But what if it was true? What if the Church could heal and grow? What if *he* could heal and grow?

"Do you think we did more good than harm here?" Angelo said, breaking the silence.

Sawyer nodded, acknowledging Angelo's sentiment with a knowing look. "It never gets easy living with the dark deeds we do. But remember this: light pushes out darkness." He leaned forward, emphasizing his words. "Darkness cannot stand in the presence of light."

Angelo met Sawyer's gaze, searching for clarity amid his own turmoil.

"The light you brought to Sister Cohen when you saved her from that situation should be a bright spot in everything that happened here," Sawyer added. "What you told me about Lucia de Freitas and her family, that should be a bright spot too. The tens of thousands of murders you prevented by destroying Casa Forte, freeing the Morro from the oppression of

Fogo, eliminating corrupt officials, those were all bright spots of light."

Angelo mulled over those words. He had saved lives, stood up to bullies, and protected the innocent—a victory among so much loss—but he couldn't shake the feeling that it came at too high of a price. Rockwell's death still echoed through him like an unresolved symphony, each note heavy with regret and anger.

"I just wish…" Angelo struggled to find the words. The shadows in his mind fought against any sense of redemption.

Sawyer remained silent for a moment before speaking again. "We can't change what's happened. What we can do is move forward and find ways to bring more light into dark places."

A spark flickered within Angelo as he contemplated those words—a glimmer of hope mingling with resolve. Perhaps there was still time to honor Rockwell's memory by bringing about change instead of merely seeking revenge.

Chapter 23

THE LAST P-DAY

Angelo and Shawn emerged from their bedroom in the missionary apartment. Elder Parkman was midstory, his hands gesturing animatedly as Elder Stein, Elder Marcus, and Elder Lawrence listened.

Elder Stein spotted them first, his face lighting up. "Oh, you guys are finally up! We didn't even see you come home last night. We were so worried after we heard about the lockdown."

Parkman picked up the narrative thread without missing a beat. "Yeah, man, it was wild. We were just getting a referral at a member's house when the phone rang. Old school, like a real telephone tree. They were looking for the missionaries, said everyone had to head back to their apartments ASAP. Now we're on lockdown for the next three days. Something about that tragedy that happened in the favela. Crazy, right?" He leaned forward, lowering his voice. "I heard we're getting a new mission president too. The rumors are flying. The office even said we get to call home today to reassure our parents that everything's all right. Can you believe it? Normally, we only get to call home on Christmas and Mother's Day." A flicker of something painful crossed Parkman's face. "My mom...she doesn't really talk to me anymore, so I get to call my dad."

Stein, ever ready to inject some levity, chimed in, "Hey, Parkman, can you still do that great impression of President Hatch? You know, from the Quorum of the Twelve?"

Parkman's grin returned. "You know it!"

"Dude, you should totally call my mom pretending to be President Hatch congratulating her because, like, I've won an award or something!" Stein said, bouncing with excitement. "And then, like, give the phone to me."

Parkman's eyes lit up at the prospect of the prank. "Oh, that's golden, Stein! Consider it done when the time comes."

The attention then shifted to Angelo and Shawn.

"Speaking of time," Angelo began, his "Elder Rockwell" persona firmly in place, "Elder Martinez and I have some news. Our time here in the North Mission, the exchange program, it's...well...it's ended."

Shawn nodded with a somber expression. "Yeah, guys, it's time for us to say goodbye."

A wave of disappointment washed over the other missionaries. Even in their short time together, Angelo and Shawn had made an impression.

Elder Marcus looked crestfallen. "So soon? Man, we were just starting to see you guys hit your stride."

Elder Lawrence nodded, his usually stern demeanor softened. "We were certainly benefiting from your perspective and dedication. It was...refreshing to see such fire."

Elder Stein pouted. "Aww, man! Elder Martinez, we were just getting started! I had a whole list of pranks cooked up that needed your particular brand of genius!"

Elder Parkman clapped Shawn on the shoulder. "Yeah, what he said! The hotdog muffins were just the appetizer! We were hoping you could join us for the main course of mischief!" He sighed. "It's gonna be less fun around here without you guys."

The goodbyes were brief, laced with the unique, fleeting camaraderie forged in the shared experience of missionary life, even if, for Angelo and Shawn, that experience had been a complete lie.

Angelo stood slightly apart from the farewells, a fleeting wistfulness touching him as he looked around the familiar, yet now strangely distant, Leblon apartment. This was where Rockwell had lived, breathed, and served. These very rooms had likely echoed with his brother's quiet determination, his gentle laughter, perhaps even his solitary prayers. He'd known these very missionaries, shared meals with them, maybe even engaged in some of their innocent, goofy antics.

A pang, sharp and unexpected, went through Angelo. He thought of Rockwell's heart, so different from his own, yet capable of wielding a powerful influence. The baptism of Ricardo de Aparcido, a man of considerable sway, a virtual king in his own sphere, was a testament to that. He recalled the genuine respect in Brett Sawyer's voice when he'd spoken of Elder Barnes, and even the fear-tinged admiration he'd sensed from President Peterson during their brutal interrogation. They had all, in their own ways, acknowledged the light Rockwell had carried.

For a moment, Angelo allowed himself a flicker of a parallel life. He saw a younger version of himself, not in a drab army barracks but perhaps in a simple chapel, crisp white shirt and tie, the Book of Mormon open in his hands. A life of earnest study and hopeful proselytizing, a life of service instead of destruction. What if things had been different? What if his birth father wasn't such an abusive bastard? What if he'd chosen that path or if that path had somehow chosen him?

The daydream shattered as Elder Parkman's voice, giddy with anticipation, sliced through his reverie. "It's ringing, Stein! It's ringing, get ready!" Parkman was practically bouncing, phone pressed to his ear, a mischievous glint in his eyes as he prepared to unleash their prank on Elder Stein's unsuspecting mother. The mundane, boyish energy of the room snapped Angelo back to the present, the imagined white shirt and tie dissolving into the reality of his own concealed identity and the bloody path he walked.

Elder Parkman, channeling his inner apostle, spoke into the phone, his voice a nearly perfect imitation of President Hatch. "Hello? Is this Sister Stein, the mother of Elder Stein in the Rio de Janeiro North Mission?"

The voice that came back through the speakerphone was starstruck, dripping with an awe that made it clear she believed she was speaking to a member of the Quorum of the Twelve. "Yes! Yes, this is she! Oh my goodness!"

Parkman continued, the thrill of the impersonation growing. "I have some news about your son."

"Oh, how wonderful!" Sister Stein responded, her voice brimming with excitement and pride. "I'd love to hear anything about him."

Parkman started with good intentions, aiming for a triumphant, award-winning sort of announcement, but the imp of perverse improv took hold. "Your son is...or, rather, *was* a great missionary." A beat of silence, then the dark twist: "Elder Stein, unfortunately, found love in his last area, and they've run off to the middle of the country to be married. It's only appropriate, considering she's with child."

The other end of the phone went utterly silent... Parkman looked up, expecting to see Elder Stein sharing in the hilarity. Instead, he saw pure terror etched on Stein's face. His friend was horrified, the color draining from his cheeks.

The silence stretched, thick and heavy, feeling far longer than the few seconds it actually was. Stein suddenly shot up.

"What are you doing, you flippin' idiot?!" he whisper-shouted at Parkman.

The mirth vanished from Parkman's eyes, replaced by horror at his own miscalculation. He'd definitely gone too far. "I'm sorry, I'm sorry, I'm sorry!" he babbled into the phone, his voice a frantic, almost incoherent rush. "It was just a prank! This is his friend, in his apartment, and he's fine, and everything's okay, and he's fine, and he's right here! Here, talk to him!" Parkman shoved the phone into Stein's hand.

Stein, still stunned, took the phone. "Hi, Mom," he managed, his voice weak. He gave Parkman a quick thumbs-up and a nod as he retreated into one of the bedrooms to undo the damage, a silent signal that, somehow, he'd manage.

Parkman sank onto the edge of a chair, looking deflated. "That is by far the worst thing I've ever done," he mumbled, remorse coloring his tone.

The tension hung in the air for a moment before Shawn let out a hearty laugh, slapping Parkman on the back. "Well, at least you didn't tell her that her son *died*," he boomed. "I can't imagine getting *that* news."

A moment of stunned quiet, then the other elders erupted in laughter. Angelo, the Operator, sensed a phantom smile flicker across his features as he exhaled a gentle laugh.

President Hatch sat at his expansive desk, the late-afternoon sun casting long shadows across his corner office. Below, Temple Square bustled with a quiet reverence. He'd been engrossed in a passage from Alma, his pen scratching furiously as insights and connections filled the margins of his study journal. The weight of his calling as president of the Quorum of the Twelve Apostles and the secret stewardship of the Nazarites felt particularly heavy that day.

His desk phone rang. He lifted the receiver. "Yes, Sister Albright?"

"President Hatch, you have a Heartfelt message on line one, sir. One of the Rio operatives."

Hatch's posture straightened. A "Heartfelt message" was code, a channel reserved for the most sensitive communications, for matters concerning the soul of the Church. He'd been anticipating this call. "Thank you, Sister Albright. Put her through."

He switched lines, the familiar click a prelude to a conversation that could shift destinies. On the other end, a voice emerged—calm and professional, its cadence measured, the unmistakable timbre of a Nazarite field report. "President Hatch."

"Sister," Hatch replied, "is the line secure?"

"Triple-encrypted, sir. Swept for anomalies before initiating contact. We're clear."

"Good," Hatch said, leaning back in his chair, his gaze drifting toward the spires of the temple. "Is he in?"

A slight pause, then, "Not yet, President. But the seeds are there. Firmly planted and starting to sprout. It's only a matter of time, a season of watering and a little more sun before it takes root. Angelo, the Operator, Mr. Barnes...he's on the path. He will become the Sword of God."

Hatch nodded, a satisfaction settling. The loss of Elder Rockwell Barnes had been a tragedy, a pure soul extinguished too soon. But from that darkness, a new, albeit unconventional, implement might be forged.

"And how, Sister, were you able to set all this in motion? To guide him to this summit?"

The voice on the other end was devoid of emotion, honed by years of executing complex, morally ambiguous tasks. "Scrambling the GPS in their vehicle was simple enough, sir. Ensuring there was only one viable route—one that led directly into the heart of Morro Diabólico—required a bit more finesse with the local infrastructure and digital pathways. But after that gentle nudge...the rest of the pieces fell into place. Human nature, grief, and a thirst for vengeance are powerful catalysts."

A spirit of a smile crossed President Hatch's face. He picked up his scriptures, his finger tracing a familiar passage. "Alma, chapter thirty-seven, verse six," he murmured, more to himself than to his operative. "'Now ye may suppose that this is foolishness in me; but behold I say unto you, that by small and simple things are great things brought to pass.'"

His gaze lifted again to the temple, a bastion of faith in a world increasingly shadowed by deceit.

"Indeed, Sister. Indeed."

ACKNOWLEDGEMENTS

A novel is never the work of one person, and this one, in particular, owes its existence to the people and places that inspired it.

This story is a work of fiction, but its heart was born in Brazil. To the wonderful, vibrant, and resilient people of Rio de Janeiro, thank you. Your city is a place of breathtaking beauty and profound complexity, and I hope this story, in its own small way, captures a fraction of the spirit I came to love. My deepest gratitude to the many friends and acquaintances I made there; your warmth, kindness, and *jeitinho* left an indelible mark on me.

To my missionary companions: thank you for your brotherhood, your faith, and your humor in the face of long days and endless hills. The experiences we shared, the lessons we learned together, and the bonds we formed are the bedrock upon which this story is built.

A special and heartfelt thank you to my brother and sister. Your unwavering support and love have been a constant in my life. Thank you for your patience, your encouragement, and for being the very first readers of this novel. Your thoughtful feedback on those messy, chaotic early versions was invaluable in shaping the story into what it is today.

Finally, to my mother. You once told me, "I understand my children don't want my advice, but they want my support."

You gave me that support in boundless measure, but I was also lucky enough to get your advice, which I have always cherished. Thank you for your wisdom, your unconditional love, and your tireless care in raising me. Your guidance is my foundation.

To my stepfather, who has always taught me what it means to be a man. You have shown me and taught me more about how life really works than any school education ever could have. Thank you for showing me how amazing and important the friendship of a father figure can be.

To my father, who has passed away: I am endlessly grateful for the life lessons and gifts you blessed me with. Your memory and the values you instilled in me continue to be a source of strength and inspiration.

To my incredible wife: you are my greatest inspiration. Thank you for your endless love, and for carrying me through the darkest times to see the light of love and appreciation. I could not have done this without you.

And to my children: you are my reason for existence. I love you unconditionally and forever, no matter what. I want nothing more than for you to succeed, be happy, and enjoy everything that this amazing life has to offer.

I must also extend my deepest gratitude to my life coach for his invaluable assistance. He gave me the tools to climb out from the bottom of the "pit of despair" and find a place where I could see myself succeeding. He helped me envision a life where I love, where I am surrounded by loved ones, and where I can be in a spot that I truly want to be—a spot where I seek my truth and no one else's, a spot that is true to the core of my being. FOR REAL reach out to me at brighams t.one through the contact page I will share the program that changed my life!

To all the influencers, content creators, and seekers of truth who have bravely shared your voices: thank you. You have opened my eyes and challenged my thinking, helping me become the author I am today. More importantly, you have helped me grow into a better person, one who strives to love all people unconditionally, regardless of what tribe they belong to.

This book would not be in your hands without the hard work of many talented individuals. My profound thanks to my editor for their sharp eye and insightful feedback, and to my cover art designer for brilliantly capturing the novel's spirit. To my beta readers, who waded through early drafts and offered invaluable perspectives, and to everyone else who helped with this endeavor—thank you.

My sincere thanks to all of my Advanced Reader Copy readers, my fans, and my loved ones. And to every person who purchased this book: thank you for supporting the cause of entertainment and fun in the face of dogmatic repression. Your support means the world to me.

ABOUT THE AUTHOR
Who IS BRIGHAM STONE?

From the Temple to Tarantino:

Brigham Stone is the kind of author who can quote both the Book of Mormon and *Pulp Fiction* in the same breath—and enjoy every word.

Raised in the heart of Salt Lake City, he checked all the boxes of a devout Mormon life: graduating Seminary, serving an honorable two-year mission, meeting his wife in Provo, and marrying in the Temple. But beneath the white shirt and tie beat the heart of a kid raised on the explosive, irreverent films of Quentin Tarantino and Robert Rodriguez, the sharp-witted dialogue of Kevin Smith, and the biting satire of *South Park*. He strived to be the best Mormon he could be, all while nurturing a darker, more twisted sense of humor.

Today, Brigham proudly calls Utah County—the Mormon capital of the world—his home. He identifies as a "broken-shelf" Post-Mormon, a term that will resonate with anyone who has navigated the complex journey of a faith crisis. He cherishes his cultural heritage, the memories of his mission, and the community he loves, but cannot reconcile his conflicting feelings of the institution that shaped him.

Writing is Brigham's way of colliding two worlds: the rich mythology and unique culture of Mormonism with the high-octane, action-packed thrillers he adores. His novels are not anti-Mormon tracts or historical documents; they are completely fictional explorations of "what if?" They are a space for the true believer, the Ex-Mo, and the curious onlooker to share a thrilling story.

www.ingramcontent.com/pod-product-compliance
Lightning Source LLC
Chambersburg PA
CBHW050524110726
47899CB00005B/1580